CW01082938

DELTA-MIKE

A NOVEL BY

EDWARD (NED) BLACK

BOOK TWO OF THE
KNIFE SOLDIERS CHRONICLES

FriesenPress

Suite 300 - 990 Fort St
Victoria, BC, V8V 3K2
Canada

www.friesenpress.com

Copyright © 2021 by Edward (Ned) Black
First Edition — 2021

All rights reserved.

No part of this publication may be reproduced in any form, or by any
means, electronic or mechanical, including photocopying, recording, or any
information browsing, storage, or retrieval system, without permission in
writing from FriesenPress.

ISBN
978-1-03-910067-1 (Hardcover)
978-1-03-910066-4 (Paperback)
978-1-03-910068-8 (eBook)

1. FICTION, SCIENCE FICTION, MILITARY

Distributed to the trade by The Ingram Book Company

Dedicated to my wife Nancy and children:
Edward, Christopher, Bernadette, Kevin and James.

Special thanks to my daughter-in-law Shannon Lainie Black
for her computer tech support.

"Once more unto the breach dear friends
Once more. . . . For he to-day that sheds
his blood with me shall be my brother. . . ."
Henry V. Shakespeare

PROLOGUE

Another day toward retirement he thought walking out of his house to the unmarked police car parked in the driveway. When Frank Farrell started the engine the police radio came on and he listened to the radio jobs with one part of his mind; with another part of his brain he thought about his coming work day. As he drove away, the dark sky had an ominous mix of white and dark storm clouds racing across that usually signaled the weather will get worse.

Only a few cars were in the parking lot when he pulled into his assigned parking spot in front of police headquarters. It was his habit to arrive early each morning in the quiet time before the shift change developed during his six-years in the Marine Corps.

He stepped out of his car, and stretch his back as he scanned the sky. Then he closed the car door to begin the walk to the elevator and his office on the top floor. An odd tingling like a mild electric shock ran completely through his body as he stepped off with his left foot toward the front of the car.

What the hell?

As his right foot touched the ground a mental flash of light knocked him to his knees with severe vertigo, nausea, and retching. He leaned forward onto his hands sweating as his vision began greying out, random thoughts shot through his mind: *I've had a stroke!* . . . *Get the phone for medical help . . . Someone should see me soon!*

He was on all fours next to his car trying not to panic. *Please God. Not like this!*

As the vertigo and nausea passed, his vision cleared and he became aware of noise and people around him, *Thank you, God!*

SIX-HUNDRED YEARS LATER. EARTH PRIME REGION-ONE. PROPOSED TRANSIT PORTAL NUMBER 851

Thirty-nine-year-old-Doctor Sam Lamont, tall and ruddy faced with ginger hair offsetting his green eyes, was born in the Region II area of Earth Prime called Scotland. Not only did he have PhDs in astrophysics, quantum physics, nanophysics; but also, perpetual motion with an astute understanding of non-locality in intergalactic travel. Oddly, his favorite hobby was Earth's history between the Seventeenth and Twenty-first Century. He usually wore a one-piece work suit with waist length blue lab coat as did his assistant Dr. Mira Starfold, a willowy, light brown twenty-seven-year-old of mixed ancestry. She resembled a well-tanned model with a wide smile that made everyone who saw it smile back. Like most of the workers at the facility, she was native to Earth Prime.

The physicist in charge of constructing Earth's newest transit portal was called Sam by friends. He was excited, and slightly anxious, entering the control room to conduct the first test of the morning.

I hope there are no malfunctions. Relax, this will be just another day.

The brightly lit room had numerous auto adjusting chairs that form fitted to any body position, the main technician sat in the most comfortable of them. Sam, sat beside her to begin the first preliminary test of the quantum gravitational forces to open a parallel universe that would connect this portal with another in the Scutum-Crux Arm. One of the longest moves attempted across the Milky Way; but it would still take more than one transit to get to the far outer ring.

Just beyond that, the buffer zone rim region, was the outer edge of the galaxy.

This portal program was progressing quicker than normal because six months earlier the United Worlds government learned of the arrival of a non-human species on the furthest human world, named Planet Sunset. A sparsely populated, mostly forested, world beyond the edge of the galaxy in the beginning of what was termed the Rim Region. The area that was part of the buffer zone of planets, gas clouds and stars surrounding the Milky Way. So far, this alien species had refused all attempted contact by humanity.

Those in the government aware of the landing of what was *de facto* an alien army hoped that Sunset would not be a metaphor for the fate of the human race. Especially if the new species proved hostile, and continued its movement Coreward into the Milky Way.

At the same time, they were excited that someone else *was* out there, but that quickly turned to worry when the intentions of the visitors became apparent.

Inside the Milky Way itself, other than humankind, no intelligent life had been discovered. Although, humans had settled one-hundred planets since the breakthroughs in understanding gravity and non-locality; along with the further evolution of nano technology, quantum computing and perpetual motion that made travel through the transit portals possible.

Sam, settled into his seat to begin viewing the test data running behind his eyes. "Power up," he ordered the technician. His ordinary day abruptly ended when the technician initiated maximum power. It caused an unexpected shock like tingling, and rippling distortion around everyone in the room who all cried out in surprise or fear. The images running behind the technician's eyes like a movie, faded into a colorful kaleidoscope making her dizzy, nauseous, and disoriented. She swayed in her seat holding onto her chair until it passed. So, did Sam.

Mira, sitting near Sam, squinted through the control room window as the distortion passed and noticed the man on his hands and knees in the main area of the transit portal.

Who is that?

"Sam!" she exclaimed.

Still slightly disoriented, Sam looked at her uncomprehending until she began stabbing her finger toward the kneeling man.

"Stop everything!" he shouted to the technician now back in control and activated his own implanted communicator. "I need a medical tube in the Eight Fifty-One-portal immediately!"

He took Mira by the arm, "Come with me." and ran into the adjoining room toward the man kneeling on the floor.

Five seconds after the event . . .

Frank was disoriented, but felt better and pushed himself upright, immediately realizing he wasn't in the parking lot.

I'm indoors?

He glanced around at the interior walls then focused on the completely smooth, glass like, light tan floor he was kneeling on.

What just happened?

He could distinctly hear people shouting, but he couldn't quite understand what they were saying. It confused him even more. But one thing he knew, *I feel much better . . . no . . . I feel great, better than I have in years.*

He attempted to stand and someone grabbed him; in a reflex, he struggled ready to throw a punch. Then his subconscious realized *probably first responders coming to my aid.* So, he relax ed and let them lay him on a small shiny slab they slid out of a human sized tube they rolled in resembling an enclosed stokes basket.

"Hey I feel fine . . . really."

One of them looked at Frank strangely, but continued sliding him into the tube. When they closed a hatch behind him, he felt a shot of anxiety.

What's going on?

He knocked on the side of the tube and yelled. "Hey, I'm fine!" A pleasant sterile aroma filled the tube making him tranquil. As he dozed off, he saw a pretty young woman staring at him through the small observation window on the tube. She appeared troubled.

I'll worry about her later was his last thought.

Sam Lamont was extremely worried. He turned to Mira while the medical technician continued monitoring the tube containing the stranger. "I am beginning to believe something alarming has occurred," he said.

"What do you mean?" Mira replied, perplexed.

He ignored her, and began talking through his implant again.

"I want this new transit area sealed off, no one in or out without my permission. I need a medical doctor in here."

That done, he walked to the med-tech monitoring the tube.

"How is he?"

The med-tech concentrated on the data stream crossing behind his eyes and replied.

"Everything seems. . . normal . . . well not precisely. As a matter of fact, his readings are all excellent, above the expected normal range. For now, the medication from the tube is keeping him asleep."

Just then the MD arrived and linked with the med tube. He too began studying the information then stood in thought for a long moment.

"Well?" Sam asked, slightly impatient.

"What is most unusual, is I cannot identify him."

"What do you mean you cannot identify him?" Mira asked.

The MD shrugged.

"His DNA is not in any of our medical or identification files. Apparently, he does not exist."

"That is impossible, yes?" Mira pressed.

"I thought so too, until now." The MD sounded puzzled.

"Every human born in the last four hundred and fifty years had their DNA registered at birth." Worry lines creased between his eyes.

"This, is unheard of."

Sam stood staring at the far end of the transit point not focusing on anything.

"Are you entirely sure he is a human?" he asked.

The MD, surprised by Sam's question, nodded then re-examined his information. "All the scans verify that he is."

"If you are satisfied that he is a human, could he have been born elsewhere? Does history record any lost colonies? In your knowledge, if you are born on a planet other than Earth Prime is it possible the DNA is not recorded?"

The MD paused, his eyes narrowing. "There is no doubt about it! He is a human born on Earth Prime. All the data verifies that. But it is extraordinary that his DNA is not recorded since it is required on every human world."

"What did your readings indicate?" Sam probed.

"I could not find any record of his DNA. What is odd, I did find records on a number of others who have markers that would only make sense to me if I was dealing with an extremely distant ancestor of theirs.

"He has no neural, language or communication implants; nor does he have a military chip. As implausible as it sounds, his body was rapidly rejuvenating before he was put into the tube; but we were able to get some initial readings that indicated major injuries and wear to his bone joints. Frankly, I have never seen anything like it. I would like to have time to study him further."

He paused frowning a silent question, then said to Sam, "Physically, he is in exceptional condition. Due I think to the med tube that seems to have assisted in continuing the physiological changes begun before he was put inside. My initial readings indicate his body mass has decreased by twenty six percent from when he entered the tube . . . and he is approximately eighteen standard years of age. Though his brain storage patterns, for the storage of episodic memories, indicate a person at least three times older." He paused again and grimaced. "It is all very peculiar. He needs further study!"

"Sam?" Mira touched his arm. "I checked our data base. There are no known or suspected lost or undocumented colonies. I …"

Sam abruptly turned bumping into her.

"Sorry, I was thinking," he mumbled but didn't elaborate and walked to the tube to look through the observation window again.

"Mira, could we have mixed up our test with another portal somewhere? Is it possible we caused some type of entanglement? Sam asked.

She thought for a long moment.

"No, I do not see how? We had everything meticulously checked and rechecked. Someone else would have also noticed that problem by now and reported it."

Sam nodded *She's right!*

"I agree. Still, I want you to recheck for reports of travelers not reaching their destination, or if any other unusual event has occurred in the system. Perhaps there was a mix-up elsewhere."

Sam continued to study the man's features and clothing as far down as he could see. The more he saw the more trepidation he felt. *Where did you come from, and how did you get here?*

Mira touched his arm again. "Sam, there are no reports of anything unusual anywhere in the transit system."

"Doctor Lamont," the MD interrupted his contemplations. "He can be awakened and removed anytime. Do you have any instructions?"

Sam nodded and rubbed his hands together.

"Yes, wait fifteen more minutes, I have some research to do."

"If that is your wish."

Sam Lamont, considered what had transpired, and made a mental list then turned to Mira and said, "I want to present my thinking to you, and the doctor, then you can give me your opinions."

"Of course," the MD replied. Mira nodded.

"First: Our mystery man is a human. Do you agree?"

Mira nodded. "Agreed." The MD said "Yes."

"Secondly, he did not come from anywhere else in the Transit system or we would know."

Mira nodded again. "I verified that."

"Third, the doctor is certain he was born on Earth Prime."

"Yes, that too is correct," the MD said.

"And finally, there is no record of his DNA. But there are other DNA markers indicating him as a distant ancestor of some."

"That is probably the oddest reading," the MD replied.

Mira nodded. "Yes. As strange as it is, I agree with every point you made."

Sam stood in thought. "Now, this is important. For all of these statements to be true we must consider Occam's Razor."

Sam and Mira both knew that Occam's Razor used as abductive reasoning said, the simplest solution to a set of observations is most likely the right one.

Creator. Could this really have happened? Did our test bring him? Sam was getting excited.

He called his boss, Dr. Mason Park and didn't waste any time with pleasantries. "Mason, Sam here; there has been an accident in the bay of Eight Five One. I think you should come here as quickly as possible. I will brief you when you arrive."

Sam Lamont couldn't remain still. He began pacing with his hands clasped behind his back as his mind raced.

" I do not think he is from here," he muttered.

Mira heard the comment. "Who? Who is not from here, Sam?"

Surprised by her remark he stopped his pacing. He looked at Mira for a moment before he indicated the med tube with his thumb.

"Him."

Mira crossed her arms and looked a question at Sam. "We know that! Did you mean not from Earth Prime, not from here in the complex, from another planet?"

"No Mira. Remember Occam's Razor. I believe he could be from another time!"

CHAPTER 1

"Now this is not the end.
It is not even the beginning of the end.
But it is, perhaps, the end of the beginning."
Winston Churchill

Frank wandered across the huge drill field to the "E" Company barracks on the other side before continuing on to his assigned quarters. As he walked into the building foyer, he saw Alicia sitting alone on a bench watching the passers-by who were all in high spirits since their graduation officially made them marines. He sat on the bench next to her; she reached over and took hold of his hand interlocking their fingers then put their interlocked hands in her lap as she ran her free hand through her hair. "My orders give me three days to report to First Recon," she said without turning her head, "When are we going?" Frank looked at her profile with a slight smile. "When do ya wanna leave?"

She squeezed his hand and looked at him seemingly lost in thought. "I have an idea," she said brightly, "Let us get our gear and get a room off the base for twenty-four hours. Then you can escort me to First Recon."

Frank could feel her warmth, and reluctantly unlocked their fingers and removed his hand.

"Alicia, you're now a member of a unit where I'm an NCO and we can't have the same relationship we had in boot camp or on R&R. Maybe when ya make sergeant," he said with a wry smile.

She looked at him with regret. "I know."

She stood up. "Can we at least get a drink together?"

"Absolutely!" he replied. "But I have to locate Blanco first. I was instructed ta bring ya both back with me. Frank reached out with his communicator, "Private Blanco this is Sergeant Farrell, report."

"Blanco here Sergeant!" came the immediate reply.

"Blanco you're now a member of the First Galactic Reconnaissance Battalion. I'm your escort to Planet Sunset. Meet me and Private Macalduie in the waiting area of the Midway transit portal at sixteen hundred local time tomorrow. Understood?"

"Aye, aye, Sergeant."

"Good . . . Macalduie and I are on our way ta have a drink at the club. You're welcome to join us if ya wish. If not, I'll see ya tomorrow. Farrell out."

Blanco was waiting at the club when Frank and Alicia arrived. After ordering drinks Frank spent the rest of the time telling them what to be prepared for when they arrived at Recon on Planet Sunset. Impressing on them that their success was entirely in their hands and his belief they would both do well.

The next afternoon the three marines walked up to the Planet Midway Terminal and had their neural implants checked for orders. Then they stoically stood in the crowded line waiting to walk through the Transit portal, and from there through another portal back to First Reconnaissance Battalion on Planet Sunset.

Frank let his mind drift. Reflecting how profoundly his life had changed since the event that brought him to this future against his will almost nineteen months before. Unexpectedly a well-known quote by Winston Churchill during World War II, now so many hundreds of years in his past, entered his mind and he judged it fitting for this new chapter of his life.

◆

REFUGE SYSTEM in relation to Sunset and nearby worlds

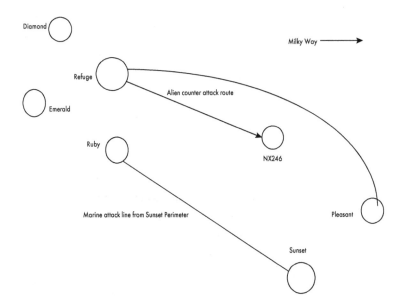

SEVERAL MONTHS LATER.

The United Worlds of Earth Starship *Argon*, escorted by the Battle Cruiser UWS *Taiwan*, slowly approach Planet Ruby in the Refuge System, in stealth mode. The Argon's captain and her bridge officers were concerned about being detected by their target, the lone alien ship in orbit around the planet. or, by one of the other one-hundred-eighteen alien ships scattered throughout the systems three other planets.

The past year and a half, had been one of vicious fighting with high causalities around a human enclave on a portion of Planet Sunset, designated the *Sunset Perimeter*. Located in the Rimward-Spinward quadrant at the edge of the Milky way.

It was from there the hostile landing by aliens, originally labeled

'Dogmen' by the human military, were driven with great loss of life. During the fighting, for ease of communications, the original label morphed into DMs, then later into the current "Delta-Mike."

When the DMs withdrew from Sunset, they stopped at a system of habitable planets fourteen light days into the Coreward-trailing quadrant of the far outer rim of the galaxy. An area they had discovered on their initial approach to Planet Sunset. It was unknown and unexplored by humans.

They were shadowed during their retreat by human stealth ships. As a right of human discovery, the Squadron Commander named the primary planet in the new system sheltering most of the one-hundred-nineteen DM ships, "Planet Refuge." Spread in an arc less than one Astronomical Unit, or eight light minutes, away Spinward-Coreward were three other planets also suitable for humans that were christened Ruby, Diamond, and Emerald.

The Argon's Captain wasn't the only one anxious about this action designated *Operation Filch*. So was now twenty-year-old Sergeant Frank Farrell, United Worlds Marine Corps, as he pondered his role in this upcoming planetary assault. He and his squad were the Pathfinders ahead of the main landing, and in view of humanities long history of pacifism, he was optimistic about this aggressive operation. After first arriving in this era, he learned that during the epoch of his birth, his nation, the United States, had a civil war that spread worldwide. It destroyed civilization as it had been known, and killed over three quarters of all humanity, creating a staunchly pacifist human race for the past six hundred years. Then the alien invasion arrived.

This was Frank's second planetary assault from the Argon, famous for launching the first one in human history twelve months earlier. At that time, he and his reinforced reconnaissance squad landed on an unnamed world closer to Planet Sunset, designated only as NX246.

A planet in the beginning of human colonization by three-hundred men, and women, that was invaded by the DMs as a ruse to draw troops away from the fighting at Sunset Perimeter.

In several days of intense combat, he and his squad earned renowned by destroying an entire DM special landing team of two-hundred troops, that had tortured, raped, or murdered, more than two thirds of the colonists. It was a minor battle in the overall war; but it became a watershed event that increased military enlistments and made Delta-Mike infamous. Their atrocities became commonly known as The Rape of NX246, that alerted the entire galaxy to the real intentions of the invaders.

Operation Filch, now tasked the Marines 1st Recon along with a navy destroyer, and a battle-cruiser, with a planetary assault here on Planet Ruby that would initially land the pathfinders. They were followed later by "D" Recon and two-platoons from "A" Recon from the Battle-Cruiser Taiwan. Their mission was to neutralize any DM crew dirtside. At the same time, the two remaining "A" Recon platoons along with a naval boarding party would seize the target ship in orbit.

The computer chip in Franks brain alerted him. "All Marine officers and NCOs report to the landing bay for a briefing." When he and his four team leaders arrived in the landing bay, they were greeted with a nod by the platoon commander, Lt. Nikowa. They sat down behind him and the platoon sergeant, Staff Sergeant Valdez.

"Attention on deck!" the First Sergeant yelled when the CO, Captain Nagoto arrived. To everyone's surprise he was accompanied by the Recon Battalion Commander, Colonel Rham. "As you were," the colonel said.

"The captain stood waiting as the group settled down while the colonel moved into the background with the First Sergeant. "This meeting is my way of making a list and checking it twice," Captain Nagoto quipped to scattered chuckles. He held up his hands for quiet.

"According to dirtside scans, we believe that only a small watch crew is still aboard our target. Scans also identified a small outlying camp by a stream near the main crew camp. Just before local dawn tomorrow, Sergeant Farrell, and his pathfinders, will begin this operation in a stealth landing craft. It will approach to the opposite side of the planet matching the orbit of our target, while staying slightly below the curve of the planet. They will land within ten K of the main crew camp."

The captain looked around, and found Frank sitting in the group. "Sergeant Farrell, you and your squad are designated as Pathfinder-One. You will identify any strong points for the main landing team following twenty-four hours after you. You will also stop any attempts by the DMs to get back to their ship when, and if, they see the landing coming.

"If you can get prisoners, we need officers. But do not get hurt getting them. If they are resisting, you know what to do. Alpha's Third and Fourth Platoons will attack and board the DM vessel as soon as their First and Second Platoons drop dirtside with "Delta" company.

"Any questions? Sergeant Farrell ?"

"No questions sir!" *Damn, now we're hunting DMs outside of our galaxy, and landing on an unknown planet to do it. We've come a long fuckin way in year and a half. Alicia is in Delta Company. I hope she'll be ok on the drop.*

He and Alicia Macalduie, were lovers in boot camp. Assigned "Training partners," a euphemistic term for sex buddies, a training concept developed several hundred years earlier. Every few months partners changed to prevent problems of the heart or hate relationships; but he and Alicia had remained in touch and he was responsible for her getting into Recon at her request.

"Any questions from Second or Third platoon?" Captain Nagoto was greeted with silence. "Okay. As soon as the Third and Fourth Platoons have control of the ship, the naval personnel will get it moving toward Sunset. At that time the Argon will send three landing craft to evacuate Alpha company, the Pathfinders, and any prisoners. The Taiwan will pick up Delta company. We want to get out fast!

There is no doubt we will have bunch of angry DMs coming after us from *Refuge*.

He looked toward Frank again. "Pathfinders, be back here at zero three hours. Until then, get all the rest you can. That's all. NCOs are dismissed. Officers stand-by."

Frank walked back to the berthing area with his four team leaders: Cpls Olney, Kim. And Drugba veterans of the battles on *Sunset* and NX246. The fourth member of the group, Cpl Gupta, was new to *Sunset*, but a qualified recon operator.

Frank considered what they would be facing. Delta-Mike was a vicious warrior race that invaded the Planet of Sunset; a human world in a Coreward-Trailing section of the outer rim of the Milky Way. They were bipedal, six feet tall and walked with a slight stoop. Their fingers had sharp three-quarter inch fingernails capable of causing nasty wounds. Their faces were flat like humans with a light hair, almost beard like, covering most of their features. They resembled a Neanderthal as close as anything else and had proven themselves to be tough, sadistic and, committed to their mission and Pack. The Pack, was how they organized themselves. Ironic considering their nickname, Dogman, bestowed by an unknown soldier on Sunset early in the fighting. It quickly caught on and was in general use until the marines shortened it to DM.

Surprisingly, these invaders had rifles and machine guns resembling Earth's Twenty-first century, and were organized in units similar to humankind. A similarity disturbingly familiar at times.

"Make sure your teams know their assignment when we land." Frank said. "You four will each carry a slug thrower along with your regular weapon in case we confront any of their War Beasts. I know they said scans did not show any other major life forms, but better safe than sorry."

"I'll definitely keep mine close," quipped Corporal Kim. "I still have nightmares about the last time those fucking things came at us." The other veterans nodded grimly.

The DM War Beast resembled a prehistoric animal from human history. An elephant sized giant sloth shaped carnivore. Two fangs came from the top of its mouth that gave its face the look of a saber tooth tiger. It was covered by a natural armor, that was impervious to any individual pulse weapon in the human arsenal.

The human weapons shot pulses of energy using a power pack. Frank still didn't understand the physics. All he knew, was it instantly shut down all the targets bodily systems and rarely left wounded, unless the hit was the residual of a near miss. It was the single most important advantage humankind had in fighting this enemy, but it proved useless against the giant beasts.

"Okay. Make sure everyone tries to get some sleep; tomorrow is going to be a busy day." Frank moved around the marine berthing area speaking with each member of his squad then went to the chow hall for a quick cup of coffee and sandwich thankful that the UWS *Argon* had food for the crew and marines 24/7.

He sat pondering friends killed in action that he sat here with just last year. Especially his best friend Ram Rena. Frank shook his head to rid himself of the ghosts and muttered "Feels like twenty fucking years ago."

"Want some company, Marine?" asked a female voice behind him. He turned and saw Petty Officer Manuela, the cute Philippine dirty blond he'd shared several quickies with beaming at him. She was one of a very few people who actually fought a DM hand to hand during the NX246 operation. He grinned back at her. "I'm glad to see ya, have a seat!"

She sat and took a sip of coffee with a gleam in her eye. "When you get back from this landing maybe we can inspect that empty storage space again . . . just to unwind."

His grin broadened "Yer on." *I love space travel!*

Frank gathered his twelve marines in the landing bay for a final briefing. "You may feel lonely dirtside with Delta-Mike but remember god will keep command up-dated on what's happening during the operation."

The Main Computer Entity, called god, was a self-aware Artificial Intelligence created by breakthroughs in physics to assist the surviving humans of the cataclysm, known as *The Final World War*, rebuild their world and move forward. "Also remember not to step on each other when using your chip." The chip all members of the military had was a neurotransmitter connecting their brain with the *Entity*. Since the brain itself was a transmitter for thoughts using electromagnetic impulses with the help of nanobots in the implant, the brain impulses were turned into real-time holographic events collected directly into the *Main Computer Entity*. "You replacements will be excited and likely to talk over someone who may be trying to answer, and help you. Even though you will still be able to hear, it makes things less jumbled if ya use procedure. You veterans know what I mean. Another thing . . . watch for those big light benders the DMs have; they'll probably be hiding some kind of craft." He was referring to the seven-foot-high poles with multiple arms at the top that provided invisibility to cover troops, landing craft, or anything else the DMs wanted hidden.

Frank saluted as Captain Nagoto and Lieutenant Nikowa walked up to the assembled marines. "We're ready to go sir!"

Captain Nagoto nodded. "Good luck in the landing Sergeant. Good luck Marines." A chorus of "Thank you, sir! " ran through the assembled troops.

"Pathfinders to your landing station. All crew prepare to land pathfinders." was heard in their heads. It was time. Frank led the squad into the front of the landing craft that disappeared to board them. It reappeared as the last marines passed the threshold and secured themselves.

"This is the pilot. We will be in stealth mode all the way down. I will give you a twenty second warning for landing. I will put you down six K from the smallest alien camp near the blue line," a term referring to a creek stream or river.

The drop from *Argon* went unnoticed and unopposed. After what seemed a longer trip than expected the pilot announced, "Twenty seconds to landing."

"As soon as we land, get fifty meters away from the craft and we'll put in a quick perimeter" Frank said to his squad, who sat waiting as the pilot gave the countdown. "Landing in five . . . four . . .. three . . . two . . . The front of the craft disappeared and Frank led the squad at a run for fifty meters then directed them into a Three-hundred-sixty-degree perimeter.

"Pathfinder-One to Alpha-One over." Even though god tracked them the marines kept their chain of command advised of everything in the time-tested manner.

"Go Pathfinder-One."

"Pathfinder-One is down and moving . . . out." Next, he switched to the squad channel. "Let's go people it's time to earn our keep. Corporal Olney, you have point. Take us to within one K of that DM camp on the blue line.

"Roger."

"Corporal Gupta, you're behind Olney's team followed by Corporal Drugba. Corporal Kim, you have our six. Let's move out."

The smell and feel of the wind on Frank's face were reminiscent of Hawaii and other South Sea Islands. Trees and plant life grew in a jumbled mix with unfamiliar flying insects. He saw what he thought of as birds flying in the distance.

With the pathfinders safely landed, *Argon's* Captain, Lieutenant Commander Fong, along with Captain Nagoto, assembled the rest of

Alpha Recon along with the forty sailors that would attack the ship in the boarding party.

Lieutenant Commander Fong stood before the assembled troops. "I'm going to defer to Captain Nagoto, due to the experience and training of the marines in these types of operations." She looked at Nagoto with a lop-sided grin. "Even though this will be the first real world evolution on something like this for any of us."

Nagoto, took Commander Fong's place.

"Thank you, ma'am," he nodded to her. "At zero three-thirty tomorrow the naval landing force, along with Third platoon, will attack and breach the hull of the DM vessel in orbit around this planet. I'm going to show you each section of the ship we will attack, so pay attention."

The marines and sailors saw a schematic of the vessel in their heads. The air lock that was used for boarding troops and supplies was brightly outlined, along with the suspected crew quarters. The bridge and engineering glowed in different hues for ease of identification. All of the attacking force studied each of the outlined areas.

"The First squad will breach the forward hatch here" the outline began flashing. "As soon as First squad is inside, they will move to the bridge of the ship and secure it." The bridge of the ship began flashing.

"The naval bridge ratings, with a chief, will accompany first squad marines. As soon as the area is secure, they will get the ship underway. At the same time, the navy ship engineers will accompany two teams from the third squad and takeover the engineering spaces. They began flashing.

"Second squad, will breach at the aft hatch. They will secure the crew spaces as soon as they are in. You naval damage control people attached to the breachers will have to work quickly to get those hatches resealed.

"Gunners mates, I haven't forgotten you. You will have to ID the weapons and hopefully be able to use them if needed. Any questions so far?" The room stayed completely quiet except for the slight hum of working systems.

"No question? Good. By this time in the raid, the second platoon should be planet-side near the main camp. They will hit any targets identified by the pathfinders, especially any landing boats or other craft. Then they will generally harass the DMs as much as possible in a short period of time. Once the captured ship is safely away you will be withdrawn at the same time as the pathfinders. First platoon will stay aboard *Argon* as a reserve reaction force if needed.

"Remember people. This is a raid, not an invasion. You do what damage you can; make sure that Delta-Mike cannot launch anyone back to their ship, and get out. As soon as the captured vessel is underway, the *Argon* will move to support and recover the troops on the planet. If everything goes according to plan, we will begin to evacuate our planet-side troops with any prisoners back to Sunset before the DM fleet descends on us from around the system. The captured vessel will be met one AU from here by fleet ships and escorted back to *Sunset*." He turned to Lieutenant Commander Fong giving the meeting back to her. "Ma'am?"

She nodded.

"I expect all naval personnel to understand their tasks, and try to anticipate what it will take to achieve their missions with a minimum of time and trouble. Good luck to all of you."

"Attention on deck, captain leaving !" the senior chief yelled as she stepped down

"As you were." she said on her way through the group.

Two stealth landing craft from UWS *Argon*, each containing a marine and navy boarding party slowly approached the DM destroyer in orbit around the planet. They drifted the last One-thousand meters to within fifty-meters of the hull matching its velocity.

The Senior Navy Chief of the two-landing craft, sitting in his seat in the rear of the first one was dressed in a standard uniform, and wearing an oxygen face plate the same as the rest of the navy and marine attackers strapped into their seats. Everyone sat in three columns facing forward. The first marines approaching the ship were the two sappers. They used impulse packs to push themselves toward their targeted hatches until they gently came to a rest against the area to be attacked. They placed magnetic cups on the ship's hull that were attached to an extremely strong micro-cable extending back through the open front of their craft, connected it its rear bulkhead. It enabled the marines and sailors to keep together for the crossing into the target vessel.

When the two sappers completed their assignments, they communicated almost simultaneously, "Breachers up!" to their respective boat pilots. The chief, anxiously anticipated the go command and was relieved when the pilot ordered, "Breachers away." As soon as chief of the flight crew in the back of the boat heard the pilot he said, "Stand up!"

The attack force lined up facing the almost invisible line stretched the length of the boat that could be drawn in instantly. Each held a clip in their hand that was attached by a short piece of micro-cable attached to the front of a harness they wore. "Hook up!" the Chief ordered; everyone snapped the clip into place.

"Boarders Away!" he communicated to the *Argon* as seventy-seven marines and sailors left their respective boats toward the alien ship.

Along with the boarding harness they wore, each Marine had a twelve-inch recon knife and two extra power packs for the pulse rifle slung across their chest in a combat sling. The navy crewman dressed the same except for the boarding cutlass they carried in a scabbard instead of a knife.

Navy breachers led the attack force passing between the two vessels. They wore a lightweight power pack with a six-inch-long nozzle for their powerful cutting laser attached to a cable. The breachers knew, they had roughly fifteen seconds to cut a six foot by four-foot plug for entry. They had to restrict the response time of any crew still on the ship. Both breachers also wore strong magnetic boots they locked down to the ship's hull keeping them in place to work in zero gravity.

Beginning at the top of the plug they made each clockwise cut until arriving back at the top. Then the number two Breacher that was behind the first and attached with an additional magnetized belt used a padded four-foot-long steel ram to knock the hanging plug inside the ship away from the attacking raiders, and into anyone who could be waiting on the other side. His boots and belt kept him firmly on the hull. Otherwise, in a void, he would have shot away from the ship with force equal to what he applied to the hull.

The breachers made their cuts. The plugs were pushed inside followed by the attacking force who got through the forward hatch with no trouble. But at the rear hatch one of the three remaining DM watch crew doing a routine inspection saw the beginning of the breach. He ran for a communicator attached to the bulkhead at the end of the passageway as the hatch breached. It is unclear if vacuum, as he was sucked toward the breach, or the first marine through the breach, killed him.

The entire boarding party was aboard in under fifteen seconds. The navy damage control team quickly began to attach a membrane over the plug that would harden into a metal seal. The attackers spread out to their assignments throughout the ship.

"Instruments indicate two hull beaches!" Minor Crewman Zokfin reported with a raising voice.to his team leader, First Crewman Fen-golen, on the bridge of the Destroyer Enemy killer with him.

Fen-golen looked up from his own station and replied, "And Glog is excited about something, but was cut off before he could finish his report. He is working on the side where the breaches are indicated.

Check on the situation quickly. It could be micrometeorite hits and we do not wish to lose too much atmosphere!"

Sometimes Glog is more trouble than he is worth Zokfin thought as he moved to the bridges' main hatch to carry out his orders. "I will contact you with conditions immediately. Give me five minutes before you contact the Ships leader."

"According to my readings the hull breaches are gone." called Fen-golen at Zokfin's retreating back. "Perhaps something is wrong with the sensors."

Or perhaps that idiot Glog finally did something constructive Zokfin turned toward the elevator and walked into a marine pointing a pulse rifle at him. Clearly imprinted on the marine's suit was the emblem of a human skull with a dagger piercing it vertically from top to bottom. The Marine Galactic Recon Emblem.

"Knife Soldier!" Zokfin screamed and raised his arms in surrender. First Crewman Fen-golen reached toward a control panel when he heard Zokfin's warning and was pulsed dead by a second marine who stepped onto the bridge.

"Recon-three to Recon-three Actual . . . the bridge is secure. I have one DM prisoner . . . over."

"Roger that Recon-three . . . let's see how fast we can get out of here . . . Three-actual . . . out."

"Naval bridge-crew up!" Recon-three communicated.

Ten minutes after the Breacher began the first cut the DM ship was moving toward *Planet Sunset* with the navy chief and his bridge crew pumping the prisoner for information on the ships systems.

11 HOURS EARLIER . . .

Frank, and his squad moved toward the minor alien camp by the blue line. This part of the planet was tropical, heavily overgrown, and humid. Much like the south seas on Earth Prime affectionately known as Mother Earth.

Strange blue hummingbird size life forms flew about but did not bother the marines who kept a wary eye on them none the less, and listened to other strange animal sounds as they moved toward the enemy camp.

"Team-one to Farrell" Frank heard in his head.

"Go one."

"I am at the one-K mark and my scanner is indicating signs of DMs . . . over.

"Do you have a direction one . . . over."

"Indications are at the blue line . . . over."

"Stand-by I'll be at your position shortly . . . Farrell out."

"Squad get down" communicated Frank as he moved up to Olney's squad in the point.

"What do you think? "he asked Olney when he squatted down beside him.

"I think they are by the blue line. How about I take my team up using our light benders and see what we can."

Frank thought about the problem and listened to the sounds of the planet around him. "According to the briefing there's a DM camp around here. If your sensor is not showing it right now I'm thinking it's on the other side of the blue line. Be real fucking careful moving up there. I'll follow with the rest of the squad five minutes behind you. Contact me as soon as you have any information."

"Roger that."

Olney stood. "Let's move out," he communicated to his team. He was veteran of some of the fiercest fighting around the *Sunset Perimeter*, and a cautious scout who knew not to rush. He set the pace toward Delta-Mike that took over an hour to cover the one-K to the river. While Frank trailed him with his chip, moving at the pace Olney set.

"Team-one to Farrell."

"Go one."

"You are not going to believe this. I have a small DM camp on the other side of a stream maybe a meter deep and ten wide . . . break . . . I have twelve DMs bathing here I think you should look at. . . over."

Frank scowled at the message. "Team-one, if they have weapons kill um . . . over."

"Team-one to Farrell, they are unarmed, undressed, and female . . . over."

"Fuck me," Frank muttered. "Team-one do you see any activity in their camp . . . over."

"I see one armed over-watch on a platform outside of the camp guarding the bathers. . . over."

Frank communicated with his squad. "Drugba, Kim, move your teams up to get on line with Olney break . . . Gupta you have our six, break . . . take out anything that approaches us from that direction . . .Farrell out." Five minutes later, ten marines were watching the bathers who other than their facial features were extremely well-built females.

DM HEADQUARTERS ON PLANET REFUGE . . .

Supreme Pack Leader Glgoffen finally had some good news after the disastrous operations on *Planet Sunset*, concluding in one horrific morning with the loss of the entire 5th Great Pack. Before that, almost Twelve-thousand others were lost in the general fighting around the *Sunset Perimeter*. Now, finally, something was going his way. The operation to get prisoners had been successful with one male and one female now in route to his headquarters. He looked forward to their interrogations.

The two young soldiers, eighteen-year-old Privates Rajan Sonde, and Joan Maa had recently arrived on *Sunset* as replacements. They were shocked to be captured by a DM reconnaissance unit that killed all the others in their routine patrol.

The DMs, had stayed behind to gather intelligence and prisoners after the withdrawal of their forces. Somehow, they managed to keep themselves and their small ship hidden. The Minor Pack Leader in charge of the reconnaissance effort knew the importance of prisoners so they were not mistreated after their capture.

The *Main Computer Entity* experienced their capture as it occurred, and notified a military Command that was too slow in organizing a rescue. The prisoners were lifted off world by the DMs that managed to evade all the human ships during the three-day trip at 4C between *Planet Sunset* and *Planet Refuge*.

As soon as the frightened prisoners were aboard the alien ship god began whispering into their minds. "*Observe everything you can see of the ship especially the controls and how they operate them*".

The AI god, warned "*you may tell them anything they ask to make it easy on yourselves, except for the Travel Portals. On your lives, never mention them to your captors. They must be kept secret for the safety of all humankind.*"

The military chip implant in each of them allowed the familiar voice of their platoon leader to keep in communication with them during the captivity. It was calming, and comforting, for them to have friendly voices in their heads during this ordeal. Plus, being in contact allowed others to assist them with answers and evasions; permitting them to be spies hidden in plain view on the DM ship.

SPL Glgoffen's intelligence chief, and old friend, Waltzz came into his office and stood waiting to be recognized. Glgoffen looked up and nodded his head in silent permission.

"The captives are outside; do you wish to participate Supreme leader?"

"Yes Waltzz, take them to the interrogation chamber. Are you sure our translators are capable of speaking with them?"

"Yes, the one message I was able to receive from the small pack I sent to the world *Pleasant* indicated among other things that our team could communicate with them."

SPL Glgoffen nodded "I will be there presently." *I hope they will prove useful; I need information on this enemy.*

Ten minutes later the two humans stood dwarfed by six DMs looking at them with shark eyes, unspeaking. The room had several hospital style tables and some other unrecognizable machines with chairs next to them. Waltzz look at Glgoffen who sat in one of the chairs for permission to begin.

Glgoffen nodded.

"Identify yourselves and your unit" he demanded. Sonde and Maa glance at each other "I am Private Rajan Sonde of the Third Company in the First Battalion United Worlds Army." Waltzz walked very close to Sonde inspecting his uniform and hat. He did the same to Maa looking closely at her features and stature and frowned. Then he patted her chest and reached down and squeezed between her legs.

"This one is female. Identify yourself" he ordered.

Maa visibly gulped "Private Joan Maa Third Company in the First Battalion."

Glgoffen inspected the prisoners then looked at Waltzz. "Are they truly soldiers? They appear frightened children!"

The intelligence chief nodded. "It is their weapons that make them so fearsome in battle. But these two do not appear to be Knife Soldiers."

Waltzz faced the prisoners again. "What are your duties?"

"We are infantry. We do what we are ordered to do."

"How long have you been with your Army?"

"One week. We just arrived" Maa answered.

"Arrived from where?"

"From MW."

The intelligence officer frowned again. "What is MW?" he asked

Sonde. Maa looked down at her feet. Sonde hesitated for a moment and he was struck in the back of the head hard enough to snap his head forward by a DM standing guard behind him.

"It is an abbreviation for a planet known as Military World where everyone trains" Sonde cringed expecting another blow.

SPL Glgoffen stood up. "You expect me to believe you have an entire world dedicated to training your military?" *This is troubling news. If this species has an entire world dedicated to fighting and knowing their ruthlessness on the battlefield it is enough to make me re-think what we are doing here.*

Sonde nodded.

"What unit in your army are the knife soldiers?" Glgoffen asked.

Creases formed between Sonde's eyes he looked at Maa who shrugged. "I have never heard of such a unit" he replied bracing for another blow. But the intelligence chief had been watching him closely and realized he was probably telling the truth. He raised a hand to stop the guard from hitting him again and ordered the guard "Bring me a knife soldier head covering."

When the guard left, he looked at Maa "How large is your military?"

"I do not know. It was small . . . but is getting larger since you invaded."

The guard returned and handed over a boonie hat with the Galactic Recon emblem embedded on the front; the intelligence chief gave it to Sonde. "This came from a knife soldier. What unit it is?" he demanded.

Sonde examined the hat and emblem. "I am fairly certain this is from the marines." He handed the hat to Maa who nodded. Her agreement. "Yes, I believe it to be their Reconnaissance Unit emblem."

"Marines . . . not army? What is the difference?" probed the intelligence officer.

"The marines, usually fight from ships in small units and their entire organization is much smaller than the army. Their reconnaissance units, travel in front of everyone else looking for the enemy." Sonde replied.

The Intelligence chief turned to Glgoffen. "They sound like our Special Landing Teams. Now the reports we have from NX246 and Planet Pleasant plus what we know of them from Planet Sunset make sense to me."

Glgoffen nodded in agreement. His own Special Landing Teams were fierce elite warriors who landed first into the worst situations and were ruthless fighters. "How many of them are on the Planet called Sunset?" he asked Maa who shrugged and was staggered by a smack from the guard.

"I think by now they have a division there" Sonde quickly added to help Maa.

"A division!" blurted Glgoffen shocked. He locked eyes with his Intelligence chief. From previous prisoner interrogations and intelligence information both knew it was the equivalent of a Great Pack. Almost Eighteen-thousand fighters.

We are going to need help, but I am not ready to admit it yet. "How did you arrive on Sunset?"

Maa knew she had to be careful with her answers. "By ship."

"Impossible!" The intelligence chief slapped her across the face knocking her to the floor. It made her nose bleed, eyes water, and left a large welt. "Do not try to lie. We have ships monitor all areas of space. None have detected ships bringing troops to that world."

Maa stood squeezing her nostrils to stop the bleeding. Sonde again interjected to help her. "That is because our ships can render themselves invisible. It is how we and all the replacements landed."

Glgoffen sat down in his chair again *is it possible? Could they stay that hidden. We will have to investigate this closely.*

"How many soldiers do you have on the world called Sunset?" the Intel chief continued. "Three Divisions, I think. I am not sure. I am only a private, it is the lowest rank in the military."

Glgoffen sat considering what he had heard *I still have the advantage in numbers now how to use them.* He looked at the intelligence chief. "If they are like out low ranks, I'm surprised they know as much as they do. End this."

The intelligence chief nodded then looked at the prisoners. "Is there anything else you wish to tell me?"

"No . . . that is all we know" Sonde said, and Maa nodded her agreement.

The intelligence chief motioned to the DM standing behind Sonde who quickly placed a garrote around his neck and killed him.

Maa began crying.

"Strip her "he ordered. Maa tried to struggle and was punched in the face stunning her. When she was naked, she was thrown onto one of the tables. Glgoffen looked at her for a long moment. "Her parts do not look much different than one of ours" he observed and pointed to the gathered guards. "you six may begin" Then he walked from the room.

The guards began raping Maa. When the first one of them was done, the Intelligence chief said to him "Go ask any others in the building if they wish to participate."

Two hours later Maa was nearly dead from the abuse and injuries she suffered and begged: "Please stop hurting me and I'll give you more information."

"What information?" asked the intelligence chief who tapped the DM on top of Maa to get off. She lay quietly with her eyes closed.

"What information" repeated the intelligence Chief who dug his nails into her breast drawing blood.

"How we really travel!" she shrieked.

"Leave" he ordered all the DM's in the room. Then he communicated with Glgoffen. "Supreme leader I may have a breakthrough in the interrogation."

"I will be there immediately."

Maa was scarcely conscious when Glgoffen arrived. The intelligence chief held her by the chin and shook her head to revive her. When she opened her eyes he demanded, "How do you really travel."

Maa was disoriented and did not answer right away. The intel chief dug his nails into her again.

"Through the portals," she whispered.

Glgoffen felt his excitement building. "What portals?" he asked.

The ones we walk through," she moaned.

"Is that how you arrived at Planet Sunset? he pressed. The Intel chief dug into her flesh again. Maa shrieked, quivered for a few seconds and died.

"See if she can be revived, hurry" ordered Glgoffen who sat watching as medics worked on her. *Ancestors was she coherent enough to mean that they walk through a door of some type to arrive at a destination?*

The Intelligence Chief approached him "Supreme leader she could not be saved."

Supreme Pack Leader Glgoffen nodded "We have much to discuss and study. It was an important interrogation."

AT THE SAME MOMENT. . .

The Entity correctly reasoned, since private Maa said she used a portal coming from MW to Sunset, the DMs would try to locate one to obtain any information they could. It knew the closest candidates for their attack would be Planets Sunset and Pleasant; It instantly flashed an alert to all military and civil leaders. "The secret of Transit Portals is discovered. Plan to defend them throughout the galaxy. Imperative to have forces heavily guard and defend portals on MW, Pleasant and Sunset. If any of these found and successful taken the fighting could spread into the core of the galaxy at Planet Midway."

The 1st Marine Division was ordered to send a regiment of troops to Planet Pleasant to guard the travel portals and research buildings along with another regiment that would land as reinforcements if needed. At the same time, the Army put two divisions on alert in the event of a worst-case scenario.

Unlike humans, the DMs did not name any planets in the system. They simply referred to them by the name of the senior ship in orbit around it. On *Refuge* itself, where the main fleet was in orbit, the world was referred to as *Warbeast,* the name of the Supreme Command ship.

A communication specialist approached the First Deputy Supreme Pack Leader and stood waiting to be recognized. After several moments the Deputy looked up "What?"

"Deputy leader the Destroyer *Enemy Killer* has left orbit. It is slowly moving toward Planet Sunset. Since I have not been notified of a movement I thought to report."

The First Deputy leaned back with a thoughtful look. "Did someone forgot to notify us of a routine move? Odd. Determine the circumstances!" The communication specialist nodded and left. The DM communication specialist on Planet Warbeast was still trying to raise the Destroyer *Enemy Killer* when he received a message from its crew camp that they were under attack by a Hooman landing force. He hurried to notify the First Deputy Supreme Pack Leader who raised an eyebrow as the specialist approached him again.

"What have you found out?"

"Deputy Supreme Leader, the camp of Enemy Killer reports they are under attack by Hoomans. I am still unable to . . ." The First Deputy cut him off.

"They said they are under attack?"

"Yes, Deputy Leader and I cannot contact the ship itself . . ." He was cut off again. "Follow me, " the Deputy ordered and walked toward the Supreme Pack Leaders spacious quarters bypassing an orderly sitting outside.

Supreme Leader Glgoffen and the Intelligence boss were in deep discussion about the information from the dying woman and annoyed at the intrusion. But he was surprised to see his First Deputy. "I do not wish to be disturbed old friend."

"Hoomans are attacking the main base camp of the *Destroyer Enemy Killer,* the first deputy said."

"Why would they attack a far-removed unimportant target like Enemy Killer when our main force in system is here?" Glgoffen asked rhetorically causing the Intelligence Chief to suddenly straightened up in his seat.

"The ship!" he exclaimed, "they want the ship for its secrets. If they obtain any of our home world charts and maps of the tunnels . . ."

"It will be very serious" Glgoffen interrupted and turned to his First Deputy. "Get an update on the status of the ship immediately. The First Deputy turned to the communication specialist behind him. The man came to attention. "Supreme Leader "the ship itself has left orbit and the system without permission. I was trying to make contact when I received word of the attack."

"They have taken it!" the intelligence chief, exclaimed. "Now they have a ship to study; we must get it back!"

Glgoffen banged his hand onto his table "Get me an update from that world now! Find if there are reports of attacks on any others in this system."

The communications man left at a near run and Glgoffen glared at his First Deputy. "How long ago did this happen?"

"The ship was first noticed moving between the third and fourth hour just before local daylight. It was contacted to see why the captain was moving. While we were trying to contact the ship, a message was received from the main crew camp that they were under assault."

Glgoffen shook his head in disgust. "How soon can we mount a force to that world?"

"It will take several local hours. All we have around the system are some picket ships."

"Cursed Hoomans! We are giving them too much time! It has been hours now. Order all the pickets to go to stealth mode and determine where they are taking *Enemy Killer*. Then: Send one quarter of a Great Pack to relieve the survivors of the camp and defeat any Hoomans still there. Next, send two hundred fighters to each of the other worlds as security. And notify the fleet to begin preparations for departure from this system. We must respond."

The First Deputy hurried out. Glgoffen took a deep breath and sat in thought for several moments then leaned forward and said to the Intelligence chief, "Have all Deputy Pack leaders report here immediately for a strategy meeting. We must counter this move. I did not expect them to follow us here much less attack us. It was an underestimation. If they followed us once they will do so again; and you understand where that could lead if they have our star charts." *If we are to prevail, I must stop underestimating these beings.*

The Intelligence Chief fully understood the seriousness of the situation and turned to gather the others when Glgoffen said "I need your thoughts for our planning."

The Chief nodded and left almost bumping into the First Deputy who hurried back into the room. "The Hoomans have withdrawn from the planet. The Enemy Killer is moving Coreward toward Sunset. I do not have any additional information yet."

Glgoffen nodded and smacked his fist into his thigh." We must destroy that ship before they get it to their space."

Two minutes later the First Deputy was back.

"Well?" said Glgoffen.

"Supreme Leader, a Knife Soldier has been taken prisoner seriously wounded but alive."

Glgoffen stood and punched his right fist into his left hand three times. "Bring him to me as speedily as possible. See he is cared for."

Word of the attack and loss of the ship had spread. The

commanders of the Five Great Packs along with their First deputy commanders, the Fleet commander, artillery and Intelligence, made a somber group when they gathered.

There had been six great packs. But the entire Fifth Great along with its attached units was destroyed. A loss so deeply felt throughout the army that Glgoffen wondered *can the damage to the psyche of the packs who have never suffered significant losses ever be repaired. And now another blow of a ship being snatched from a place I thought secure. Perhaps I should offer my life in atonement for my failures. It may be forfeit anyway when word of our losses reach home. Ancestors curse the Hoomans!*

Supreme Pack Leader Glgoffen stood and regarded his gathered subordinates. "Packmates. We must regain the initiative from our enemy that has become increasingly bold since the loss of the Fifth Great, and has now attacked us in this system.

"All indications are they have captured the Destroyer *Enemy Killer*. My latest information is that they are withdrawing from the planet. A quarter of the Sixth Great from the Sixth-third Attack Group is moving toward that world as reinforcements.

"We have learned several important facts from some Hooman prisoners. Firstly: they have very good stealth capabilities. A fact that I have sent to our ships. Secondly, and more importantly, they have alternate methods of traveling that we were completely unaware of. The prisoner described it as a portal, and also said they have an entire world for just the military.

"Unfortunately, she died during the questioning so we have no way of knowing if that is truthful. But it is imperative for us to find out more about the doors and mount operations that will have them reacting to us.

One other item. For the first time we have taken a knife soldier alive although he was grievously wounded. He is being brought here for questioning. Now give me your thinking."

The leaders began talking among themselves at his disclosure.

Glgoffen held up both arms for silence. "Our expedition of expansion has changed. Now in the short term it is the defense of our home-land worlds."

"How is such a thing possible?" challenged the First Great Pack Leader amid another babble of conversation.

"Quiet, you will maintain discipline!" Glgoffen yelled . The room became deathly quiet as he walked back and forth in front of them. The anger evident in his eyes; each knew he had absolute power over them.

"We came to this galaxy because of a message collected from one of our exploration probes and we sat undisturbed for months while I dispatched a small reconnaissance pack to another well-developed Planet near-by. As it turned out that world was called *Pleasant*. Our packmates had some initial success there and we gained information.

"Since that time, the Hoomans have mobilized against us on *Planet Sunset*, and have destroyed almost seventeen percent of the force I brought here." He glared around the room. "They seemed to have unlimited troops even though we have killed them in almost equal numbers. Do any of you still doubt that this adversary who we joyously mocked as Hoo-hoo-man's when we first encountered them are not warriors equal to us?"

Hoo-mans was the extremely insulting nickname given to human-ity by some alien troops after their first contacts. A play on words linking humans and a small mammal from their galaxy that made a "hoo-hoo" sound as it fearfully scurried to hide from most things.

SPL Glgoffen stopped his pacing and stood with his hands on his hips looking around the still room. "Now I believe we know why they had so many fighters that we did not know about on that world. . . the doors revealed by that dying prisoner are the secret."

He began pacing again. "Another prisoner said that they have an entire world dedicated to training their military. If both statements are true, I doubt we win with our current force. I am considering sending to the home-worlds for help."

One of the commanders stood to be recognized and the supreme leader nodded to him. "Why not take our force home and return a greater one." Glgoffen considered the question for several moments.

"Remember . . . the Hoomans have followed and attacked us here in our sanctuary. As we speak, they are attempting to captured a ship that has invaluable information of our worlds along with the location of a tunnel used to get there. If the ships I sent in pursuit cannot recapture that ship I am afraid that our enemy, if able to understand this information, will use it to follow us home."

His comment created another babble of conversation he allowed to continue for a minute before holding up his arm. "Which is why I now re-define our role here as defensive. It is critical we discover the truth of the doors. A task that we would have a much more difficult time achieving on *Planet Sunset*."

CHAPTER 2

"Fair is foul, and foul is fair."
Macbeth. William Shakespeare

ON RUBY WITH THE PATHFINDERS . . .

Frank, and his squad watched the bathing DMs for several minutes. "Squad Pull back" he ordered. "Corporal Kim, I want you and your team in position to kill the overwatch then grab one or two of those females. Do as much damage to the rest of them as you can as quickly as you can. You may be able to get them all and still have time to gather any intelligence data. Meet us with your prisoners before the main landing in the morning"

Kim nodded. "Right."

"Corporal Olney, take us downstream a few hundred meters. We'll cross there then continue searching for their ships or strong points."

"Roger that."

Later:

"Squad down," Olney transmitted from point as he approached the DM camp. "I see one of the big light benders on the outskirts of their camp . . . break . . . I can see six prefabricated buildings and numerous DMs in the area . . . over."

The light bender, was a pole roughly seven feet high and three inches in diameter. Its top half had small arms like a clothing tree. It was technology that bent light rays around a person or object making it, or them, invisible. The marines had small individual units that were very effective; and while the DMs had more or less the same technology, they only deployed it around large items such as ships.

"Stand-by I'm moving toward you," Frank replied. He moved up to the other marines that were watching three-hundred-sixty degrees. When he reached Olney, the team leader indicated with his head toward the large light bender situated outside the camp. Frank studied it for a minute. "Ten to one there's ships hidden there. For some reason, no matter how safe they feel they always hide the ships. This is the third time I've come across one of um."

"Corporal Gupta, you have point. Move back two hundred meters . . . break . . . Corporal Olney you now have our six." They left the area as quietly as they arrived.

The marines set up a perimeter, and Frank met with his team leaders. He took off his hat and wiped his face with it. "Olney, I want your team to pulse that light bender and knocked it out. As soon as the boats or anything else becomes visible start bouncing pulses around. Drugba and Gupta your teams will position yourselves with me to pulse anyone trying to reach the boats I expect to see."

Both team leaders nodded.

Frank cautioned Corporal Gupta: "You've never fought um before. Remember, they're fast and aggressive. Don't ever underestimate um, and try not to pulse them head on. If they're wearing their helmets they'll see a disturbance from your pulse if you're head on to them when ya shoot."

The DM helmet resembled the Roman Coolus helmet with a clear face shield. Early in the war Frank discovered that even though human pulse weapons were completely silent, when a DM had the visor on his helmet down the pulse made a shimmer when observed from the front.

Frank looked around. "We have a good location here everyone try ta rest. We'll keep one person on watch for thirty minutes each. That'll give us all a breather. The watch will repeat until zero two thirty when we move to our assigned positions."

Frank looked at the calm faces around him "Any comments, suggestions, questions?" The team leaders remained quiet. "Okay."

Frank settled in under a large tree "Pathfinder-one to Alpha-six . . . over."

"Go Pathfinder-one."

"Pathfinder-one we have a possible location of the Delta-Mike crew landing boats . . . break . . ." and Frank outlined his plan of attack and withdrawal in the morning.

"Roger that Pathfinder-one good luck . . . out."

One of Gupta's team shook Frank "It is zero two thirty Sarge."

"Right"

When everyone was up and alert the teams moved to their assigned locations. Frank lay in the thick forest at dawn watching the alien camp when he heard "Landing force away" and communicated with his squad "The landing force is coming down. Let's do it people."

He began pulsing the large light bender that was immediately knocked out revealing three landing boats that the ten marines also began hitting."

They all saw the landing craft coming in behind the buildings in the camp then immediately shooting up out of sight. And from the sound of it, the DM resistance to the landing was fierce. Frank winced when he heard the *Rrrriiipp* sound of one of the rapid-fire weapons that was able to put out a huge amount of fire power like a Gatling gun. He had been under fire by them before, and he had a healthy fear of it.

As he lay there with his squad, he saw a group of twenty DM's jogging in formation toward the landing boats. They were led by an officer that halted them momentarily when he realized the boats were now visible, and something was wrong. He began looking around for a threat. It was a pause that cost them.

The leader had just issued a command when Frank and his squad began pulsing the formation that were sailors who had never experienced the silent death of a pulse weapons in a direct fire situation. They were all killed before they could react.

The marines took a moment to root through the bodies for any obvious intelligence information. Frank opened a small haversack the leader carried and found what he recognized as a flag from one of the DM home worlds that their fighters liked to carry with them. He took it for a souvenir, along with a naval helmet he thought may have intelligence value. But the fighting on the other side of the camp continued as fierce as ever and he realized they had to move quickly.

"Kim to Farrell" Frank heard in his head.

"Go Kim."

"Kim to Farrell the camp only contained fifteen DM's. All female . . . break . . . I have five prisoners . . . break . . . we are moving toward your location."

"Roger that. Good job. . . Farrell out."

Just as he finished, he heard a chilling transmission from groundside command to the naval ships in orbit.

"Landing team command to *Argon* command . . . the DM's are fighting from building to building. It will take us too long to attack each one to get them all . . . break . . . in addition, our pulse weapons are not penetrating through the buildings . . . break . . . send down the boats we are going to withdraw back to the ships . . . out."

"Roger that. Boats away."

"Landing team command to all groundside troops. Move to your evacuation positions. I say again, move to your evacuation positions."

Shit they're resisting much more than expected Frank worried. He opened a map in his head, saw that Corporal Kim's team was now close to the camp. He communicated to the squad: "Farrell to pathfinders, move to the right front of the camp to meet our assigned boat . . . break . . . all teams acknowledge."

After they all acknowledged, he moved the squad toward the landing craft that were taking heavy fire when they tried to land as the landing force began to disengage. He and his squad reached their boat without too much interference and prepared to embark. Frank shook his head in surprise. *The fucking DM squids are resisting harder than their fucking army did.*

"Delta-three" Frank heard "we are pinned down by the rapid-fire guns and have many causalities. Our pulse fire will not penetrate the buildings the DM's occupy."

Oh shit! No one saw this coming Frank realized . . . then quickly decided on a plan of action. *Our slugs will probably penetrate those buildings and every team leader has one. It may help.*

"Corporal Kim, give me your slug thrower then get those prisoners aboard now. All team leaders rally to me with your slug throwers. Everyone else board the landing craft now!"

Franks squad ran on board prodding their prisoners while he and the team leaders moved a short way looking toward Delta Companies 3rd Platoon, that was pinned down taking very heavy fire.

"Pathfinder-One to Delta-three we have four slug throwers; we'll attempt to knock out that rapid fire gun so you can evacuate . . . break . . . Move when I tell you . . . Pathfinder-one, out."

"Roger that Pathfinder-one."

Frank communicated to his team leaders. "I want ya to put as many slugs as ya can around the opening that gun is firing from. These slugs should punch through. On my command. . . fire." The shooting from inside the building stopped almost immediately.

"Move now" Frank communicated to the pinned down survivors who ran toward their evacuation craft helping those wounded they could. The dead were left.

Frank and his team leaders kept a brisk fire into and around the open windows as they maneuvered to their own craft. When everyone was seated the front snapped into existence and they shot straight up to the *Argon.* They had been the first to land on the planet, and were the last to leave.

The cost to the landing force was heavy. Worse, the command was shocked to discover that six marines had been forgotten; left behind when the force withdrew from the planet. But the team leader of that lost group kept her head and notified the ship they were going to evade capture in the forest and hope to be rescued at some point. She also notified her command that the DMs were collecting the marine bodies, gear and captured a wounded marine found among the dead. Then she gave the names of everyone still with her, including Private Alicia Macalduie.

"We will be back to get you. Evade, hide, and report when possible" were her orders. It was god who gave the name of the prisoner. Corporal Benton Simon also a member of Delta Recon. Who was unconscious when he was captured after he and his team walked into the kill zone of a rapid-fire gun, and were all shot. One slug had creased the side of his head knocking him out for a minute. It saved him, and he was the only survivor of the team; but was now a prisoner. Something he had never imagined would happen to him.

Corporal Benton Simon, born on New Hibernia, had been in the Corps eight years and in recon for the last three. He was a tough professional standing over two meters tall and in excellent physical condition. His face, and bearing, marked him for a veteran who had been in continuous combat since the beginning of the Sunset Perimeter campaign the year before.

Cpl Simon was an impressive sight. More so in his beat-up, bloody, field uniforms worn condition that was adorned with the numerous medals, and badges, he'd earned during the past year. Including the Combat Action Bar; and above it was the Recon Qualification badge of a Silver skull with a dagger stuck through it vertically from top to bottom. On His left pocket he wore the Galactic Cross in silver. The third highest award in the United Worlds military. Under that was a plane Bronze Maltase Cross next to a one-inch-high representation of a red blood drop symbolizing a wound in action. And under those was the round Planetary Assault Badge and the silver Nuclear Veterans Badge with its representation of a mushroom cloud. Finally, his right cuff had corporal chevrons, and five inches above the cuff on his left sleeve was the one-inch-high white trimmed in gold cuff band "RIM WORLDS"

Simon had been in close contact with DMs many times and had no special fear of them. He'd certainly killed his share over the past year and knew they were sadists who enjoyed torturing and killing humans. *I am already dead. It is just how long they want to keep me. Stars help me stay strong.*

He was very surprised that what he took to be a DM medic treated his injuries before they escorted him to a waiting boat. It took him to a small ship that left for Planet Warbeast/Refuge. He was kept in isolation in a small compartment that had a guard outside, but he remained unmolested during the journey. When he was taken from the ship and saw the amount of activity and landing boats coming and going, he realized, *they brought me to Refuge. But why? Whatever it is I cannot show weakness. Ancestors help me.*

Suddenly he had an idea. *Hey god are you still with me?*

Simon felt a tingle inside his head and heard his own mind *I am with you marine. Look and gather what you can. Your comrades know of you.*

He was marched alone in the middle of four armed guards who stayed at least four feet away from him to prevent any surprise attacks. The group entered a large prefabricated building amid the stares and comments of everyone they passed. They halted at a large office and turned the prisoner over to the Intelligence Chief who had his own guard with him. "Bring him in" he ordered his guard. The others waited outside.

Inside the room Simon saw two long tables one with blood stains from the two unfortunate soldiers. Sitting behind a desk in front of the room was an older DM who regarded him with more curiosity that hostility. Simon stared back at him, and then at the other one standing next to him as he continued to look around taking in as much as he could.

I hope you are getting this.

"Are the translators in place?" SPL Glgoffen asked.

"We are ready when you are Supreme Leader."

Glgoffen stared at Cpl Simon who met his eyes. Surprisingly it was Glgoffen who looked away for a moment after they held eye contact for almost thirty-seconds. Then he looked back continuing to study the man standing in front of him. *There is no mistaking him. This is a killer. A warrior. Not a child like the other two, and he is a knife soldier.*

Glgoffen nodded to the Intelligence chief to begin. The intelligence officer walked up and stood next to the Supreme Pack Leader. "Soldier, what is your name?"

Simon eyes clicked between the intelligence chief and Glgoffen, but he said nothing.

"Are you unable to speak!" demanded the intelligence officer.

Glgoffen sat watching, then he remembered that the young soldier said the knife soldiers were called marines in their army. *Could there be such a difference?*

He stood up next to his intelligence chief who looked at him curiously. Glgoffen stood looking at Simon and said, "Marine, who are you?"

Simon looked at Glgoffen and raised his chin. "Corporal Benton Simon United Worlds Marine Corps."

Fierce proud and unafraid. "Marine what do these devices on your uniform represent" Glgoffen asked.

Simon looked at him and grinned. "They are awards for killing a lot of DMs like you." The guard behind him was so incensed he instinctively punched Simon in the back of the head knocking him to his hands and knees stunned.

"Stop or you will be executed!" Glgoffen shouted at the guard who left when the intelligence chief made a shooing motion. Two additional guards came into the room carrying Simons utility belt. They laid it on Glgoffen's desk.

"Help him into a chair" the intelligence chief ordered. The guards lifted Simon off the floor and stood on either side of him and lowered him into a chair. Glgoffen and his Intel chief both regarded Simon. "How did he refer to us?" the Intel officer asked.

"Marine. What is a DM?" asked the Supreme Leader Glgoffen.

Simon shook his head trying to clear it. He had a headache and felt groggy. The blow had also reopened the wound on the side of his head that was bleeding freely again. "Wh . . . what?"

"You called me a DM. What is that?"

"I don't think it's a secret. DM is the abbreviation for Dogman."

"What do you mean?" asked the intelligence officer clearly confused.

Cpl Simon gave him a feral smile. "To us, you face has a resemblance to Pug dogs. Four legged creatures we keep as pets. It is a stretch but you get the meaning."

The Intel officer was insulted and furious. "You dare insult us like that you Hoo-man slime!" he yelled. Then he stopped realizing what he just said.

He and Glgoffen shared a look. "Hoo-man . . . and . . . Dogman. We have much similarity" commented Glgoffen. The Intel officer nodded.

Glgoffen walked over and looked at the utility belt on the desk. He removed the twelve-inch recon knife and studied it along with the recon emblem prominent on Simon's chest. Then he walked to inspect Simon closer.

"What is your rank?"

Simon looked up at him "I am a Corporal."

The Intel officer said to Glgoffen "He is a very small unit leader." Glgoffen nodded.

"What is your unit?" he asked, and Simon stared at him but did not answer.

"Stand up when you address the Supreme Leader and answer him." The guard prodded Simon in the back with his rifle and Simon stood quietly.

"Where is your unit from, and what is your job."

Simon stood watching the two men but did not answer. Glgoffen still holding the long recon dagger tapped its point several times in the middle of Simon's chest hard enough to draw blood. "Marine. Suppose I told you today was the day of your death unless you speak to us." He put the point of the dagger up under Simon's chin.

"Well?" Glgoffen demanded. He was confused when he saw a glint in the prisoner's eye. *Is his mind gone?*

Simon drew himself up almost at attention and said "Since no one knows the time of their death all that can be done is to control how we die. Hopefully it will be well."

In a flash of his hands, he snatched the dagger from Glgoffen. Because the DM standing beside the Supreme Leader was the easiest follow through target Simon sunk the dagger into the right eye of the Intelligence Chief penetrating into his brain instantly killing him. The entire movement was so quick that the guard did not act to shoot Simon until he saw the Intel Chief sag to the floor with hilt of the dagger sticking from his eye.

Glgoffen jumped back and was immediately surrounded by other guards who ran in at the sound of the guard's gunshot. He was shocked looking at Simon, now dying, laying on top of the dead Intelligence Chief.

"Check him" Glgoffen ordered still shaken by the speed and ferocity of the attack. *Spirits of the ancestors. He has killed an old and trusted friend who is irreplaceable. Spirits help if there truly are a Great Pack of fighters like him.* He continued looking at the body of his Intelligence Chief and close advisor *you are the third old comrade and deputy to die at the hands of these cursed Hoomans.*

The guards dragged Simon a few feet from his victim and checked his wound that was clearly mortal. Although his heart was still beating.

"He still lives Supreme Leader" one of the guards said. Glgoffen nodded then looked at the body of his friend again. "One of you pull that weapon out and give it to me. Then take the Deputy Leader and prepare him. We will morn him later."

A guard pulled out the dagger holding the remainder of the eye in place as he did so. Then he handed the weapon to Glgoffen, who stood studying it while listening to Simons labored breathing. Now more of a rattle.

He knelt beside Simon and held the dagger over Simons right eye. *This warrior wished to die well . . . and he has.*

Glgoffen pushed with all his strength jamming the dagger into Simons eye and out the back of his skull. The marine shivered and died. The instant before his death, the Computer Entity told Marine Command of his bravery then recommended he be awarded a posthumous Galactic Starburst. Cpl Simon had killed a very important enemy combatant in extreme conditions. His last words were also reported by god; and in later years they were slightly modified as a training slogan: "We don't know if we will die in battle. If so, die well."

SPL Glgoffen stood waiting to begin the meeting with his Great Pack leaders thinking about the loss of his friend. More importantly, he knew he had lost a brilliant theorist, annalist, and advisor without whom he felt directionless. Glgoffen brought himself back to the present and muttered. "He was right in his thoughts of alternative methods of delivering troops. That dying female soldier said they use some type of door." *I must determine how they do it.*

The Assistant Intelligence Chief, now the new Deputy Supreme Leader for Intelligence, reported to the Supreme Pack Leader and stood nervously before him. Glgoffen scrutinized him. "How much did your predecessor confide in you?"

"Very little I am afraid Supreme Leader. He kept his thoughts and information to himself." The new intel chief, whose name was Herckel replied.

"Did he discuss the existence of the Hooman doors?"

Herckel thought for a moment. "Once he told me he suspected they had another method of travel. I was in the room when the dying soldier confirmed that. But you were there also, and heard the same." Glgoffen nodded and asked, "Did he speak of his plans for a counter offensive to the Planet Pleasant?"

The new Intel chief thought for a moment. "He told me to begin a grid plan of the city of New Glasgow on that Planet. He said he had indications from the Reconnaissance pack sent there over a year ago that a travel hub may be on the south side of that city. Near a river. But they never sent additional information before contact was lost.

"Neither of us thought much of it; until the talk from that prisoner of alternative methods of travel. Supreme leader, I am beginning to believe that we misunderstood the information from a year ago .Since our team was probably destroyed, and unable to clarify, we allowed ourselves to think in conventional terms. Perhaps, they reported it because they *had* learned of the alternate travel."

Glgoffen sat in thought again. *He seems intelligent enough. Perhaps this loss will not be as crippling as I feared. He has just provided me with a direction for our offensive.* "Herckel, you and I will be working very closely. I will act on your recommendation of an attack to New Glasgow. Keep working on the plan you began and be ready to discuss it with me in full in three days. Now let us address our packmates."

The two walked to a meeting room and to the front. Glgoffen pointed to Herckel. "Packmates! This is our new Intelligence Chief. You all know him. Now . . . we must react to the hoomans quickly before they become too aggressive, but we need much more informa- tion. I propose the following plan, its object will be the discovery of one of their traveling doors that, as she died, a prisoner told us she used to come to Planet Sunset. I believe it critical to verify this information one way or another.

"The first phase of the plan: is the successful recapture of *Enemy Killer* by our picket boats. While that is happening, one third of the fleet will leave this system when they are ready. They will follow an arching route Trailing-Rimward to the *Planet Pleasant* for a raid in force. The purpose is to gain intelligence information on the doors that we can use later. It is reasonable to postulate, that a world such as *Pleasant* that has government buildings and is major a learning center will have one of these doors . . . if they exist

|"This action, will be conducted by half of the First Great and half of the Second Great Packs. Almost eighteen thousand fighters and attachments should be enough for this type of attack. To support this plan a smaller force will make a diversionary attack on another Planet called *NX two four six*. Now listen to the Intelligence Deputy who will now explain the plan. I want you to be ready within two weeks."

The new intelligence chief stepped forward. "I do not have information of conditions on Planet NX two-four-six since our original attack with the Special Landing Force. It is prudent for us to expect some type of military presence there. I am hopeful Hooman reinforcement ships will concentrate on that world, while our real invasion fleet proceeds to *Pleasant*. There, they will attack a city called New Glasgow identified by one of our reconnaissance packs as a center of study and learning."

He looked around the room at the assembled commanders. "Is this clear so far?"

The commander of the First Great Pack stood. "Why have we targeted that world? If we are to make headway here, we must destroy their fighters who are on *Planet Sunset*. If they travel by mysterious doors might not one be there? Are we afraid to confront them in battle to avenge our brothers and sisters of the Fifth Great Pack?" he shifted his gaze to SPL Glgoffen who not only sensed the challenge to his leadership, he understood it.

Glgoffen stepped forward and put a hand on Herckel arm to stopping him from answering. He addressed the group. "Packmates . . . the focus has changed. We came to this galaxy with expectations of quick victory and have found another hunting species." The grim looks on the assembled faces told him they agreed.

"The information gained from the prisoner answers a number of questions first raised during the fighting on *Sunset*. Mostly about their capabilities, and it has given other information useful to our cause. We all wish to avenge the loss of the Fifth Great, but I do not believe we have the capability to do it here and now. Does that answer your question?" The commander of the First Great sat down more from surprise than courtesy.

Six DM picket ships, and one stealth ship, joined up and were able to locate and catch *Enemy Killer* and its escorts. The Battle Cruisers *UWS Resourceful* and *Dreadnought* moved in formation with *Enemy Killer* well below half C, on a trajectory toward the Planet Sunset. The bridge crew on the captured ship worked feverishly to understand the control sequences to gain speed. "We are crawling" complained the bridge officer, "if we can't figure this out, we are fucked!"

"Sir," answered his chief, "there are still some computers and systems we cannot access without the correct codes. As close as I can tell they are specific to traveling at C. They seem to increase in increments that require a password. From what I can see there are twenty settings that would equal five C, at full speed."

"Shit chief!" spat the bridge officer. "At this rate it will take forever to get back. The DMs will be all over us!" The chief shrugged. The bridge officer sighed. "Do your best chief. I will communicate with fleet to see if we can get some help."

"Aye-aye, sir."

The first DM picket ship fired its missiles immediately followed by the others that quickly turned to evade the defensive fire of *Resourceful* and *Dreadnought*. But not before two of the smaller picked ships were destroyed. The Gunners mates on *Enemy Killer* were able to destroy the last of the incoming missiles as the four remaining DM ships turned to reengage.

The *Dreadnought's* main pulse weapon quickly shut down all the systems on the attackers then fired a missile into one of the helpless ships that catastrophically exploded. At the same time the remaining three DM boats concentrated their missiles on *Enemy Killer* trying to destroy it at all costs.

The captain of UWS *Resourceful* realized the importance of the captured ship to humanity; and he placed his ship into the trajectory of the incoming missiles. His gunners were able to destroy all but two of them. One hit forward, the other midship, causing severe damage to *Resourceful* with heavy causalities to the crew. The captain called for assistance.

The UWS *Dreadnought* re-engaged the three-alien picket ships: destroyed one, crippled a second, and forced the third to withdraw. But they missed the stealth craft that stayed out of the battle and continued to follow.

"Sir!" yelled the senior helmsman on the captured ship, "I have the sequence! We can move to C or faster on your command."

"What is the maximum?"

"It looks like five C sir."

The officer nodded "Take us to three C until we are two AU from Sunset; then reduce our velocity to a normal approach."

"Aye-aye sir. Three C until we are two AU from Sunset, then reduce our velocity to a normal approach" the helmsmen replied. An AU, astronomical unit, equaled ninety-three million miles or eight light minutes, the distance of Earth to its Sun.

The captain communicated his information and intentions to the other ships. Military command sent a second battle cruiser, the UWS *Mother Earth*, to insure their safe arrival. The Naval boarding party on the alien ship was able to successfully attain geostationary orbit on Sunset, away from the Perimeter, above Camp Gonzales located on the other side of the planet. There, a score of navy engineers, and physicists, came aboard to begin studying every inch of the ships data bases and systems. They began compiling a significant picture of DM technology.

It was a costly successful operation. Although the raiding force had achieved its mission of cutting out a ship and getting prisoners, the landing force itself had been badly bloodied. Mostly because their pulse weapons would not penetrate a solid object. If not for Frank, and a few others using slug throwers it would have been much worse. But it had a positive aspect also . . . the lessons learned.

CHAPTER 3

While Operation *Filch* was in progress in the Refuge system, a discovery was made that shocked the Intelligence and scientific communities involved. So, they dug deeper, to reinvestigate scientific experiments, and studies, that were hundreds of years old. Their conclusions were inescapable. Delta-Mike, originally came from Mother Earth. They were direct descendants of Earths Neanderthals believed extinct for over forty thousand years. The leading scientists of the one-hundred planets comprising the United Worlds of Earth held a symposium to discuss this discovery.

"How is it even possible?" one asked.

The head of intelligence replied "When we first saw the DNA scan results, along with the other blood work studies, we thought we had done something wrong. However, you ladies and gentlemen may or may not know that at gods suggestion, a military implant was placed into our prisoners to verify the truth of answers they give."

"How did that help in these DNA results?" asked the representative from Planet Pleasant.

"Well . . . what we did was have god search their downloaded memories for any mention of how they viewed their own evolution, history, religious beliefs, traditions, and things like that." The head of intelligence paused knowing he had everyone's attention. "And guess what was discovered. A tradition bordering on religious belief, that a spiritual being put them in an ark, then transported their almost extinct species from a land of ice, cold, and large beasts to Andromeda. Where they were taught how to survive and thrive before their saviors left them on their own.

"Ladies and gentlemen, we know from Mother Earth's history of the glaciers covering much of its surface a hundred thousand years ago, up until they thawed from a meteor strike into the glacier, roughly fourteen thousand years ago. This may also explain the speculation of how and why the Neanderthals disappeared, and why so few remains of theirs have been found."

The same representative from Planet Pleasant followed up and asked, "How sure are we of these facts". The intelligence officer deferred to another woman sitting on the stage with him who was a geneticist from the University of Pleasant; and a colleague of the one asking the question.

She cleared her throat.

"After seeing the DNA scans, we began studying research from the Twentieth Century ignored since the Final World War. We also re-reviewed the studies and findings from some Neanderthal bones that were then thirty-nine thousand years old. Primarily we found that, at the time, they sampled the mtDNA or Mitochondrial DNA that follows the mother. That mtDNA research of those twentieth-century studies showed that homo sapiens, and Neanderthal mtDNA, split into separate lineages from a last common ancestor over six hundred and twenty-five thousand years prior. They concluded that Neanderthals were unlikely to have contributed significantly to the human genome."

She paused and took a sip of water.

"However, in the early Twenty-first century, evidence of ancient liaisons with Neanderthals and other extinct branches of our species, like the Denisovan's, came to light and *could* be found in the DNA of some homo sapiens population.

"In the second decade of that century, research concluded that

Neanderthals, and Denisovans, had at times, much later than thought, mated with homo sapiens. The researchers estimated that the DNA of living Asians and Europeans in the Twenty-first century was on the average two-point four percent Neanderthal.

"Needless to say, they wondered how much inbreeding would be necessary to end up with so little Neanderthal DNA. Further study concluded all that was needed would have been for a human and a Neanderthal to create a baby roughly once a generation."

She took another sip of water. "Of course, the Final World War almost wiped-out humanity on *Mother Earth*. Our population since then, on all one hundred of our worlds, is still not as high as it was just in the county known as China before the final war."

The prime minister of the Unite Worlds cut in "Thank you Doctor. For the purposes of *this* war, we know now we fight a more human than alien enemy. One that originated from our ancestral home. Now . . . what does that mean for us and our strategies?"

ON MILITARY WORLD:

The Marine Commandant, General Thomas, was notified by the Army Commanding General, the overall commander on Sunset, that Dr. Lamont and his team had quickly solved the ineffectiveness of the pulse weapons in Urban combat.

The Army CG told General Thomas "I do not know why we did not address this when we could not kill those monster beasts used at the Sunset Perimeter." It was rhetorical. He shook his head and answered his own question. "We wanted a quick solution and went with the effectiveness of a slug thrower. Doctor Lamont will brief us in an hour."

An hour later the two general officers met with Doctor Lamont, who after some small talk told them, "What I discovered as I considered this problem was available to us the entire time. I have tested the answer in the laboratory and it *is* effective. We can tinker with it if necessary after you use it in actual field conditions,"

"I never knew you were a weapons specialist" the Army Commanding General remarked. "I always associated your name with our transit system."

Dr. Lamont nodded. "It is new for me too. But I am a physicist first, and as it turned out our weapons are just another physics problem. Yes?"

The two generals sat considering him. Sergeant Major Brown and the army command sergeant major both sat inscrutable. Dr. Lamont began to pace as he lectured the men. "The problem was the pulse weapon could not penetrate a hard surface. Since we never really had any sustained warfare before this invasion it never became an issue. Even this wars early fighting, as I understand it, was in the open woods and fields. Other than when confronted with the war beasts, our troops were never blocked by obstacles and the flaw remained unknown until the landing on the Planet Ruby."

General Thomas was slightly impatient. "Tell us how you have remedied the problem Doctor"

"Oh yes . . . sorry. Well, the problem was how to adapt our weapons to be used in an urban environment. Essentially it was merely a matter of adding radio waves then adjusting frequency. The lower the frequency, the more the penetrating power."

General Thomas had furrows form between his eyes. "Could you be a little more specific doctor. I do not know about General Hayduf, or the Sergeants Major, but my knowledge in this is limited."

The General Hayduf chuckled. "Do not feel alone."

Lamont sat down again and took a deep breath. "What my team and I did was as simple as ancient basic radio. We encoded the information for the pulse weapon, that has a rectangular wave, onto a radio wave in effect creating a non-sinusoidal wave form.

"Then we piggybacked the amplitude modulation onto the pulse.

Once the modulation was completed, it became a simple matter of the frequency of the original pulse. Remember the lower the frequency the more penetrating power. After you convert them, your weapons will penetrate most unshielded obstacles."

General Thomas chuckled. "Thank you for that simplified version doctor." Dr. Lamont did not get the joke.

"Oh, I almost forgot. Lamont said." We also developed a sort of sighting device that can be rotated from the side of the pulse weapon to the top as needed. It works on the same principle as a Radio Tomographic Imaging device, RTI for short. Essentially it will see through some walls by measuring the shadows created on the radio waves when they penetrate a person. It should make a target visible depending on conditions." Even Sergeant Major Brown looked impressed.

"How long will it take to convert our weapons?" General Thomas asked.

"It should not take long at all. The applications can be loaded into a basic tester, then be plugged into a weapon the same as doing field maintenance. It will only be a matter of how many your armories can adapt in a day. The converters are being made as we speak as fast as we can turn them out. I'll make sure your marines get some of the first ones. As for the RTI scope, that will take slightly longer."

As General Hayduf stood to leave he said, "You have done an amazing service in a very short time. Thank you, doctor. Your work will save many human lives" He left followed by General Thomas and both sergeants major.

ON PLANET SUNSET . . .

Frank and the other squad leaders of 2nd Platoon met with Lt. Nikowa and Sgt Valdez in a lesson learned session from the raid. Nikowa looked around his office at everyone. "Well, we had a nasty surprise when we discovered that our weapons would not penetrate a hard structure. But the think tanks have worked on it and say they have a solution."

"How did they solve it so fast sir?" one of the squad leaders asked.

"It had to do with frequency and waves. At any rate, we will begin getting our pulse rifles updated beginning early tomorrow. Supposedly it's a quick process. Not only that, the skipper told me we are having a meeting of all Battalion NCO's and officers. The Colonel himself will give the briefing."

There must be some big shit coming for the colonel to brief every NCO. "When is it sir?" Frank asked.

"Tomorrow at the ninth hour. Everything will be discussed then. Until then you're dismissed."

"Attention on deck!" yelled the battalion Sergeant Major when he saw the colonel enter the back of the room. The assembled NCO's and officers of the 1st Recon Battalion jumped to their feet.

"As you were," the colonel said as he continued up to the raised platform in the front of the room. He stepped up and looked over the assembled marines all waiting to hear what caused this unusual meeting of the battalion leadership.

"I know you ladies and gentlemen are waiting to hear the word. First: as far as we know, the pulse weapon issue has been corrected by the think tanks. The problem had to do with frequency. When the weapon was first developed it was always considered an anti-personnel weapon. There was no concern with hard targets because we have never been in a major urban conflict in the Perimeter much less a major war until now.

"I know some of you are asking yourselves why did we not figure all of this out when we encountered those monster beasts on the Sunset

Perimeter for the first time." The colonel looked over the sea of faces. "And I do not have a good answer. We did not. But that was then, and this is now. Now we know.

"The problem without too much physics talk was all about combining waves. They added radio waves to the current pulse wave then adjusted the frequency. The lower the frequency the more penetrating power there is. If you want to know all the scientific jargon access your chip later on your own time. The bottom line is that after we do the conversion your weapons *will* penetrate most unshielded obstacles and kill your target."

He smiled at the growl the greeted his comment.

"Not only that, they went one better, and developed a type of sighting device called an RTI that stands for Radio Tomographic Imaging Device. And again, without going into the physics the RTI should allow you to see your target through walls."

There was a burst of conversation around the hall.

"As you were!" the sergeant major yelled. The colonel looked around with a satisfied expression. "I agree. I was impressed too when I first heard it."

The colonel became ominous. "This battalion left six marines behind on the withdrawal from Ruby. In the confusion of that fighting withdrawal they were not missed until the landing boat had lifted off. It was a navy decision not to endanger the boat to return for them."

Some grumbles began from the NCO's.

"As you were," the colonel said silencing the meeting. He looked over the assembled troops. "Things happen in the fog of battle. It was no one's fault. I can understand the navy decision not to endanger a landing boat crew and the full load of marines it was evacuating under heavy fire.

"The good news is that the team leader is keeping her head. She and the four marines with her are moving toward high ground to await rescue . . . and we *will* rescue them people." His remark was greeted with a roar. The colonel held up his hands for silence.

"Unfortunately, another Marine, Corporal Benton Simon who was captured while unconscious from a head wound was later killed by the DM's during questioning. But not before he was able to kill one of the highest-ranking officers in their army. For his action he has been posthumously awarded the Galactic Starburst."

The hall became tomb quiet. "Regrettably, two new soldiers were captured here on Sunset; and during unspeakable torture one of them mentioned our Travel Portals."

If possible, the silence felt weightier.

"Because of the mere mention of the portals we have to assume Delta-Mike will try to locate one of them. The most likely targets at this time are the ones on Pleasant or here on Sunset. The one here has already been reinforced. The feeling is that any attempt they make will be made for the one in New Glasgow on Planet Pleasant.

"Now before I go into the New Glasgow operation, I want to share one more piece of information that I personally found shocking. This has been verified to the satisfaction of the galactic government." He paused drawing out the anticipation he could feel coming from his audience. "It has been proved beyond a doubt that Delta-Mike came from Mother Earth."

Instead of noise he was greeted with continued silence. "Apparently Neanderthal humans were removed from Earth almost forty thousand years ago by some unknown force, and taken to Andromeda. So . . . it seems we are fighting distant cousins. Now we know why they seemed so familiar at times."

Frank was as shocked as the others. *I knew it! I said more than once, the more I see those ugly fuckers the more they seem like us.*

"Now ladies and gentlemen for the main topic." Colonel Rham waited as the shock of his last statement wore off and he could see people beginning to quietly discuss what they heard.

"How do we prepare to face a DM landing on Planet Pleasant in city of New Glasgow?" A rhetorical question that he immediately answered. "Initially, one-regiment of the First Marine Division will be involved.

"Tomorrow, General Thomas along with the CG of the First Marine Division will be briefing all officers on the coming operation. Our role here in Recon will be duel. First: I am sending a rescue team to Planet Ruby to find our missing marines in an operation named *Enduring Fidelity*.

"Second. The remainder of this battalion will be on Planet Pleasant involved with the1st Division in another operation named, *Strong Door*. I want you to watch as I show you our AO." Everyone relaxed as a graphic appeared behind their eyes the same as watching a large screen movie. It was a tactical image of the City of New Glasgow as seen from higher altitudes. Everyone heard the colonel in their heads.

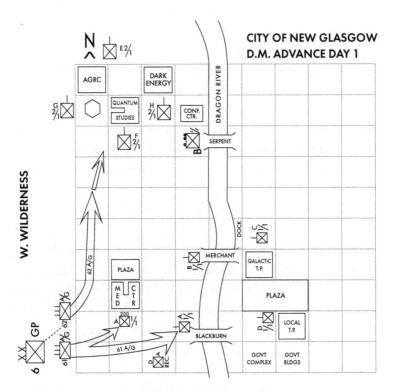

"A year or so ago Delta-Mike sent a recon platoon to Planet Pleasant. They were able to cause some trouble there until being discovered by a team from this Battalion. Our own Sergeant Farrell was part of that two-man team. They battled those DMs in the wilderness outside of the western boundary of the city. That is important for several reasons. The main one being that Delta-Mike may, and I emphasize may, have passed information back to their command about our transport system. No one knows for sure. What we do know is that a prisoner did mentioned Portals to them before she died. So, we must assume they are not stupid. They will make a SWAG that one of the portals is in the City of New Glasgow on Pleasant.

"As you see, New Glasgow is as much university as a city. It is roughly ten standard blocks by nine blocks square. The blocks themselves are square at six hundred and sixty feet. Eight blocks equal a mile. That makes New Glasgow close to a mile and a half square. That's a lot of ground to fight over.

"The city is cut in half by the slightly wavy Dragon River. It flows north to south and is two hundred and twenty meters wide and between twenty to forty deep." An identification tag appeared on the feature. "There are no shallow fording places. On the northwest side of the city is the University and critical research centers such as the Dark Energy Center. Next to *it* is the Advance Gravity and Non-Locality Research Center known locally as AGRC. In the middle of them is the Quantum Studies Center. The small hexagon shaped building is part of the AGRC. "The other smaller buildings are additional university buildings comprising most of that side of the river. That large building you see in the southwest is the medical research center and hospital.

"The prize is on the southeast side of the river. The planetary government is housed in the complex butting against the river, next to them is the local travel complex. Just across that large plaza roughly two hundred meters to the north is the galactic transit system." Both critical centers began to glow a deep red.

"There are three large bridges spanning the river. The one furthest south by the government complex and closest to the Transit complex is *Blackburn bridge*. The middle span is *Merchants bridge* and you can see why, since it is in the middle of the shopping district. The far northern bridge is *Serpent Bridge*.

"Immediately west of the galactic portal plaza is the shopping district encompassing almost four-square blocks. It includes waterside docks with restaurants recreational piers and boat rentals. East of the river to the wilderness is private residences local clubs and drinking places. There are no large main roads in the City but the grid shape is also a through street in all directions. It is thought that Delta-Mike will most likely land in the western wilderness. That is what their recon team used before and they are familiar with.

"So . . . based on that assumption, the First Battalion First Marines, are assigned the mission of securing the three bridges along with both travel portal centers, and the government buildings. If it appears at any time that Delta-Mike may take a bridge it will be destroyed to prevent them from using it.

"The Second Battalion, will secure the Energy center and the AGRC buildings tucked up next to the northwest wilderness. In the event of an attack those units will hold to the last marine, or until our supporting counterattack arrives that will comprise the entire Second and Third Regiments."

"Any questions?"

"Question sir" the captain of "D" Company vocalized. His name and unit appeared in the lower left of everyone's projection.

"Yes Captain?"

"Sir, what is the Recon mission while the First Marines are securing these areas?"

"We will be running patrols around the entire area out to one hundred K from the city. Especially in the western wilderness where Delta-Mike had a camp before. If we are notified of an inbound alien fleet, or a major landing, we will help repulse the landing then do what we did on Sunset to wreck their day. If they come in stealth mode, hopefully we discover them before they make it to any of the bridges. We will just have to wait and see what develops. Some small teams may be roaming the city itself."

"Thank you, sir," the captain said.

"Anyone else?"

When no one answered the colonel said "I am tasking "A" company for *Operation Enduring Fidelity* to get our people. Captain Nagoto it will be your job to put together a platoon size rescue to land in Stealth mode on Ruby. Get something to me in the next twenty-four hours."

"Aye-aye, sir".

"That's all ladies and gentlemen you are dismissed."

"Attention on deck!" the sergeant major yelled as the colonel stepped from the stage.

"As you were!" called the colonel as he left.

EARLY MORNING ON RUBY . . .

"Everyone follow-me and keep your light benders on" the corporal ordered as she led her lost patrol that was left behind when the raiding forces left Planet Ruby "We are going to make a base camp and gather as much intelligence as we can before we get picked up. Make sure you stay on your toes. We are going to make our camp on top of that hill in front of us" the corporal said.

Alicia had point. She moved through the semi-tropical flora, and trees, that became denser as she climbed higher up the hill. She was followed by another marine then her team leader. The other two behind them continually watched their six as they moved. The five stranded marines had continued running patrols around the large DM camp and had a good idea of what was going on. *I wonder how Frank is? Does he know I'm still here?* Alicia mused. She was not as frightened at being left behind as she imagined she would be.

The DM activity on Ruby had been minimal since the raid. Soon after the attackers withdrew they were followed by most of the DM reinforcements, although there was still a naval presence camped in the town from the now stranded crew of *Enemy Killer*. Those DMs hoped their ship would return for them soon, but until then, were charged with taking care of the dead and collecting everything human they could find from the battle.

"Stop in the next clearing "Alicia's team leader communicated with her.

"Roger that."

The team leader moved up and sat next to her. "What do you think?" she asked. Even though Alicia was new to Recon the team leader knew she had been an analyst on MW that had very good instincts on DM behavior.

Alicia picked up a stick and began scratching in the dirt. "We are about one-klick from their main camp. As far as I know they are still policing up the area. I have not seen any patrols looking for us so they must believe that we all got out except for the bodies they picked up along with that prisoner. The number of DMs in the camp is equal to a standard ship crew like the one we took. My guess is they are the crew stranded groundside when the ship was taken. That's why they have been left with cleanup for the time being. I don't see them as being overly aggressive or eager to patrol. I think we should get higher on this hill, find a clearing we can bring a boat into, keep our heads down and ask god to send a rescue."

The team leader suddenly sat up intently listening for a full minute.

I wonder what that is about Alicia mused.

Her team leader relaxed, smiled at Alicia, and communicated "Team up to me." In a few minutes the five marines sat in a circle. "I actually had a communication from god the team leader said. A rescue from "A" Recon will be coming to get us. All we have to do is get where we want to be picked up and eyeball the area so god can forward a picture to the rescue leader." She looked at Alicia "I want you to stay on point. Find us a place we can land a boat. That's it people. Be alert and let's get ready to haul ass out of here."

ON PLANET SUNSET. . .

Captain Nagoto met with Lt Nikowa and Staff Sergeant Valdez to plan the rescue mission to Ruby. When Lt. Nikowa came into the meeting he said to Nagoto, "Sir I would like Sergeant Farrell to be included in this meeting since he has the pathfinders and has already experienced two hostile planet landing . Captain Nagoto nodded. "You are right I should have thought of him. Get him in here." The four men sat in Nagoto's office. "So far, we know there are five survivors who are not only evading, they are sending back intelligence on Delta-Mike; who they report have recovered the remains of four marines and seven sailors killed during the withdrawal. And we all know about Corporal Simon.

"Sit back gentlemen and look at the area then give me your thinking." They allowed the picture of Ruby around the large alien camp to fill their head. One klicks to the south of the camp a red dot flashed on the top of a hill. After a long moment the captain looked at Frank.

"Sergeant Farrell you first."

"Well sir, it seems like a straightforward rescue or raid. That site selected on the hill is good, and we can go in stealth with two squads and pick everyone up. Our biggest worry will be getting from here to there through the DM ships that must be on full alert. I think we could do some damage to that navy camp, and maybe recover all the remains before we leave if you want too."

Captain Nagoto shook his head. "This is strictly a survivor recovery and out. Does anyone have another option?" He looked around. "No? That is it then. Lt Nikowa you will take two squads and get our people back."

"Aye-aye, sir" Nikowa looked at Frank. "Meet in my office in twenty minutes."

"Get ready, they are coming in" the team leader communicated to her stranded team who all felt the overpressure from the stealth craft as it landed before they could see it.

"Move to your left on the double" came a voice in their heads. The five marines ran left and the inside of a landing boat appeared. As soon as they belted in the craft shot straight up.

"Lt Nikowa leaned over and said to the now grinning team leader. "Good job Corporal. Welcome home Marines."

At that moment Alicia noticed Frank sitting on the other side of the boat *I knew it would be you.* He gave her thumbs up and a smile.

The rescue mission landed at 1st Marine Regimental headquarters on Planet Pleasant fourteen hours later. According to tradition the five survivors were told they would be decorated for their continued reconnaissance even when they knew they were marooned on Planet Ruby. Frank stood in ranks with the others as they were all awarded the Planetary Assault Badge. Then Alicia and the other four were awarded the Galactic Cross in Bronze, the squad leader got it in silver. At the conclusion of the ceremony Frank went over to congratulate Alicia. "You had me worried for a while."

"Me too."

He reached out and touched her Galactic Cross, then her Planetary Assault Badge, Combat action bar, the Ribbon for Ruby combat and her Rim Worlds cuff band. "You look like the combat veteran you are. Still glad you're in recon?"

"Yes, but I also discovered how my intelligence background was a help on Ruby." She stopped and listened to a message in her head then said "My Lieutenant wants to see me for a minute. I'll contact you later."

As he watched her walk away, he was joined by Lieutenant Nikowa who asked "Is she the one you spoke to me about giving a Recon Trial."

"Yes sir." Frank nodded

"I can see why you recommended her."

"She's a good marine Sir."

"Yes, I see that . . . and very attractive as well."

"Come on sir!"

"Relax Sergeant. I am just kidding. As a matter of fact, I was speaking with her CO who said they are meritoriously promoting her to corporal for her actions on Ruby."

"No shit! I knew she'd do well!"

Doctor Lamont, was one of a team of Physicists studying the DM ship that ascertained C5 was the maximum speed of the ships. Good news, since humanities level of technology, using portal type knowledge, was increasing and could achieve the equivalent of ten times the speed of light. They also discovered that Delta-Mike did not have anything close to a portal, and they recovered star charts codes and routes used in folding space from Andromeda. They reported the findings to the Universal Government and military high command.

CHAPTER 4

DM COMMAND CENTER ON PLANET WARBEAST/REFUGE AT THE
SAME TIME . . .

Herckel and his assistant, who held a small holographic projector to use in his briefing, stood nervously outside of the Supreme Pack leader's office waiting to be recognized. They could see the supreme leader sitting at his table intently looking at a screen. After several minutes he looked up and waved them into the office. Herckel sat quietly watching his assistant set the projector between himself and the Supreme Leader.

"Well?" inquired SPL Glgoffen as he steepled his fingers looking intently at Herckel.

Herckel took a deep breath. "Supreme leader, I will outline the plan of attack on Planet Pleasant first conceived by my predecessor, Deputy Supreme Leader Waltzz."

SPL Glgoffen stood and walked from behind his table to sit closer to the intelligence chief. "Proceed." Herckel nodded to his assistant who created a holographic display in front of them. It showed the rim region of space containing the seven planets that constituted the current war zone.

"Supreme leader, I proposed that the raid on Planet Pleasant begin with a ruse landing and demonstration on the NX planet one local day ahead of the main thrust into the city of New Glasgow on

Pleasant." A thin red arrow stretched from Planet Warbeast, known as Refuge to humans, directly to NX246.

Glgoffen was confused. "Why there? You realize that world was reinforced by troops after the knife soldiers left and is being re-colonized."

Herckel nodded. "Supreme Leader, I have seen the Ho-man propaganda broadcasts. It is why I feel our demonstration to that world will draw a major response from Sunset to give us the time needed on Pleasant. I recommend units of the First Great Pack land from six ships to attack the military and settlers currently on that world. Our demonstration will hopefully disrupt the military on Sunset and have them concentrate on repelling us from NX. Our next phase will begin one local day later."

The Supreme Leader studied the hologram. "Why have you assigned the first great pack to that world? I have already alerted them to land in the Pleasant raid. What do *you* have in mind?" "Leader, my Predecessor and I both thought the Pleasant raid should begin with the Sixth Great Pack because of ... ."

"Why the Sixth?" interrupted the supreme pack leader.

Herckel faced him. "Since the destruction of their battle brothers in the Fifth GP they have felt the loss more than any others. It is reflected in their actions. This endeavor will be helpful to their prestige and confidence."

Glgoffen nodded *He is right they do need encouragement.* "Continue."

Another arrow moved from Warbeast in an arc around NX striking at Planet Pleasant. "I have reviewed the available data from the small pack sent to Pleasant. Unfortunately, they only sent one detailed report before they were apparently destroyed." He motioned to the technician and the scene changed. A large holographic image of New Glasgow hovered in the room. "This view was sent by the lost Recon pack when they first arrived over that city. I have labeled it as accurately as I am able based on the one report we had from them and my conversations with the former Intelligence chief.

"New Glasgow, is a learning center with a city built around it. It is, from the report, one of the most respected learning centers in this arm of the human galaxy. As you see it is cut in half by a wide river flowing in a north to south direction spanned by three bridges that are visible in this picture."

Each of the bridges began to glow.

"According to the scouting report, the critical study centers are located on the west side of the city . . . here." The AGRC and several other buildings around it glowed. "Their report also mentioned that the planetary government buildings are also in this city but did not give a location. I will assume that the government would want to stay close to the important studies and is also located on the west side. Possibly this large complex visible here in the southwest." The indicated segment began to glow. But Herckel had it wrong as had his predecessor. They weren't looking at government buildings. They were actually looking at a hospital and medical research center.

"As for the *Doors* mentioned by the dying prisoner," continued Herckel, my hypothesis is they will be located at or near the government complex for convenience to the leaders and traveling scholars coming to the university buildings." A small area situated midway between the illuminated AGRC buildings and medical research complex began to glow.

Herckel looked at Glgoffen for his reaction.

The supreme pack leader continued studying the panorama floating in front of them. After several minutes of scrutiny, he asked, "Then what is this on the other side of the river?" pointing at the actual Government buildings and the business district on the other side of a large plaza situated between the two.

"We believe it to be another merchant's district with other university buildings and dwellings," replied Herckel. The supreme leader studied the view again. "Your hypothesis has merit. What is the rest of your recommendation?"

The intelligence officer created two bright yellow arrow heads next to each other on the southwest portion of the landscape in what appeared to be fields at the lower edge of the western wilderness. Then he slowly rotated one arrowhead due east toward the river. The other he pointed north toward the AGRC.

The first arrow marked *61ˢᵗ Attack Group,* called an AG, began to glow then moved east through the city branching into a smaller arrow aimed at what was believed to be the government buildings. The main arrow continued to the river and branched again crossing the first two of the three bridges.

Herckel narrated, "The Sixty-first Attack Group with six thousand fighters will attack to the east and capture the government buildings along with the first and middle bridges at the river. We do not know how deep the river is. That can quickly be determined when we have them."

The second arrowhead marked *62ⁿᵈ AG* expanded to the north toward the AGRC and other critical scientific centers. "At the same time the Sixty-second AG with another six thousand fighters will attack north and capture the scientific centers. The remaining troops of the Sixth Great consisting of the Sixty-third AG will stay in the western wilderness at the landing site as a reserve force.

"Most importantly, as far as can be determined, this world does not have a military presence of any size. We should have no trouble holding these locations as long as we wish to find a door or other transitway if one exists."

Supreme leader Glgoffen, sat looking at the glowing avenues of attack through the city and their target areas considering the plan. *No military? Then how did we lose a reconnaissance pack here?* "What of the population? How much resistance do you anticipate; and how do you explain the loss of a reconnaissance pack here?"

Herckel gave a fierce grin. "Certainly not enough resistance to be any concern for twelve- thousand fighters hoping to avenge their dead Battle Brothers. Remember, there is no significant military presents on the entire planet. I cannot explain what happened to our reconnaissance pack. Perhaps it was law enforcement like those we destroyed on Sunset."

Glgoffen studied the holographic projection floating in front of them for several more minutes. *Yes, that was our first great killing and victory.* "I am concerned that you have not planned to occupy all those bridges and completely secure the area. Why?" He looked at his new intelligence chief . . . waiting.

Herckel looked from the supreme leader to the image and back. "Respectfully Supreme Leader . . . this is an intelligence gathering raid, not a conquest. I plan to have intelligence operators with the warriors at each of the target sights to find any travel ways, and to interrogate the Hoomans we round up. It is my opinion that the population will be moving away from our troops not toward them. We can occupy the last bridge with a small unit from the AGRC attack any time we wish."

Glgoffen nodded. "How long will it take for you to make all arrangements?"

"Our Great Pack leaders should be ready to attack in four days."

Glgoffen sat quietly deliberating. "I am making one change to the plan. Our stealth boats have reported the location of Enemy Killer at Planet Sunset. It is in a fixed orbit on the far side of that world away from the battle area. At the same time we send a diversion to planet NX have four hundred special landing shock troops aboard a stealth craft re-capture or destroy Enemy Killer."

Herckel nodded. "Anything further Supreme Leader?"

Glgoffen shook his head. "Let us meet with the other deputies and finalize this plan. I do not want to be in that city any longer than three days after we land."

It was a bright pleasing morning in New Glasgow as Company "A" 1st Battalion 1st Marines, with their engineer support, landed at Blackburn Bridge. The troops remained as unobtrusive as possible at the request of the City/University Council to avoid a civilian panic. The 2nd platoon of that company quickly moved north to Merchants bridge; while the Third platoon continued further to Serpent Bridge. They all began preparing defensive positions with rigged demolitions under each bridge for a worst-case scenario.

At the same time, Company "B "took positions and secured the surrounding area of the local planetary portal. While Companies "C" and "D" tied into "B" and put in a strong defense around the galactic travel portals. All positions had at least two large pulse cannons that were added to the inventory as a lesson learned, after dealing with the large DM mass charges around the Sunset Perimeter.

On the northern end of the city the 2nd Battalion 1st Marines situated themselves in and around the AGRC and Dark Energy Centers in strong well concealed positions with "E" Company touching the western wilderness. F, G, and H companied stretched almost to Serpent Bridge.

1st Recon Battalion assigned Company "B" Recon to the SE Forest to watch for stealth landings and "C" Recon to patrol the western wilderness paying special attention to the area of the battle the year before. There Frank and another recon marine named Muleovich helped destroy a platoon of DMs operating from the western wilderness that were involved in a sabotage campaign against human research centers.

At the same time, "D" Recon took the eastern forest while Two platoons from "A" Recon were also tasked to patrol the ten by nine block city for any suspicious characters; and would be joined by the 2nd Platoon when they returned from *Operation Enduring Fidelity*, on Planet Ruby.

By evening the Regimental Commander of the 1st Marines reported the area was as secure as he could make it and understood his orders to hold his position until his last marine. Or until help arrived from the 2nd and 3rd Marine Regiments on standby to assist along with some army units.

When the 2ⁿᵈ Platoon reported back for duty, Lt Nikowa met with Frank and the other squad leaders. "For today at least, you and your squads will patrol east of the River to the eastern wilderness. It is fifty square blocks from the river to the wilderness, so send out small two-person teams to keep an eye on the area. That should allow you to work out a rest schedule for your people."

Still undetected, and on station in the Space near Planet Refuge as the eyes of the fleet, UWS *Whisper* was one of the original stealth craft that followed Delta-Mike from Sunset. A job both stressful and exhilarating for its crew who were constantly on alert.

"Captain." communicated the officer of the watch to the ships CO. The captain groaned. He had just gone to his quarters for some rest after almost twenty-hours awake. *What now?*

"Captain here, this better be good."

"Yes, sir it is. A large portion of the DM fleet is moving toward human space. I make it sixty-three transports and warships."

The captain jumped from his bunk. "Stand-by I'll be right up." He quickly communicated with his headquarters and gave them an alert. "Possible DM attack force of sixty-three ships moving from Refuge system. All ships and stations stand to" was relayed throughout human space.

Delta-Mike made their opening move of the Pleasant Campaign using the 1ˢᵗ Attack Group. Known by friend and foe alike as an AG . It was the equivalent of a human Regiment, and reinforced with a quarter of the 2ⁿᵈ AG and their support units. A total of over 8000 troops from the 1ˢᵗ Great Pack in the feign directed at NX246.

"Where do you think they will strike Sir?" asked the young soldier on watch on NX when she heard the alert. Her watch commander, a new lieutenant, shrugged. "A guess from you is as good as anyone's. We are in a backwater here soldier, even though we are the closest human world to the *Refuge System*. If Delta-Mike wants us they can make it here quicker than anywhere else. I would not worry too much. We are not a strategic strong point. But stay alert."

As soon as the words were out of the lieutenants mouth a second alert arrived. "Trajectory now indicates a possible strike against NX two four six."

An hour later the same young soldier in the control room of the base on NX yelled, "Sir! Twenty, that's two zero DM ships just appeared at three AU coming toward us. I estimate they will be here in twenty-four minutes or less!" to the watch officer standing a few feet away,

The army base itself called Fort Das, was named after the first colonist killed in the invasion of eighteen months earlier. It was built around Colony Town, the main town of over a thousand residents, on the newly re-colonized world. A far cry from the few survivors of a year ago. At the end of the fighting then, the army landed to relieve the marines and established a base of several thousand soldiers. They became a permanent force. Since then, the surviving colonists felt secure enough to grow their numbers and expand.

A buzzing sounded in everyone's head for four seconds. Followed by: "All personnel prepare for an incoming attack." The army troops had already moved to their positions that began with a perimeter in depth beginning one klick from Colony town that had additional hardened fortified positions reaching into the town itself. Other smaller enclaves were scattered around the entire planet.

The defenders of NX waited for the first blow that soon began with a bombardment from DM warships in space; a prelude to the landing craft beginning to drop on human positions planetside.

The colonel put all his assets on alert to engage the DM ships as soon as they were within range. The modifications to the pulse weapons had not been started on NX so the garrison held their fire until the landing craft were on the ground. Although anti-ship missile batteries were able to successfully engage the ships in orbit.

"The alert said sixty-ships. Where are the others?" the watch commander asked rhetorically. "Massed landing craft are moving from the ships and coming down. I make it One hundred and sixty-five boats" called a communication specialist.

The watch commander did some quick math. "Ancestors that is over eight thousand troops. This is a major attack people." At that moment covering fire from the DM warships began hitting the selected targets on the planet.

Anti-ship weapons firing from around NX246 targeted the troop ships in orbit while the DM fired counter battery at every system they could locate.

"First landing craft are on the ground, contact imminent!"said the communications specialist holographically linked to human units in positions preparing to block the advancing DM who had not detected their invisible positions,

AT THE SAME TIME IN SPACE ABOVE FORT GONZALES, PLANET SUNSET . . .

The civilian engineer brought aboard the captured ship to study one of the consoles on its bridge saw a signal coming from the control computer he did not immediately recognize.

"Hello, what are you about?" he murmured. It only took him a moment to grasp what he was seeing. "Oh Shit!" he blurted and felt a shot of adrenalin. It was a Friend or Foe recognition signal. He realized that the ship had automatically begun to recognize another DM ship close by. Since no warnings had been received, he theorized it came from a stealth ship routinely broadcasting its own position to any friendly vessels.

The engineer called the captain. "Sir a DM stealth ship is approaching!"

"What? What makes you think that!" the surprised captain replied with a concerned look as he walked to the engineer who pointed to the incoming signal and said "This ship is automatically recognizing what I believe is a FOF from another vessel in close proximity." The Captain realized the possibility of a raid to re-capture or destroy the ship and didn't hesitate, he broadcast to everyone. "Security force to your combat stations. All civilian personnel to the boat bay for immediate evacuation" Then he notified his command on the planet below.

As the civilian engineers were leaving the ship the fifty-person navy and marine crew that had captured it deployed at the weapons stations. They began getting under way covered by the *UWS Dreadnought* that moved in to pinpoint and engage the DM ship.

ON BOARD THE DM SHIP SLASHER, APPROACHING SUNSET

The watch officer called, "Leader, *Enemy Killer* has automatically recognized us and has begun moving. A Hooman war ship is moving toward us."

"Pack gods!" cursed the ships Leader. "The signal will alert any Hoomans on board that we are in the vicinity. Turn it off!"

The leader turned to his executive officer. "We must assume they know of us. Now we must destroy rather than board that ship. Energize Weapons." As the *Slasher* energized its weapon systems it lost some of its stealth and was made discernible to *Dreadnought*, and other scanning equipment on Sunset.

"Fire all anti-ship missiles as we come to bear," ordered the captain of *Dreadnought*, "and prepare a second spread of anti-missile ones for the return fire."

The watch officer on *Slasher* yelled, "Fourteen incoming missiles!"

The captain sent a message to his headquarters. "*Enemy Killer* is over an unknown major military installation on far side of Sunset. I am under attack by a capital enemy vessel. I will attempt to destroy *Enemy Killer.*"

The captain looked at his gunnery officer "Target Enemy Killer and fire. Then Fire missiles at that Hooman ship and come about at full speed." He sadly shook his head *too late, too late; I can't outrun and avoid them all. We die for the Pack homeland.*

"Hits on DM ship. It blew up but they managed a spread of incoming missiles." The CIC on *Dreadnought* reported calmly.

"Deploy anti-missile defense," the captain said watching as the ship computers began targeting and destroying the incoming missiles faster that a human mind could react; hitting all but one. It detonated very close causing damage and causalities on the bridge of the ship that began to drift until control was reestablished by the XO and a new bridge crew.

Although the fighting was still severe on NX246, Delta-Mike's screaming charges under their pack, world flags, and banners into the pulse fire of human troops had drastically changed since the beginning of war.

After their battles, and losses on Planet Sunset, they learned to first kill as many Hoomans as possible with artillery and indirect fire before assaulting them. Now their rushes were by squads, platoons, and sometimes by companies with fire and maneuver. No longer did they attack in a screaming horde to overwhelm with weight of numbers.

"Sir, Colonel Martinez reporting with a sit rep." came the voice in the Commanding Generals head inside his command bunker in Colony Town.

"Go colonel."

"We are holding them sir. They made some penetration and destroyed some outlying positions; but they are fighting in smaller groups and using lots of indirect fire on us. Sir, I have an observation that they do not seem to be seriously trying to break our perimeter . . . over."

"Thanks for the information colonel. You are doing a good job, keep me informed . . . CG out."

He turned to his second in command. "Colonel Martinez says the DMs are not trying hard to penetrate his perimeter. I am wondering if this could be a feint."

"I agree sir, but then what is their real target?"

The general received another communication then said to his XO and Intel Chief, "Colonel Martinez was correct in his observation. That was god, who believes this attack is attempting to draw forces from responding to Planet Pleasant. It also reported another attack just began against that captured ship, over Fort Gonzales."

"Sounds like this is the opening move, Sir." The intelligence chief observed.

The general nodded "Now let's get rid of the ones we have on this Planet."

The XO stood listening. "Sir, I was just notified that a naval battle is in progress in space nearby. Some of our reinforcements are beginning to land behind the DMs already dirtside."

"Very well. Let's press them gentlemen."

The attack information was flashed by god to the forces on Pleasant. When the Regimental Commander of the 1st Marines received the word, he met via his chip with all his battalion commanders. Shortly, the 1st Marine Regiment with 1st Recon readied themselves.

Colonel Rham of 1st Recon linked with his officers and NCO's.

"Delta-Mike has attacked NX two forty-six with as much as half a Great Pack."

Holy Shit! Frank thought as he listened.

"The army is sending a regiment along with a fleet of ten warships from Sunset to reinforce the garrison, and beat back the attack. This is a warning alert for all our people here in case the attack is a feint hiding another one that could fall on us. There is still a large DM fleet out there somewhere; and there is an ongoing attack over Sunset apparently to destroy the ship we captured. It appears our enemy is moving. Get prepared."

All around New Glasgow the marines worked on their positions making them as invisible as possible, and considered strategies to meet any attacking force. The next twenty-four hours passed in quiet expectancy. There was an evacuation to the eastern wilderness of anyone who wished to leave the city. But a great many chose to stay a take what cover they could in their homes and work areas.

CHAPTER 5

"I am a soldier, and unapt to weep or to exclaim on fortunes fickleness."
William Shakespeare. Henry the Sixth

Forty-three DM ships in stealth mode drew close to Planet Pleasant, then swept aside the human ships in the region and began launching stealth capable landing craft oriented toward the western wilderness area of New Glasgow.

Upon landing unopposed, their scout teams moved toward the western fringe of the city and were only detected when a patrol from "C" Recon was entering the woods from the city. The squad leader quickly alerted his command. "Charley three to Charley Actual. Have spotted DM landing craft . . . break . . . many troops . . . break . . . Advance teams almost in New Glasgow . . . break . . . the axis of advance appears to be toward the southwestern section of the city . . . Charley three, out."

The warning went to all marines "Delta-Mike on the ground and moving toward us. Stand- to."

Frank was checking his squad when contacted by Lt. Nikowa. "Sergeant Farrell, get your team moving toward to the southwest where the advance is heading. Ambush and fall back toward Alpha One-One by the bridge. Good luck . . . out."

As the marines prepared to receive them, the lead elements of the 6th Great Pact consisting of the 61st and 62nd Attack Groups of six thousand fighters each approached the city. The remaining six thousand of the 63rd AG remained as a reserve force in the wilderness.

The two lead AGs approached the outskirts of the southwest corner of the city where they split. The 61st AG detached One-hundred fighters to occupy Blackburn Bridge Seven-hundred meters further east. Then broke into smaller units taking two different streets through the town toward the medical center, and what they thought were the government buildings containing a Transit Portal.

At the same time the 62nd AG made a left turn to advance a click and a half toward the Science buildings in the northwest section of the city. But the speed of their attack slowed to a crawl as they began to kill, rape and plunder in the buildings as they advanced. It was their way in war. Since no real opposition was expected the leaders allowed, and even encouraged, it. They slowly continued along the western boundary to attack the ARGC, and other science buildings creating their own havoc along their route of march.

Frank and his squad double timed west toward the DM's until he saw their first troops looting a building about a hundred meters to their front. He halted to brief his team leaders. "Olney, Kim, get your teams into the upper floor of the buildings here. Get some of them busy knocking holes through the wall big enough for you to get through. Get any remaining civilians out of here. If they won't go it's on them.

"After you make your first kills, move through the walls and get out at the end of the row. Then fall back to Drugba, and Gupta's teams that will be set up another block back. If the pursuit gets too close were gonna fold in with 'A' One-One at the bridge. Any questions?"

They all shook their heads. "Okay, let's kill these fuckers!"

Frank joined with Corporal Olney, watching as DM soldiers moved in and out of the houses a block away. He heard the screams of victims in the buildings from where he was, and observed an advanced scout group of fifteen DM coming down the street toward him then took aim. "On my mark" he communicated to the others.

"Mark, mark."

"*Pulse, pulse, pulse, pulse.*"

All fifteen DMs fell dead and the marines shifted their fire to others they could see advancing behind the first group. When they too began to drop, those behind them realized from their experiences on Sunset they were in contact with fighting troops. They took cover to return fire to their front mostly into the lower floors of the buildings.

Frank knew *once they shift their fire higher, we gotta move.*" How many do ya think we got?" he asked Olney.

"I make it twenty-two."

"Team-two, we are being flanked to the right" communicated Kim who saw the lead of the group moving to occupy the medical center.

"Roger that. Hit any you can see. All teams move back . . . break . . . Corporal Drugba we are falling back toward your position" Frank replied.

"I have it."

"Corporal Gupta did you copy?" Frank asked.

"Roger that."

Frank and the eight marines with him moved along the block of houses through the holes in the walls looking out of the windows as they passed to see how close the DM were.

The small group leader in the 1st Company of the 61st AG on point of the Attack Group contacted his large pack leader. "Pack leader we have come under fire by troops hidden in some buildings, but I do not know where yet."

"What kind of troops? You must determine that immediately," the large pack leader who was the equivalent of a company commander ordered, "then continue to lead us to the bridge".

The small group leader stood up and waved his platoon forward. "Attack into those buildings before we move on." He pointed at the row of buildings Frank and his two teams were trying to get out of.

As the DMs ran forward one of Corporal Kim's team yelled "They are attacking!"

Frank stopped at the next window and looked then communicated. "Everyone shoot four pulses, and get out of here." The marines quickly got to windows and fired four pulses at the attacking DMs before evacuating.

The small group leader leading the attack was a veteran of some of the heavy fighting on Sunset, and he hit the ground as soon as he saw his first fighter fall followed by others.

Pack ancestors we are not attacking civilians, this is military! He looked at the bodies around him and called to one of his senior pack men now taking cover behind some steps near him. "Get me a casualty count quickly!" he ordered. Then he yelled to his platoon "Concentrate your fire into the upper windows, and get some rapid-fire guns into action!"

The weak amount of fire that followed was an unexpected response, and he began to get a bad feeling. He had faced Hooman troops before and knew the army tended to stay in place and usually fought until an attack was beaten back or they were overrun. But he had also, more than once, seen the aftermath of knife soldier ambushes on Sunset. Always where least expected, and they usually disappeared only to reappear somewhere else to kill more. His experience told him *this feels like the knife soldiers. If it is, we may have to change our tactics.*

His senior pack man interrupting his thoughts "Leader we lost nineteen fighters"

The small group leader contacted his large pack leader to report.

"Have you found the Hoomans who shoot at us?" demanded his commander.

"No, we have been ambushed and I have lost almost half of my unit. I beg to report that this ambush and the killing has the feel of the Knife Soldiers."

The large pack leader considered *He is an experienced leader not given to panic. This must be reported.* "Contact Attack Group head-quarters" he ordered his communicator.

Frank and the others came out of a back door at the end of the block and were able to link up with his other two teams. "All teams, we are going to fall back in a fighting retreat, break . . .. Corporals Drugba, Gupta, we are going to move through you and take up positions about fifty meters further on . . . break . . . you two engage the DMs. Pull back through us if they get too close to you . . . break . . . we are going to leapfrog back to the Alpha company perimeter . . . break . . . Corporal Olney do you copy."

"Roger that."

"Kim copy."

"Copy."

"Drugba."

"Got it."

"Gupta."

"Aye-aye."

"Good luck, Farrell out."

At almost the same moment another scout team of the 61St AG approached the medical center complex guarded by a platoon of A/1/1 marines in fortified positions inside of the complex. They had a force multiplier of one heavy dual barrel pulse cannon.

A two-person outpost situated at the end of the street saw Delta-Mike moving toward the medical center and enhanced their contacts to be binoculars for a better look. They not only saw the approaching scouts but noticed several others begin to fall further back just before the entire column hit the ground and began firing into the buildings around them.

"It looks like Recon is doing their thing" the senior marine in the OP said to his partner.

"Fuckin right! That should take some pressure off of us for a while. Report it, and let's get out of here. They are getting closer." He began to pulse any DM he saw moving around to engage the Recon troops, hitting them from the side.

The senior marine communicated with the platoon leader. "OP-two to Bravo-actual. I have approximately one hundred that's one zero, zero Delta-Mike advancing toward the med center . . . break . . . the scouts are only about one hundred meters away . . .. break . . . it looked like their column was ambushed further back, and has halted for the time being . . . break . . . we are pulling back now. . . out."

"Roger that OP-two" replied Bravo-actual who alerted his entire company "Get ready we have DM's moving our way." Then he alerted Battalion.

As OP-two began to move from their cover toward the medical center it was bad luck that a sharp-eyed gunner of a DM rapid fire gun team saw them and opened fire hitting and severely wounding both OP marines who fell about twenty fire meters short of the building. Several advancing DM scouts ran to take them prisoner and were killed with fire from the med center. The commander of the one-hundred troops in the lead column deployed, and returned a heavy Fire. The leader of the 61st AG heard their firefight begin and contacted them. "What have you encountered. Report."

"Leader" the commander of the one-hundred replied "we lost a number of fighters in an ambush and have killed two knife soldiers by the government buildings. I tried to take them prisoners by have been driven back by others inside those buildings."

"How do you know you face knife soldiers?" the surprised Commander asked.

"I can see the bodies."

"Hold at that location for now. I will contact you with additional orders." The 61ˢᵗ AG commander turned to his XO. "Contact Great Pack headquarters. It seems we are fighting knife soldiers."

"Are you absolutely certain!" demanded the leader of the 6ᵗʰ GP.

"Yes. The leader on the scene said he was looking at their bodies as we spoke." The leader of 6ᵗʰ thought for a moment and replied "I am sending three more large packs to you. When they arrive begin an attack to take that location." A large pack was company size. After the order was acknowledged the Great Pack leader said to his communication team "Contact the Supreme Pack Leader for me."

SPL Glgoffen was working in his office on Warbeast with Intelligence Chief Herckel when advised of a message from the 6ᵗʰ Great Pack. He was pleasantly surprised. *They have completed their mission in record time. I must congratulate him.* "How did my Sixth GP leader do everything so quickly" SPL Glgoffen said in a jovial voice. The commanding Officer of Sixth winced, and hesitated for a moment.

"Unfortunately Supreme leader, the 61ˢᵗ AG has only advanced three hundred meters and has already suffered approximately sixty causalities."

"How is that possible?," demanded the Supreme leader, "intelligence felt that the civilian population would flee not fight. Are you telling me you and your great pack cannot push aside these Hoomans?" Glgoffen said in a cold voice.

The commander of the 6ᵗʰ swallowed hard "Supreme Leader let me report; and if you are not satisfied you can relieve me." The commanders tone made Glgoffen calm down. "Report"

"We began taking causalities at one hundred meters into the city. Until then our soldiers had had their way with everyone encountered. After our first losses we continued toward the government building objectives and came under heavy ambush type fire for a second time.

"My lead elements killed two persons outside of the government complex and the leaders advise me they are knife soldiers. That is probably who has been ambushing us. I have stopped in place and sent reinforcements for an attack. That is my report."

Pack gods! Knife soldiers on Pleasant? "Commander is there any possibility you are mistaken" asked Glgoffen who had a mental image of the Marine Corporal who killed his old comrade as he stood beside him

"Supreme leader, the advance element said they were looking at the bodies, and they are knife soldiers."

Glgoffen directed an angry glance at his new intelligence chief. He ended his communication with the 6th GP Leader. "Commander you have my trust and confidence. Use whatever force is needed. Keep me informed of your attack and anything else you find noteworthy."

Herckel had overheard the message and stood nervously waiting. Glgoffen sat down and studied him for a long moment. "You assured me there was no military on that world, especially in that city. Now I find the 6th GP engaging knife soldiers. I want you to contact your people with the 61st and 62nd AG's and get me some hard information . . . quickly."

"At once Supreme Leader." Herckel fled the room.

A 61st AG battalion commander had his entire command in positions surrounding what he thought to be government buildings, and called his unit leaders for a quick meeting before his attack. When the four large pack leaders representing almost seven-hundred fighters arrived the commander studied them. "We have evidence that knife soldiers are present in this city. It was not anticipated. But now we must deal with the actuality of what we face."

The Battalion Commander himself was a seasoned veteran who had fought on several worlds in different galaxies. One of them had urban type fighting and he had an idea of what to do against the

Hooman's facing him. One of the lessons learned in that situation led to the development of a heavy caliber rapid firing weapon the equivalent of a .61 Cal machine gun used to suppress hard targets for assault.

"Twenty minutes after the end of this meeting, all fighters will begin firing into every window door or other opening in that building. The weapons unit will target them too, but also move their fire along all walls in between to try and punch through adding to the disorder and casualties inside. As soon as the massed fire begins, the special assault company will attack from the north and attempt to break into the building complex. If they are successful, reinforcements will follow them inside. I have ordered the fighters advancing to the Bridge to move as fast as is possible. Now go prepare yourselves."

As the different leaders went to their units the 6th GP Leader contacted the 62nd AG still plundering their way north and advised him of the coming attack by the 61st AG and to be prepared to meet Hooman troops. The 62nd AG Commander halted to brief his subordinate leaders giving the defending marines in the AGRC and other buildings a little extra time.

"Bravo-two to Bravo-Actual" communicated the platoon leader inside the medical center watching the swarms of DM soldiers deploying in front of him.

"Go ahead Bravo-two" replied the company commander.

"Bravo-two, I have enemy troops probably a full Battalion in positions around this complex . . . break . . . Recon Two-one who is operating in the area estimates close to one thousand fighters moving on us. . . break . . . I am going to need support . . . over."

"Stand-by Bravo-two" said the company commander who checked his chip for the time out of habit and contacted the 1st Battalion 1st Marines commander. It was 1420.

"Shoot!" ordered the DM Commander, beginning a thunderous

fire into the medical building instantly blowing out all windows and shredding the doors as the heavy machine guns blew chunks from the building wounding a number of defenders inside. The incoming fire was so heavy that few if any of the defenders could raise their head to shoot back.

"Start chopping some holes in the wall to pulse through!" the platoon sergeant yelled as he attempted to enlarge a hole made by the concentrated heavy machine gun fire.

The 61st battalion commander turned to his number two. "They are not causing us many casualties. Order the attacking force foreword." The DM's attacking from the north went forward in platoon rushes and were soon at the north wall and blew a breach. When they began to enter, they encountered the first marine defenders that pulsed the area as quickly as they could killing the first dozen DMs through the breach before being riddled with bullets themselves.

The area inside the breach hole was a large cafeteria that became a fatal funnel for the attacking DMs entering the building. The two surviving marines took positions in the long wide hallway leading from it and managed to hold up the attack long enough to call for help. "OP-four to Bravo-Two actual. We have DMs in the building through a wall breach. Send help . . . out."

The platoon commander Lt. Martinez, heard the firefight begin and had just sent his first squad to investigate when he received the message and contacted his Company commander. "Bravo-two to Bravo-actual the north wall of the building has been breached . . . break . . . we have DMs inside our perimeter, over." The Bravo captain contacted his colonel again but before he could say anything the colonel said, "I know you want to send troops to help them. So, do I, but we have to wait for Two-one. I have been notified that one-hundred DMs are about two-hundred meters away from the two platoon's "A" has at Blackburn bridge. Another estimated regiment of DMs is moving north to attack the AGRC complex. Tell your platoon commander he has to hang on for a while."

"Aye-aye Sir," replied the Bravo CO, and contacted his second platoon and passed the word. After he spoke to the CO, Lieutenant Martinez turned to the platoon sergeant. "We are on our own for a while. Get help to barricade the main hallway from the dining hall. We will fight room to room if we have to."

"Aye-aye sir. Looks to be a long day." The platoon sergeant began gathering some troops to help, while Lieutenant Martinez made his way to the crew leader of the Dual pulse cannon. "Chop a hole big enough to site the gun, but try not to let the barrels protrude outside. It may give us and edge for a while. You pick your targets and fire when ready."

"Aye-aye Sir."

Five minutes later the dual barrel weapon was pulsing any DM foolish enough to stay in the open up to four-hundred meters away. But they were only effective against those in front of them; and more and more were entering through the breach in the rear.

It was the recent upgrade of the pulse weapons that made surviv-ability possible for the marines who were taking steady causalities from the alien weapons. Now at least the marine weapons could pen-etrate the tables and chairs the DM's attempted to take cover behind; but it was a losing situation. The surviving marines were being pushed back toward the front of the medical center where the pulse canon was still causing major causalities.

The DM company leader now inside the medical center with his troops had a chance to look into various cleared rooms and at some of the equipment then contacted his battalion commander who immedi-ately asked "Have you conquered the government building yet?"

"Leader "our information has been mistaken. This is not a govern-ment building. It is a medical one."

"Are you certain?" asked the battalion commander.

"Positive."

Curse the stars above! The battalion commander gritted his teeth. "Contact me when you have taken complete control."

"Alpha recon two-actual to Patrol-two I have a change of mission for you," Lieutenant Nikowa communicated to Frank. "I see you are almost at Blackburn Bridge. I want you to move up toward the medical center. It is under heavy attack at present. There is no other assistance available . . . break . . . see if you can do anything to disrupt the attack . . . break . . . your focus should be a breach on the north side . . . out."

"Two-actual, I have it. . . out."

"Farrell to squad, we are going to move around the DM's to the north side of the med center . . . break . . . the building has been breached and under heavy attack . . . break . . . Corporal Kim, you lead out followed by Corporal Grupta, then Corporal Drugba . . . break . . . Corporal Olney, you have our six. Keep alert. Many DMs in the area . . . break . . . activate light benders. Farrell out." Kim carefully led the squad along the Dragon river to the Merchants bridge where she turned left, proceeding west, to approach the north side of the medical complex. The sound of the ongoing fighting was plainly heard assisting in her navigation.

"DMs ahead get down" communicated Kim's point marine.

Frank worked his way up to the point team and saw the large numbers of DM's collected around the complex. *Fuck. They're in deep shit in there!* "Corporal Kim, take your team another hundred meters north, hit um from behind. We will use Merchants bridge as our rally point if needed.

"Squad, we're gonna disrupt um. Keep light benders on as long as possible . . . break . . . Corporal Grupta, work the north side with Kim. Clear what you can . . . break . . . Corporal Drugba, hit um from this side ... break ... Corporal Olney, move slightly south and do what ya can ... break ... Merchants bridge is the rally point ... Farrell out."

"Patrol-two to Alpha-one we are set to hit um."

"Good luck Sergeant Farrell," communicated Lieutenant Nikowa.

Farrell and his squad began pulsing the DMs from the rear causing chaos because the invisible marines with silent weapons were a ter-rifying combination to DM who watched people just falling dead around them.

Kim, Grupta, and their teams caused enough damage around the breach that the DMs stayed away from the piles of bodies and began spraying their weapons where they thought the attacks were coming from. Their volume of fire increased dramatically against the invis-ible enemy.

Inside the complex it was a different story. The one hundred-fifty DM who already made it into the building had killed or wounded most of the marines. They were pushing the few survivors toward the front by the pulse cannon that has just stopped firing; when the con-centrated fire from the heavy machine gun punched through the wall, and knocked out the crew.

The break in the pulse cannon fire was all that was needed to start a general assault on the front of the building that overwhelmed the defenders who fought to the death.

"Alpha-one to Alpha recon-two."

"Go, Alpha-one" answered Frank."

"Be advised the building has been overrun and all our people killed ... break ... continue to harass and do what damage you can ... break ... re-enter over Serpent Bridge at dusk. They will expect you. . . Alpha-one out."

Fuck! Forty good marines killed by those bastards. We're going to make them pay. Frank passed the word to his squad.

The lead element of the one-hundred DMs moving to occupy Blackburn Bridge ran into the fortified positions of the two platoons of A/1/1 and their engineers and died almost to a man in their approach before they could take cover. Two prisoners were taken.

A shaken Intelligence Chief Herckel stood in front of Supreme Pack Leader Glgoffen who glared at him. "Well?" demanded Glgoffen.

"Supreme leader I . . ." Glgoffen cut him off by holding up his hand in a stop motion.

"Before you begin let me tell you what I know. First: there *is* Hooman military on Planet Pleasant. Second, the Government building you pointed out in your briefing was not what you said. It was a Medical facility guarded by a platoon of marines. You may have noticed that I did not say knife soldiers. The on-scene Pack leader, realized after checking the forty bodies of the defenders that none wore the knife soldier emblem. They all wore the marine emblem, like the one I also noticed on the prisoner we had here; but he wore the Knife Soldier one too. So . . . what does that tell you?"

Herckel began to sweat, momentarily lost for words. After a short pause Glgoffen said, "It tells me that we are now meeting main force marines that all fought to the last. They must be part of that Division those young soldiers spoke of. Do you know they killed almost two hundred fighters inside that building alone? And are you aware that in ambushes outside we lost another one hundred-seventy-fire. Most likely from a small knife soldier unit. And are you also aware that the small pack sent to the first bridge has been wiped out. In total, close to five hundred pack mates of the 61st AG are gone."

Glgoffen continued to stare at Herckel. "My first reaction was to have you executed for stupidly." Herckel begin to shake and Glgoffen said in an exasperated voice "Calm down. If I executed everyone that misunderstood this species, I would have to begin with myself.

"I want to go over our intelligence information again and see if we can adjust to still achieve our mission. We have lost one day and far too many troops already. And the Knife soldiers are roaming among us."

All that night, Frank and his squad, along with other recon teams caused as much damage as they could to the DMs west of the river. So far, east of the river remained quiet.

Early next morning, after a few hours of sleep, Frank and his squad lurked inside a building a block west of the river, just south of Serpent Bridge, watching. Waiting to hit the DMs when they carefully began to advance toward the river bridge, using tactical formations and rushes in an early morning mist.

"They are moving!" communicated a lookout in Corporal Guptas' team.

"Let um get close," Frank said. "We'll hit um with four pulses each and haul ass through the buildings. Then we'll move to that platoon at Serpents Bridge."

"They have learned," observed Corporal Olney, "they are not raping and looting like they were."

Frank nodded. "We've gotten their attention; and from the bodies, and prisoners, we verified we are fighting the Sixth Great Pack. That's eighteen thousand soldiers. We're in for one hell of a fight before this is over. Okay . . . here's what we're gonna do."

He was interrupted by the noise of a large fire-fight beginning on their right. Then by a communication from Lieutenant Nikowa. "Alpha Recon-one to team-two . . . over."

"Go One." Replied Frank.

"Be advised that a major assault has begun on the AGRC and other scientific buildings. Two-one is holding the perimeter and reported large numbers of DMs attacking break . . .."

The 1st Marines Commanding General contacted Colonel Rahm. "First Regiment-Actual to Recon-Actual."

"Go ahead sir."

"Colonel, we have learned from a prisoner that we are fighting the Sixth Great Pack. . . break . . . two of their Attack Groups, the Sixty-first and Sixty-second, each the equivalent of a regiment are currently engaged . . . break . . . the prisoners report the Sixty-third Attack Group is in reserve to the west. . . break . . .I want you to have "C" Recon concentrate on finding those reserves to determine if they are moving toward the fighting . . .break . . . I also want you to task "D" Recon to assist with as much information and ambushing as is possible to confuse those people . . . break . . . I will use artillery on any large concentrations found . . . break . . . after the artillery strikes have your two companies fold back into the perimeter around the Science Centers and help out hitting the DMs when they least expect it. . . break . . . Colonel I have requested the Second and Third Marines to land to assist us. I am also reinforcing the Bridges somewhat. It is only a matter of time until the DMs try to force the river. Good luck. First Regiment-actual over."

"Aye-aye sir. You can count on First Recon; we will move immediately. . . Recon Actual out."

Colonel Rahm turned to his XO. "Get Charley and Delta moving to find, track, and interdict any DM reinforcements in the west wilderness. You can pass on that we are fighting the Sixth Great Pack comprised of the Sixty-first, Sixty-second, and Sixty-third Attack Groups. About eighteen thousand troops."

The XO let out a long whistle.

"Me too, so get busy."

"Aye-aye sir" replied Major Lamb.

CHAPTER 6

INSIDE THE DM COMMAND CENTER . . .

Intelligence Chief Herckel, and his assistant, waited for Supreme Leader Glgoffen to recognize them. After a moment Glgoffen waved the two over. "Well?" he asked.

"Supreme leader, my staff and I have spent time reanalyzing the image that our small reconnaissance pack sent from space when they first approached New Glasgow a year ago." A holographic image of the city and its environs appeared in the air.

"We know now that the complex first believed to be a government building is in fact a large medical and research center that was defended by only forty marines. We have recovered all their bodies and inspected them to confirmed that none are what we have been calling Knife Soldiers.

"So, we have learned that Knife Soldiers are apparently elite reconnaissance marines whose duty is to operate among the enemy. While the main force marines are shock troops used in first landing situations."

SPL Glgoffen was getting impatient. "How they fight is known, we need not spend any more time on it. But all indications are that so far, they are the only troops we are engaging. Except on the NX demonstration where we did meet regular army formations.

"Before going further, I think it prudent to note that the staff and I have wondered how the Hoomans determined that an attack would fall upon this city. What could have predicted it?"

SPL Glgoffen sat in thought *I have wondered the same thing. Was it just luck or have other stealth ships discovered us . . . or . . .? is there something here they want to protect. Like a doorway?* "I agree with that assessment" said Glgoffen "and we will have to study it further. Continue with your briefing."

Herckel nudged his assistance that hi-lighted the AGRC and other scientific buildings as well as the arrow representing the 62nd AG. "What we are currently attacking is the Advanced Gravity Research Center, and other science buildings, that I am convinced neither house the government nor the Doors. My staff and I believe that the key to everything is actually on the east side of the river. That is why the bridges are so heavily defended."

The large buildings surrounding the open plaza along with the shopping district were highlighted. "I believe these to be the actual government buildings that probably house one of the doors."

Glgoffen studied the holograph projection for a moment. "Why?"

"Supreme Leader. I believe the clue is this large Plaza connecting these two buildings. On our worlds transportation centers all have large open areas near them to assist travelers. And although the Tradesman's district is several blocks of residential buildings away, they are close enough to that plaza to be convenient.

"Also, the bridges are more heavily guarded than expected and must be considered important by the Hoomans; and so far, most knife soldier activity seems to be along the approaches to the first two bridges then up toward the science centers.

"All of this argues that our original intelligence was misunderstood. That finding any of the doors will be in this area."

"Anything else?" asked Supreme Leader Glgoffen.

"A recommendation sir."

"What is it?"

"Supreme Leader, the axis of our attack needs to change with all Packs moving toward those bridges as soon as possible. Also, reinforcements should land in the eastern wilderness and surround the city.

"I realize the fleet is busy keeping Hooman ships away from the raiding force while they are in that city. But as risky, and possibly suicidal as it seems, I would recommend attempting to drop landing craft on the other side of the river. It may give us the advantage needed."

Glgoffen was pensive. *I would not have thought him capable of bold thinking like this. I am pleased.* "I am ordering the First Great into the fight. And I am willing to discuss a landing from space . . . it could be very costly. I am also ordering the Sixty-second AG to change the axis of their arrack to the east and that last bridge." He gave Herckel a penetrating look. "It seems your raid has turned into a meeting battle we were not prepared to fight. I do not want another Fifth Great Pack disaster."

AT HEADQUARTERS MARINE CORPS ON MW . . .

General Thomas met with his reserve regimental commanders, their executive officers and the Sergeants Major. "Ladies and Gentlemen, the battle in New Glasgow is growing but it does not feel like an invasion. It is completely localized to that city and its environs. The landing on NX two forty-six has ended. Delta-Mike has withdrawn. It is believed that was a ruse to draw assets away from assisting this current move by Delta-Mike. There is no doubt in my mind that they are attempting to locate a portal on Pleasant. I want your regiments to deploy for combat operations there immediately." He paused. "Ensure they are ready for combat as they step from the portal. Now here are your assignments."

The projection of the New Glasgow battle area appeared in their heads and General Thomas first addressed the Commander of the 2nd Marines. The different areas of the image and unit symbols of

Delta-Mike and the marines lit up as he spoke. "Colonel I want you to have One-Two and Two-Two dig in and fortify the entire waterfront and bridges. While Three-Two and Four-Two reinforce the troops defending the buildings and grounds around the Transit Plaza and government buildings."

"Aye-aye, sir" replied the Regimental Commander.

"Third Marines. You are to dig in along the entire eastern wilderness approaches to New Glasgow.

"Aye-aye, sir."

"Fourth Marines. Keep one of your Battalions here on MW. Get the other two ready to be lifted to a naval transport as a ready reserve if they are needed anywhere in the battle zone."

The briefing ended. "That is all Ladies and Gentlemen. If there are no questions you are dismissed."

"Sir!" called the colonel of the 2nd Marines.

"Do you have a question Steve?"

"Are things as close as they seem, Sir."

"Sounds like it, Steve. You will know when you get there. Get to it Gentleman."

"Aye-aye, Sir" the colonels replied.

On the way-out Steve said to his XO, and Regimental Sergeant Major. "Here we go gentlemen. If we have to come out of the portal fighting any suggestions on the leading unit?"

The sergeant major spoke up. "Sir I know from the NCO's in First Battalion they are probably the most ready and eager. The Fourth Battalion is a close second."

The Colonel looked at his XO. "What do you think?"

"I agree with the sergeant major's assessment. First Battalion has first rate officers. In my opinion the Third Battalion officers impress me almost as much."

The Colonel thought for a moment. "All right, first battalion will lead us out of the portal. I want them ready for one-hour mount out. Now contact the battalion commanders to be ready for a chip briefing", he said to the XO. "Sergeant major, have the Commanders of Logistics and artillery contact me ASAP. It sounds as if things are getting very hot on Pleasant."

While the XO and sergeant major moved to get things ready the Colonel communicated with the Battalion commanders. "Move your commands to the transit portal with full combat load out. You must be ready to begin combat operations the instant you step through the portal. The order of march will be First Battalion followed by Fourth Battalion, Second, then Third. Light artillery and supply will move behind you. Initially I will go in with First battalion and decide where to put Regimental headquarters when we get to Pleasant."

The small unit leader of the recon pack from the 61st AG moved his squad completely around the south edge of the city until he was stopped by the Dragon River that he found un-fordable.

He had one of his soldiers climb a tall tree to look over the Blackburn Bridge. The soldier realized he could also see into the plaza between two large complexes on the east side and saw troops coming from one of the buildings in the area before moving to other locations.

The soldier knew, because he was in a recon pack, they were looking for some type of a door and felt he may have located it. He looked further down river to the south and saw a small pier with a few boats tied up and quickly climbed down and reported to his unit leader who said "Very good observations. I agree with the conclusion. We must get those boats so we can cross this river."

He moved his recon squad a quarter of a mile to the deserted pier and the DM soldiers rowed two boats across the Dragon River unseen. On the other side they moved north again and into an abandoned house two-hundred meters from the Blackburn bridge with a sight line into the plaza and the avenue leading from the transit complex.

When he contacted his Pack command and reported the stream of troops moving from that area he was ordered to stay on the east side of the river and report what they could. That information was passed up to his command who passed it to the intelligence section.

Herckel felt almost faint when he received the report. *The concentrations are around the government plaza probably coming from one of the doors. And because this is only a raid, we did not bring artillery and cannot take advantage of the information. If he does not execute me now, he never will.* Herckel went to notify the Supreme Leader.

"Alpha-one to Patrol-two" communicated Lieutenant Nikowa. "Go one" replied Frank.

"Patrol-two mission change . . . break . . . cross river through Merchants bridge and move toward East woods . . . break . . . access your chip for Company HQ . . . Alpha-one out."

"Farrell to squad our mission has changed . . . break . . . Corporal Kim, take us to Merchants bridge. Break . . . we will take out any targets of opportunity along the way . . . break . . . use light benders until we hit friendlies. Out."

A short while later Frank heard a burst of buzzing in his head that meant an important message for all hands followed: "All commands and units, DM ships have pushed past Fleet vessels over New Glasgow . . . break . . . a major landing force is dropping from transports now. . . break . . . landing areas are the East and Southeast wilderness."

Fuck every time I think things can't get worse; they do.

"Alpha-two to Patrol two" communicated Lieutenant Nikowa.

"Go two."

"Move into Eastern woods to locate large troop concentrations and disrupt what you can . . .

Two out."

The 62nd AG was suffering mounting causalities as they probed the 2nd Battalion 1st Marines Main Line of Retinene surrounding all the science buildings that stretched from the west woods to the river.

Platoon size rushes along a small front was the largest attack they could mount with any expectation of success, and even then they were taking too many casualties. Most of their success came from moving behind massed rapid firing guns that raked the marine lines with frightening effect.

When the leader of the 62nd AG was notified by 6th Great head-quarters to change his axis of attack and take the river bridge he felt a scene of relief that shamed him. But he quickly contacted each of his four small attack group commanders and told them to disengage and pull back one block then report to his command post for a briefing.

Thirty minutes later he looked over his dirty battle worn small attack group commanders. "We have been ordered to change our axis of attack. We will move to the river and cross the last bridge and move east into what has been identified as the government buildings, and the Doors. I expect everyone to do their duty."

"Group leader can we pull back another block east before we move to the river" asked the 1st Small Assault Group commander "I fear we will be moving across the front of the Hoomans after we make our first turn and it could prove costly."

The 62nd AG Group leader looked around. "Do any disagree with his assessment?" The four other small assault group commanders, equivalent to battalion commanders, sat quietly as he glared around at them. "I never thought to see the day the leaders of this Assault Group would be afraid of facing an enemy. However, considering what we face, I can understand the concerns, *and I shame myself*, but we have been given our orders. The fate of the battle and success of this raid could depend on us. Now, go cover us with glory."

It was the captain of F/2/1 who first contacted his regimental commander that the DMs had pulled back and turned right. They were moving across his front toward the river. "Sir it could be they are trying to link up with the ones reported to be dropping in the east woods. They may be trying to use a pincer to move on the Portal areas."

"Good observation captain. You could be right. Stand-by for orders." A minute later the colonel sent a transmission to all of his company commanders "All companies push forward to disrupt the DM movements as they pass across your front. One-actual out."

Human anti-air defenses along with fire from ships caused major causalities to the landing of the 1st Great Pack, that for all their prior battle experience had never landed against determined anti-air fire. The commander of the shuttle fleet on station in space was alerted by his second in command. "Leader we have lost almost one quarter of our landing craft, crews and the fighters they carried."

The leader did not hesitate. "Land ten K further back to get away from the incoming fire." The boats quickly laded and immediately shot back into space to their mother ships. The battalion commanders of the 2nd and 3rd AG's of the 1st Great units were considered the cream of this army, and began to organize when everyone was down. It was a shock when they realized the 3rd AG had lost almost a small attack group of troops in the drop.

They had already started with slightly less than two full Attack Groups because the 1st AG along with several thousand extras from the 2nd Great had been sent to attack NX 246 in the subterfuge there. And they lost almost one-thousand more in that opposed landing from space and the fierce perimeter battle that followed.

On the ground the Leader of the 1st GP held a quick meeting with his AG commanders. "Pack mates as you know the landing was costly to us and we lost eleven landing boats coming down; over five hundred fighters. But our mission remains and we will move west toward the bridge to link up with the Sixty-second and destroy any Hooman's we encounter. Go and do your duty."

They moved quickly to cover the ten kilometers from their drop zone, unprepared for the camouflaged fortified positions of the 3rd Marine Regiment screening the city. But the Leader immediately ordered his Great Pack to attack into the Eastern city and advance on the government buildings. At the same time the 63rd AG began moving from reserve and east through the west woods following the route of the 61st and began to encounter "D" Recon.

CHAPTER 7

Delta Recon's three platoons, broke into small patrols to cover the entire western side of the city and moved into the woods. Alicia and her team found themselves in the NW sector in the general area that Frank and Mule first fought the DM over a year earlier when Mule was killed.

"Light benders on" her squad leader ordered. Alicia and the rest of "D" Recon continued west for almost an hour before they found the first outposts of the 63rd AG Consisting of two squads of troops sitting in place.

"Down" communicated Alicia's point marine leading her team and the squad. She carefully moved up to his position, followed shortly by her squad leader that nudged Alicia and whispered into her ear, "Get your team on line Corporal, and be ready to pulse them."

Alicia nodded, and began moving them into place. Her Squad leader contacted the Platoon commander. "Delta recon-two to Delta-one, over."

"Go, recon-two."

"I have two DM squads to my front . . . break . . . I count twenty-four that's two four. . over."

"Roger that Recon-two stand-by . . . break . . . I have other reports of more DMs. . .break . . . Delta-actual is sending Delta-one around them since they have not yet made contact" the platoon commander said.

"Roger that, Delta-two out."

Alicia and her team, still in point, lay watching the DMs. She heard her sergeant in her head. "Team-three we are standing-by in place while First platoon checks to see what else is in the area."

"Team-three roger" Alicia said listening to the continuous sounds of fierce fighting coming from the city *I hope we do something soon.*

The CO of Delta Recon contacted Major Lamb. "Two of my platoons have DMs in front of them. I sent my First Platoon to determine the size of the unit the outposts are screening and to see what else is in the area. We can destroy the outposts encountered at any time."

Major Lamb thought for a moment and said "Use caution. According to our prisoners you could have as many as six thousand DMs in front of you. After your First platoon reports back do what you can to harass them. Then try to locate any large concentrations we can hit from space or with artillery. Good luck."

"Fuck me," muttered the Captain and Communicated with his 1st Platoon and other platoon commanders to pass the word on what they could be facing.

"On my mark" said the company commander over his command net and everyone prepared to pulse the DMs in front of them.

"Mark, mark, mark."

"*Pulse, pulse.*" Began the fire into the DMs who responded quickly when the first fighters fell down. They knew what they were facing now, and laid down a tremendous base of fire killing and wounding several marines. The DMs were advancing through a field, and recon called in a fire mission from space that wiped out most of them.

But the DM had learned too, and the survivors called in ship fire around their entire front killing or wounding over half of "D" Recon. Alicia and her team survived because only they were so close to the DM line. They slowly withdrew with Delta-Mike cautiously following.

The Leader of the 2nd AG of the 1st GP contacted his counterpart in the 62nd AG. "I am moving toward you but will be late because we dropped much further away than expected." The 62nd commander grimaced. "Join as soon as possible. We are being punished as we move east."

At the same time . . . 2/1 and B recon pushed forward into the buildings lining the road toward Serpent Bridge, and were inflicting severe causalities on the 62nd AG. Who, after losing almost a small attack group as they crossed the front of the 1st Marines began chopping into the ends of the building rows on each of the four blocks they had to travel. They were learning from the marine's tactics, and hacked their way through the walls to avoid the human pulse fire. An unintended consequence of the move was a number of vicious close, and at times to hand to hand encounters with human troops already inside the buildings. The dual pulse cannons were having a devastating effect; making it the equivalent, for the DMs, of attacking into canister fire in earlier times

The newly developed RTI's recently placed on the pulse guns was paying off for the marines that could now see the DMs through the walls, and were able to shoot through most of them. Forcing the 62nd to withdraw back another block further south to take them out of contact as they slowly continued toward the river, still chopping through the blocks of buildings.

The 2/1 Marines continued to press, while B recon used their light benders and began sniping at the 62nd AG from some of the building they just abandoned. It pushed them even further south and into the outposts of 1/1 Marines holding Merchants bridge. The 62nd AG was now being hit from both sides.

The commander of the 62nd AG contacted the Leader of the 6th GP. "My leader, I have suffered at least forty percent causalities, and still have not reached the bridge that my scouts report is heavily fortified."

"What are you suggesting" bristled the 6th GP Leader.

"I believe I should hold in place until you can support me with the 63rd AG reserves."

The Leader was barely able to contain his anger. "Is your next in command with you?"

"Yes, leader but he . . ."

"Let me speak to him." The GP leader cut off the 62nd commander who realized he was going to be relieved, and hung his head as his second in command spoke to his GP leader.

"Yes, my leader."

"Can you get this Attack Group to the bridge?" the GP Leader asked.

"My leader, this group is down to three-thousand-six-hundred fighters at last count. We have one more block to advance through the Hooman's fire before we can attack their fortified positions at the bridge. I can only promise to advance as long as I am able."

"Why are you not taking cover in the buildings?" demanded the Leader.

"My leader we did; but the Hooman's have the ability to shoot through walls and we are engaging in touching close contact. That ability with the fighting inside has pushed us out the other side into other Hooman's outposts."

Pack ancestors. I had no idea things were so bad "Give me your commander again."

"Yes, my leader."

"Commander, do what you can to fortify your position until I can get some of the Sixty-third AG to you. I am going to request assistance from the fleet on targets around the bridge and buildings to help you. Stay ready to attack again when directed."

The 62nd AG commander stood staring at his communicator. Then he looked at this second in command. "Have them fortify in place and stand by. He said he will ask for help from the fleet."

"Alpha-two to Alpha-actual."

"Go two."

"I have DM's who are being pushed by 2/1 pressing against us from the north. . . over."

"Alpha-two what is your status . . . over."

"Alpha-two, we are good. Delta-Mike seems to be trying to disengage from us . . . over."

The 61st AG was still attempting to penetrate the marine perimeter encompassing both Serpent and Merchants bridges. The commander knew that the 62nd on his left was in trouble and that the 63rd was also suffering serious causalities in the West woods. So, he and his second in command were trying to devise a strategy when he was contacted from GP headquarters. "Commander pull your troops back a little. The fleet has managed to drive off the Hooman ships for the time being and we will bombard the entire river front. Attack at the end of the bombardment."

Ten minutes later, space weapons began hitting in and around the marine positions at the bridges. It caused enough causalities and damage that the DMs were able to fight across the two bridges until they were stopped again by two companies of the 1st Marines dug in on the east side, along with two companies from the 2nd Marines sent from 3/2 that was situated in the south woods. However, the volume of fire hitting the marines from the DM fleet made it obvious they could not hold-out for long without help.

"Bravo-six to First Marines-actual we are losing Blackburn Bridge. The DMs will force it very soon. I am going to detonate our charges and destroy it . . . Bravo- six, out."

"Ancestors!" exclaimed the 1st Regiment XO when the Regimental commander repeated the message. "Are you going to stop him?"

The regimental commander shook his head grimly "No. He is on the scene and a proven leader. It must be very bad for him to feel the need to do it."

"Blackburn Bridge; fire in the hole, fire in the hole!"

The message went out over every communicator along the river before the bridge blew up in a shattering explosion killing or wounding almost six-hundred of the 61st AG on and near the bridge. As soon as the bridge detonated the DMs who had just captured Merchants bridge, abandoned it and ran for the safety of the west side of the river fearing it too was about to be blown up. As they withdrew the Battalion commander of 4/2 counterattacked. They retook the bridge in a sharp fight that killed almost two-hundred more DMs still on the east side of the bridge. But 4/2 suffered almost as many causalities themselves in the attack. The marine survivors quickly re-occupied their old positions, and barely beat back another DM attack.

SUPREME DM HEADQUARTERS.

Supreme Pack Leader Glgoffen, angry and anxious, sat inscrutable listening to his Intelligence Chief.

"Supreme leader at this time our ships have a slight advantage in space. However, indications are they could soon be fighting a larger Hooman's fleet . . . perhaps within hours. Our raid to find the doors is a major meeting engagement that is stalling. The reinforcements from the First-Great lost eleven craft to Hoo-man's ships while coming down into the eastern wilderness. When they began moving toward the city, they encountered a large unexpected unit of marines that were dug in. Some gains were made, but they have been lost in a counter attack that cost hundreds of dead and wounded. Those added to the losses in the landing from space indicate that the First Great has suffered a total of close to thirty percent causalities on Pleasant, plus the hundreds more during the NX raid. Its Third AG suffered the worst and must be considered very close to combat ineffective."

"That is the First-Great. What of the Sixth?" Glgoffen leaned back in his chair and rubbed his hands along the tops of his thighs looking at his intelligence chief.

Herckel took a deep breath. "Supreme leader, the Sixty-second AG must be considered combat ineffective due to losses. The Sixty-first AG has suffered almost one thousand causalities. But it is still combat effective The Sixty-third AG is engaged in heavy combat in the west wilderness"

Glgoffen smacked his hands on his thighs and stood up. "How are our fighters holding up to this."

Herckel hesitated a moment, and hung his head waiting for the worst. Glgoffen held up his hand and snapped "I told you earlier you will not be punished. What of our fighters?"

"I am told they refer this place as *the Galaxy of Death*."

Glgoffen shook he head and rubbed the side of his face. "Both you and your predecessor badly blundered the information we had on this galaxy. But we must learn from this, and we must withdraw while our fleet holds some advantage in space."

He turned to his Deputy Supreme Leader. "Begin a recall and withdraw to Planet Warbeast. Order the fleet to defend and patrol in depth in that system. I will decide what to do when we arrive there. Packmates we have bloodied the Hoomans also, and in a way this raid has been a success by the observations of the Recon-pack that managed to cross the river. They are still observing numbers of troops coming from one of the target buildings that we will soon totally destroy.

"We can infer a door is there and so have learned an important fact about our adversary." *At a dreadful cost to the Pack.* "We must plan carefully for what comes next. Go and carry out my orders."

Herckel nodded and quickly left. Glgoffen held up his hand stopping his Deputy Leader, and watched as Herckel left. *I cannot have another fifth Great disaster during this withdrawal.* Glgoffen looked into his Deputy leader and old friends' eyes. "Select one Large Pack from each Attack Group to stay behind as a rear guard to continue engaging the Hoomans as we withdraw. Tell the leaders of the rear guard they will be notified when the majority of our forces are off world. Assure them I will send stealth landing boats to get their survivors. Then have all other troops, disengage and move as quickly as possible to their landing positions for pick up. I want the landing areas bombarded immediately to destroy any Hooman troops who may be in the area before the arrival of ours.

"Finally: Have the fleet target every large Hooman position they can see and destroy the buildings we were trying to reach on the east side of the river."

"At once Supreme Leader" his deputy left to carry out his orders.

Supreme leader Glgoffen walked to his door and call to his aid. "Have the Chief of Engineers come here immediately. If he is not in the general area send me the senior engineering leader who is in the area. And send in that Intelligence technician with his projector."

Five minutes later, the Chief of Engineers and two aids waited to be recognized by the Glgoffen who was communicating with one of the Great Pack Leaders. When he finished, he waved the engineers into his office and addressed the intelligence technician. "Put up the visual of the Warbeast system." The tech hit a command and the front of the office became a hologram of the Planet Refuge/Warbeast system in relation to the other three human worlds being fought over.

"How can we serve," asked the chief engineer as he and his aides looked at the hologram with curiosity.

Glgoffen motioned the men to sit while he stood thoughtfully studying the hologram for a moment before he replied. "As you know, the raid has ended. I am attempting to disengage our packs from the Hoomans. The fleet has begun bombarding the Hoomans to destroy as much of their army and suspected location of the doors as possible.

I wish to insure we do not suffer another Fifth Great Pack disaster as we lift the First and Sixth from the planet.

"I have sacrificed a brave rear guard to keep the Hoomans occupied as we leave. The fighting is reported to be at touching distance and causalities are high on both sides." He stood looking at the three engineers who seemed confused.

"How can engineers serve in this?" Asked the chief engineer again.

"Let me pose a tactical problem to you." Glgoffen pointed at the hologram and instructed the technician "Indicate the fleets line of movement." A red line moved in an arc from Pleasant, past NX 246, to bend back into the Warbeast/Refuge system where the fleet ships took station to defend all four planets in the system.

A second line moved back from NX to join those already there. "I intend to disembark the Great packs around the system for the short term. Two will fortify Warbeast, and one each will fortify each of the other three planets.

"I anticipate the Hoo-mans will follow us and attack this system when they feel able. So, I need a way to slow them and make them cautious. That is where the engineers can serve. I want you to design a . . . type of bomb we can seed in the space around us that will slow the Hooman and possibly destroy some ships. Can you do that?"

"Supreme leader, can we have some time to study it?"

Glgoffen thought for a moment. "Time is short. I need something in a day. Report back tomorrow with your plan." The engineers came to attention and left leaving the Supreme Leader staring at the hologram of the system he now had to defend for the short term. *Ancestors, how the fortunes have changed.*

CHAPTER 8

The DM troops sacrificed as a rear guard moved to cover as much area as they could, and began engaging the marines to cover the withdrawal. But the drop-in contact and firepower was noticed by Frank as his squad moved further into the Eastern woods.

"Farrell to team leaders do you get the feeling they are disengaging . . . over." Corporal Olney, was the first to reply when a one second alert buzz sounded in everyone's head followed by "Take cover, take cover. DM space bombardment imminent."

"Get some cover!" Frank yelled to his squad and found a small ravine he rolled into. He quickly realized he and his squad were outside of the primary impact area. "Squad be alert for DMs pulling back. This may be another withdrawal."

The DM ships drove off the small human fleet and began pulverizing the City of New Glasgow along with any identified marine positions. It went on for almost an hour keeping them undercover as the 1st and 6th Great Packs disengaged and moved to their landing sites in the east and west woods outside of the impact areas. Explosions, making the ground shake like an earthquake, seemed ubiquitous to the marines.

The large packs left behind engaged the groggy marines that survived the bombardment; and for a while a series of fierce close quarters small unit firefights were fought near the government buildings, transit portals, and plaza along with the science centers in the north-west part of the city. The entire area was transformed into urban rubble allowing the combatants to get very close to each other and more than once they fought hand to hand.

"I see some movement east. . . over." Corporal Olney reported.

"Roger that" Frank replied. "Squad get on line and hit um as they pass."

"D" Recon was also outside of the impact area in the west woods where they had taken Cover. After the bombardment ended, they saw the very end of the 6th GP rapidly moving across their front through the trees toward their pick-up zone.

Alicia's squad leader communicated. "Teams this is a general withdrawal of Delta-Mike . . . break . . . we are going to engage any targets of opportunity that are still here. . . out.

Alicia's team, in point, saw the steady stream of DM landing boats coming down in the distance and immediately shooting up again. "Team-three we have boats landing about half a click away."

"Roger that team three" replied her squad leader "Engage any target of opportunity . . . break . . . Reports are coming in that most remaining DM's have gotten away from here, and the east wilderness, in a general withdrawal. . .out."

Alicia adjusted her contacts to study the DMs she saw and noticed one group of four wearing the markings of high-ranking officers on their sleeves. They were the very last of the column accompanied by three others, obviously acting as body guards. She watched them and the surrounding bushes for a full thirty seconds for additional threats then communicated her suspicions. "Team-three to Squad leader; I have what appears to be a command group moving across my front. I am going to try to capture them . . . three out."

"Roger that team-three. I will pass the word up."

The 62nd AG had advanced the furthest of all the AG's and now had the furthest move back to their pick-up point. Plus, they had to re-fight past some marine strong points and suffered additional causalities as they hurried back west. As the cover bombardment came in it became easier for them to withdraw, and the leader of the 62nd began to relax somewhat when he reached the wilderness area. *Thank the stars I know that the remnants of my AG will survive this battle.*

"Leader I see the pickup boats," his second in command reported, as their headquarters group followed behind the last of the 62nd fighters, who suddenly began jogging toward their pick up.

Pack gods they shame themselves! He and his group were forced to jog also to stay in touch. *Spirits I feel like I am running from my enemy. The only thing making this bearable is that I am the last to leave this battlefield, a point of honor for my fighters. But I can feel those cursed Hoomans around us.* He tried not to appear anxious as he, his second in command, and personal communications specialist surrounded by four security men stayed roughly one hundred meters behind the last of the troops.

Alicia and her team used light benders to move within twenty meters of where the DM command group would pass. She communicated, "Team, hit the security men first. Give the other three a chance to surrender but don't let them get you. Anyone who does not immediately give up we kill . . . break . . . Long, Jones, you hit the security; copy?"

"Roger that"

"Get ready on my mark."

"Mark, mark, mark."

The leader of the 62nd turned to his communicator, "Get GP headquarters." The soldier handed his small COMM device to his leader who said to the 6th Great Pack commander "Leader I can see the pickup zone and I am the last out of the city. Most of the Sixty-second is coming up now. I will be . . . Knife soldiers!"

The leader of the 6th Great heard the commotions.

"Are you there?" He asked. The comm device was silent. He turned to his deputy commander and said with concern "I fear we may have lost the Sixty-second Command group. If they have been captured . . .."

TWO MINUTES PREVIOUSLY:

"Mark, mark, mark." Alicia whispered, and the three security men fell dead one after the other. The marines now appeared pointing their pulse rifles at the three astounded DM who stood completely still. It saved their lives. Alicia motioned with her rifle and indicated for them to raise their hands which they did. "Search them. Bind their arms and let's get them back. Team-thee;" she communicated. "I have two high value prisoners with their communications specialist. Where can we pass them off?"

"Team-three . . . move to company CP."

"Roger that. Team-three moving."

The Battle Cruiser *Mother Earth*, and other ships pushed past the alien destroyers and allowed the two transports they were escorting to land the reserve battalions of the 4th Marines. They began engaging the remaining DM's of the rear guard and were already being hard pressed as soon as they hit the ground. Soon the remaining DM finally began to surrender.

While the destruction of New Glasgow continued Frank and his squad quietly engaged as many of the 63rd AG as possible when they passed. After a lull of thirty minutes with no further contact, Frank and his squad began following in the same direction and arrived in time to see the last landing boats shoot up to disappear in the heavens. "Alpha patrol-two to Alpha-one."

"Go patrol-two" Lieutenant Nikowa replied.

"Patrol-two. . . the DMs have withdrawn from this area . . . over."

"Alpha-one to patrol-two . . . indications are that the DM main force has withdrawn from the planet . . . break . . . small groups up to large pack size may still be in area as a rear-guard break . . . return to my location at Merchants bridge . . . break . . . locate and destroy any DMs you encounter who do not immediately surrender . . . Alpha-one out."

Frank looked around. He checked his chip for the most direct route to Merchants bridge. "Team-three you have point . . . One, you bring up the rear . . . Keep alert people we're going back through the city break . . . there are reports of loose DMs still in the area."

He and his squad were sickened by the destruction of New Glasgow. To him, it resembled Berlin at the end of World War Two. Rubble made the journey much longer, and more dangerous than previously. The smell of death and destruction was ubiquitous. Broken furniture and bodies were visible in the wreckage, and at times the marines had difficulty recognizing areas they worked through when they first arrived a week ago. Frank saw the bridge. *Okay we can relax and start to clean up I guess.* "Team gather on me ta . . ."

The shock was like being hit in the chest with a large bat. It staggering him back a few steps before he fell backwards aware of his squad moving around him pulsing an enemy to their front. He heard the return gunfire from the DMs who had ambushed them.

Corporal Gupta and his team were the first to assist him and call for medical help. Gupta put a Nano dressing on his shoulder then rolled him over to place one on the exit wound in his side "We will have a med unit here soon Sarge. Shit! None of us saw them in the rubble."

Frank felt more and more lightheaded and had trouble getting a full breath. "Keep me sitting up" he gasped I don't want to lie down. Don't feel bad, I didn't see the fuckers either. Did you get them?" he gasped.

Gupta nodded. "We killed six of them but lost Private Chang

who took multiple hits in his head and could not be saved. Corporal Drugba and Olney are rechecking the area with their teams."

Frank nodded. "Tell Corporal Olney he has the squad until I get back," Frank gasped.

"Roger that Sarge."

Frank passed out. He came around when he was tapped by a corpsman. "I have a tube coming behind me. After I get you in it you are going up to the ship. Your vitals look good. I'm going to give you something to relax you and begin getting more fluids back in." It the last thing Frank heard as he blacked out again.

He woke up in the sickbay of the *Argon*, and felt good enough to sit up and look around the crowded room at the other wounded in various stages of recovery. A corpsman approached him.

"How do you feel Sergeant?"

"I feel good doc," he moved his arm around, "and everything seemed to be working. When can I get back to my unit?"

"That is up to the doctor, and here she is now." They both watched the exceptionally trim lieutenant commander coming toward the bed. "How are you feeling Sergeant?"

"I feel fine ma'am." Frank could see her reviewing something from her chip. After a moment her eyes cleared and she ran a scanner over his wound, chest and side. "You are very fortunate. The bullet hit the shoulder rode along the clavicle then down through the tops of your lungs just missing the heart. It came out of your side. "Everything looks good now, but with conditions as they are groundside, if that bullet had hit your heart and you did not get into a tube almost immediately you would not have survived. I am keeping you aboard tonight to ensure complete healing. You can rejoin your unit tomorrow. Enjoy the rest."

"Thank you, ma'am."

Frank got out of bed and stood stretching his shoulder by moving his arm back and forth then took several deep breaths and heard Lieutenant Nikowa say "Glad to see you are fit Sergeant."

"Did you get hit too, sir?"

Nikowa shook his head. "I am checking on second platoon wounded. The ship is full of wounded, and Recon has had their share. I saw the doctor, I'm glad to get you back tomorrow."

"Me too sir. What's the word? Is anything happening?"

Nikowa shrugged. "Delta-Mike managed to evacuate the majority of their surviving forces back to Refuge. "D Recon captured a couple of high value prisoners. One is the equivalent of a regimental commander, along with his XO. They are currently being interrogated. You may be interested to know they were captured by that female corporal you recommended. They made her a sergeant and awarded her a Galactic Cross in Silver."

"Alicia? No shit! I told ya she was good! "Frank blurted and smiled.

Nikowa laughed. "Do you remember the morning of the DM landing"

Frank nodded. "Of course, sir."

"Well, your squad was the first to engage the DMs. You inflicted so many causalities that it slowed down their advance long enough to be helpful not only to the defenders at the bridges, but you also gave those marines we lost in the medical center a little extra time to make the DMs pay a high price to get in there. For that contribution all your men have been awarded the Galactic Cross in Bronze. You get it in silver, along with another wound badge and a second award star for your Pleasant campaign ribbon.

"Thank you, sir," I know the squad will be pleased. They responded very well the entire time. But you don't have to give me anything. I didn't do anything special."

Lieutenant Nikowa put his hands on his hips. "I am not giving you anything Sergeant; god makes the awards. Just take them, be grateful, and say, Aye-aye, Sir."

Frank came to attention. "Aye-aye, Sir."

"One other thing" Nikowa said "when you get back you will have a replacement from "C" company for Private Chang. It is the other one you brought back with you from MW."

"Who? Private Blanco?"

Nikowa nodded "I will see you dirtside tomorrow Sergeant." He left the room.

WARBEAST/REFUGE SYSTEM A DAY LATER.

Supreme Leader Glgoffen stood in front of all of his Senior Pack Leaders. His first after action meeting from the battles on Pleasant and NX world. They had just heard the reports from the 1st and 6th Great Pack leaders on their losses. Added to the earlier destruction of the entire 5th Great Pack on Sunset, it was an unimaginable defeat for the Pack Army in this galaxy, or any other in their recorded history.

A gloom hung over the meeting room. Glgoffen realized *I must do something to help their confidence for what we still must face in order to withdraw from here.* "Pack mates!" he called to get everyone's attention.

"As reported, the recent fighting was as times fiercer than that we experienced on Planet Sunset. Our forces have covered themselves in glory with their warrior spirit. We know now that the hoomans have a capability to transport fighters, other than by ship, even though we do not know exactly what it is. We also know they are a warrior race. That must be considered in all further actions against them.

"I intend to fortify this system for the short term, then return to the home worlds to report my failure to conquer this galaxy. I will then help with planning if further involvement becomes an option. For the present, I plan to withdraw in stages so we can stop any pursuit of our ships as they withdraw."

Glgoffen pointed to the Chief Engineer. "What have you discovered to assist me?

The Chief waved to a technician standing in the rear of the room who came forward, and created a hologram of the seven planets the war had touched so far, in front of the group . Inserted into that image was what looked like a Twenty-five-gallon tank with several protrusions sticking from it that everyone studied with curiosity.

"Supreme leader the container you see holds a small missile that when awakened is activated if one of these protrusions senses the kinetic waves from any ships in motion up to three light seconds away from it. The missile will lock onto the target and is capable of light speed travel with a maximum range of four light seconds. The impulsive force on hitting something at that speed is catastrophic."

The chief Engineer nodded to the tech who added a thousand tiny points around the Warbeast /Refuge system. "These should be a benefit to you depending on where and how you wish them deployed. My shops can manufacture as many as needed in a few weeks. It should never be forgotten, that when awake, these are as dangerous to our ships as to the hoomans. Just a few of these will cause grave concern to the hoomans and I would caution against using too many. A small amount will slow them down."

Glgoffen and the others continued to study the hologram of the strange looking rounded tank. The Engineer continued, "If these are put in the approach space around the planet, they will cause enough confusion for the Hoomans to give us time for our departure."

Glgoffen sat in the now quiet room studying the hologram. "I am pleased with your efforts" Begin manufacturing them immediately."

He looked around the room. "Any questions?"

"What do you call them?" Herckel asked.

"I wondered that also" the 3rd Great Pack Leader said. Several others called "I also."

Glgoffen looked to the Chief Engineer. "Well?"

"The engineers call it a *Hoobar* Supreme Leader."

Glgoffen tilted his head and gave the Engineer a puzzled look. Before he could say anything, the engineer continued. "Supreme

Leader, it's an abbreviation for Hoo-man Barrier." Several of the commanders chuckled.

Glgoffen nodded. "A fitting name. We will place our Hoobars in their path to give them a difficult journey to meet us. Now let us plan the defense of this system and our return to Andromeda."

CHAPTER 9

". . . Freedom is a noble thing!"
John Barbour. Freedom

The highest-ranking prisoner in the war to date, equal in rank to a full colonel, was the angry Commander of the 62nd AG, Attack Leader Wolflazgl. Who sat in a chair, flanked by armed guards, in the center of a secure room on Marine Commandant General Thomas's command ship, Battle Cruiser *Mother Earth*.

He had not spoken to his captors at all and continually scanned his surroundings. *I do not see a way out. I will resist telling them anything as long as possible, then perhaps I can be untruthful.* He closed his eyes waiting for his interrogators expecting the torturous type of treatment routinely given to prisoners by the Pack.

As fate would have it, when his command was destroyed by a team from "A" recon the year before he was the first to identify the human pulse weapons for what they were. It was a very important observations in the early days of skirmishing around the Sunset Perimeter on Planet Sunset. And although he lost most of his command at that time, his fighting ability since then led to his rapid promotions as DM causalities grew. *What are they waiting for?*

Wolflazgl opened his eyes when he heard footsteps approaching. He watched a sailor walking toward him and knew enough to realize *not a leader. Is it my interrogator?* The sailor walked behind Wolflazgl, took a hand size tube from his pocket and pressed it behind his ear. *What did he just do to me?* He worried, but he quickly realized *I feel no different than before. Whatever it was did not seem harmful.* He closed his eyes again, and god began scrutinizing his mind.

◆

In a room across from the prisoner, a number of naval and marine officers along with two Astrometric Celestial Mechanics experts, and a physicist discussed what had been learned from the captured charts off the DM Ship, *Enemy Killer*.

The briefing was begun by General Thomas. "Here is where we are Ladies and Gentlemen. Our prisoner in the next room, is the equivalent of a Full Colonel in our forces, and is called an Attack Group Leader. He is the Commander of the Sixty-second Attack Group. As most of you know that is the equivalent of a reinforced regiment. That attack group was involved in most of the fighting in New Glasgow. So, he is a very high value captive that we have not yet spoken to. Along with him we have his second in command our equivalent of a lieutenant colonel, and their communicator, a senior NCO.

"At gods recommendation, we placed a military grade implant and translator into each of them to draw down most of their immediate military and personal memories. Then we may or may not remove the military chip leaving the translator to begin our questioning from the information we harvested. Mostly, we will be asking him questions that we will already have the answers to; but we may get other useful information and clarify unclear matters."

General Thomas looked around the room "Astrometrics, do you have anything to report?" The senior scientist replied "Sir, the star information from Andromeda we recovered from the ship is extremely detailed. It gives information on their route not only marking the navigational Pulsar signals, but the Astronomical Unit drift between the navigational points. It also shows the effects of gravity streams, and other forces, on their ships while inside the wormhole bridge This information along with our own portal navigation will allow us to backtrack them to their worlds of origin whenever we wish." The General nodded his thanks, "Physics, do you have anything to add at this time?" The lead physicist shook his head, "Not yet sir."

General Thomas smiled. "Thank you ladies and gentlemen. We will meet again when we begin our actual interrogation.

Frank was back with his squad, continuing the sweep through the rubble of New Glasgow when his chip alerted him to a personal call. "Sgt Farrell sir."

"Frank it's me," Alicia said.

"Alicia? Where are ya?"

"I'm in New Glasgow looking for my parents. I was told they survived the fighting but I can't find them."

Frank glanced around at the destroyed buildings and devastation with fires still smoldering in places; he grimaced smelling the bodies and wreckage .*Is she wondering around here alone?* "Who's with ya Alicia?"

"No one. I was given permission to search for a few hours and hoped we could get together." "Be careful Alicia, we're still looking for surviving DMs hiding in the rubble to cause trouble. Tell me exactly where ya are."

"My parents live in the far Northeast section of the city. Fighting there was not as bad as everywhere else but the area is still in bad condition."

"Stand-by Alicia, I'll get back to ya."

"Alpha patrol-two to Alpha-one," communicated Frank.

"Go patrol-two" answered Lieutenant Nagoto.

"Alpha-one. . . I would like permission to move from the AGRC area down to the northeastern area on the other side of the river to assist a member of Delta Recon in a survivor search. . . over."

Nagoto replied "Are you assisting a new Sergeant in Delta . . . over."

"Roger that."

"Permission granted. Move your search to that locality. . . Alpha-one out."

Frank looked down toward the river. "Squad we are moving across the river to assist Delta Recon . . . Break . . . Corporal Gupta, you have point take us over Serpent bridge . . . Break . . . Corporal Kim, you have our six."

"Gupta Roger."

"Kim roger."

An hour later, Frank and his team along with Alicia were helping survivors; inquiring about her parents that they finally found huddled with a group hiding in the northeast woods.

Alicia ran to them and hugged her mother then her father who seemed stunned to see her. "Thank the ancestors you are well" she hugged her mother again. Her father just stood looking her over from head to toe. When Frank walked up beside Alicia her father glared at him and Alicia. "See what you and the military have done to our home and friends."

Alicia was speechless; but Frank replied angrily, "Look to yourself! Your daughter didn't do this. Your uncaring attitude about the aliens who invaded our galaxy and killed its people did this. And if you were nearly as intelligent as you think you are you would realize it and thank your daughter for her dedication and courage. Quite frankly, Mister Macalduie you and your ilk disgust me. Your daughter is one of the finest people I've known."

Alicia's father stood pale and looked around at Frank and his marines in their filthy and some bloody clothing. Then perceiving that his daughter looked the same; he sat down and began to quietly cry. Alicia sat and put her arm around his shoulders, and cried with him.

Later . . . Frank escorted Alicia's parents to a shelter set up for surviving civilians. After ensuring their welfare he took her back to her Unit. As they moved through the devastation of the city and university Alicia said angrily "It will take years to repair the destruction done here. The fucking DMs have a lot to answer for."

Frank looked sideways at her, surprised by her tone and vehemence. "Yer right. But don't let your anger destroy ya by taking it personal."

"Oh? And how would you handle the destruction of your home!" she answered hotly.

"Alicia, you have to make a place in here." He tapped the side of his head. "Never forget; and plan on how to kill as many of the fuckers as you can. But do it coldly and professionally. It may not make you feel better, but it will keep you alive and well longer." He gave her a feral grin.

Alicia stopped and stared at him for a long moment . "You never cease to amaze me. For the first time, for some reason, I feel that I'm seeing the real you." She began walking again. "I know ya have always given me good advice, and I'll think about it. Ya already have me using that silly Earth accent of yours." She punched his shoulder lightly .

Frank laughed out loud. "How about we try to get together when we get back to Sunset?"

"I'd like that I think."

"Alpha-one to Recon-two . . . over" came the voice of Lt Nikowa in his head.

"Go Alpha-one."

"Are you still assisting Delta recon? . . . over"

"Recon-two . . . I just delivering their personnel back to them . . . over"

"Alpha-one to Recon-Two, meet me at Merchant Bridge CP for information and personnel.

Alpha-one out"

I wonder what this is about? "Corporal Gupta!," Frank called to the point team, "take us to Merchants Bridge." Then he communicated to the rest "Squad, team four has point we're moving back to Merchant Bridge to the platoon CP. Stay alert."

It took almost forty minutes to move thorough or around all the destruction before they got to Alpha recon's makeshift command post. "Corporal Olney, place the squad facing West" communicated Frank "I'll see what's going on"."

"Roger that."

Frank ducked under some rubble into the basement of a partially collapsed building and saw Lieutenant Nikowa. Private Blanco was sitting on some debris in a corner. Frank nodded to him then saluted Lieutenant Nikowa. "What's going on, sir?"

"Get a mug of coffee and sit-down Farrell; we have a few things to go over."

Frank got coffee and sat near Nikowa enjoying his first cup since the battle began.

"Amazing how good it tastes during something like this" observed Nikowa.

"You've got that right sir." Frank took a sip."

Lieutenant Nikowa finished his mug and sat it between his feet.

"I have several things for you: first Private Blanco there will go to your squad to replace Private Chang." Frank looked over at Blanco. "Get a mug of coffee then go find Cpl Olney, and tell him you are replacing Chang." Blanco nodded and left.

"What else Sir?" Frank asked. "Wait one" Lieutenant Nikowa got another coffee. When he came back, he asked, "Which of your corporals would you recommend for sergeant?" Without hesitation Frank answered, "Corporal Olney."

"Very well get him in here"

"Farrell to Corporal Olney, report inside immediately."

"Roger that"

Olney entered the Command Post a moment later and gave Frank a 'What's going on look.' Frank tilted his head and raised his eyebrows in a 'I have no idea.'

"Get a mug of coffee Corporal," Nikowa said.

When he returned, Lieutenant Nikowa said, "Sergeant Farrell says you will make a good sergeant. So, congratulations. Effective immediately you are promoted to the rank of sergeant. Here are some stripes I scavenged for you. The skipper will give you the certificate when we get back to Sunset. You will take the First Squad. You and Sergeant Farrell decide if we can promote a corporal from within the squad or have one brought in."

"Sir?" Frank was surprised that he was losing the squad; but Lieutenant Nikowa held up his hand stopping him. "With all the fighting and moving you two might not know that Charley Recon lost most of their Third platoon including the Platoon Commander and Platoon Sergeant in the east wilderness. It was bad luck during the DM landing that several landing craft came down on top of them."

Frank and Olney both winced.

"Staff Sergeant Valdez, has been moved to "Charley" as the acting Platoon Commander for now and will probably end up a Lieutenant. And effective immediately, you Sergeant Farrell are promoted to Staff Sergeant, and will be my Platoon Sergeant. The skipper will give you your certificate with Sergeant Olney. Here are Staff Sergeant stripes that Valdez left for you. Do either of you have any questions?"

Frank and Olney looked at each other, "No Sir."

"Very well. Sergeant Olney, report back to your squad and stand by for orders" After he left Nikowa turned to Frank. "If nothing changes, the army is due to land here and in every other large town on the planet tomorrow. The Corps will turn over all combat operations to them. They will establish a permanent base here like the one on NX. I want you to make sure everything is ready to make our move that will be by ship. I understand it could take a few months to get the portals here up and running again. Oh, and before I forget. You are supposed to contact Dr. Lamont when we get back to Sunset. Any idea what that's about."

Yea I might. "No Sir. Maybe it is about the pulse modifications"

General Thomas and other senior military leaders, along with Sergeant Major Brown, straightened up after listening to, and watching, imagery from the data dump given by god that was taken from the prisoner AGL Wolflazgl. General Thomas said in a reflective tone "The randomness of war is indeed surprising at times. To think our prisoner had his first command destroyed by a squad from the First Reconnaissance Battalion in what was the first combat action they had on Planet Sunset. Then to be capture by a squad from that same battalion over a year later, and several worlds away." He looked at a Navy Commander who would do the interrogation. "Perhaps you will be able to goad him with some of that information."

"It may prove useful Sir," the commander replied.

"Very well Ladies and Gentlemen. Let us get to the business at hand. What do we wish to know first?"

Two hours later Wolflazgl looked up as the hatch disappeared and the Commander stepped into the room. *I will tell them nothing and not speak until the torture becomes unbearable.*

Commander Cummings sat on a chair given to him by one of the guards. "Thank you" he said to the sailor, sat down and examined the prisoner. "Well Attack Group Leader Wolflazgl, I hope you have not been too uncomfortable."

Wolflazgl felt a head rush and blurted, "You know nothing about me. You are using a name you made up." Commander Cummings smiled. "We have a lot to discuss Attack Group Leader. We have been watching you for a long time, since you survived the destruction of your large Pack by the stream on Planet Sunset a little over a year ago. Remember?

Wolflazgl felt faint. . . . *This is trickery of some sort. Pack ancestors how does he know that? What am I to do?*

Commander Cummings saw the uncertainty and fear in Woflazgl's eyes. "You have achieved great stature since then. Your family on First World will be honored by you."

They know the world I come from. Is he a mind reader or is this all a trick? Wolflazgl was a superstitious man who felt he may be up against something he could not comprehend. He began to sweat. Commander Cummings noticed.

"Can I offer you food or drink Attack Group Leader." Woflazgl shook his head. "Well then let us get started." As Cummings began the interrogation, his prisoner quickly realized that his inquisitor knew so much about him he saw no reason not to answer all questions and he spent hours doing so. At the end of the session Commander Cummings said "Did you know Attack Group Leader that we come from the same world."

"What nonsense is that! We are not even from the same galaxy."

Cummings smiled. "Think of your history. I understand your religion speaks of rescue from the land of ice cold and beasts."

"What is your point?" Woflazgl asked.

"My point, is that the world you evolved on and were carried from by your rescuers so many thousands of years in the past is our prime world. We were a separate tribe when you were taken away; and we were left in the cold with the beasts."

Woflazgl stared at him with his mouth open unable to say anything. "I completely understand" Cummings said "That was my reaction when I first learned we were related as it were. We will talk again Attack Group Leader."

CHAPTER 10

SUNSET PERIMETER.

Operation *Strong Door* was a brutal twelve-day battle with high causalities. The returning marines settled in to their old bunkers and after cleaning their weapons were given three days leave to help them decompress from the operation even before they began the process of getting issued new gear, replacements and training.

Frank spent his time arraigning for the platoon replacements and giving the veterans as much leeway as he could. He was in the platoon office when he received a call from Lieutenant Nikowa. "Sergeant, the skipper and I have been called to see the colonel. I'll let you know what is happening when I get back. By the way, the skipper mentioned that you have not contacted Doctor Lamont yet. Make a point to do it today."

"Aye-aye Sir."

DELTA-MIKE H.Q ON WARBEAST/REFUGE.

"Quiet pack mates!" called the second in command and conversation ceased.

SPL Glgoffen stood before the gathering of senior officers. "You fought a long difficult campaign against a fierce relentless enemy covering yourselves in glory. But too many us are now gone. Some of our Attack Groups have almost disappeared, and the Fifth Great Pack was annihilated."

He stood with his head lowered for a moment. "I am the blame. It is all my fault and I will answer for it when we get home. Until then," he said in a commanding voice, "we have more to do. This is the beginning of our defense of the home worlds. Unfortunately, we awoke a hunter-warrior species that is unforgiving and savage.

"The battle on the world of Pleasant is over. Those left behind as a rear guard have been picked up. Regrettably, only a third of them survived death or capture." He nodded to a technician who displayed a hologram of the Refuge system. It extended to the first of the Space Stations guarding the region of space containing the tunnel back to Andromeda. "Packmates, this is our first formulating session for the move back home, and the probability that it will be a fighting withdrawal. I will outline some thoughts for you to comment." He turned toward the hologram.

"Hello Doc. How have you been?" Frank said when Doctor Lamont answered his communication "I imagine this invasion has knocked ya off yur schedule."

Doctor Lamont snorted. "Unfortunately, you are correct. Nonetheless, Mira kept working on your issue and we have some news for you."

Frank's heart quickened. "About possibilities of going back?"

"No. You have already resolved that issue, yes?"

"Yes. So, what's the news?"

"I would rather tell you in person. Mira and I are working at Camp Gonzales, come by at noon tomorrow. We will talk then." The transmission ended.

What was that about?

Frank was still wondering about his cryptic conversation when Lieutenant Nikowa entered the platoon office and announced, "You will be getting a new platoon commander."

"Why?" *Is this somehow tied in to Lamont's news?*

Nikowa grinned at Frank. "I have been promoted to captain."

"No shit? That's great Sir! How about I buy you a few beers."

Nikowa chuckled. "Later." First, we have to see the skipper. By the way, he made major and is being transferred to a new battalion being formed. I imagine he'll tell us about it."

Suddenly he held up his finger in wait motion listening to a transmission for a moment. "Yes, Sir I am with him now. We are on our way."

A short time later: Major Nagoto said, "Sit down Gentlemen", handing Frank his promotion papers and brand-new stripes "Congratulations Staff Sergeant Farrell. It is well earned."

"Thank you, Sir; and congratulations, on your promotion."

Major Nagoto smiled. "Down to business gentlemen. Within a week Captain Nikowa will assume command of "A" Recon." Frank turned and smiled a congrats to Nikowa.

"In my case, Staff Sergeant your congratulations are somewhat premature. I was notified before you arrived that I have been jumped two grades to Lieutenant Colonel. Along with Major Lamb jumped to full Colonel. This war has necessitated changes and promotions inconceivable last year.

"Not only that, the United Worlds Military Counsel and Civil government is considering conscription if the war continues much longer. And I am reliably told the Military Counsel will limit boot camp training to just sixteen weeks for most conscripts before assignment."

Captain Nikowa blurted "No disrespect sir; but that is crazy! Colonel Nagoto nodded with a frown.

Frank sat quietly. *I'm the only one here who knows people can be very effectively trained for basic service in that time.*

"It will take some getting used to," Major Nagoto said. The next reason you are here, and this affects you Staff Sergeant, is that the Corps is forming a new battalion within recon; but it will not be conventional recon. It is designated the First Raider Battalion with plans for a second raider battalion in the near future."

Frank was as surprised as Captain Nikowa. *Fucking Raiders. How quickly a real war changes things. What goes around . . .*

"Not only that gentlemen, two modified naval vessels the UWS *Vengeance* and the *Retribution* are attached for primary duty with us in what is designated as First Galactic Reconnaissance Brigade. Colonel Rahm is now the Brigadier General commanding. Colonel Sing from HQ will be the Brigade XO, and I have the First Raiders."

"Holy shit!" Frank muttered.

Colonel Nagoto overheard his comment. "I agree."

"Sorry Sir."

"Do not be sorry Staff Sergeant Farrell. I am taking you with me to First Raiders as a Platoon Sergeant in "A" Company, and depending on your continued outstanding performance, I expect to have you commissioned as a lieutenant after the reorganization. You gentlemen are ordered to keep that information to yourselves. That's all for now. Staff Sergeant please stay a moment."

Colonel Nagoto sat back in his chair and smiled at Frank. "We are a long way from our first fight in Pleasant's west wilderness. It seems like another existence"

"It was another existence Sir, especially with what we are still facing."

The colonel nodded. "Sit back." An image of the second defensive line of the Sunset Perimeter with a section highlighted filled Frank's mind. "This is our new home, and before you ask, the Fist Reconnaissance Battalion will continue in the traditional mission. The Raiders will do what the name implies. We are going to harass Delta-Mike everywhere and way."

Their meeting lasted an hour and finished when Colonel Nagoto said, "Move over there in three days, and help them get ready to receive new troops. I will let Sergeant Major Hoysaia know you will be available."

"Did you say Sergeant Major Hoysaia?"

"You seem surprised. Do you know him?"

"Yes Sir, I do. He is an old friend."

"Good. It should make things easier for you. Good luck Sergeant."

At noon the next day Frank was greeted by Mira who gave him a tight hug. "I am so glad to see you have stayed well since I last saw you."

"Thanks Mira."

"Come with me." She put her arm through his and led him thru the large underground complex toward a laboratory where Dr. Lamont was working. Frank smiled to himself, "Ya know Mira, ya always seem to be taking me through deserted halls to hidden rooms." She squeezed his arm with hers and he felt the curve of her breast with his arm. "Stop Frank, be good," she chided with a smile. When he entered the laboratory, Dr. Lamont stopped his work and extended his hand straight out to shake hands making Frank smile at the gesture.

"What do you have to discuss with me Doc?"

"Sit down Frank. Do you recall that I told you we may be able to locate some descendants of yours if you were interested? Frank felt a chill run up his spine and had goosebumps on his arms.

"Yea I remember."

"Well, Mira has been working on it and has located a number of persons throughout human space that are a match for you to be a distant ancestor of theirs."

Holy shit! "How many?" Sam Lamont looked at Mira and raised his eyebrows.

"Approximately one thousand two hundred individuals" she said. "The nearest, in a geographic sense is here on Sunset in the military. A colleague who deals with DNA said he appears to be your

Twenty-fourth great grandson. I afraid I cannot tell you from what last common ancestor of your children or grandchildren he descends. But I have listed all Twelve hundred and where they can be found."

"Holy Shit!" Frank muttered. "Who is this military person on Sunset?"

Mira checked her chip. "Well what a co-incidence, he is a marine in the Reconnaissance Battalion."

"What!" exclaimed Frank "who is he?"

Mira checked her chip again. "He is a Marine Private named Alonzo F. Blanco."

Frank was stunned. Unable to speak he just stared at the wall.

Mira and Sam looked at each other. "Frank?" Mira said.

"Tell me yur fucking kidding."

"Is something wrong?" Sam Lamont asked.

Frank took a deep breath and composed himself. "No nothing is wrong. I am acquainted with him and just surprised."

"There is a caveat attached to all this Frank."

"What caveat?"

Dr. Lamont seemed disappointed Frank did not grasp the implications. "Obviously, you cannot tell any of them you are their direct line ancestor."

Frank sat quietly for a moment. "You're right. Thanks for the information, and if Mira will send the information to my chip I will at least have it." Mira hugged him again, tighter this time, and he felt her breast brush his arm. "Of course, I will. Perhaps we will have time to have dinner together." Frank nodded. "I'd like that."

He had a lot on his mind as he walked back to the Recon area.

CHAPTER 11

Frank entered the First Raider Battalion Headquarters bunker that was organized chaos of people moving in and setting up different offices. When he found Sergeant Major Hoysaias office he pounded loudly on the door frame.

"Sir! Staff Sergeant Farrell reporting as ordered Sir!"

Frank heard something being dropped and Hoysaia appeared. "Fuck me seven times Farrell! Let me look at you. A fucking Staff Sergeant?"

Frank grinned at Hoysaia's surprise. "It's good to see you too."

"Come in and try to find a place to sit. Are you by chance assigned here?" Sergeant Major Hoysaia asked.

Frank nodded. "The colonel told me I was to be a Platoon Sergeant in "A" company, and to come over and help you with the start up."

Hoysaia grinned. "I knew I had a Staff Sergeant coming over but not a name. "Fuck me seven times Farrell. I've wondered about you since I last saw you back at the Graduation. I guess you were on Operation *Strong Door*, Yes?"

Frank nodded. "Along with *Filch*, and *Enduring Fidelity*. But *Strong Door* was the roughest so far. It was a bad one Sergeant Major."

Hoysaia laughed out loud. "I'm still getting used to it. Well Farrell, I can definitely use the help. We are getting a lot of new, and I mean brand new, people of all ranks. Your new CO is coming from MW and is a virgin in line operations. His name is Captain Johnson. He has been at HQ most of his career as I understand, and will be here within a week. I do not know who the Platoon Commander is yet. And I have only met the new Battalion Commander once so far, but I am meeting with him this afternoon."

"I know um Sergeant Major. He's a professional. Do ya remember when I left training and ended up on Pleasant?"

Hoysaia nodded.

"Well Colonel, then Captain, Nagoto, was the CO of the company that landed and finished off the DMs in that firefight. He also led the landing troops in NX246 for the mop up. You don't have to worry about him."

"That is good to hear. Let us get some coffee and I'll tell you what I need you to do."

A week later Frank was assisting in personnel and unit billeting when he received a communication from Sergeant Major Brown, his old mentor at HQ Marine Corps. "It seems I am still watching your back Farrell."

"What do ya mean Sergeant Major?"

"First off, congratulations on the current promotion and upcoming commissioning."

"Thank you."

"The main reason I am contacting you is because you are assigned to "A" Raiders and I am very familiar with your CO, Captain Johnson. He is a sharp palace guard type individual, if you understand my meaning. Be careful what you say to him."

"I got it Sergeant Major."

"Very well. I had a word with him when I found out you two will be in close contact. If he tries to press you on your background more than you feel is pertinent to your relationship let me know. I will deal with it. Good luck Farrell"

"Thanks again for everything Sergeant Major."

Several hours later Frank received another communication and answered crisply, "Staff Sergeant Farrell, sir."

"Staff Sergeant Farrell, Captain Johnson here. I have just arrived from MW. Report to me in the Company office at 18 hours local time and we will have a chat."

"Aye- aye sir." Frank checked his chip *I've got a little over six hours yet.* Then he went back to work.

Later:

Captain Johnson raised his hand in a traditional greeting. "Come in and have a seat Staff Sergeant." He studied Frank from head to toe. "I was surprised when the colonel informed me that you will have one of my platoons. But since I have now reviewed your service records several times I understand why. However, my biggest surprise was a back-channel call from Sergeant Major Brown at headquarters. I know from past experience that he speaks for the commandant. He said you will be commissioned a lieutenant as soon as the battalion organization is finished and I was not to discuss it with anyone but you. He also told me about your background in black ops. So, I am up to date, correct?" He sat waiting for Frank to respond.

Get to the point. I'm not playing yur waiting game.

After a long pause the captain smiled. "Do not worry. I understand what I was being told . . . or more importantly, not being told. I am giving you my First Platoon. Frank nodded. "Aye-aye, sir"

"Every other lieutenant for the company is coming from basic school and you will be my only veteran platoon leader. I also learned you and Sergeant Major Hoysaia, as well as the colonel, are old friends. I'm sure they told you this is my first infantry assignment. I will need to rely on your experience for a while."

"I'll help you in any manner I can Skipper."

"Very well. I count on it."

A month after Recon left Planet Pleasant, the Raiders were formed and into intensive training. Frank, now a commissioned officer did the majority of training on close fighting with Delta-Mike and was also, De Facto, the "A "Company XO since one still had not yet been assigned.

On April 26th. UWS Whisper had been back on station in the Refuge system for over a week after relieving their sister ship the UWS Echo now returning to Planet Sunset. The Whisper observed and reported the gathering of half of the alien fleet but had no indication of what it was preparing for.

When next they observed landing craft moving troops up to the gathered ships the captain contacted Fleet Headquarters and reported. "Whisper to command . . . I estimate that half of the DM fleet is gathering in the space around Planet Refuge loading troops and other attachments. I will notify of the axis of attack when they get underway. I recommend that when we leave the Echo returns to watch the other half of the fleet still spread around the system"

"Roger Whisper. Report in every eight hours unless the situation changes" replied the admiral on duty. He motioned to his Aid. "Advise the Echo what is happening and to return immediately to the Refuge system to contact the Whisper."

"Aye-aye Sir."

The watch officer in the Combat Intelligence Center of Whisper communicated "Skipper we have a lot of new activity over and above the preparations we have been watching."

"What type of activity?" the captain asked walking toward the CIC.

"It is odd sir. They seem to be dumping elongated barrels around the system."

"Barrels? What kind of barrels?" At that moment the captain reached CIC and approached the watch officer. "Show me what you mean."

The watch office motioned to the sailor on duty and a panorama of the Refuge system opened in their heads and began running a track from when first noticed. The Chief with the sailor said "You can see Skipper, they have about forty ships dropping those things in the space around the four worlds of the system. The computer estimated at least a thousand have been dropped so far.

"What is your best guess Chief?" the captain asked.

"The way they are being careful Skipper tells me this is something they are nervous about themselves. That worries me. We need to find out what they are dropping."

The captain looked at the watch officer. "What do you think?"

"I think the chief is spot on Skipper, we need to make this a priority."

"Good job gentlemen, I concur. Let me kick this to fleet. Chief, get some holos and include them in the tracking information to be sent to fleet headquarters. And Chief send holos down to engineering along with the tracks. Let's get their thinking too."

"Aye-aye Skipper."

*MAY 1*ST*. SPL GLGOFFEN'S HQ.*

SPL Glgoffen and Deputy Leader for intelligence Herckel, sat discussing the upcoming move and plan for defending the system with their remaining troops. "What are your thoughts of the Hoo-man's next move?" SPL Glgoffen asked.

Intelligence chief Herckel thought for a moment. "Reports from our scouts left behind in Hooman space are that Planet Pleasant is now heavily reinforced with fortifying Army units as the city begins rebuilding. Their main Army on Sunset is up to strength, undamaged, and currently has the equivalent of seven great packs or Divisions as they refer to them. As far as can be determined, the Knife-Soldiers, and for our purposes I am including all marine units in that category, have pulled back into their main fortifications on the Planet of Sunset and are engaged in repopulating their units. Some of them suffered far more losses than we realized; But they are training continuously.

Glgoffen was intrigued. "Why have you included all marines as knife-soldiers?"

"After interviews with commanders who fought on Planet Pleasant, and reading after action reports I have come to the conclusion that the marines are all the same except for the type of assignment they have. They are all shock-troops, and so far, we have engaged them more than their main army. I believe that will change if they come here."

Glgoffen nodded to himself then stood and stretched his back. He gave a signal to a waiting technician on the other side of the room and a hologram of the refuge system appeared around them. "Let me outline my thinking for the defense of the system."

He spoke to Herckel for thirty minutes highlighting areas on the different planets. When he was done he asked, "What is intelligence's best guess of the Hooman intentions and capabilities for the near future."

Herckel swallowed. "Leader I believe they will continue to train until they feel ready and then they *will* come for us. I have no doubt they already have scouts in this system as we have around their planets. They will know when our army moves toward home, and they will probably know our defense strategies and strengths on each world.

"The one surprise we have are the Hoobars. We must bleed them badly when they decide to attack; but I do not think we can prevent them getting a foothold somewhere."

SPL Glgoffen looked at Herckel for a moment. "Even with over Fifty thousand fighters here?"

"Supreme Leader, it will be close."

Glgoffen sat with his chin resting on his chest for a moment. *Gods of our ancestors. I agree with his bleak assessment, but we must make the best of it.* "I agree with you. Let us brief the Pack commanders.

"Quiet and come to attention!" the Assistant Supreme Pack Leader yelled as SPL Glgoffen entered.

"You may sit," the SPL called and stood looking over his commanders for a long moment. "Pack mates, our move back home is ready to begin by the First, Sixth, and half of the Second GPs. The Third, Fourth, and other half of the Second GPs with roughly half of the fleet under my personal command are the rear guard to defend and hold this system as a base of operations for our returning forces.

"I am sending the First and Sixth GPs along with the other half of the Second GP home because of combat causalities they suffered on Planets Sunset, Pleasant, and NX world. Along with them will be most of our support units under command of the Assistant Supreme Leader. Those forces will wait at the tunnel space station with the fleet until I, or the home worlds, order otherwise. When, and if, I am sure this system is secure I along with the intelligence Unit will join those waiting at the space station near the tunnel.

"Five local days ago, the engineers began seeding space with their Hoobars to a distance of fifty million K. It should make any approach, or pursuit, slow cautious and will hopefully inflict heavy losses on an attacking force. Until then our remaining forces will be deployed as follows: The entire Third Great will defend Planet Warbeast. The world Enemy Killer in a Rimward-Spinward direction from here will be held by the Forty-third Attack Group. World Forty-one in the Spinward-Coreward quadrant will be defended by the Forty-first, Forty-second, and Twenty-First Attack Groups. World Twenty-two also Rimward-Spinward, will be defended by the Twenty-second, and Twenty-Third Attack Groups. In total we will have over fifty thousand fighters on the ground in system and half of our fleet spread throughout.

CHAPTER 12

The United Worlds of Earth Government called for a symposium on the conduct of the war Attended by representatives of all one hundred worlds, along with the Military High Command and Counsel. The Main Computer Entity monitored and made suggestions for debate.

After the military finished their presentation and stated goals, the worlds that had major concerns were heard next. It was decided that First: The *Refuge system* was critical for the early warning and future defense of the Milky Way. As such, it must be captured from Delta-Mike. Secondly, that human forces should follow the DM fleet as far as the first known fold space tunnel used by them. There, if practicable, establish an early warning outpost near the terminus of that tunnel. Third, the Refuge System having no high-level indigenous life, and being ideal for human habitation should be annexed by the UWE for human colonization. Further it should be heavily fortified as a bulwark against future invasions. Finally, how to achieve these aims was the responsibility of the Military with the continued assistance of the Main Computer Entity.

At the conclusion of that symposium, the military convened a major planning session on how to achieve the stated goals in a three-day workshop on MW. It was attended by every Colonel and above in the theatre of operations

One of the first issues was the current shortage of officers and

NCO's due to combat loss, along with military growth. Since the military was just beginning to advance to the needed levels of staffing, they increased the number of promotions from the ranks and upgraded existing officers while continuing to increase the conscription levels for enlisted personnel.

"Attention on deck!" the Brigade XO called as General Rahm entered the hall. All of the officers of the Recon brigade, including Raiders jumped to their feet. General Rahm walked to the dais.

"As you were, take your seats ladies and gentlemen." He looked over the assembled officers, then he glanced at his executive officer and a large holograph of all the space between Planet Sunset and the Refuge system appeared.

"I know you are wondering about this," he pointing up at the hologram over his head. "Forget about it for now. I will get to it at the end of the briefing."

He paused again in thought. "Ladies and gentlemen, things are changing so quickly it becomes almost difficult to comprehend. The military life we know, and have lived, is rapidly changing as the needs of this war become obvious.

"You all know of the symposium on the conduct of the war for three days on MW; and that symposium is what we will discuss today. First on the agenda is the expansion of all the Armed Forces. As we speak, the Second Marine Division is forming with plans for a Third Division in approximately six months." The hall became a buzz of excited conversation for a few moments.

"Furthermore, the United Worlds Government has ordered the conscription of every qualifying person, male and female, ages eighteen to twenty-eight" The surprised chatter was louder this time. "Ladies and gentlemen your attention please. This conscription is needed not only for the additions of the two Marine Divisions, but the increase of the fleet and creation of twelve additional Army Divisions along with replacement of combat losses.

"To date ladies and gentlemen, we have lost almost forty-four percent of our total pre-invasion military" There was an audible gasp around the room. The Marine Corps has borne the majority of combat losses. And information learned from the captured high-ranking DMs has given us additional cause for buildup and preparation.

"Now before I continue, one item that every marine should be proud of is that the citizens of New Glasgow have re-named the bridge destroyed in the fighting there as "Marine Bridge." The assembly began applauding, and after a moment the general raised his hands for quiet. "This is the largest expansion of military in roughly six hundred years since the end of the Final World War. With such large expansion comes necessary major accelerated promotional and assignment changes. A list of these changes has been put together by the Main Computer and submitted to the military and civil councils for approval or change. A list of promotions effecting this brigade will be sent to your chip at the end of the brief. It is lengthy and will be surprising to you. They are listed by command and future assignment. You will notice a new Unit called Career advisory. Their function is assisting in putting the round peg into the round hole.

"Ladies and gentlemen, by one June everyone in this room, and I literally mean everyone, will be at a new rank or assignment. Things are changing. You are the beginning of a new era in the UWE military. Unfortunately, our slow-moving, career oriented, professional military will be gone, eclipsed by the conscripts, and one can only wonder at the unintended consequences.

"By the first week of July, the UWE will begin an offensive against Delta-Mike." The meeting erupted into conversation again and after a minute the general continued. "You may have noticed the absence of some Brigade officers. They are already in the *Refuge system* involved in determining DM unit strengths and location. That is all for now ladies and gentlemen. There will be another meeting of all Brigade officers in a week."

"Attention on deck!" the Assistant Brigade Commander called as General Rahm walked out. Captain Johnson looked at Frank. "Ancestors! Let us see what else is going to change." Both men accessed their chip.

"Holy shit!" Frank muttered as he read and re-read the changes *the general wasn't kidding about the end of the old and beginning of the new. This fucking war has changed everything. And I now have "A" Company Raiders and promotion to Captain. But where did Captain Johnson go if I have "A"?* Frank searched and found *Johnson promoted Major XO of 1st Recon Battalion.*

"Damn"

Then he saw another name. wow *Alicia made Captain to "E" Raiders and Fuck me seven times Hoysaia is a Captain in Second Raiders too!*

Some of the other changes that stood out to him was General Rahm getting a second star and Sing to BG. Along with Alonzo Blanco commissioned a Lieutenant. Nikowa now a Lt Col *and* CO of the 1st Raiders. While Nagoto was a full colonel of the 2nd Marines.

As he checked further, he saw all of his team leaders were promoted to sergeant, and Olney, commissioned as a Lieutenant.

"Well, what do you think?" now Major Johnson asked him.

"Sir, there are no words. I better contact my new boss." Frank called Colonel Nikowa. "Sir, Captain Farrell here. I thought I should touch base with you."

Nikowa chuckled. "I cannot keep up with who is who captain. And yes, I am glad you contacted me. I received a call about you from Headquarters Marine Corps. Stop by Battalion this afternoon sometime and we will discuss it."

"Aye-aye Sir"

Frank walked into his new office. "Congratulation's Captain" the First Sergeant said with a grin.

"Thanks Top. I'm glad to be staying with "A." Are any of the platoon commanders around?"

"Not yet Skipper. We lost some and gained some, everyone is still getting sorted out." Frank chuckled. "No problem Top. If you need me, I'm going over to battalion and see the colonel."

At battalion the sergeant major escorted Frank to see Colonel Nikowa who grinned on seeing him. "Look at us now Captain." He quipped.

"I'm lost for words Sir."

The colonel chuckled. "Captain I was told to have you report to Major Brown on MW as soon as possible. Any idea what it is about?"

"No sir. I haven't spoken to the Sergeant Major in a while."

"I did not say sergeant major captain." Frank looked at him blankly for a moment.

"He's been jumped to major?"

Colonel Nikowa nodded. "But he is still the gate keeper and even more of a confidant of the boss. At any rate you better get to MW to see what they want. "

"Aye-aye, Sir"

Later: Frank reported to Major Brown and saluted "Captain Farrell reporting sir."

"Good to see you again Captain. "Come with me." hey walked into the commandant's office. General Thomas looked up and smiled. "Nice to see you Captain, sit down."

When Frank was settled the general nodded to Major Brown who said to Frank "Way back when you were still in our little school here you told me of a space probe that possibly contributed to the DM invasion. Do you remember?"

"Sure, the Pioneer mission."

"Captain" interrupted General Thomas "Due to your unusual background, you had information that none of us did and it helped.

Now we are faced with another unknown that Major Brown and I hope you will also have some insight on from that time before you arrived here. Sit back and watch."

Frank sat and a section of deep space opened in his mind followed by a number of ships on line apparently seeding space. He heard the general saying "These images are from the stealth scout UWS Echo that captured them roughly Fifty Million K from *Refuge system.*

"The Echo's captain sat in place watching this and managed to get some close-range images of the seeds or whatever they are. There are a number of theories here on MW about them; but at times you have demonstrated a special knowledge and I want to hear your thoughts. These are some close-up images."

When Frank saw the first one, he felt a cold chill run up his back. *Oh shit! This is not good if it really is what it looks like.* He continued studying the images that were long and barrel shape rather than round. *I wonder why they made them that shape. Are they self-propelled?*

"I do not like the look on your face Captain. What do you know that we do not?"

Frank looked from the Major to the Commandant. "Sir, I suspect what they could be but I could be wrong."

"Do you think you *are* wrong?" asked the commandant.

Frank took a deep breath. "No sir, I don't think I'm wrong. We called them Mines. They were used at sea to destroy, or disable ships. They were also used on the land to destroy vehicles kill and disable troops or block areas of approach.

"Most mines I'm familiar with were round or flat, except for the smaller anti-personnel ones that had a shape more like these. The protrusions on this device are sensors and are triggers more or less the same as used against ocean going vessels. When a ship brushed up against, or hits, any of the sensors the mine detonates. In a space void environment with the distances involved I don't see how these can be that much of a factor unless they deploy them almost in atmosphere. They must think they can do something with them. It's important to get one of these to study. I know of magnetic ones that puled toward any metal mass passing at a certain distance. But again, in a space environment the odds of a ship hitting one of these is astronomical. Also, we don't know if the DMs have any type of trigger except for the contact spikes we can see. I wondered if this shape is because they could be self-propelled or command detonated somehow. They must think they can use them even with the distances involved. My opinion would be they will use these in system and close to planetary atmosphere.

"Sir, what these are going to do, is slow us down to become targets some other way. But ideally, I think they hoped our ships or landing craft would get into the mine field at normal speeds and be destroyed by hitting any number of these things before they realized what they were. That's the bad news. The good news is mines are as deadly to those who put them down as to an intended victim. And, now that we know a mine field is there you can develop ships to remove or detonate them, or it can be avoided. On a personal note, I really hated the things both in the water and on land."

"How were they dealt with?" the Commandant asked.

"How many are we talking about, Sir?"

"From the intel we have from UWS Whisper, the Echo, and other recon stealth vessels in the system we think the number could add up to more than a thousand."

Frank sat back stunned. Holy *shit1 This could be a fucking mess.*

"Captain?" Major Brown said after a moment.

"Sorry Sir it took me by surprise."

"Well?" prompted the commandant.

"I've never heard of numbers that large being cleared at once. What I know, is that in mass mine situations lanes were generally cleared that were then well marked and followed by everyone else for the short term. This was generally done by the Engineers who usually blew the path through. But that was on land or in water. We are discussing things in a huge area. I think it would be almost impossible for them to think they will have a ship hit one in a void of space. They must have figured a way to cover vast distances and that does not seem feasible to me but I'm sure we have good people who can come up with ideas

"The unfortunate thing is that you never get every one of them, and losses should be expected. I'm sure that our engineering people can come up with something."

"Captain Farrell, you seem to have proven your worth again" the commandant said.

UWS ECHO BETWEEN NX 246 AND REFUGE SYSTEM.

"Aye-aye, Sir. I will get busy, and we will rendezvous with the *Vengeance* at NX Two forty-six" the captain of the *Echo* replied after a long conversation with the fleet admiral. She looked around for the XO. "Commander Paplay, have officers and chiefs assemble on the mess deck please."

"Attention on deck!" the senior chief yelled fifteen minutes later as the captain and XO entered the mess deck.

"Sit and relax ladies and gentlemen. Get some coffee if you have not done so yet." She and the XO walked to a coffee earn and poured a cup each then walked to the front of the room. There was an undercurrent of excitement in the room; they all knew that fleet headquarters had given the captain orders they were anxious to hear.

The captain looked around at the two dozen officers and chiefs then began "Those barrels we have been watching the DMs drop are apparently explosive devices. Engineering, have you by any chance encountered references on anything like this?"

"Skipper," Lieutenant Commander Kee the engineering division chief answered, "the only combination of explosive and mines I know of are in some cratering type operations."

"Thank you, Commander Kee. Commander Paplay please put up the hologram." A large representation of one of the barrels they have been watching floated behind the captain.

"The fleet calls these things Mines. Those protrusions on this thing are sensors, or triggers, that detonate the device if It is bumped or even brushed with sufficient enough force. The chance of a ship actually hitting one of these in the vastness of space is mindboggling, so the DMs must have a way to make it possible. The admiral thinks they will be encountered close to planetary atmosphere.

"Fleet reports that based on the dimensions of this there is enough explosive inside to damage most ships to various degrees, and perhaps destroy those of our size, depending on where the explosion occurs. One thing we definitely know, is that on most ships the hull will probably be breached enough for some causalities and a serious escape of atmosphere.

"Fleet also has a number of questions that have to be answered. Such as: is gravity or magnetism involved in pulling them toward a ship. Are these self-propelled due to their shape." The captain gave a bright smile. "By the expression on some of your faces I expect you know where this conversation is going. We have to get one of them."

"How are we going to do it skipper?" asked a chief sitting in the back.

The captain looked to the engineer division chief. "Commander Kee, what is the maximum range of our Towing beam?"

"Three thousand meters."

"Do you think our beam will detonate it?"

"Skipper, it depends if the Mine really is magnetic or if gravity is involved, and how it interacts with our gravitonic beam. But we should be alright."

"Do you think three thousand meters is a safe distance for us?"

"Given the size of the device; it is if it is not nuclear."

"Thank you, Commander, you and your people get a plan to capture one of these and give it to me by Eighteen hours. Does anyone have anything else? No? Thank you, ladies and gentlemen."

All of the Officers and Staff NCO's sat chatting while they waited for Major General Rahm to arrive at this first meeting of the Brigade since the mass changes.

"Attention on deck! the assistance brigade commander called when he saw the General enter the auditorium.

"As you were." General Rahm walked up on the stage and looked over his audience. "Hopefully everyone is settling in on their new duties. But time is not a luxury we have, so sit back for the upcoming operational plan." Everyone sat back as the view of the seven planets involved in the fighting and the deep space beyond appeared in their heads.

"This is a two-phase operation, ladies and gentlemen. A major joint services attack on portions of the *Refuge system* commencing on thirteen July. Our goal is to destroy the DM forces there and open the way for further operations wherever they go."

Frank sat among the other Raiders officers and NCOs. *Holy shit! I wonder what they'll do about the Mines?*

"First, I want to discuss Phase-Two of this endeavor, the main focus of our attack against *Planet Refuge*. It is called Operation *Black Beach*. We know by the intercepts made by intelligence, and by the stealth ships sitting in the system that Refuge is defended by the Third Great Pack. It consists of the Thirtieth, Thirty-first and Thirty-second Attack Groups. For those just joining us, that equates to eighteen thousand troops that according to scans are positioned to respond rapidly to most areas of that planet. And I warn you ladies and gentlemen, do not to think of distance as a detriment for Delta-Mike. It will not be a problem for them to rapidly move to wherever they wish on that world. It is their main base of operations that until recently was the home of all their Great Packs. You veterans involved in Operation *Filch* some months back know that the other three Planets in this system did not have any significant numbers of troops." The general paused and looked around. "Unfortunately, that has changed."

A flattened close up of Planet Refuge appeared and was a surprise to some of the audience. "Like Mother Earth, Refuge is a water world, Earth size with one gigantic land mass, and several other islands on its periphery. It is the same, I am told, as Mother Earth was three hundred-thirty-five million years ago during its Paleozoic era with the super continent of Pangea."

It looks like a rabbit in the fetal position thought Frank studying the main land area.

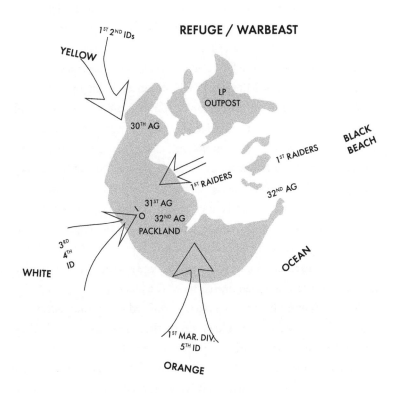

"All right that's enough history that you can immediately forget." He received the expected laughter. A view of the entire system appeared. "Planet Diamond, called Planet Forty-one by Delta Mike, is now defended by the majority of the Fourth Great Pack composed of the Forty-first, Forty-second, and twenty-first AG's. That is another eighteen thousand troops.

"Planet Emerald, called Planet Twenty-three by them, has one half of the Twenty-third AG, roughly three thousand troops. And Planet Ruby, now called Planet Forty-three, instead of Enemy killer that a lot of you are familiar with, is defended by the Forty-third AG. Another Six thousand."

The general looked around the room. "They also have significant naval presents around the area that our fleet will have to deal with before we can begin landing operations. But of a major concern is Phase-One of this endeavor, called Operation *Drum Roll*.

"Along with battling the DM fleet, the navy will clear lanes through the devises known as Mines that will detonate if hit by a ship or landing craft. For a small ship or landing craft it more than likely will not be a survivable event. Intelligence believes that a thousand plus of these Mines *could* have been seeded. Considering the vastness of space, and, to have any impact on us at all, they are around, and very close, in relative terms, to the four planets in the Refuge system.

A red line encircled the Refuge system. "Anywhere past the Red Line we have to assume mines. How will we get through them you are wondering? That is a problem that has kept a lot of folks awake at night." As he spoke the image of the Refuge system was completely encircled by a second green line closer to the planets.

"Recon Scouts already in system, reported numerous accidents involving Delta-Mike being blown up by their own mines while they deployed them, or accidently strayed into them. It is obvious they are also on a learning curve with this invention of theirs. As a result of an apparent healthy fear of them, they have left a safe margin of what we calling the Green Line.

"This Green Line, will hopefully turn out to be our salvation ladies and gentlemen, it represents a distance of two and a half light seconds, approximately four hundred-sixth-five thousand miles from the outer boundary of each of the Refuge system worlds;. It also represents the boundary of the mines to those worlds. As far as can be determined, all the mines sit between the red and green Lines. It enables the DMs to move from planet to planet and around their system without fear. But it appears that they have sealed themselves into that system.

"We owe thanks to the Captain and crew of UWS Echo, who watched a number of DM ships being damaged by the mines they were trying to remove. It quickly became apparent to the Echo that the DMs were clearing pathways through the mines so they could get out.

"Two pathways have now been identified by Echo, here and here." The two paths began blinking in yellow and were entered fifty thousand miles Coreward-Trailing of Planet Diamond and was the beginning of the route through the mine and away.

"These mines must be dealt with if we are to successfully invade. The navy is working on a plan that will allow them to clear three lanes through this red area. Each of these lanes will be an attack vector I will discuss shortly." Three Yellow arrows appeared on line through the mine field; until they passed the Green line. Then they oriented to different points on the East side of the main continent that was now referred to as "Packland" by Delta-Mike in their communications.

General Rahm looked around. "Any questions so far? No?"

"Now, as the navy is engaging the part of the DM fleet operating outside of the Red Line, they will also be clearing a path through the mine field. When through, they will begin a space bombardment on troop concentrations, and fortifications, identified over the past months at, and near, the landing zones. The landing craft will follow the bombardment in to the ground. The drawback is that the landing craft will be funneled on a set of cleared vectors. That will give Delta-Mike time to target and get to where we are landing. Notice our landing vectors are nowhere near the cleared lanes made by the DM's. Because we are giving them a route of retreat if they wish to withdraw."

The general paused. "Take ten and be back here to continue."

Ten minutes later, General Rham walked back onto the stage. "Let us begin." There was a momentary rustling in the hall as everyone readied themselves. "I know you have been waiting for unit assignments, so I will begin with the broad outline on how we get through the mines."

A Navy Lieutenant Commander sitting to the side of the stage walked to the center. "Good morning. I am Commander Dubni from Fleet Headquarters on MW. My unit's specialty is ordnance, space debris and wreck recovery. We are the lead in Operation *Drum Roll*. You should know that no one has ever dealt with this type of problem before. Therefore, everything I tell you should work as it has in our models . . . in theory." His comment caused a groan and an undercurrent of mumbling in the audience. "I completely understand," he said quickly, "and I will personally be directing this Operation from one of the lead ships." The murmuring stopped. Commander Dubni walked across the stage looking at his audience.

"The Captain of the UWS Echo obtained one of these mine devices at great risk. I do not wish to get too technical. In simple terms, each of these barrels, or shells, holds a small missile, "C" speed capable with a set target detection range when activated, of two light seconds. That may not seem far; but with an ability to travel up to three hundred seventy-two thousand miles a second, at C, the time to target is almost instantaneous. The impulsive force, upon striking the target at that speed is not survivable for the crew of any size ship.

"The good news is that these weapons are not hardened, and they are sleeping until activated by one of several transmitters attached to their shell directing them to the intended target. All of these weapons are located between the red and green lines around the planets in the system enabling us to attack them simultaneously with our EMPs system wide. With the mines killed by the EMP we are going to use a flexible linear explosive device. The plan is for three stealth command ships to each carefully guide out hundreds of drones through the mines between the Red and Green Lines along our three attack vectors. These drones are connected by a continuous thin flexible linear explosive going through each. The physics took the most work to cope with nonlocality in dealing with distances and instantaneous blast. For you marines who do not deal with ships navigation on a daily basis, or any other astrophysics, non-locality that was finally proven one hundred years ago describes the ability of objects to instantaneously know about each other's state even when separated by thousands of light years. Check your implant if you need more information.

"When detonated, all three paths should explode more or less in a series of linear stages due to the distance involved. It is expected, and hoped, that the blast and chunks of metal hitting others near them, and *their* subsequent detonations, will continue to have a sympathetic wave effect to clear the paths for us. Keep in mind there are residuals sometimes left. If one of the residuals for some reason wakes up, it will destroy whatever vessel is closest inside the two light second neighborhood."

"Thank you, Commander," the general said. "Ladies and gentlemen back to your implants again" A close-up view of the DM fortifications, docking facilities, buildings, and missile batteries appeared, glowing white.

"As soon as ships in the invasion force cross the Green Line into clear space, we begin *Operation Black Beach* and proceed to our targets. Remember there will be more conventional opposition by DM ships, and surviving, anti-ship missiles batteries on the planets. While we quickly cross the distance to the main landing at *White Zone* on Planet Refuge in the center of the main continent. We will land beside the Army's Third and Fourth Infantry Divisions.

"The Frist and Second Infantry Divisions, will land at *Yellow Zone*, on the left, while the Fifth Infantry Division with the First Marine

Division and all of its attachments, and that means us, are landing at *Orange Zone* on the right.

"At the same time, other transports coming in behind us will move to Planet Diamond where the Sixth and Seventh Infantry Divisions, along with the Second Marine Division and all of its attachments will land.

"For the time being we are bypassing Ruby and Emerald. Other than space bombardment we are isolating those troops unless they attempt to move off world.

"That is it ladies and gentlemen," General Rahm said. "You now have the overview of Operations *Drum Roll* and *Black Beach*. Specific mission and movements of our Brigade will be given to you in a few days.

L -DAY MINUS 24.

HEADQUARTERS 1ST RAIDER BATTALION PLANET SUNSET.

Colonel Nikowa stood in the large meeting room near his office facing his Company Commanders and Platoon leaders. Some new lieutenants fresh from training in their pristine uniforms, and relaxed features, made a marked contrast to the veterans in the room who knew what to expect.

The room had six long tables with a dozen chairs each situated horizontally facing a lectern. Against the wall behind the lectern stood a group of flags representing the United Worlds of Earth, the Marine Corps, the 1st Marine Division, 1st Reconnaissance Brigade, and the Raiders new Regimental Colors. When everyone who wished had coffee tea or water from the serving table in the rear of the room Colonel Nikowa walked to the lectern and began.

"Ladies and Gentlemen, Operation *Black Beach* has given us an interesting assignment for our first outing."

A hologram of Planet Refuge began to float in the front of the room. "Some of you new people may not know that when Raiders were formed, we had two ships assigned to our operations, the *UWS Vengeance* and the *Retribution*. These ships have been refitted to hold thirty landing boats each. Enough to land an entire battalion. We are assigned to the *Retribution*.

"This Battalion, along with Second Raiders assigned to the *Vengeance*, will not land in *Orange Zone* with the rest of First Division. We have been tasked with the critical mission of destroying Delta-Mikes main missile fire control targeting, and tracking complex, located on this peninsula roughly two-thousand K to the south of east of the Orange Zone. Our landing zone is designated *Black Beach*. We land prior to the main landings." A peninsula sticking out from the bottom of the main continent and shaped like the rabbit's foot began to flash.

"According to intelligence, this entire peninsula is two hundred and fifty K long by thirty K wide. It is hilly and has ocean beaches on three sides covered with sand and dark pebbles. Our targets are located at the very tip of the peninsula close to the beach. Most large vegetation has been cleared from the area but a number of bigger trees have been left adding to the camouflage; along with flower gardens planted in front of every building or bunker.

"It begs the question, why did they plant those flowers? For the aesthetic value? Maybe to relax their troops, or for a feel of home? Perhaps all of the above, who knows? It was a surprise considering the nature of our enemy. An oversite we will make them regret since those flowers clearly mark the front of all of their camouflaged buildings that are more or less invisible, and our targets."

A fierce smile quickly passed over Frank's face. *We're gonna stick flowers up their asses! I love it.* He came back to the moment.

"As you can see by the gardens, this complex is a series of six buildings mostly below ground level. So, we will have to be as quick as possible to limit the destruction and causalities to the fleet and troops coming into the other zones caused by any fire control batteries that survive the initial bombardment. Our main problem, ladies and gentlemen, will be the surviving troops of the roughly twenty-five hundred from the Thirty-Second AG of the Third Great Pack that are on rotation defending this end of the peninsula. Their camps have been identified further down the peninsula; but on the same side as our target.

"We must stop them, and their landing boats, from joining the fight at the main landing zones. That will be the primary mission of Second Raiders who will land down the peninsula twenty K away from us. They will first establish the anti-ship battery they have with them then attack toward us.

"Sit back white I go through *our* landing plan. We have five full strength companies and weapons attachments; along with a platoon of engineers who will destroy what we capture. The space bombardment will begin just before the invasion force crosses the Green Line. We and Second Raiders will be the first stealth ships through the Green Line and will follow closely behind the bombardment. As soon as we clear the green line our ship will turn right still staying behind the bombardment and will land on the north side tip of the peninsula immediately after the bombardment.

"Captain Farrell, your "A "Company along with the engineers platoon is responsible for securing the main command bunker that co-ordinates every other on this world. It is the largest building on the site, surrounded by the five smaller ones. Infrared Scans show your target to be thirty by fifty meters with two levels above ground. Unfortunately, and we have no idea how deep they go.

"Aye-aye sir." *Every time I think things can't get worse they do.*

"Captain Boece, "B" Company is responsible for the next two smaller flower gardens to the right of "A" the colonel said with a smile causing the room to erupt in laughter.

"Aye-aye sir."

" Captain Kim, "C" has the next gardens to the left followed by

Captain Sing, and "D" with the last one situated slightly behind them. When we have secured these buildings and while engineers are destroying everything inside, we will push on down the peninsula to help Second Raiders. We will be the anvil to Second Raiders hammer or ,if necessary, act as reinforcements for "A" inside that main building that could well be a labyrinth connecting everything."

Colonel Nikowa pause, and looked around the room. I am not going to tell you how to achieve your assignments. That is up to you. Just get the job completed as quickly as possible. If we are lucky the bombardment will do most of it for us. Questions ladies and gentlemen? None? You are dismissed."

Frank walked with his platoon leaders. "Get your troops fed then meet me in my office with your platoon sergeants and squad leaders."

An hour later he sat with his lieutenants and sergeants "Okay gentlemen our target is certainly big enough to stand out for us and bless the DMs love of flowers. Sit back."

The intelligence pictures from stealth recon ships filled their minds. "There in the center is our target." The view went infrared. "It dwarfs the others buildings and has quite a few heat signatures; but we know where to aim when we land even if the bombardment destroys all their flowers.

"When we attack, First-platoon, with Lieutenant Olney, will lead. Before anyone wonders why a newly promoted lieutenant will lead the attack, know he has been in non-stop combat for eighteen months and is the most experienced combat leader here. His platoon will be followed by Lieutenant Zaman's Second-platoon. I will be traveling with him until we get inside and I can see what things looks like.

"Lieutenant Ivanovic, put your platoon in a perimeter around our breach. Lieutenant Ainsworth, follow Zaman's Second-platoon in, but be ready to give help to Ivanovic or the others inside as needed. Does anyone have questions, comments, suggestions?"

Lieutenant Zaman asked "Sir what is the priority after we get inside?"

Frank smiled at him. "We find a way down and kill every DM we see that does not immediately surrender. Now let's take a look at the infrareds and see what we can figure out." Later, Frank had a plan for his attacking platoons to separate by squads if able and move down to attack along each subsequent level as soon as they hit the building. "Whoever hits the bottom level notifies me immediately. If anyone finds passageways leading out of the building footprint contact me and let the engineers know. They can send a mapping drone into it to show us what we are facing."

CHAPTER 13

Frank and the other company commanders were awakened by a priority call from Colonel Nikowa. "Just listen up Gentlemen, I have been told that god notified the High Command that the *UWS Invisible,* one of the stealth ships in *Refuge system,* hit a sleeping mine in situ that blew up. The invisible was destroyed with the loss of all but two of the bridge crew. The captain and Astro-navigation officer were captured in space and taken to *Planet Refuge* for interrogation. According to god they have been well treated but communicated they were being given some type of injection. Apparently it ether accidentally or deliberately turned off their chip. The Main Computer Entity has no idea what is being asked or answered during their interrogation and is trying to analyze their physiology as much as possible to discover what has caused the blockage. Both of these officers have information that could have serious consequences to the invasion. As a result, our landing timetable is being moved up by several hours. Notify your troops."

Frank felt a chill run up his back. "Fuck me," he muttered. Every time I think things are gonna get better they get worse. When I think they are gonna get worse they do."

The trip was slow until the Naval engineers activated the EMPs then blew the Linear charges and the *UWS Retribution* picked up speed following the detonations. Sometime later a buzzer sounded throughout the ship and in everyone's head with a message. "Now all landing force move to your boat stations."

Frank opened his command net and said "That's it ladies and gentlemen, let's move. Meet me at our boat station." He was answered with a series of "Aye-aye sir."

L DAY.

APPROACHING BLACK BEACH. 13 JULY.

Frank sat in the lead of the six boats assigned to his company. It wasn't until they entered the atmosphere of the planet their silent trip changed. Now he could feel the concussion and hear the deep rumble of the space bombardment. He thought about the aftermath of the 5th Great Packs destruction and wondered what sights would greet them upon landing. *Not much can survive this. Don't' get cocky expect anything.* In his head he heard the pilot say "Landing in ten seconds."

Frank opened his chip. "Company we are coming in now, now, now." The front of his boat disappeared and he ran out with Lt Zaman and his platoon and saw the mostly destroyed top of his target bunker. Then he noticed that the area, while cratered and partially destroyed, was in better condition than he expected.

"*Rrrriiipp,*'" came the sound of a rapid firing DM gun.

"Oh fuck!" *Where is it?*

"Alpha-One to Alpha-Six . . . over."

"Go One" he replied to Olney.

Frank heard an explosive charge go off. "Alpha One, Olney said. We have some DM infantry in the building , Break . . . have just destroyed a rapid-fire gun, but it took out two teams that walked into it. We have cleared the front."

When you least expect it. "Alpha-One . . . you know what to do now that we know what we are up against . . . out.

"Roger," Olney replied.

"Alpha-two . . . move down and clear as much as you can" Frank ordered.

"Aye-aye," Lieutenant Zaman replied.

"Alpha-Six to all platoons . . . be advise First platoon is meeting infantry opposition . . . Beak . . . Alpha- Four keep a sharp watch out there."

"Roger that." Lieutenant Ivanovic said.

"Alpha-Six to First Raiders Actual."

"Go Alpha-Six."

"Be advised we hit some infantry inside our target wearing the insignia of Thirty-Second AG, and have destroyed one rapid firing gun so far. . . break . . . I have two KIA and four WIA. . . Alpha-Six, out."

Frank and "A" company continued moving through the building that was four floors deep. They were involved in fire fights on each floor as they killed, captured, or pushed the 32nd AG troops further levels down killing fifty DM, and taking another twenty prisoners at a cost of nine more marines killed and as many wounded.

All of the rooms were full of targeting and communication computers with their technician's dead around them. Some that the engineer's thought it should be saved for study." As long as they can't use it do what you want," Frank said moving to the bottom level to meet with Lieutenant Ainsworth when he heard another fire-fight begin from the other end of the level.

"Six to Three what's going on down there . . . over."

"Three. . . we had some more DM infantry pop out of a hallway on us. . . break . . . we got them all . . . break . . . I think I may have one of the tunnels they mentioned . . . over."

"Six to Three stand by and secure it. . . Break . . . I will be there with engineers and a drone ASAP."

Frank turned and motioned to the Engineer Lieutenant who was moving with him and his command group. "Are you ready with the drone Lieutenant Yaxley?

"Yes Sir."

"Alpha-Six to Raiders actual . . .over."

"Go Six." Colonel Nikowa replied.

"Six . . . have found a tunnel on bottom fourth level of our target . . . break . . . have been continually engaging infantry throughout building . . . break . . . engineers are sending in a drone . . . break . . . depending on the imagery we get back I will continue attack into tunnel. . . over."

Colonel Nikowa said to the battalion sergeant major, "That is the third building that had some type of surviving guard. I am surprised." The sergeant major nodded, "They are dug in like ticks sir."

"Roger Alpha-Six" the colonel said," keep me advised. . . break . . . what is Cas rep . . . over."

"Alpha- six . . . I have twenty-two KIA eleven WIA . . . break . . . have killed sixty that is six zero DM . . .break. . . have forty, four zero POW. . . Alpha-Six out."

Frank sat with the Engineer lieutenant and his sergeant who was setting up his drone that looked like a large Bat. The sergeant sat in chip contact with a dark colored box. "Sir have you ever seen one of these in action?" The lieutenant asked.

Frank shook his head and the lieutenant smiled. "You are in for a treat. This will connect directly with my sergeant the same as any chip show. It will give him a complete picture of what is inside, how far it has gone, and projected distances etc.

"The box he has next to himself will also capture everything for us to watch, or if you wish I can get it directly into your head the same as any briefing. Your decision."

Frank asked "Can you hook up my XO also, along with yourself, so we can deal with it in real time?" The Lieutenant nodded.

"Alpha- six to Alpha-One . . . over.

"Go six."

"Meet me ASAP on bottom level. Follow you chip. . . out."

"Alpha-One, Aye-aye."

Five minutes later, Olney squatted down beside Frank, Lieutenant Ainsworth, his platoon sergeant, and the engineers. They were all peeking down a pitch-black tunnel that that had built in sensor illumination. It lit up as the marines approached the mouth of the tunnel but only gave a very dim light for about four meters into the inky blackness.

"Frank pointed to one of the engineers and said to Olney, "Lieutenant Yaxley here will explain what we are going to do and connect you into the drone feed. Your platoon will lead the advance into the tunnel. You know the drill. Don't let your squad leaders take any chances. If you find any side branches of this tunnel stop in place and myself and the engineers will be up to your location."

Frank looked down the tunnel again. "Not a lot of room. How do you want to advance?" Lieutenant Olney looked down the tunnel. "I make it about five meters wide. I will keep normal combat interval, but I'm going to stagger each team port and starboard and have a ten-meter gap between squads. I will follow the second team in and I'm using light benders."

Olney stopped and looked at Lt. Yaxley in thought. "Do you think the benders will work if there is zero light source?" he asked.

The Engineer shrugged. "If it is sensor, the Bat may or may not activate it depending on where they are placed." He stood in thought for a moment. "I can program the Bat to fly the height of a DM for the first ten meters. If other sections illuminate the light benders will probably work too."

Frank nodded and said to the two officers "Sounds good, try it. We'll know really fast if it helps or not. Lieutenant Yaxley, be ready to slow that bat down if it doesn't work so they have some light in there."

"Aye-aye Sir" the officers replied in unison.

"I am sending the Bat in," the engineer sergeant reported.

Frank was surprised at its speed as the little drone activated illumination as it went. But it only illuminated four meters. Then the tunnel behind became dark again. Luckily it hit another sensor almost immediately.

The Bat, flew about fifty meters further down where it suddenly bent to the right rounded the bend to the mouth of a longer tunnel and stopped.

"Go." Frank said to Olney who waved up his point team and pointed down the tunnel that the marines cautiously moved into.

"Alpha-One to Six, the benders seem to be working . . .out."

"Six roger. Alpha-Six to all platoons, Sit Rep . . . over."

"Alpha-Four . . . no outside movement but there is gunfire to my east. . .out

"Alpha-Three . . . the inside of the building is now cleared on all levels. I am doing another check as the engineers wire the place for destruction. . . out."

"Alpha-two . . . we have all the prisoners contained. . . out."

"Alpha-One . . . no contact yet. But the bat has stopped ahead again will advise. . . out"

"Six roger that." Frank nudged the engineer lieutenant who looked startled until he realized who it was. "Why would the Bat stop?" asked Frank.

"I stopped it the first time to check the light benders. This time . . . probably another tunnel.

EIGHTEEN HOURS EARLIER.

DM COMMAND BUNKER IN THE HILLS ABOVE WHITE ZONE. L DAY
MINUS 1 HUMAN TIME.

Intelligence Chief Herckel entered SPL Glgoffen's office and reported. "A Hooman stealth ship hit a Hoobar. It was blown almost in half and destroyed. There were only two survivors picked up. The ship was just inside the edge of our safe zone when destroyed. The survivors are in route here and are obviously intelligence gathering scouts."

"I want them well treated. "I am not going to make the mistake I made with the others and loose more critical information. How do you plan to proceed?"

"Supreme leader, we have a drug that will make them completely uninhibited and willing to obey any command or answer any query without hesitation. I will have them injected as soon as they arrive so we can begin."

Glgoffen smiled. *He is becoming a thoughtful asset for me*

"We will use the regular interrogation room. Call me when they arrive."

Two hours later Herckel communicated with SPL Glgoffen. "They are here Supreme Leader both are navy personnel. One male, and one female."

"I am on my way." SPL Glgoffen walked into the room and saw the prisoners sitting on folding chairs in the center of the room.

"Stand up," Herckel said to the prisoners."

SPL Glgoffen looked them both over noting the naval uniforms and asked "Who is senior?"

Captain Jane Folkroy took a step forward. "I am."

"What are your duties?" Herckel asked.

"Senior crew member," Folkroy answered.

Herckel was skeptical and turned to the man. "Tell me your duties."

"Junior crewman." Replied Lieutenant Wong, the Astro-navigation Officer."

"Enough of this, inject them" Glgoffen ordered.

Herckel nodded to the soldiers standing behind the prisoners who put each into a bear hug. A third soldier pressed a tube against the back of the struggling prisoners head who immediately stopped moving and stood docile.

"Can I count on this drug for complete truth and compliance?" Glgoffen asked Herckel.

Herckel turned to Captain Folkroy. "Strip naked." She complied and stood waiting. "Touch your female parts" Herckel ordered; and Captain Folkroy did. Herckel looked at Wong, "Rub her female part." Wong did.

"Enough! Have her sit." Glgoffen ordered.

The naked Captain Folkroy was sitting next to Wong and Herckel asked again "What is your position on the ship."

"I am the ship's captain."

"What is your position" Herckel asked Wong.

"I am chief Astro-navigation officer."

Glgoffen looked at Herckel who grinned at him. *Thank the ancestors. They could truly be a treasure of information* realized Glgoffen.

"Tell me your assignment in this space, and the reason for it. He said to Captain Folkroy." After fifteen minutes of listening to the captain Glgoffen felt frustration and the beginnings of fear, and asked, "When does the invasion begin."

"It begins early on Thirteen July."

"When is this Thirteen July?" Glgoffen asked. At that moment Folkroy sneezed wetly on the arm and hand of the DM guarding her that from habit, hit her a hard blow to the side of her head that knocked her from the chair hitting her head on the floor. For her it was like waking from a bad dream that she remembered, and she realized she was naked. At the same time, she heard the main computer in her mind again. She laid still for a moment and advised god what had happened and her fear she gave the entire invasion plan to the DM. The Computer Entity whispered back.

Still slightly groggy Captain Folkroy stood and faked a stumble toward Wong who she began punching in the head as hard and fast as she could. When he fell from his chair, she kicked him in the side of the head until she was restrained.

"When is thirteen July by your calendar" asked Herckel who looked at Folkroy's eyes and realized he no longer had control of her. "The blows to her head have neutralized the effect of the drug."

Cursed fools, not again! Glgoffen shouted in his mind and pointed to the guard. "Execute him."

He looked at Wong. "When is 13 July by your reckoning.

"Wong still groggy stared back and did not answer.

That cursed woman was very quick in understanding what happened. "Herckel, quick find out when that is by Hoo-man reckoning."

A few moments later a researcher handed Herckel a tablet. He glanced at it and went pale.

"Well?" demanded Glgoffen.

Herckel handed him the tablet "It is in eight hours by their counting."

SPL Glgoffen stood looking at the device unspeaking. *Cursed hoo-mans. If not for the prisoners they may well have destroyed us here. There is very little time.* "Get my First Deputy in here" he said to Herckel, "and set up a communication conference with all leaders down to the Large Pack level hurry."

Glgoffen then contacted the senior navy leader told him of the invasion and invasion lanes and had him sortie his fleet toward the attack lanes.

"Supreme leader," the navy leader reported, "almost half of the remaining half of the fleet is spread between *Planet Sunset*, this system, and beyond. I cannot get them here in the small time before invasion."

SPL Glgoffen gritted his teeth. *Are the gods against me! How do I save the army?* "

I know you will do your best. Stand by for further orders."

The First Deputy Leader came into the room and asked, "How do you plan to beat them?"

Glgoffen looked at Herckel. "What say you?"

Herckel did not hesitate. He pointed to Captain Folkroy sitting under guard. "She gave us our strategy."

"Speak plainly." Herckel winced at his tone of voice.

"Supreme Leader, she told us the plan was to leave open the lanes we made for ourselves so we could withdraw. We should make Planet

Forty-one our main line of resistance and get as much as we can through those lanes."

Glgoffen sat nodding to himself. "Herckel, give her to the guards to use, and execute the other one."

Both sailors jumped up and tried to fight the DM guards who quickly killed Wong and dragged Fitzroy from the room. At the same moment the Main Computer Entity notified human command of Wong's death and the continuous rape and other abuse Fitzroy was being subjected to; along with what it had heard up to that point.

Glgoffen looked at his First Deputy. "Your thoughts."

"I agree with his thinking but we are running out of time. You must start moving now."

Supreme Leader Glgoffen contacted his fleet leader. "When you are able, I want you to assemble behind Planet Forty-one where I am going to make our stand. For now, assign half of your remaining fleet in this system to defend that world. I realize that only leaves a quarter of our original numbers to oppose the invasion. Do your best."

Glgoffen waited as his conference was set up. "This is Supreme Leader Glgoffen. This emergency conference is because of intelligence information gathered from prisoners off a ship destroyed by the Hoobars. The Hoo-mans will invade this system any time after the middle of local night here on Planet Warbeast. It will begin with a major space bombardment. All leaders of the Third Great begin getting your troops into deep shelters and as separated as possible. Landing craft should be expected when the bombardment ends. The Twenty-third and Forty-third AG's begin moving to Planet Forty-one to join the Forty-first AG for evacuation to the space station as soon as possible. I am moving my headquarters there also. The First Deputy will defend here on Warbeast with the Third Great. He will bleed the hoomans as they have never before experienced. Go do your duty."

◆

Frank and Lieutenant Yaxley controlling the Bat worked their way up the tunnel toward Lieutenant Olney who stood with his platoon sergeant. As they approached the Bat went down the new opening and came back in a matter of seconds to continue following its original course.

"What just happened?" Frank asked Yaxley.

"It was short empty supply tunnel," replied the engineer, "but the Bat just made another turn to the right." The marines cautiously followed watching the illumination go on and off in the wake of the Bat. "The bat has stopped again, a hundred meters down" reported Lieutenant Yaxley. "It must be another shaft but it is also showing a large wide room or some other void."

"Team-one . . . move up and find out why the drone stopped." Lieutenant Olney ordered.

"Team-One . . . to Alpha-one. . . over."

"Go Team-One." Replied Olney."

"Team one . . . There are six tunnels all converging on a large room that has a wide stair way leading up. . . Break . . . As far as I can tell the area is secure. . . over."

"Team one stand-by. . . out"

Frank was monitoring all the company tactical frequencies and said to Lieutenant Olney. "Move your platoon up and get a watch on those tunnels; then we'll check topside." Olney nodded. But the Engineering Lieutenant spoke up. "Sir, before the lieutenant moves out can I make an observation:"

"Absolutely."

"Sir, the Battalion has assaulted a complex of six buildings. This being the largest. I find it more than a coincidence that six tunnels come together here."

"Because they are coming from each of the other buildings?" Frank asked.

"Yes Sir, and I think we should be ready for contact when we go out that door up there."

Frank and Olney shared look. "He is right Sir" agreed Olney. His platoon sergeant nodded too.

I agree, Frank thought. "Lieutenant Olney, send two men down each tunnel no more than fifty meters to make sure they are clear. By then most of the company will be ready to see what's at the top of these steps."

As the scouts were cautiously moving down the six tunnels Frank communicated with his Fourth Platoon. "Six to four . . . send two squads and your platoon sergeant to the tunnel on the bottom level . . . break . . . you continue to hold the front . . . break . . . let me know if situation requires more troops . . . six out."

Alpha-Four, Aye-aye."

"Alpha-Six to Alpha-Three . . . move to bottom tunnel with three squads. Keep one squad with your prisoners. . . Six out."

"Alpha-Three, Roger."

Frank walked to the bottom of the steps and looked up. They went a long way. "Send up the Bat," he told the engineers. It only took a few moments for them engineer to report. "Sir, the steps go up thirty meters. They stop at what look like double blast doors."

As Frank stood looking up the steps, Lieutenant Olney walked up to him. "Scouts report all clear down fifty meters."

Frank nodded, and communicate, "Alpha-Six to Alpha-Four. . . I want you to have two men guarding each tunnel after we move up. . . Break . . . Your platoon will be our reserve if its needed, Six out."

"Alpha-Four . . . Roger that." Lieutenant Ivanovic answered.

Frank looked at Lieutenant Olney, and motioned upward with his thumb. Olney began moving his teams forward and upward until he reached double steel doors where he called for an engineer, that arrived in a minute.

"Check for hidden explosives around this door," he said.

After a careful check the engineer reported."You are good to go, sir."

"Alpha-One to all squads . . . we will form into a one eighty perimeter after we go through the door." He nodded to his first squad leader who pushed the doors open and found himself inside another room. It too had steps, in the middle, leading to a door that had to be pushed upward like a cellar storm door. "Open it and be ready for anything" Olney cautioned the point squad leader. Frank followed at the rear of the Platoon.

The team leader pushed the door upwards just enough for him to look under a crack and reported to Olney "I see a field, cleared to a lightly wooded hill with some type of pillar or device sitting near the crest."

Lieutenant Olney looked under the door with him and paused. "Alpha-one to Six . . . meet me at the top door. . . out."

"What do ya have?" asked Frank when he met Olney.

"One of those giant light benders like we had on Ruby and NX."

Frank looked under the door. *Son of a bitch!* "Ya know what's probably hidden there."

Olney nodded. "Landing boats."

"Yep. Scan the area with your thermals for hidden positions. See if there's troops guarding um."

As Lieutenant Olney's platoon sergeant was scanning the area Frank communicated "Six to all platoon commanders. . . met me and Alpha-One at the second set of steps ASAP. . . out"

Then he contacted Battalion. "Alpha-six to Raiders Actual. . .over."

"Go Alpha-Six" answered Colonel Nikowa.

"Sir, we have control of the entire building, at least forty prisoners, and killed seventy-two DM infantry. We found a system of six tunnels all ending at my present location. Break . . . outside near the hills we have a very large light bender that I've encountered before on Pleasant, NX, and Ruby . . . break . . . they usually hide ships and supplies but could also have troops . . . break . . . the tunnels indicate that it all comes through here from other buildings. . . break . . . I intend to attack, and knock out the light bender. What is status of other buildings, and any remaining infantry . . . over."

"Raiders Actual to Alpha-Six . . . all secured except for Delta that is mopping up as we speak . . . break . . . the battalion has killed roughly your total in the other five buildings . . . break . . . that is much more infantry than we were expecting . . . break . . . Second Raiders are having a busy time . . . break . . .finish ASAP so we can move to assist them . . . Actual out."

Frank joined his gathered lieutenants. "Listen up, we are going to assault and knock out that giant light bender. We have to do it quick because the colonel said Second Raiders are having a rough time further down.

"Here's the plan. Lieutenant Olney, have a squad begin pulsing that bender as soon as we open these doors. As they are doing that have one squad out and down on the deck to the right and another on the left ta begin pulsing the areas to either side of the pole. Even if they can't see anything, they can still kill what they may not see. As soon as the bender becomes visible, I will lead second and fourth platoons out to assault the hill. Make sure yur people don't pulse each other.

"Lieutenant Ivanovic, you're on the right. Lieutenant Zaman, you have left. Lieutenant Ainsworth, your people are in reserve. Assign a squad to the tunnels, and watch our six on the chance that someone sneaks in. Any questions? All right we go in three minutes on my mark."

"Mark, mark, mark."

It was always the silence of the attack Frank couldn't get used to. Without return fire it was deadly quiet. Inside of a minute the light bender shorted out and six landing craft in two rows of three became visible. *Shit if they were all full there are still a shit-pot full of DMs around somewhere.*

"Move" said Frank and ran toward the boats followed by the

Second and Fourth platoons who reached the boats quickly and put a 360° perimeter around them.

"Six to all platoons . . . it was too easy . . . Break . . . be ready, there should still be a few hundred of um around."

"Six to Alpha-One and three . . . We have boats here for three hundred troops. Be ready for anything. Alpha-Six to Raiders Actual . . . over."

"Go Six, but be advised I have been monitoring . . . break . . . we are interviewing prisoners and re-sweeping all buildings and tunnels for bodies living or dead . . . Break . . . Move to occupy the hill behind the boats until you her from me . . . Actual out."

"Six to one . . . get your platoon and move to the top of the hill and dig in. We are going to hold it for a while . . . Break . . . Place the others as they get up to you. . . out"

"One, Aye-aye."

"Six to three . . . yur holding our lower end. . . Break . . . Watch those tunnels and our six. . . out."

"Three, aye-aye."

"Six to two and four . . . move up the hill and tie in with First Platoon. Alpha-one will place you. . . out"

Frank took the time to look into some of the boats and found a flag he had never seen before and took it for a souvenir before following his men up the hill. As he approached the summit, he saw activity and Lieutenant Olney pumping his arm at him in a hurry up motion. *What the fuck has him excited.*

Frank jogged up to Lieutenant Olney. "Ivanovic found another set of the type of doors we just came through on the back side of this hill. I have two squads covering it. I figure we could have maybe a hundred plus in there." Frank looked down the hill at another partially cleared field leading to heavier woods with older trees, and said to Olney, "I want to check those woods before we bunch up around that door."

"Do you think there are troops in there, sir?" Lieutenant Ivanovic asked.

Frank and Olney both nodded and Frank said, "If I were them, I'd cover my six and lines of retreat. Wouldn't you Mister Ivanovic? Have a squad check out that woods in front of us."

"Aye-aye, Sir."

The three officers watched the squad moving down the hill to cross the field in Team rushes."

"Rrrriiipp, Rrrriiipp"

Tracers from a rapid-fire gun in the woods began sweeping over the advancing team and two marines fell. The other three teams began pulsing the area the tracers came from when a second gun opened fire from their right along with rifle fire.

"Rrrriiipp"

"Crack, crack, crack

" The rounds came over Frank and the others laying on the hill top.

"Get the rest of your troops deployed!" Frank said to the two lieutenants "I'm going to get a fire mission on the woods. Cover our people and see if they can work their way back from the blast area. As soon as the rockets hit, we attack. Get ready.

"Alpha-Six ta Recon Actual . . .. I need a fire mission into the woods directly behind the hill we occupy . . .Break . . . we are under fire by multiple rapid firing guns and several squads of DMs . . . over"

"This is fire control Alpha Six . . . I have your location; it is on the way." A minute later Frank heard the "Whoosh" of the incoming rockets.

"Kaboom."

"Kaboom."

They impacted along the woods throwing trees, bushes, and pieces of DMs into the air.

"Go now, now!" Frank jumped up and started down the hill. The two marine platoons charged across the field and into the woods covered by those on the hill. The fight was over in five minutes.

Frank stood by a destroyed rapid-fire gun watching a corpsman working on the marines laying in the field while Lieutenant Ivanovic checked on his other men. He was joined by Lieutenant Olney. "We have two destroyed rapid fire guns and their crews along with twelve more riflemen. Most were killed by the rockets the last three were pulsed as we entered the woods. Total of eighteen more DMs."

Frank nodded. "Check for intelligence info then meet me by the door." He said and walked over to Lieutenant Ivanovic and asked. "What's the count?"

"Four wounded, and one dead from the gun that caught them in the field. I should have told them to use light benders"

"There is nothing you could have done. Those fuckers have probable been watching us since we got to the top of the hill. They wanted us to open the doors before they hit us which leads me to believe there are more troops waiting on the other side."

Ivanovic grimaced. "I agree, Sir."

"Engineers up!" Frank communicated. Lieutenant Yaxley, and three of his men joined Frank who pointed to the marines spread in a half moon around the doors that ,although well camouflaged, could be seen from ground level. "Lieutenant, do you have anything that can breach those doors?"

"Yes Sir, and it will blow inward and push those doors into anyone waiting on the other side."

"Okay. Lieutenant Ivanovic, as soon as the door blows in have a team fire four pulses each down the steps. Lieutenant Yaxley you let the Bat fly in. We will adjust depending on what the Bat sees."

"Aye-aye, sir."

The engineers quietly set the charges and backed up "Fire in the hole!" yelled the sergeant.

"*Kaboom!*"

Both doors blew inside and four marines began to pulse the steps "*Rrrriiipp.*"

The return firs from a rapid-fire gun hit two of the marines.

"*Rrrriiipp.*"

The incoming fire continued, marked by tracers. The other marines who were holding their guns around the opening kept pulsing back.

"Fire in the hole!" Yelled Lieutenant Yaxley, who ran to the door and threw in his field made package the size of a medium pillow far enough that it went to the bottom of the steps. He spun around to the side of the doorway and hit the deck.

"*Kaboom!*"

Grey smoke and dust flew from the stairway along with concussion washing across the marines near the opening.

"Move out! Move out! Keep pulsing as you move!" Frank yelled.

Lieutenant Ivanovic led his squad down the stairway followed by Frank along with Olney and his squad. Bodies were piled along the first five meters of the tunnel along with the destroyed Rapid-fire gun.

"Olney, go until you hit a cross tunnel or the end" communicated Frank then contacted Lieutenant Zaman "Six to two . . . get a count of these bodies . . . Six out."

"Alpha-one to Alpha-six."

"Go One."

"One, I have reached another door like the other tunnel . . . break . . . also have a lot of dead along the tunnel . . . break . . . the blast over-pressure and concussion was focused down the tunnel and by our count they are fifty-two dead not showing any wounds except for bleeding from ears eyes and nose; probably from blast concussion in the confined space. . . over."

Shit it must have hit them like an in-line wind. "Roger that, I am having Fourth Platoon relieve you . . . Break . . . they will attack through those doors with Second Platoon. You and your people move back and take a break . . . six out."

Frank walked outside and watched two corpsmen working on the wounded. The dead marine was wrapped and laying to the side with the other.

Olney has had the brunt of this entire fight and the most causalities and deserves a rest. His thoughts were interrupted by Lieutenant Zaman "There are nineteen bodies at the bottom of the steps Skipper"

Frank nodded his thanks. *That's a total of eighty-seven more of them leaving a platoon running around here somewhere.* "Alpha-Six to Engineer-Six meet me up front."

About three minutes later Lieutenant Yaxley reported to Frank who asked him, "Can we use the same type of explosive on these doors as well.?" Yaxley grimaced. "You saw what over-pressure did to the DMs strewn along this tunnel?"

Frank nodded "That's what I thought ya'd say."

"I have a suggestion sir. I can use the same explosives with a command detonation. As soon as it blows, I can fly the bat straight in and hopefully get some data while they are still groggy if anyone is there at all."

Frank smiled. "Lieutenant Yaxley, you re definitely an asset. Set it up I'm gonna talk ta Battalion."

When everyone had been withdrawn from the tunnel the engineers blew the door

"Kaboom."

The Bat flew and imagery of fleeing DM began coming in.

"Alpha-three to Alpha-Six priority, over!"

Shit that's Ainsworth at the other tunnels, Frank thought. "Go Three."

"Three . . . we had an attack here . . . break . . . a bunch of DMs came out of a tunnel and we killed and captured them and I have wounded!"

"Alpha-Six to Three, relax . . . break . . . first give me your Cas rep then define Bunch . . . over." Lieutenant Ainsworth winced, and saw his platoon sergeant giving him a sardonic look and realized he had acted like the newbie he was.

"Alpha-Three to Alpha-Six . . . I have four WIA . . . break . . . we had a large group estimated at twenty-five plus try to force the port side tunnel closest to the steps . . . break . . . we have killed seventeen and taken seven prisoners. A few others ran back into the tunnel . . . break . . . they all wear the same insignia on their sleeve. It is a blue shield with a hollow yellow diamond in the center. The points of the diamond cross as spears . . . over."

"Six to Three outstanding job . . . break . . . I believe we are at the other end of that tunnel and I have met this unit before on Sunset . . . break . . .. Now I know who they are. Stay alert . . . six out."

"What does the Bat show" Frank asked Yaxley.

"In infra-red I can make out only two or three signatures."

"Raiders-Actual to Alpha-six . . . over."

"Go Raiders-Actual."

"Actual . . . I have been monitoring everyone in your operation and I am satisfied we have gotten the bulk of them. Leave one platoon to find any survivors and you move with the rest of the battalion to assist Second Raiders . . . Actual out."

CHAPTER 14

General Hayduf, Commanding General of the invasion forces sat at a meeting table inside a surviving structure in White Zone with five other Army General officers, two Marine Generals, and two Admirals.

When everyone was situated, he said "Ladies and Gentlemen with the first item on our agenda for discuss is the reminder that it is still top-secret Ultra.

"On the recommendation of god, we released the attack group commander taken prisoner at New Glasgow after getting everything in his head. Since his chip remains in place it is hoped god can follow developments as this senior officer reintegrates with the DM leadership. But not only that, we are letting them know we all originally come from the same world."

"I do not know what good it will do" one of the Admirals said "but I do hope we get hard actionable intelligence back."

General Hayduf nodded. "I agree. Now here is a brief of where we are in this invasion; and we will discuss what we still need to do. First: The eight hours warning the DMs received from their two prisoners was unfortunately used to good effect by them in some places. One of those being their local anti-air defenses that initially had a punishing effect on our landing craft.

"It was also an unpleasant surprise that they chose to fight burrowed below ground. We are all aware of the difficulties and casualties incurred fighting in tunnels, caves, and rubble they learned on *Pleasant*. Both of these items contribute to why the battle here is taking longer than anticipated.

"Who here would have thought we would miss the mass charges of eighteen-months ago; when we could see what we were fighting. Now unfortunately, we are doing the attacking and they are defending."

The other senior officers sat nodding, and General Thomas said "Sir I would like to point out we have learned some lessons. I would like to commend Lieutenant Yaxley, an Engineer attached to the First Raiders who made such a contribution during a tunnel battle back on L Day at Black Beach when he devised an explosive charge in a bag that can be thrown into whatever you wish. It turned out to be a main tunnel clearing tool for the infantry. Who knows how many troops his idea has saved; and god has awarded him a Galactic Cross in silver."

General Hayduf nodded. "It was not only the marines he saved general. His bag is now in use Theatre wide. Now please sit back ladies and gentlemen." The *Planet Refuge* appeared in their heads with the Landing Zones and troop concentrations marked. In a panel on the right side was the entire *Refuge System*.

"The Third and Fourth Infantry Divisions, have been the most fortunate to date. Our bombardment from space did what we had hoped here in White Zone where half of the Thirty-First AG took severe causalities; but they fight on. Approximately two thousand of their survivors have been evacuated to *Planet Diamond* leaving only a few remaining fragments of them that linked up with the still dangerous Thirty-Second AG minus the one quarter of their troops lost to the Raiders at Black Beach. Now they are acting as a rear guard tenaciously resisting at Orange Zone, and are slowly being wiped out or captured.

"The First ID from Yellow Zone, has been ordered over to Orange Zone along with the Fourth ID from here. They will assist the Fifth ID, and First Marines, that are mostly fighting underground slowly digging out the Thirty-second AG that is causing them severe causalities. This area was turned into a labyrinth of passages and strong points; but I expect it to be secured by L plus nine. At that point I am leaving only the Third ID in White Zone for any needed mop up.

"The Second ID from Yellow Zone will stay in place as a reserve since the Thirtieth AG withdrew from Yellow Zone to *Planet Diamond* ahead of the invasion. Hopefully by L Plus Ten or Eleven at the latest the Planet will be secured.

"One other positive note from white Zone. Captain Fitzroy who was captured on L minus One has been found still alive, although critically abused and beaten. Apparently, she was locked in a room as a prelude to more abuse but was forgotten at the start of the invasion and god directed troops to her location. I am hopeful that she will soon recover enough to give some insight into the DM leadership she met.

"As you ladies and gentlemen already suspect, the battle for this planet is mainly won and will soon end except for the mop up. The DM troops bypassed on *Planet Ruby* identified as the Forty-third AG was able to evacuate to *Planet Diamond* during the initial days of the landing. Unfortunately, so were the Twenty-second and Twenty-third AGs isolated on *Planet Emerald*. There, Delta-mike made a daring stealth ship rescue and transported the survivors to *Diamond*.

"Now to *Planet Diamond*. Things there are not going well. Delta-mike has consolidated all their remaining troops on that planet in underground fortifications that, we believe, equals at least three great packs. They are bleeding us for every inch of movement."

L PLUS 8 LATE IN THE AFTERNOON.

SUBLEVEL 4. DELTA-MIKE TRANSIT HUB IN ORANGE ZONE.

Frank and his officers sat beside a monorail that led down a darkened tunnel toward the DM ship landing platforms thought to be one-hundred kilometers away. 1ˢᵗ Raiders was tasked with the capture of the Transit center that intelligence told them may exist. Finding the monorail at this bottom level was an important discovery; but a costly one in the intensive close-up fighting through the building then down four levels.

"Alpha-Six to Raiders Actual . . . over."

"Go Six," answered Colonel Nikowa.

"Cas Rep sir, seven KIA, and seventeen WIA that the corpsman says are all returnable . . . break . . . by count we killed Forty-three DMs here, and have three POWs . . . break . . . we've reached the bottom and found a monorail leading, we believe, toward White beach. . . break . . . there is a three-car train sitting roughly fifty meters up the rail; and I'm sure the engineers can figure how to get it moving if you want us to continue the attack . . . break . . . Charley Company is above us on Sub three . . . over"

"Raiders actual to Alpha-six stand by . . . ."

Frank looked at his officers and senior NCOs. "We are on hold for now. Let's get as secure as we can down here. Lieutenant Olney, send a squad to scout down the tracks roughly one K." See if they find anything of interest."

"Yes Sir"

"Lieutenant Zama, do the same on the track in the opposite direction."

"Aye-aye Skipper."

"Staff Sergeant Imlay, you and Lieutenant Ainsworth will stay here with your platoons."

Both nodded to Frank.

"Everybody get all the rest you can."

Frank sat, popped a ration pill and drank some water. *This is worse that New Glasgow. It's been a tough eight days . . . Shit thirty-four killed and sixty-four wounded so far. The fucking DM are dug in here like roaches.* His musings were interrupted by a personal call on his chip.

"Captain Farrell."

"Fuck me seven times are you always this formal," asked Hoysaia.

Frank laughed and asked, "How are you holding up?"

"Good so far, but the fucking DMs are making things tough. We are about half a K from you still digging the bastards out. We are lucky to be above ground at this point, and that is the reason I contacted you. Your friend Captain Macalduie was wounded serious enough to be moved up to the fleet hospital ship this morning. I heard she has been awarded the Galactic cross in gold. I thought you would like to know."

"Thanks for the heads up. Watch your six."

Frank tried to contact Alicia. *I wonder how bad she was hit this morning. I remember my trip up from New Glasgow. Shit. She should be able to talk by now.*

"Captain Macalduie." Alicia sounded tired and weak.

"Hey, did I wake you I heard you were up taking it easy with the fleet."

Alicia chuckled. "You're a wise ass."

"I love it when you use an Earth accent. It gets me aroused."

She laughed out loud.

Frank was quiet for a moment.

"I guess they will be sending you back into this shit soon. Maybe I can get to see you."

Alicia didn't reply.

"Hey, did you fall asleep again."

"I'm not coming back down Frank. I'm being sent to MW."

"Why is that?"

"I need a bit of work on my injuries is why."

What the fuck happened to her? "How bad did you get hit Alicia?"

"I lost my right leg above the knee."

Holy shit! He felt his stomach drop and sat silently.

"Are you there, Frank?"

"Yep absolutely. They do all kinds of things with injuries. I'll bet they're already thinking of growing ya a new one."

"Yur right, that's why I'm going to MW" said Alicia sounding like her perky self.

Frank was surprised. "I am? You are? A new leg? No shit?"

Alicia laughed.

"Not only that, I'm going back into intelligence. When you get a chance, come see me to take me dancing on my new leg. I have to go now Frank. Take care."

Frank sat staring down the dark monorail tunnel, feeling very lonely.

"Raiders Actual to Alpha-Six.

"Go Actual."

"Alpha-six, I want you with as many of Charley Company as can fit in with you to get that monorail working. See where it takes you. You are correct that it is oriented toward White Beach. The First Marines and the Army's Fifth Infantry are still facing stiff resistance there. If you hit heavy opposition, either hold in place until we can get up to you, or withdraw at your discretion. . . break . . . if you are lucky you will arrive under the DMs and give them a nasty surprise . . . break . . . let me know when you are moving. I have already notified Captain Kim. . . out."

"Platoon commanders up" Frank communicated to his and to Charley Company leaders.

He continued looking down the tunnel, smelling the dank air and a line from Shakespeare suddenly popped into his mind: One *more into the breach, dear friends, once more.*

Captain Kim was the first down from Charlie and walked to Frank. "Trying to see problems down that long dark road?" he asked with a wry smile.

Frank nodded. "Guess I was Kim. Any words of wisdom for me?"

"Not even one" Kim replied with a grimace "what is your plan if you get hit along the way?"

"One of my patrols found another two cars further up the track" Frank replied. "You and battalion can pinpoint exactly where we are with your chips. I'm thinking you can probably fit over two platoons in those two cars if you pack um in tight. I'm also thinking of asking the Colonel to have the rest of your company follow us at a distance of twenty minutes at whatever speed we are traveling."

Kim whistled in surprise.

"Yea I know, it could get close to two hundred K per hour if we can determine we have a clear track; but at least I'll know somebody is already in route. If two Marine companies can't hold some fucking DMs in a tunnel for a while, we should be ashamed. To be safe, I'll have the engineers find, or rig-up, a forward-looking sensor somewhere in this car."

As the platoon commanders gathered around it was Kim's turn to stand looking down the tunnel deep in thought

Forty-five minutes later Frank and his composite command stopped two K from the end of the line and cautiously moved through the tunnel to avoid being surprised at their destination. The Shipyard station was set up with a circular ramp leading topside.

"Lieutenant. Ainsworth, you lead out with Third-platoon" Frank ordered "followed by the First then the Second. Staff Sergeant Imlay, you have our six. Keep a watch down the tunnel."

Frank looked up toward the brightness above them. "Lieutenant Ainsworth, have a team scout up and see if any DMs are in the vicinity. It seems too quiet here."

"Aye-aye, Skipper."

"Alpha-six to Raiders Actual."

"Go Alpha-Six."

"Alpha-six . . . we are below the yards. The station is secure. A four-tier circular ramp leads upward and we are beginning to move now . . . Alpha-six out."

An hour later there was no doubt that Delta-Mike had withdrawn while the fighting was raging underground. The 31st and 32nd AG's again performed their sacrificial mission as a rear guard allowing the survivors of 3rd Great Packs escaped to *Planet Diamond* to fight again.

"Alpha-six to Raiders Actual."

"Go Six."

"Six, the Shipyards are abandoned and DM gone . . . over."

"Roger that Alpha-Six, they have slipped away again . . . break . . . dig in there. I am moving Battalion command to your location . . . Raiders Actual out."

CHAPTER 15

Frank and his Platoon Commanders were inspecting the company perimeter when he received a terse order from Colonel Nikowa. "Alpha-Six and Alpha-One report to Battalion CP immediately."

Frank and Olney locked eyes, and Frank shrugged *What the fuck is this about?*

"Lieutenant *Zaman*, Lieutenant Olney and I have been summoned to battalion. You're in command until we return."

"Aye-aye Skipper."

Frank and Olney began walking to the Command Post.

When they entered the bustling room, Frank looked around and saw the colonel standing in the far corner in what appeared to be a heated conversation with another lieutenant colonel dressed in a clean, un-faded, and un-adorned, uniform that looked out of place. He marked him as freshly arrived.

Colonel Nikowa saw Frank and Olney looking his way and waved the two men over as the other colonel walked away nodding to them in passing.

"Want coffee?" Colonel Nikowa asked, gesturing toward a large urn sitting on a box.

"Thank you, Sir," replied Frank who said to Olney" Relax I'll get yours too."

He re-joined Olney and the colonel in a medium size room the colonel was using as his office. Its only furnishings were a few chairs to sit on and a box. The rest of the room was dingy and smelled like Delta-Mike.

Frank looked around and quipped, "Nice office sir."

Colonel Nikowa took a sip of coffee and regarded the two filthy, exhausted looking, officers.

"Right this minute which one of your lieutenants would you recommend to command a company?" the colonel asked Frank.

Oh shit! I've heard this before. What's happening?

Frank indicated Olney with his thumb, and the colonel shook his head.

"He is being relieved of command."

"What!" Frank shouted, and stood up. "Tell me what's going on!"

"Sit down captain," ordered the colonel, "you are being relieved of command too."

Frank heard Olney gasp. *Something else is in play here. Be cool and wait to find out everything.* "In that case sir, Lieutenant Zaman is a very competent officer."

"Sounds like you have calmed down captain" the colonel said with an ironic smile. "As a matter of fact, I am relieved also."

Frank and Olney looked at each other.

"Did I . . . fuck up sir?" Frank asked

"Relax captain. I was teasing you and it got out of hand.

"Frank and Olney exchanged another look.

"Does that mean I am not relieved of command sir?" Olney asked.

Colonel Nikowa chuckled. "Before this gets any more fucked-up let me explain, and apologize for kidding with you."

He sat back and took a gulp of coffee. "The *Main Computer Entity*, has determined based on a variety of factors that it is detrimental for anyone to serve more that eighteen months in close ground combat. The reason is it could affect future actions, attitudes, and individual mental status. Furthermore, god has also determined that the average recovery time needed to get back into prime mental and physical conditioning is one year. From the state of you two sorry characters I now believe it.

"Gentlemen, the three of us have been in almost continuous contact and combat with Delta-Mike for close to two years on four worlds. We have been relieved of combat duty effective immediately, and transferred to MW. That colonel you saw me speaking with is *my* replacement. I will get Lieutenant Zaman in here and promote him to captain. Then we three are getting on a landing craft and going up to the *Argon* that has also been pulled out of combat. Go get what gear you have and meet me at the landing dock. Our boat is waiting."

Colonel Nikowa stood up and raised his hand in the traditional greeting and said "It has been an honor serving with you gentlemen."

MILITARY WORLD 24 JULY.

Frank and Olney walked out of the transit hub into the morning sunshine of MW after spending two days resting, replacing equipment, and cleaning up on Planet Sunset. They were met by a sergeant who salute and asked, "Sir, are you Captain Farrell?"

"That's right."

"Sir, I have transportation to take you gentlemen to your temporary quarters. Then to the Commandant's office at Headquarters Marine Corps."

Frank and Olney exchanged a look. Olney raised his eyebrows and Frank shrugged back.

"Lead on Sergeant," Frank said.

An hour later the two marines arrived at Major Browns office. When they entered the office, the major looked up and scrutinized them both for a long minute. "You two look like you need some rest" he said to them as a greeting. "Grab a chair and sit."

Major Brown sat considering the two men again. "I do not make a habit of meeting everyone rotated back her for rest. But you would be dismayed how few from the very beginning here on Sunset Perimeter have managed to last as long as you two.

"Your performance during Operation *Black Beach* was outstanding. As a result, Captain Farrell you get the Galactic Cross in Gold. Lieutenant, you and the other platoon leaders of "A" Raiders get it in Silver. Congratulations."

"Effective immediately, you are both on ten days leave to any world with a Portal to get you back here. Your new assignments for the future will be sent to your chips at the end of your leave." Major Brown looked at them with a gleam in his eye. "But I will give you a hint. Lieutenant Olney, you are promoted to Captain effective today, and will be assigned as a Company Commander with the Third Marine Division now being formed. They will be training here on MW for close to a year."

"Aye-aye sir" said Olney grinning widely, "

Major Brown looked at Frank.

"Captain Farrell, you are promoted to Major. The boss still has not settled on your assignment. Enjoy your leave and report here when you get back.

"Aye-aye, sir."

CHAPTER 16

DELTA-MIKE UNDERGROUND HQ ON PLANET DIAMOND/PLANET 41.

Intelligence Chief Herckel came into SPL Glgoffen's bunker and stood to be recognized.

"What is it Herckel?"

"Supreme leader, Attack Group Leader Woflazgl who was captured during the withdrawal from New Glasgow is on his way here. Apparently the Hoomans released him."

SPL Glgoffen straightened up and looked thoughtful. "Why?"

Herckel shrugged. "If he does not get caught in the fighting again, he will be here soon."

Two hours later . . .

Attack Group Leader Wolflazgl stood before Supreme Pack Leader Glgoffen being closely scrutinized by him and his Intelligence Chief. "You do not look injured or distressed to me. What did you tell them that they released you?" Glgoffen asked with a penetrating stare.

Wolflazgl began to tremble. "Supreme leader, on my honor I told them nothing because they already knew everything. They knew me, what and where I was in the first days of the invasion; they have intelligence information about us that is difficult to comprehend."

"Why do *you* think they released you?"

"Supreme leader I think it was to convey a message to you."

"What message!" the Intelligence Chief demanded.

SPL Glgoffen held up his hand silencing Herckel.

"Continue," he said to Woflazgl, "but before we get to the message, since they impress you so, give me your assessment of them. Apparently, they treated you well."

Glgoffen looked at his intelligence chief. "

What do you think Herckel?"

"Supreme Leader, he should have died fighting instead of surrendering."

Woflazgl felt his insides turning to water by the look on the supreme leader face, and the angry stance of his intelligence chief.

Glgoffen looked at Woflazgl spreading his hands. "Continue Attack Pack Leader."

Woflazgl swallowed. "Supreme Leader. I was taken by knife soldiers who appeared almost at arm's length from the undergrowth approaching our landing zone. They killed everyone around me except my assistant commander and our communicator and overpowered us. We are only alive because they recognized a command group.

"They took me up to a very large war ship, possibly a Battleship, where I waited for my torture. I have not seen my second in command, or my communicator, since that moment of capture.

"My first interrogator was a mid-level naval officer who was polite and respectful. He called me by name and . . ."

"How is that possible?" the intelligence chief interrupted.

"Let us hear his story first!" admonished Glgoffen and looked back at Woflazgl.

"And then he named my home world and recounted my first battle against knife soldiers back on Planet Sunset at the beginning. When I kept silent, he smiled and told me I may as well talk with him since he already knew everything anyway. He went on to discuss our home worlds traditions and myths."

Clearly confused, Glgoffen asked "What myths?"

"He spoke of the legends of the cold time and beasts on an old world. Then he asked if I knew how we left there."

"Why do you think?"

Woflazgl shrugged and said "He already knew the answer to every-thing he was asking. But he wanted *us* to know something."

"Do not make me pull this from you one piece at a time" Glgoffen warned.

"Supreme leader on my honor and past record as a warrior of the Pack. He told me we have met before and lived near each other on that old world of snow and beasts that is the Hooman's home world.

"He told me they too were a hunting tribe but were left behind when we were taken. He said the proof of his words is in our DNA that we can test against any prisoners we have. One final observation. We should not misunderstand their kindness. They are as ruthless, vicious and courageous in battle as the packs."

SPL Glgoffen stood and began to pace the room in thought. After a few quiet moments he Turned to Herckel. "Do you have an opinion?"

"Supreme Leader, we have a number of prisoners. Let us test them and ourselves. The results will help us decide what to do."

Glgoffen nodded. "See to it."

When the intelligence chief left Glgoffen looked at Woflazgl. "I am aware of your service to the pack and I believe what you have told me. For now, do not discuss your captivity with anyone but myself and Intelligence Chief Herckel. When the testing is completed you will attend the High Command briefing with me."

SPL Glgoffen looked around at his surviving Commanders. *How will they react to the news that the majority of human prisoners tested all have around three percent of our DNA. And a number of Pack troops have roughly the same amount of theirs. This information should not be shared for the immediate future.*

"Pack Mates we will begin a stealth withdrawal from this world to our space fortifications at the bridge to Andromeda. There we will rebuild the pack army. The Fourth Great will continue the battle here during the withdrawal. When the army has gone the Fourth Great will make their way back to us as they are able."

He looked at his assembled commanders, and especially the Leader of the 4th Great. "The Fifth Great gave all on Sunset. The First and Sixth gave unreservedly on Pleasant. The Third Great gave fully on Packland where it's Leader along with almost every senior officer was killed leading them against the Hooman's attack. I intend to rebuild around their survivors who made it possible for us to come here."

He motioned toward Woflazgl.

"Attack Group Leader Woflazgl of the Sixty-second Assault Group. For service and bravery in advancing the furthest of all units fighting in the New Glasgow battle, and for intelligence gathered by you I promote you to lead the Third Great Pack. Always do your duty."

The gathered senior commanders stomped their feet in recognition of the promotion. Woflazgl was stunned.

The Main Computer Entity listened to it all.

ON MW.

Limping only slightly, Alicia reported to Major Brown at Headquarters the next morning and was taken to see General Thomas who looked her up and down. "You are looking fit again Captain," the general said.

"Thank you, sir."

"Captain, you are being assigned to G-One Ultra."

Creases formed between her eyes and she looked confused. "I have never heard of that unit sir."

"I would be surprised if you had Captain. G-one U is the highest most secret Galactic Intelligence division we have. It is multiple layers above normal military intelligence. In order to maintain our secrecy, you are in the records as the Executive Officer of your old unit the Marine Intelligence Battalion. But you will be on a very loose leash as it were, so you can also be involved in your G-one U duties. As such you will be privy to many things; and so, *the Main Computer Entity* will monitor you more than usual to make sure you do not divulge anything you should not. It is something we must all live with. I do not think you will have any problems but you need to be told. Do you understand, and do you accept the assignment and its conditions?"

Why does he think I would divulge anything I learn? Sounds serious. "I understand, and I accept the assignment sir."

"Very well. I am going to turn you over to Major Brown. Remember. Everything you discuss is G-one U." The commandant called Major Brown into the office. "Captain Macalduie is now G-one U. I have another meeting, you finish this." The commandant stopped at the office door and looked back to Alicia. "I almost forgot. The rank of major goes with this assignment. Congratulations."

Major Brown smiled at Alicia's surprised face.

After the commandant left Alicia looked a question at Major Brown who said "As I recall, you and Major Farrell were training partners in boot camp . . . and then some. Yes?"

Frank is a major too? "We've had an on and off relationship because we're good friends. Why is it an issue?"

Major Brown sat looking at Alicia "Friends and lovers. Yes?"

What is going on here. Why is he treating me like I may be a problem? After she hesitated a few more seconds Major Brown said "You do not have to take the assignment and promotion."

This is some sort of test. "I do want this assignment sir; but I'm confused why you think I may have a problem with it?"

Major Brown tilted his head. "Did I detect some Earth accent in your speech patterns. It is not usual."

Alicia did not know how to respond and shrugged.

"Major Brown smiled. "What is your assessment of Major Farrell?"

"I think he is one of the best marines, and finest men I know. Why?"

"Do you have an emotional attachment to him?"

"Why?"

Major Brown exhaled loudly then took a deep breath through his nose and blew it out of his mouth. "Major you are going to see G-one U information on Major Farrell who, I agree with you, is a good marine and fine man. One that has made additional contributions to the war you will soon appreciated more. I have known him since he arrived here.

"Sit back Major, this will take a few hours. You are going to see a program god made on the first weeks after the arrival of a Time Traveler around the same time Delta-Mike invaded Planet Sunset."

"Ancestors" blurted Alicia. Was the time traveler part of the invasion?"

Major Brown shook his head. "It was an accident caused by a Physicist, Doctor Samuel Lamont. Now sit back. I will answer any questions you have later."

Why do I know that name? I know. He did something to fix our pulse weapons.

Two hours and thirty minutes later Alicia sat still trying to grasp what she had seen putting it together with early conversations with Frank when they first became training partners. She was stunned and asked Major Brown, "Can I discuss this with him?"

Brown nodded. "It will probably be good for him if you do; but be careful of where and when you discuss it. Now there are a few issues with this I want to discuss with you."

Later . . . Alicia answered the call. "Major Macalduie."

"Hey Alicia, it's Frank I'm back on MW. Congratulations in making major."

I knew he would contact me. So apparently did Major Brown. "Frank, so good to hear you. Were you relieved because of time in combat?"

"How'd ya guess? Oh, I remember you're back in intelligence and snooping into everything right?"

"I love that Earth accent Frank; but I'm still in treatment. My new leg is coming along fine."

"Well, when can I inspect it."

"I am at an important stage in the regeneration process and won't be able to see anyone for at least seven days sorry." *Sometimes I do not know how to handle the way he comes in and out of my life and I feel terrible for lying to him about not seeing anyone. I wonder why Major Brown was so adamant about that. I am a little angry he did not tell me he made major too.*

It's ok" Frank replied "I'm on leave for ten days and will be off world. I'll contact you when I get back. Take care of yerself."

CHAPTER 17

MW 5 AUGUST.

Frank was well rested when he returned from his leave on Joyful. Speculating about his new assignment he contacted Major Brown. "I'm Just checking in."

"Stop in and see me Farrell, I have your assignment. I know you are wondering about it."

Forty minutes later Frank sat in Major Brown's office. After the usual small talk Major Brown said "Let me give you a little background on what transpired in the Battle for the *Refuge* system after you left.

"Your old adversary The Third Great Pack, was almost totally destroyed on *Planet Refuge*. Most of that you already know since you had a hand in it. Their few thousand survivors were extracted by stealth craft and taken to *Planet Diamond* after you left along with their other surviving formations where they re-grouped with the forces from the other three worlds in the system.

"The battles for *Planet Diamond* although a victory for us was costly one. Many DM units managed to escape again. The Fourth Great Pack was annihilated there when they stayed and fought a holding-action against us until the rest of them withdrew. Now it is just a matter of time until we follow them again.

"As for you, report to Brigadier General Sing who is now the First Brigade Commander of the Fifth and Sixth Marines along with their attachments, in the Second Marine Division. Good luck in your new assignment."

That afternoon Frank was at Brigade Headquarters. "Major Farrell reporting as ordered sir" he said when shown into Sing's office.

The brigadier smiled widely. "It is good to see you Major; it has been a long time."

"Yes, sir it has."

"Have a seat."

When Frank was settled the general said "You have been appointed the Executive Officer for First Battalion Fifth Marines. I still find it amazing to say Second Marine Division knowing there is also a Third one now. I am depending on you to train the battalion until the new CO arrives."

"Who is it sir?"

"The CO has not been announced, you will be running the show until then. Get them trained to usefulness. Utilize your adjutant to assist you as needed until the CO arrives; however, I do not foresee us being deployed for at least seven months . . . if then.

"Who are my company commanders, sir?"

"They are all new but very energetic. Mostly promoted lieutenants from garrisons around the galaxy. The same with most platoon commanders. I have not given any assignments. I leave that to you. The Battalion Sergeant Major is an old timer who refused a commission. Do you remember Sergeant Major Kim Young from old First Recon?"

"Yes sir. A good man. He will be a great help, maybe even more than the adjutant in the beginning."

The general nodded. "I agree, and the Recon CO is only a lieutenant, but I am going to change that. He has been around for a while and in recon for almost two years. His name is Blanco. Do you know of him?

"Yes, sir I do. A good man."

"I am glad to hear you say that. I will get his promotion in."

✦

"Attention on deck!" Sergeant Major Kim Young called as Frank entered the meeting room. "As you were!" Frank said walking to the front of the room. He looked around for a long moment.

"Relax lady and gentlemen. This is a quick introduction meeting before we start training. I will be meeting with each of you privately as we go along.

"I'm Major Farrell the Battalion Executive officer. The Sergeant Major is Kim Young who has forgotten more about being a marine than any of you will ever know. You may or may not be aware that a Battalion Commander has not yet been named. I am responsible to begin our training. How many combat veterans do I have here?" The room became very quiet. Only one hand raised in the rear.

"Please stand up."

Alonzo Blanco stood. The rest of the group turned to look. Frank smiled. "Lieutenant Blanco, welcome aboard, it's good to see you again. Lady and Gentlemen for your information, Lieutenant Blanco has seen combat on three worlds and will soon be promoted to Captain. He is now the CO of our Recon Company. You may sit down Mister Blanco.

"As I call your name please stand for your assignment. Captain Sherington. You have "A" Company."

"Aye-aye, sir"

'Captain Woon, you have "B."

"Aye-aye, sir" replied a petite dark-haired woman.

"Captain Aeneas, "C".

"Roger that, sir."

"Captain Silvanus, Company "D".

"Yes sir"

"Captain Worrall, H and S Company."

"And as I mentioned soon to be Captain Blanco has Recon. That's it lady and gentlemen, my door is always open. Don't hesitate to contact me with a problem. You are dismissed except for Captain Blanco."

When the group left Frank said to Blanco "I'm assigning another old friend to you as one of your platoon sergeants."

"Who sir?"

"Staff Sergeant Timlin."

Alonzo Blanco smiled. "Thank you sir."

Frank was settling into his office when he received a communication from Alicia. "I need to see you Frank."

"Where and when. I still want to inspect that new leg of yours."

That evening Frank knocked on Alicia's door and was greeted with a tight hug and long kiss.

"Wow. What was that for?"

Alicia closed her door. "Just for being you, and because I wanted to kiss the oldest marine in the galaxy."

Frank stepped back and looked into Alicia's eyes. *Shit. Where did that come from? Is she being a wise ass, or does she think she knows something? Careful.* He laughed out loud. "You're such as wise ass. I haven't aged that much in the past six or so months, have I?"

Alicia turned and walked to a table with two glasses and a bottle of wine sitting on it and poured them a drink. She handed one to Frank clicked her glass to his and when they had taken a sip replied. "No Frank you haven't aged in the past six months, or in the past six hundred years have you."

Frank sett his wine glass on the table. "Are you losing your mind? I just want to look at that new leg of yours." They smiled at each other. She took his hand and walked him to a small couch. "Sit with me Frank, I need to talk to you."

If you don't talk about my history. "I always like talking to you. Hopefully you're done with the jokes." Alicia stood and pulled down the leisure pants she was wearing and spun around. "See. I don't even have scars."

"Pull um back up before I forget I'm a gentleman." Alicia laughed out loud and retrieved her wine glass. She took another sip. "Frank, I have been assigned back to intelligence. I have been authorized to tell you I am in Gee One Ultra."

Frank was confused. "Never heard of such a thing, what is it."

"Among other things, it is the unit keeping watch on you and your secret time travel."

"I have no idea what yer talking about. But my advice is stop taking about crazy things before ya get in trouble."

Alicia reached over and patted his shoulder. "Call Major Brown and report me." He gave her a long and penetrating stare then communicated with Major Brown. Before he could say anything Major Brown asked, "Farrell do you happen to be with Major Macalduie?

What the fuck is this? "How'd ya guess?"

"Listen Farrell, she is Gee one Ultra and that means she knows about you the same as some others do. Feel free to discuss anything you wish with her. It may do you some good. Do you need anything else?"

"No, I do not." Frank looked at her and rubbed his nose in a thoughtful manner. "Well . . . now ya know."

She nodded. "And now I understand many things." She got the wine bottle and refilled their glasses. "Frank, would you tell me a little about that time and what your life was like." He took a large gulp of his wine and shook his glass for her to top it off.

"Back in boot training when we were paired, I told you I was a returnee. That was true. I'd been a marine for six years and a combat veteran then. After my discharge I went into law enforcement and spent thirty-five years at it until I was caught in Doctor Lamont's experiment and somehow ended up here."

"How can that be? You're my age."

Frank shook his head. "I was fifty-eight when I arrived here. But the trip, along with being put into a med tube on my arrival, somehow made me eighteen again. They still don't know how or why. I don't know if it was General Thomas or god that made the decision to make me a returnee and give some awards from back then."

Alicia finished her wine in a long gulp. "It is unbelievable. How have you been able to cope?"

Frank shrugged. "Now tell me why you were so anxious to bring this up." She filled their wine glasses again. "They said it may help if you had someone to talk to about it."

He nodded. "Yer right. I have let it emotionally slip out several times since I got here. The first two were almost immediately after I arrived, and were good in as much as it forced me to confront my situation and realize I was never going to get back. I realized it would be devastating to my family and myself by what could result from it."

"But Frank, your family would support you and adjust, don't you think?"

He shrugged. "It not them so much. It would be the government of the time. They'd milk me dry and I'd never see the light of day again. The last time was after the first major attack on the Sunset Perimeter. Wow, it feels like a thousand years ago, doesn't it? At any rate for some reason my XO at the time had it in for me and during a patrol deep in DM territory he ordered that my team and I be sent out alone for a while. So, I thought fuck him, he wants to get me killed and the team and I found a nice hill and sat on it for a while. It was a peaceful, almost serene place and I became too introspective and had a break down. Luckily no one saw it, and if they did never mention it.

"That was the patrol where I killed the first DM War Beast, and it was where Fergie was killed, and I was seriously wounded then took over the squad survivors. It was also the time that Ram came across the body of the Nuke officer we had killed and gathered enough intel that the perimeter had some warning they were going to nuke us."

Alicia nodded to herself, and mumbled "I remember my intel unit at the time was amazed by both incidents." She took a gulp of wine and poured herself another. "Do you still miss them Frank?"

"Who? Fergie and Ram, th . . .."

Alicia interrupted him, "No Frank! Do you still miss your wife and family from the past?

Only every day. "Just in the way you remember loved one's dead and gone for a long time. Now how are you doing with that acerbic Father of yours?"

Alicia sighed. "They are busy trying to rebuild their lives from the devastation, and they no longer blame me or the military. My father is already suggesting I return to academia when my tour is up."

"And?"

"And I still gotta a war to fight. I can't make any long-term plans yet. But, It's not outta the equation." He leaned over and kissed her. "It makes me Horney when you use an Earth accent." They made love; and at some point, he really did check out her new leg; from all angles.

SIX MONTHS LATER . . .

Frank was still the acting CO of One-Five. During the past six months two lieutenant colonels had been named for the command, but the needs of the Corps took them both into the ongoing mop up operations in the Refuge system. While he was left frustrated in the rear; even though he knew he still had several months before he could actively participate in combat again. So he rigorously trained the battalion as if they *were* in combat.

One afternoon, after a strenuous field problem of attacking a tunnel complex he asked Sergeant Major Kim Young, "What do you think?" Kim Young sat chewing on a long grass stalk and looked up at Frank. "They are as good as any battalion in the line sir."

Frank smiled and nodded. "Hopefully when we finally get a CO we can keep it will be easy for him or her."

Kim Young nodded." No problem their boss." Frank was going to reply to him when he received a communication. "Major Farrell, report to division headquarters at thirteen hours local."

The sergeant major gave him an inquiring look. "Looks like someone overheard us Sergeant Major. I have to be at Division in an hour. Could be our new boss."

"We will see, sir."

Frank reported at 1300 on the dot, and was taken into the general's office. "Sit down Major. How is the training progressing?" the general asked.

Frank gave him an overview of what he was trying to achieve for whenever the battalion was called to active service. He finished with "The sergeant major and I feel we have a good unit, ready for the CO when he or she arrives."

The general nodded. "I agree with that assessment. Major, you have made an outstanding unit. When we first met, and it feels like ancient times now, you were a Colonel of Police that I scoffed at."

Where is this going? "I remember sir." When he was first brought to this century by Dr. Lamont's experiment, he was a Chief of Operations in a large metropolitan police department. But due to the transformations caused by the nanobots involved in that singularity he emerged as an eighteen-year-old in large clothing.

"Now it is my pleasure to promote you to Lieutenant-colonel, and give you command of the First Battalion Fifth Marines."

Holy shit! Frank was stunned and could only manage a "Thank you sir. I will do my best."

"I have no doubt of that. Is there anyone you would like as your executive officer?"

"Captain Olney, if it is possible sir. He's a company commander in the Third MarDiv."

"Give me a moment Colonel" the general left the room. He

returned five minutes later and sat down. "I spoke to Headquarters Marine Corps. Captain Olney will be promoted to Major, and report as your battalion XO in a few days.

MONTHS LATER:

Frank looked up when Major Olney walked into his office and said, "We received a few new lieutenants today."

"Okay, have the Sergeant Major put um where we need um." Major Olney hesitated for a moment. "There is one you may wish to interview. He petitioned Headquarters Marine Corps for this battalion and they granted it."

Frank sat back in his chair puzzled. "Why? Who is he?"

"Do you remember the name Ram Rana?"

"Of course I do!" Back in the early days of the invasion on Sunset Senior Private Ram Rana from the Planet of New India was one of the two original members of then Corporal Farrell's sniper squad who when Frank was promoted to sergeant and made a squad leader became a corporal and his first team leader, as well as his best friend.

On the day that Delta-Mike was finally driven from Planet Sunset with the destruction of their entire 5th Great Pack of Eighteen-thousand troops, Ram was shot and killed by one of the surviving DMs. A loss Frank never really got over.

"Did you know he had an identical twin brother?"

"No shit? What's his name?

"Lieutenant Ron Rana."

"Is he asking for special consideration?"

Major Olney shook his head. "He just wanted to be assigned to your battalion. I had a rather long conversation with him. I was surprised by how much Ram had communicated to him about our squad and what we were doing. He knew about me, you, Fergie and most of our Ops. He said his brother's stories made him apply for a marine commission and it seems that he has a lot of political clout on New India. The commandant did him a favor."

Frank grimaced in disgust. "Shit! Just what we don't need is a politician in the battalion." Olney shook his head again. "Sir, I interviewed him closely. I believe he is sincere. I think we should wait and see.

Frank sat for a moment in thought. "Okay. Where do we need him?"

"C" Company needs a platoon commander."

Frank nodded. "Notify Captain Aeneas but don't tell him about a past history. I want him to judge the lieutenant with an un-biased mind. Now, how is our training progress?

UWS Whisper, found the DM space-station by following a group escaping from the mop-up in Refuge system. It was an enormous wheel shaped multi-level, deep-space fortress, dock, and habitat comprising five levels, like a layer cake, surrounding a central hub. Each level had four wide passages, or spokes, crossing the central hub to the outer hull for each level of the station. Viewed from top down it resembled a cross inside of a circle. The space docks on each ring lined up on all connecting spokes of the station that maintained a constant one gravity of spin in each ring. The *Whisper* sent images to god as it went around the entire station as close as they dared, amazed at how immense it was close up.

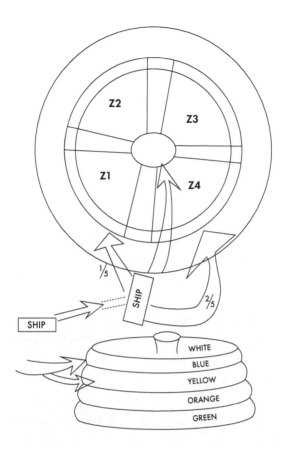

"What do you think of this station gentlemen." The captain asked the, XO, and Senior Chief standing with him.

"I would not like to tangle with that fucking thing," muttered the Senior Chief. The captain and XO both nodded. "Well, we found it." the captain said. "According to intel, the mouth of the tunnel to Andromeda should be in this quadrant too. Close by I wager. Let us go back toward the Refuge system before they discover us, and wait to see what Fleet wants to do. I have an idea I would like to propose."

Five weeks later: Frank and Olney sat with other battalion and regimental officers of the Second Marine Division waiting with anticipation for the briefing to begin. The first they attended together since being taken out of combat the year before. Although the rumor was that ultra-high-level meetings elsewhere had been underway for several days. "What do you think?" Major Olney asked Frank.

"Same as you. I think were goin back into the shit."

Olney nodded. "The battalion is in fine shape. The troops are eager, maybe it will be some mopping up. That would be a good tune-up for us. They are still finding stray DMs on three of the Refuge System worlds, especially Diamond." Frank listened absent- mindedly.

"Attention ladies and gentlemen!" called an army Brigadier General, as General Hayduf Commander and Chief of all human forces entered the hall. "As you were!" General Hayduf said walking to the front.

Frank nudged Olney and whispered, "This feels like more than a mop up operation if it brings him out." Olney nodded with a thoughtful look.

General Hayduf opened: "Since the beginning of May the stealth ships UWS *Whisper*, and *Echo* have followed and monitored Delta-Mike to what, they report, is a gigantic space-station found by *Whisper*. Ostensibly it is guarding their bridgehead back to Andromeda; and it is where all their surviving troops from our battles are waiting for reinforcement or transport to their home worlds. However, each of the ships has reported only minor troop increase that the captain of *Echo* described as a trickle. As a result, the Captain of *Whisper* requested, and was granted, permission to transit the bridge to Andromeda when the next DM ships went outbound from their location.

"The *Whisper* successfully followed an outbound convoy to Andromeda and after an extremely harrowing and dangerous month in Delta-Mike's home system has returned with quite a bit of important intelligence. All gathered in real-time using information seized from prisoners taken over the past year along with what they culled in

Andromeda itself. I want to congratulate Captain Sun Kee of *Whisper*, who has been awarded the Galactic Starburst for his exploit and bravery. Each of his crewmembers have received the Galactic Cross in Gold for being the first humans to have operated in another galaxy.

"Now the critical points for us are, first: There is another Space Station on the Andromeda side very close, only one point five light minutes, from the horizon of the tunnel. For our purposes, any further reference made to a space station is describing the one on our side of the tunnel, not on theirs.

Presently, only three understrength Great Packs, that together do not equal a full-strength one, are on the Space station. Estimates are between eleven to fourteen thousand troops in total, but that is still a lot of fighting troops. They are the survivors of the First, Third, and Sixth GPs. The Third GP is probably in the worst condition of the three, only equaling slightly more than one Attack Group. Their new GP Commander is our former prisoner, Attack Group Commander Woflazgl. That is a benefit to us since we know him.

"The *Whisper's* intelligence, shows that the Second GP was sent home as combat ineffective, and the Fourth and Fifth GPs were annihilated. Furthermore, communications they heard indicate that no major troop replacements are planned for the Space Station in the foreseeable future."

General Hayduf was grim as he looked around. "Because of this intelligence, and before the DM buildup continues, plans are being made for an attack on that Fortress/space-station as soon as practicable. We will begin planning here the day after tomorrow. All of you, and your number twos, be ready to discuss the problem then."

This one will be a-son-of- a-bitch Frank leaned over to Major Olney "Now we know." Olney nodded.

"As a point of information, we are also beginning to fortify the entire Refuge system and constructing our own early warning space station one half AU Spinward-coreward of that system as a bulwark against another incursion by Delta-mike."

"This definitely has the potential to be a son of a bitch." Frank said to Olney on the trip back to the battalion area. "Notify all company commanders, their XOs and the Sergeant Major that there will be a command meeting at 1300 local time tomorrow at battalion."

"Aye-aye sir."

The Deputy Commander in Chief of human forces, Army General Gimpsie stood with the Marine Commandant, General Thomas, who began the planning session of the Second Marine Division's company commanders and above.

"Good morning ladies and gentlemen. I just have a few housekeeping comments to begin this session. Several major command changes have been made in this division that are effective immediately. General Sing ,is promoted to Major General and now commands the Second Marine Division. Colonel Lamb, is promoted to Brigadier General and is now Second Brigade Commander. Congratulations gentlemen."

The room was filled with applause and congratulations.

General Thomas held his arms up for quiet then asked General Gimpsie, "Do you have anything before I begin, sir?" Gimpsie shook his head.

"Now to business. First: the initial landing and assault of our target will be a marine operation. Since the First Marine Division bore the brunt of Operation Strong Door on Pleasant, they will not participate in this undertaking other than as a rear reserve force. The Second Division, led by the First Marine Brigade's Fifth Marines are tasked with the initial assault on the DM station. The Sixth Marines along with the Seventh, and Eighth Marines are in what we consider a second wave, although they will in fact attack almost simultaneously.

"Secondly, on the trip out to replace *Whisper*, the *Echo* discovered that after the DM forces withdrew to their station, they deployed deep space sensors out one AU from the station as an early warning of any approach. The *Echo* was able to obtain and study one of these and discovered, surprising as it seems, they are not shielded in any manner, nor are they smart. As a result of that information, we have begun to seed our attack route all the way to the Station with a number of small sleeping missiles that, when awakened, will each produce an EMP to simultaneously knock out all of these unshielded sensors up to one light second around us. If we are lucky they may damage some on the station as well. But we are sure they are heavily shielded. I will discuss that later.

"The Third Marine Division, along with the Army's First and Second Infantry Divisions will be the active in-theater reserves if needed. Finally, most of you probable do not know that during course of the space battles above *Planet Refuge* during Operation *Black Beach*, the navy boarded and captured a huge troop ship used to transport part of a Great Pack and its equipment. We intend to use it in our attack on the Space Station in an Operation named *Trojan Horse*. You can access your chips to understand the historical context of that name when you have a chance. Added to that fact is we are familiar with a ranking Pack Leader on the station, it gives us an excellent chance to quickly achieve our mission."

General Thomas paused and looked at General Rahm. "General, your brigade will lead the landing and initial assault on the space station. Please have a plan of action ready to present for review in two weeks."

"Aye-aye sir."

Uh oh. I don't like the name of this operation. I can see where it's going. The thought no sooner passed through Franks head than received a communication from General Rahm. "Colonel Farrell you, Colonel Fromk, Colonel Blak and Colonel Tzu meet me at brigade headquarters after the meeting. You gentlemen are the tip of the spear on this operation." Frank was thoughtful as the briefing continued.

General Gimpsie took over and said: "Operation Trojan Horse." The top-down view from above of the massive space station with identifying names attached appeared behind their eyes. Next to that was the side view of the five rings of the station resembling a layer cake. Each ring had its own landing dock that began to flash clearly marking its location.

"Major Macalduie from intelligence will give the next part of this briefing." General Gimpsie said stepping aside. Frank was surprised he hadn't noticed Alicia when he came into the room. Nor had she mentioned her participation. He was further surprised that she was briefing more than just intelligence matters.

Alicia highlight the first view." I want you to examine our target. A fundamental part of this plan is we know for fact the DMs are demoralized because of their losses. The rank and file refer to the Milky Way as Galaxy of Death. They know they are not getting reinforced or replaced in the foreseeable future. It could make the difference for us in how they resist."

The top-down view of the space station glowed slightly brighter highlighting the cross of even arms with a large central hub. The other ends of the cross arms were attached to the circular inner hull of the space station continuing through the ring to the outer hull, like a wheel with four spokes, ending at a ship docking station where there was equipment for unloading. The inner hub was marked *Main core* and glowed a light red.

"For ease of coordination between us and you commanders, the outer hull ring area between each spoke of the wheel at the landing bay and dock area are our designated attack landing zones Each is marked in a clockwise direction, from the left lower area at Z-One around to Z-Four. During the fighting each of the five rings will be treated as individual landing zones.

"The circumference of the station rings is one mile each." She was interrupted with a buzz of comments and conversation. "Please give me your attention ladies and gentlemen, it gets better, and your questions will be answered. Now to continue, each ring is one hundred feet high.

When the hall quieted, she continued. "Colonel Farrell's One-Five with Colonel Fromk's Two-Five, Colonel Blak's Three-Five, and Colonel Tzu's Four-Five, will be the first wave of the landing attacking from our Trojan Horse. We hope to get One and two-five inside the dock between Zebra -one and Zebra -four unchallenged. Followed by the rest of the First brigade as soon as the landing zone is secured. If we are challenged on the approach, our Trojan horse will declare an emergency due to battle damage, then execute a slow, controlled, minor crash into the docking area, and land our troops in the confusion.

"At this time, I am authorized to tell you we are literally inside the head of Great Pack Leader Woflazgl. So we know our layer cake is divided thus: The top ring with the Fifth Marines is White Zone." It took on a pale off white color. "Under ten minutes after the Fifth Marines and Recon make their landing the rest of the division should be able to attack their targets from large landing craft simultaneously attacking through the docking area on each of the other rings.

"The top ring White Zone, is docks, missile bays, command spaces, and VIP area. Think of it as officer country. Ring two is Blue Zone," the ring became pale blue, "It has the troop spaces and training areas. We expect Blue Z to initially be some of the hardest fighting. It will be the responsibility of the Eighth Marine Regiment that will land through the landing dock of that ring at Blue Z-One. Depending on conditions in white zone, One-Five and Two- Five Marines moving down from there will support them. The third ring, Yellow Zone," that began glowing pale yellow" is civilian living spaces and government offices and will be handled by One and Two-Eleven. One-Eleven will attack and secure Yellow Z-One and Z- Two, to the left. Two– Eleven has Yellow Z Three and Four and will attack to the right.

"Ring four, Orange Zone now glowing: is stores, entertainment, recreation supply, and ammunition magazines is One and Two-Six. One-six to the left; Two- six right. .Finally, Green Zone: the bottom ring holds maintenance and support and the task of Three-Six and the Engineers. The engineers can determine what are the priority areas when they arrive at Green Z-One.

Alicia paused and looked around the hall with a smile. "I'm sure you're asking yourselves how we expect to get close enough to the station to do any of this. Fortunately, small groups of DM survivors continually limp in from the *Refuge system*. So we will let them see our captured ship coming. We hope to catch them anticipating the arrival of more of their troops. Remember, they don't know that we know the location of this station, and bridgehead.

Alicia turned to General Gimpsie. "Sir."

"Thank you Major, that was an excellent presentation."

The General looked over his audience. "As soon as the Trojan Horse is in proximity of the station, Lieutenant Commander Dubni from naval ordinance that some of you may remember from our invasion of Refuge through the mines; will wake the sleeping EMP's. Then we will begin the landing with Recon dropping on top of the station CIC located on the top of the station hub at White Zone. They will capture and hold it until Zodiac White-One thru Zodiac White-Four are secured by the first wave.

"At the same time, the rest of the Second Division will come from their holding location slightly more than one AU-astronomical unit-out and land the actual second wave of the Army's Second Infantry Division and attachments.

"Colonel Farrell's One-Five will secure all of Zodiac-White One and Two along with their ship docks and anything else in that half of White Zone. Then will move clockwise to link up with Colonel Fromk's Two-Five." All of the other battalion commanders received similar detailed instructions that covered the entire area of responsibility.

"With their CIC gone, it should degrade their resistance somewhat. At that point Recon will break up and do their thing looking for troops or other hazards throughout the entire space station. I believe that is critical since the fighting in this station has potential to be five miles of contact time reminiscent of the underground fighting on Refuge; and we all remember what that was like. Approach this as attacking a fortified mountain *full* of tunnels. Because of that consideration and the size of our target the Third Marine Division had been taken from reserve to become a third wave of the attack and a regiment from that division will follow into each ring for additional support."

His comment caused some murmuring around the room so he paused and looked around.

"I know. That is Thirty-six battalions of infantry committed to this attack. Are there questions anyone? None. Then everyone study the second hologram of our cake." It began to glow with a description of each rings purpose.

"According to god, we know Great Pack Leader Woflazgl's Third GP has less than three thousand combat troops. As a result, they have been relegated to guard and police duties around the station with a slightly heavier presence, perhaps one or two platoons at Orange Zone with the ammunition magazines until they are reconstituted. The Sixth GP is somewhat better off with roughly six thousand combat troops. They lost two thirds of their GP in New Glasgow. The First GP is in the best condition with slightly more than eight thousand combatants giving a combined strength of about one full strength Great Pack; But remember they could be spread out as small units throughout the station. The Eighth and Fifth Marines should be prepared to meet those two units at Blue Zone.

"As One and Two-Five secure White Zone they will move down the main core and attack Blue Zone where we expect the most resistance; they will reinforce the Eighth Marines."

Alicia nodded to the generals and stepped back. General Rahm said "That ladies and gentlemen is the broad outline. I want the Battalion and Regimentals CO's and XO's with your Sergeants Major and your input on this plan for your part of this invasion for a meeting in seven days.

Frank left the hall deep in thought *This could be a bitch.*

As he and Major Olney walked along, he said, "I'm thinking of those tunnels on Refuge. I'd like to talk to an engineer about clearing charges in a space station environment."

Major Olney nodded, "I agree. Do you suppose the DMs have any type of reaction force or drills that could give us trouble? Maybe Major Macalduie has an answer."

"Good thinking I'll ask." Frank replied.

He communicated with Alicia who answered with a crisp, "Major Macalduie."

"Alicia it's me. Nice presentation. Now that we know we could be in the shit; can you share any of the intel you are harvesting from that GP Leader? I have a few questions for you that will help my planning."

"Like what?"

"Like what units could be at White Zone as we begin the attack? Will the Sixth and Second GP's likely be together at Blue Zone when we attack? Has anyone planned to sow mines at the mouth of their tunnel to help defeat any counter attacks? Has Delta-Mike laid mines around the station like they did in the *Refuge System?*

"Let me check on those things Frank, I'll have some kind of answer in a day or so. Talk ta ya soon." She ended the transmission. *I love it when she uses an Earth accent.*

"What is the word?" Olney asked as they got into their vehicle to go back to the Battalion area" She's going to have something for us in a day or so, but let's get our people planning as if Delta-Mike is going to do everything we are worried about.

Frank thought for a moment. "Do you remember Lieutenant Yaxley, the engineer that helped clearing the tunnels at *Black Beac*h on Planet Refuge?"

Olney nodded."Why?"

"I'll let you know in a minute." Frank communicated with Captain Yaxley now the CO of an Engineer Company in the Third Marine Division.

"Captain Yaxley," came the voice Frank remembered.

"Captain Yaxley, Colonel Farrell here. How is my favorite problem-solving engineer these days, and congratulations on captain.

Yaxley chuckled. "I am doing well here, as a matter of fact I have been frocked to major."

"Congrats again! Frank said, "any idea of your assignment?"

"Not yet," How can I help you, sir?

"Are you aware of the upcoming operation as we follow Delta-Mile?"

"Yes sir. Third Division is a reserve force for the Second Division attack on a Space Station. But has been re tasked as the third wave."

"In case you did not know, I am in the Second Division as the Battalion Commander of One-Five. Our information is this could be like the fighting in the tunnels on *Refuge*. The difference here is, I need something that will not open us to vacuum when we use it. I suppose we need something like a satchel charge that does not have any shrapnel, only explosive overpressure. Would you object to coming over to One-Five for a few days to help us with the planning if you have the time?"

"Not at all, sir, if you can arrange it, I'll be there."

"That's outstanding," Frank said, "but I've just had another thought, Will you bring one of your Bats that worked so well last time."

"Aye, aye, sir"

"Captain Yaxley is a good man," Frank said to Olney., "Between him, Major Macalduie, and our team we should come up with a good plan."

CHAPTER 18

Since his arrival at the space station, SPL Glgoffen had been communicating with the government of the Andromeda Pack Unification attempting to get reinforcements to continue the battle against the humans. To his disgust, since the DNA revelations became common knowledge humans were now labeled *The Cousins* by the civilian government.

He and security chief Herschel, sat in his office drinking an alcoholic beverage after a busy afternoon. Herschel took a deep drink then complained: "I have been fighting Hoomans for over two years. Now they call them *cousins*, where does it end? Their attitude would change after one engagement with them!"

"I think the more important question is what does it mean for us," Glgoffen said. "I should tell you that I was told by the civil authority that no more troops will come here until the issue of the humans is unambiguous with everyone."

Herschel scoffed. "If they knew them as we do they would have no problem!" He took another swallow of his drink.

SPL Glgoffen nodded. "I agree. I am leaving for the First World the day after tomorrow to argue my case to keep fighting these. . . cousins. I will also have to defend my actions in this galaxy. You and I both know that whatever we or the council call them, if possible, the humans will follow to attack us at home."

Herschel nodded with a wry expression. "Is there anything I can do to help?"

SPL Glgoffen sighed and shook his head. "I am greatly disturbed by the loss of so much of my force here. I face an inquisition when I arrive on First World." It was the original world the Neanderthals were placed when they arrived from *Earth* and still serves as the de facto primary world in the Andromeda Pack Unification.

DM HEADQUARTERS AT ANDROMEDA BRIDGEHEAD STATION FIVE MONTHS EARLIER. . .

Supreme Pack Leader Glgoffen sat with ten of his most senior leaders and two civilians who were out of place in the group. He glanced at his Intelligence chief Herschel for a fleeting moment then said, "Packmates. I have information it is time to share with you to get your opinions. Our two guests are Scholar Immal and Senior researcher Ganglez.

He nodded to Wolflazgl. "Our Third Great Pack Leader is to be congratulated for bringing this intelligence to our attention. Now it is up to the military council, and civil government, to decide what, if anything, to do about it.

"Supreme Leader, what have these scholars to do with our operations?" asked the First Great Pack Leader who was the senior Leader.

SPL Glgoffen looked around. "I notice my comments have confused you so we will discuss what I know. I have been alerted by Researcher Ganglez that at some future date I will be summoned to the Counsel of Packs to discuss this matter with them before any further action can be taken in our endeavors against the hoo-mans."

He motioned to Intelligence Chief Herschel who stood and addressed the group. "Pack mates. The information I will give you has been checked, re-checked, and is verified. The Hoo-mans all have roughly three percent of our DNA."

"How can that be possible!" blurted the First Great Pack Leader.

Herschel glanced at Glgoffen who nodded to continue. "Pack mates, to understand we must go back into the mists of time and tradition. I believe Scholar Immal is more qualified that I to address this." Herschel motioned to Immal and sat down.

Scholar Immal was especially uncomfortable in the company of warriors, and stood quietly for a long moment. "Warriors of the pack; those of you who know history and our belief traditions will remember that our species was brought here by superior beings, or deities, whatever fits your belief system. We came from a freezing land of large beasts and were moved from that world of ice before we disappeared, overtaken by other aggressive beings we lived with for millennia. That was roughly forty-five thousand years ago, and now we know those others we existed and competed with were the humans.

"We do not know who our saviors were. Only that they settled us on *First World* in our galaxy, taught us basic science, and left. Over time the Pack settled other worlds to begin our unification until we became what we are today.

"It is now beyond debate that our world of origin, called *Earth* by the Humans, is also their home world. You should know that each of us, including you warriors, probably have at least three percent of their DNA as well. They were our old neighbors that, for whatever reasons, were left behind when we were moved. We know from oral traditions we were competing with them for the best locations and hunting grounds and they were becoming the dominate group."

Eight of the ten senior Pack leaders began speaking at once causing SPL Glgoffen to stand and raise his hand silencing them. When calm returned, he said, "I know. I had the same response. But because of this information, the Counsel of Packs has stopped any further increase of warriors to this station. They will rebuild the Fourth, Fifth and Second GPs on their home worlds. The First, Sixth and Third GPs will be re-formed here when we get more troops.

"Until I am called, we will continue to train and reform the units to our best. GP Commander Woflazgl, you have a daunting first command combining and motivating the survivors of your attack groups. They distinguished themselves in the recent fighting on several worlds in route here from the Planet of Sunset. Unfortunately they are now combat ineffective from losses.

"Packmates, I hope to learn more whenever I go to the home worlds."

Frank sat alone in is quarters, drinking his second beer while pondering the six different Delta-Mike world flags decorating his walls; along with two of their helmets, one Army and one Naval, and his assortment of over two dozen smaller unit insignia. All ripped off uniforms from the bodies of DM killed by him and his men as souvenirs; during nearly two years of active combat.

His new awareness that the flags, and unit insignias, represented only a small expeditionary detachment assigned as a token force kept him awake some nights. *Okay we are beating them, and they are running. But our troops from a hundred different worlds are still a very small military.* He took a large swallow of beer and let his eyes roam over the six flag each twenty inches square meant to be carried by individual soldiers. *Shit their unit attack flags are four feet square. You can see um coming from a long way off and I'm looking at six separate world flags. I wonder if anyone knows how many planetary armies we could end up fighting, or the size those armies?*

He finished his beer in several swallows. *I can't be the only one worrying about this shit. Can I?* He heard a knock at his door interrupting his brooding and found Alicia standing there with a smile. She had a large bottle of wine that she waved back and forth in front of him. When he stepped aside to let her in she noticed his empty beer bottles, and chair facing the flags and other emblems on the wall as soon as she entered. She looked at Frank for a long moment.

"Are we worried about something?"

"I'm worried you won't get the wine open soon so I can check out that sore leg of yours."

She laughed out loud. "I'm happy to see yur old-self again. After we have some wine ya can tell me all yur problems." It was his turn to laugh out loud, then he kissed her deeply and they worked their way to the bed room and made love. An hour later he asked," Do you secret intel types have any idea how many DMs we could potentially end up facing?"

Alicia put her arms behind her head and looked at the ceiling. "Since I've been given clearance to talk to you about your status, I don't see why I can't tell you."

He sat up facing her, so she sat up and got comfortable. "Frank when I captured that Attack Group leader, that is the same as a regimental commander, god ordered a military grade chip put into him so we could mine as much information as possible without his knowledge. It has been sifted through and for your question I remind you this information, for right now, in the same category as yours."

Frank nodded. "Got it."

"As you know, each great pack is roughly the equivalent of a Division. That group leader's memories indicate there are thirty-eight independent worlds in Andromeda populated by what we first called Dogmen, but now know to be descendants of *Earth's* Neanderthals. The important thing to remember is only ten of their worlds have fully militarize.

"When they decided to invade our galaxy each one of those ten worlds was invited, not ordered, to send at least one Great Pack for the expedition; but only six worlds agreed to help. Each of those worlds is represented in your wall collection.

"We were invaded by a small number of troops from only six worlds donated to their confederate government for the Milky-way endeavor. Apparently, they considered it a joint training exercise they believed would be another quick walk-over for them. I want ya to remember, they've never experienced anything like the *Earth* wars to decimate their populations.

"Even in what they call their wars of unification never came close to a genocide like our Final World War did. As you are aware, even after six hundred years we are still recovering from it. Also, in their history they never experienced an event like the Black Death Plague of Earth's Medieval history that was another huge loss of population for us, as you more than most of us, are aware. Frank, they have billions of inhabitants on each of those ten militarized worlds; and conceivably hundreds of billions on all thirty-eight of them.

"Several of those ten worlds, certainly not all of them, have the ability with conscription to field up to three hundred great packs. But they have never had to do that. For our purposes they probably have the equivalent of six to twenty Great Packs per planet depending on their population etc. With a combined military might that could be in the millions if not tens of millions. If they decide to militarize their entire thirty-eight planet society . . . you do the math.

"Apparently, they did not expect significant resistance much less face to face combat that shocked them; but it has been a substantial advantage for us. Things will be different as this war continues. So, our high command and civil authority along with god have to very carefully consider any future response by us beyond the capture or destruction of that space station on our side of their bridge to the Andromeda galaxy.

"We are very fortunate to literally have god on our side in this since we are in the head of the Third GP commander." As a result, we know they are not being reinforced on the space station, and his Third GP was badly mauled in the fighting and is considered combat ineffective. He is upset they are being used for odd jobs and police functions on the space station. The First and Sixth GPs are also on the station and understrength from the fighting. The remaining three GPs were annihilated and are in their home worlds to recruit and rebuild. We also know that the Primary commander of the army that invaded us is a ruthless warrior named Glgoffen. He is being recalled to justify his losses here, and things could be much worse for us than they are Frank," she said with an uneasy look.

He felt a chill. "Fuck me," he muttered, "if six Great Packs were only a landing force, we may well have to play very rough, and dirty, in the future." *Or we could be properly fucked.*

Alicia looked at him strangely for a moment then smiled. "Wanna check my leg again?

ON FIRST WORLD.

SPL Glgoffen entered the chamber *Will I survive this tribunal? I doubt it after the destruction of my force.* He marched across its highly polished stone floor accompanied by Senior researcher Ganglez and Scholar Immal with their aids. At times he glancing up at the vaulted ceiling ten meters above their heads that held an echo of their footsteps, as the group approached the representatives of the military counsel, and civil governments, of the Confederation in the large private meeting room inside the capital building of the Confederation of Worlds. The room had a number of balconies along the walls resembling an opera house or large theater for use when open public events were planned. This meeting was closed to the public.

The thirty-eight-member council representing each of their worlds sat on a raised U-shaped dais. They watched the group approach to a long table and chairs facing them inside the front of the dais.

"You may sit," said the leader of the Confederation, his voice echoing as everyone watched Glgoffen and his little group get settled before he began. "The purposes of this tribunal: first, is to understand the near total destruction of an Expeditionary Force of ours driven from another galaxy by warriors of that galaxy; a situation unique in history. And secondly, the consequences, if any, of that defeat and what we have learned from this adversary some refer to as *the Cousins.* "Finally, what blame, if any, you may personally hold in this situation.

"So, Expedition Supreme Leader Glgoffen," he made it sound like an accusation, "as leader of that endeavor please explain the destruction of most of your Force causing such grief on six of our worlds."

Glgoffen felt the need to relieve himself but took a moment to compose and order his thoughts, then began in a clear voice: "Esteemed leaders of the confederation. I commanded the Expeditionary Force sent to the Galaxy known by humans as the *Milky Way.* To see if the world pictured in the probe recovered by one of our surveys in that galaxy was viable for our colonization, since the representations of beings living there seemed much like us. You also know my lineage as a war leader who has conquered other worlds and served in our final wars of unification."

He nodded to one of the aids who created a large holographic simulation of the Milky Way Galaxy then isolated a box showing the *Refuge System* outside of the Galaxy, along with the *Planets Sunset* and *Pleasant* positioned on edge of the outer arm, with *Planet NX246.* situated between the two groups.

"Esteemed leaders, this is the seven-planet area of battle with the humans that I will discuss and present my concerns as well." The holographic view changed to the entire Milky Way. "As you see they are not even a noticeable spec in that galaxy; but for our purpose they now command a major role." The view changed back to the battle expanse.

"At the beginning of our expedition, after coming out of the tunnel at our space station we stopped for a while before continuing toward the galaxy proper. Then we continued and discovered four habitable worlds where we stopped to train for several months on the largest of them that I named *Warbeast,* after my command ship.

"I would note that human prisoners stated they refer to that world as *Planet Refuge,* and the other three planets in that system as *Planets*

Ruby, Emerald and *Diamond*. The entire system is known, by them, as the Refuge System. As a point of information, humans give a name to all their settled worlds, and a numeric designation to any in a pre-colonization state." There was no evidence of humans or any other advance life forms ever living on these worlds when we arrived.

A green line appeared from *Refuge* to *Planet Sunset*.

"As you see, I continued from *Warbeast* to the *Planet Sunset*. It is a settled world that our intelligence indicated had very few warriors and we landed to set up a number of camps. That Planet, became our first area of conflict with the humans. Our second contact was *Planet Pleasant*; where a small Reconnaissance Pack reported notable research and studies centers inside a city named New Glasgow. That reconnaissance group disappeared, apparently destroyed to the last warrior, a fact unknown until later in the battle.

"Before continuing esteemed members, since now we all know we are of the same genetic makeup, and share some DNA with humans, I need not dwell on it; I will ask Scholar Immal to address this." He nodded to Immal.

Scholar Immal stood and bowed deeply to the tribunal. "Esteemed members. Following your instructions to have a complete study of our relationship with what some call the cousins. I have collected the following information. Roughly fifty thousand years ago, our ances-tors lived on *Planet Earth* along with the human species for close to a million years. It was a land of ice-cold glaciers and large beasts. Back in that dim history before we were brought here, we apparently lived near the humans, and at times even mated with them, or, we or they became impregnated by force. The current amount of DNA in both of our genes was caused by very few contacts but, the fact remains, we did have a close social and sexual interaction with the humans in our history.

"From very early oral traditions passed down before being written down after coming here, we know the humans were an inquisitive, aggressive, intelligent species that slowly forced us to move. They were masters of ambush, hunting and constantly moving over the next hill to explore. According to traditions the humans became more numerous and we constantly moved to find more animals as the ice grew, while the humans continued to increase and push us further for thousands of years. As the last few groups of our species was in danger of extinction our saviors arrived to move us here. Why the humans were left behind by the saviors is unknown. Perhaps they knew the humans did not need help."

"Thank you, scholar Immal," said the head of the Tribunal who looked at Glgoffen.

"Continue."

"Esteemed Leaders, the scholar's information has been a help in my understanding what happened to us. At first, I approached the humans as a passive species that prisoners told us were pacifist's for hundreds of years; and we easily killed them early on. But we re-awakened the hunter warrior spirit that has risen to the fore with vengeance.

"Our first combat on *Sunset* was with a force of a thousand troops that we destroyed to the last in several hours. The fighting was so easy our pack soldiers nicknamed them Hoo-hoo mans that became their identifier at the time." Several council members smiled because they all understood what that insult represented.

"Following that battle they did not disturb us for a long period. I misunderstood that to mean they were afraid of us. I was wrong. They spent that time building a huge fortification surrounding our camps while we had continuous scouting of the progress attempting to determine weakness as it was built; all the primary battles and most of the skirmishing on *Planet Sunset* was around that vicinity.

"Before going on, I will describe their military that has three primary branches. My summary will include their weapons and the different branches of their military and how they travel and fight beginning with the *Knife Soldiers*. They are warriors called marines. They are also their reconnaissance troops, and assault forces, and so far, the most daring of the humans. They are masters of ambush and camouflage, and work closest with their space forces they refer to as the Navy. They are the smallest in numbers but became the most troublesome and merciless in battle."

"They are the only troops not referred to as Hoo-mans by our warriors. The *Knife Soldiers* name began because of the emblem on their uniforms that was our first indication we had found another hunter/warrior species."

Glgoffen nodded to his aid that put up a hologram of the Marine Recon emblem. A human skull with a dagger thru it from top to bottom. "We have killed many of them; but have only captured one alive. He was taken unconscious from a head wound. Even while dazed from his wounds, and in custody during interrogation, he managed to kill my assistant supreme pack leader for intelligence in front of myself and my guards.

"Beside their personal bravery, what makes the humans so formattable in battle is their silent weapons. They give almost no indication they are shooting at you until those around you fall dead. It is a tribute to our warriors that they continued to fight and inflict as many causalities as they do on the humans. We learned the lesson to kill them with artillery when at all possible."

The senior military leader of the ten militarized worlds in the confederation spoke up. "You say almost no indication of being under fire. What gives it away?"

"Esteemed leader, when head on to the enemy a slight vibration in the airs can be observed, but only if a warrior has the helmet face shield down prior to a pack soldier falling dead. There are never any wounded. It was a small unit of these Knife Soldiers that destroyed the Fifth Great Pack."

"How small a unit was able to do that, was it an Attack Group?" asked the senior military member.

"Esteemed leader, our information is about twelve of them."

"Hum. Twelve Attack Groups is a significant number; they could easily overwhelm a Great Pack. How did they manage to get so close to do so?

"Esteemed leader you misunderstand. It was not twelve Attack Groups; it was a group of twelve individual Knife Soldiers."

"How is that even possible!" shouted his questioner echoed by others in the tribunal.

Glgoffen winced.

The leader of the tribunal sitting in the middle of the group banged his hand on the table to restore order. When it was quiet, he said, "Continue."

"Esteemed leader, the destruction of the Fifth Great occurred as we were withdrawing from *Planet Sunset* back toward *Warbeast* that henceforth I will refer to by the human name of *Refuge*.

"This group of Knife soldiers followed the Fifth Great and located the gathering point for lift to the fleet. They called in a massive artillery and rocket strike on them.

"Esteemed members of the tribunal, as we were leaving after the destruction of the Fifth Great, I left a number of small reconnaissance packs on *Sunset to* gather intelligence and harass the humans as they were able. Most were discovered and destroyed; but one group took two young soldiers, a male and female, prisoner and brought them to *Refuge* for interrogation. As the female was dying, she indicated their troops arrived on *Planet Sunset* other than by ship: hinting that it may have been a door or portal of some type. The same prisoners stated they have an entire planet dedicated to the training of their military."

"Based on the prisoner's comment, and on earlier suppositions, my Intelligence chief and I decided that the *Planet Sunset* would have such a travel device if it existed; but would require a major effort and untold causalities to find.

Glgoffen nodded to his aid who put up a different holographic representation from his intelligence files of the City of New Glasgow. "I reasoned that this city on *Planet Pleasant,* a center of study and research, would probably have this travel capability too; and it was a soft target with no large military presents we knew of. But I had lost contact with the Reconnaissance pack I mentioned that had been on that world since we arrived in the Milky Way.

"I realized that since the destruction of the Fifth Great the moral of the fighters was lowering, and I believed that a raid into a soft target like this city could help them recover. At the same time, I sent a demonstration raid to the NX world to draw attention away from *Planet Pleasant*. I chose that world because I lost another special landing team of two hundred fighters there before the loss of the Fifth Great. My intelligence officer reported that upon monitoring human communications it was discovered that the same small unit of Knife Soldiers that were responsible for the Fifth Great also destroyed the entire special landing team on the NX *world*. I admit an element of vengeance in attacking there.

"But what began as a local raid into a soft target to find some type of transportation device became a major meeting battle on *Pleasant* that was never meant to occur. Somehow, the humans anticipated the attack and were prepared."

The tribunal members looked at one another when the senior military member asked in a condescending voice, "Was your army also driven from that world with significant loss Supreme Leader?"

"It was, esteemed member. Their navy is also aggressive and managed to follow us to the *Refuge system* then participated in the heavy fighting there. Their Army has continued the mop up fighting in that system and they garrison and hold all of their conquests. One of my fears is that the humans will follow us again and perhaps find one of our bridges."

The military member of the tribunal sat in thought for a moment. "I agree with Leader Glgoffen that it was important to find the truth of such a device if it existed. His decision in raiding that city was sound."

"Why do you consider it such a real possibility that the humans will follow us?" the Confederation leader asked, "It seems they should be glad to see the end of us."

Glgoffen sat considering the question of his fear of humans following him. He remembered a conversation with his intelligence chief months earlier who believed humans would follow them and attack them at Refuge. *He was correct then and I'm sure it is the same now. The humans will follow us. But then what? Do they even understand what they are up against?*

"Well Pack Leader, what are your thoughts," prodded the senior military member." Glgoffen sat quietly for a moment then said, "Here is why I feel it important to reinforce our Station and tunnel . . ."

Later, the head of the Confederation of Worlds looked around the table for further comments, then said 'Supreme Leader go back to your quarters while we debate your testimony. You will be advised of our decisions on this matter."

THREE DAYS LATER: ANDROMEDA CONFEDERATION OF WORLDS COUNCIL CHAMBER.

The elected leader of the Confederation of the thirty-eight worlds began the meeting. "Esteemed colleague's, my primary concern is what type of threat, if any, do we face from the humans."

An elderly senior member sitting in the middle of a rounded meeting table next to the elected Confederation leader raised his hand. The leader turned and nodded to him. The representative looked around the meeting table. "We took this war to the humans as we have to others in our history. If the expeditions Supreme leader is to be believed, and I see no reason to doubt what he has reported, then for the first time in our history we face an enemy, possibly even an old hereditary enemy, with retribution as a goal. We should consider this a very serious issue.

"I believe that if we do not try to resolve this more peacefully, they *will* try to come here bringing fire, destruction and mayhem. I think we should all give additional consideration to the information the expeditions Supreme Leader gave us that we did not pursue in depth at our hearing. We have had three days to consult with our staffs to consider options. It is my belief we must first decide if we wish to attempt diplomatic relations with them if they were agreeable to such a thing. However, neither do we . . ."

The military command representative broke protocol by slapping his hand on the table top interrupting the speaker. "We cannot be considered weak by asking them to stop!" He said loudly, receiving a glare from the Confederation leader and the senior colleague he interrupted.

The leader knocked on the table top and was going to reprimand him when he noticed *Pack spirits, I think almost half of the table agrees with him. I better wait to see what develops.* The Confederation leader nodded again to his senior member that also looked around at the other representatives of their thirty-eight worlds.

"As I was saying before being interrupted. Neither do we wish to continue a war against a well-trained determined enemy that according to Leader Glgoffen, who himself has a reputation as a fierce resourceful leader, are as ruthless and vindictive as the packs. Do we wish to subject our worlds to war? And let me make a final observation for your consideration. The expedition we sent to their galaxy had a total of one hundred twenty-eight thousand army and naval fighters. We know we have lost ships and crews there but do not have exact number yet. I do know the number of army dead. The army has lost ninety thousand warriors killed in battle. Almost no prisoners have been taken by the humans. The surviving force we have at the first station are the remains of three Great packs that equal in number about one full one."

The Confederation leader looked back to the military member. "What are your thoughts."

The military member had composed himself and responded in a normal tone of voice. "Esteemed colleagues. Suppose we do initiate contact with them to settle the issue, and while we are trying to establish relations thy attack the far bridge station on their side of the tunnel. Do we have war then? Or do we concede that side of the tunnel to them. Where do we draw a line with them?

"The military recommends searching out all the human forces and destroying them as we have done to others. We know all of their worlds are compatible for our use and we should take them. Especially their own home world that is apparently our beginning place. Tomorrow, or the next day, let us call expedition leader Glgoffen back and get his thinking and recommendations on how he would conduct a war if necessary."

CONFEDERATION CONFERENCE THE NEXT DAY.

Glgoffen sat calmly, waiting for the meeting to begin. Last night a supporter of his gave him the agenda of today's meeting and he spent the night planning his defense of the station and the tunnel it guarded.

Everyone stood when the confederation leader entered the room and took his central position. "Please sit." The Confederation leader looked at Glgoffen and said, "We left a number of issues unresolved at our last meeting. At that time, you told us that the humans will find us here and come to this galaxy. Why do you believe that?"

"Esteemed members of the Tribunal, I base my comments on personal experience with the human's past, present and future. In the past we invaded, killed them and used the women we wanted. Their men we sometimes kept as slaves then killed. For the present we are still in contact with them in the Refuge system; although now it is only by our remaining fighters still attempting to evade not fight them. And for the foreseeable future I do not expect that to change. I have no doubt that if they can follow, they will; If they locate us they will attack us. They always come for retribution, and they are aggressive, savage and brave.

"Esteemed leader, I said in my experience with them I believe that if they can find where we have gone they will follow. I also said I would not be surprised to find they have already followed us and are just biding their time. I urge the esteemed members to begin sending reinforcements to the station at our bridgehead so we can prepare for them."

The elderly member asked, "And you base your belief on what?"

I just told you. I base it on my experience with them you pompous fool. "Esteemed board member, after our initial landing they sent a force to investigate us and we destroyed a large number of them. Following that we did not have any major bother or fighting but their small reconnaissance units continually searched for us; as you know they were able to destroy the Fifth Great Pack in one day.

"They followed us to the Planet Pleasant, met us in the City of New Glasgow, then attacked the system of planets they call the Refuge System where we had major combat on all of the four worlds. They found us on the NX world. After each of these meeting they stop to train and reinforce themselves. If they discover our whereabouts, they will follow us. That is why I believe it critical to be able to build up my forces to meet the challenge as I am sure they are doing."

The military member looked at Glgoffen. "Your forces Glgoffen? Why do you think they are still yours? The expedition is over. It ended in disaster, is that not true?"

"Yes, it is true. However, we have to do something! So, whoever you appoint to defend the station is going to need more troops to do it."

The confederation leader asked "If you retain the command of this defense and it comes to battle how will you go about defeating them? We are still considering establishing relations with them; although I know there are those here in this room against it. Give us your strategy to help us decide.

"I will bleed them for every meter, wear them down, then destroy them."

"And how do you plan to do that?" We assume you do have a plan".

"Yes, Esteemed members, I do. In our early battles we used the traditional attacks of our soldiers that cost us thousands killed. By time we left Planer Sunset the AG commanders were using artillery and rapid-fire guns first. Then attacked in a series of small rushes of no more than a platoon at a time to overwhelm a position.

"When they humans followed and attacked us in the Refuge system, we were fortunate to have captured two higher ranking prisoners. By using a drug interrogation treatment on them we obtained enough warning to narrowly avoid the disaster of a surprise attack. The information gave me scarcely enough time to move the pack army below ground into the tunnels we had already established and we found it particularly effective in causing extremely high casualties among the humans. My plan is the same. Only this time, I will have the time to make every ring of the station a large tunnel of continuous barricades with large and small strong points forcing the humans to bleed for every step they take on each of the five levels."

The leader of the Confederation looked around the conference table and said "I am satisfied with the plan. and we will meet again in two days."

CONFEDERATION OF WORLDS COUNCIL CHAMBER THE
NEXT AFTERNOON

The confederation leader looked around the table. "Then we are all agreed that Glgoffen will retain command of the space station troops that we will begin to reinforce." Every one nodded or grunted assent. The leader said, "Not surprisingly each of our ten militarized worlds has offered to send some warriors if it becomes necessary." He looked to the military councilmen. "We will send reinforcements to Glgoffen to fill out the three Great Packs on the station with him. I am certain that with his plan three Great Packs can hold that station if it becomes necessary. Also notify him he has our trust and will remain Supreme Leader of the force on station to set his plans in motion. He is to remain here for another session with us with in the next six days."

When he was notified that he retained command of the forces on the Station, Glgoffen immediately sent a message through the tunnel to his second in command and the Intelligence chief. He told the second in command to notify all the GP leaders he will return in six days to resume command, and they will be up to strength within a month. Then he gave his orders on how to deploy his three Great Packs and the assigned areas to be defended by each.

CHAPTER 19

MILITARY WORLD, 10 JULY.

The three second Buzzz in his head alerted Frank something impor-tant was coming, and he stopped the work he was doing. *Sounds like the shit hit the fan somewhere. I wonder what's up?*

"All regimental and battalion commanders report to a meeting at Division headquarters in one hour. Battalion commanders bring your company commanders and their executive officers with you."

Frank communicated with Major Olney, "Come into my office, it feels like the shit just exploded somewhere." Then he contacted Alicia. "Major Macalduie," she answered crisply.

"Alicia its Frank . . ." She cut him off. "I think I know why you are calling Frank. Your questions will be answered at the briefing. Sorry, I have to go."

This is getting interesting.

Forty minutes later Frank, Major Olney, the sergeant major, and the 1/5 Company commanders with their XOs sat waiting with the rest of the Division's senior officers in the crowded meeting room that was a hum of speculative conversations. Frank received a communica-tion from Captain Yaxley and answered, "I was just thinking about you Captain."

"Sorry it took a week to get back to you sir. The good news is I have three days to come over to you and see what we can come up with. I kicked your problem around and was directed, by a friend, to a Physicist who happens to be a platoon commander in another company. if you have no objections, I will bring him with me and I think we may have a solution to our problem."

"That's great news, captain. I'll look forward to meeting with you the day after tomorrow."

"Attention om Deck!" Yelled Major Brown as Generals Thomas, Sing, and Rahm entered the hall followed by Alicia. Every officer in the Second Marine Division came to attention.

"As you were ladies and gentlemen." General Rahm said waiting for everyone to settle down." Before we begin, there are refreshments in the rear help yourselves then sit back and get comfortable." General Rahm waited for a few minutes chatting with the others on the stage. While General sing, and Alicia, walked onto the raised stage in the front of the room and waited as everyone settled down. Alicia stood behind the general.

General Sing looked around. "The reason for the sudden call out is because I have just received intelligence that requires we begin Operation Trojan Horse earlier than anticipated. I will ask Major Macalduie from Galactic intelligence to begin." He turned and nodded to Alicia. She walked to the edge of the stage and spent a long moment looking around the room. If she spotted Frank she gave no indication.

"A friend of mine has a saying I used to think quaint; but during this past year I have come to understand it. The saying goes: Every time I think things will get better; they get worse; and when I think they will get worse they do. She received some cautions laughter from the mystified audience. Major Olney elbowed Frank and gave him a wide grin and Frank heard a staged cough from Captain Blanco.

Alicia looked around again. "That saying has significance to the context of this meeting because an unsuspecting intelligence source has been giving us real-time intelligence on everything he does on the Space Station, along with those he meets with. I felt good because we knew it would make things better for us in our attack. Now remember the saying I began this briefing with: "Things may have gotten worse.""

There was a rustling and murmur in the hall. Alicia held up her hands for quiet.

"Our ability to know their strategies was the foundation of our attack plans against the Space Station . . . but that has changed in a dramatic way. Although there could be a positive aspect of this for us too. Time will tell.

"Battalion commanders. You have our original planning and know the station is barely being reinforced. That moral was low; and the three-great packs on station in fact do not equal one complete one. All of that was good news.

"So, what has changed?" she asked rhetorically. "And the answer ladies and gentlemen is that four days ago the Supreme Pack Leader of what turns out to have been just a small expeditionary force for their military was called to Andromeda to explain the destruction of so much of his force by us. SPL Glgoffen was apparently able to justify his strategy and losses and has retained his command; so, things could begin to change shortly. Think of that! We have been fighting a small force comprised of troops donated by only six of the planets that make up their thirty-eight worlds confederation.

A murmur began in the hall.

"Here is what may change and we must address: Our unwitting spy, has been informed that within two weeks from this morning new troops will begin arriving to reconstitute the Third Great Pack to the full strength of eighteen thousand fighters. We also know the First, and Sixth Great Packs will also reach close to their full strength. The only good news in this is their government will not send any additional Great Packs to the space station. We will only face the three already there. As far as can be determined, the reinforcements will not arrive all at once but over a period of one month."

General Sing walked next to Alicia and quietly said, 'I'll take over Major." She nodded and stepped back.

General Sing studied the audience for a moment. "We estimated on, then planned for, dealing with roughly eighteen thousand DM troops when we set Operation Trojan Horse into motion. Our three to one ratio of forces for the attack on this fortified position was also predicated on their bad morale, worn out equipment, and some lack of cohesion with no unity of command in some units.

"We now know that within a month there could be as many as fifty-four thousand combat troops on station. I leave you ladies and gentlemen to do your own math on the troop levels we need to have any chance at all in that case. The good news is it will take Delta-Mike at least a month to reach that level. But as Major Macalduie so imaginatively stated at the beginning: When I think things will get worse, they do. According to real time intelligence their morale is improving exponentially; and at any time during the assault, we could be faced with troop increases. Also, our old nemesis, Glgoffen, has ordered that fighting positions be established inside the Station on every level to slow us down and he is establishing specific kill boxes.

"So . . . we want to take care of this as quickly as we can to ensure that we hit them at our original projected levels. This will put more responsibility on the fleet who must plan on holding the horizon of the tunnel to this side and destroy or degrade any reinforcements.

"Ladies and gentlemen, this is your notification to begin mounting out to your assigned ships. We will begin Operation Trojan Horse a week from today on Seventeen July, when our Trojan Horse will land at the space station. We are now at L-Day minus eight, and counting down.

"Any questions?"

Frank glanced at Olney, "I didn't see this coming."

"Neither did I, sir."

Just then Frank received a communication from Captain Yaxley.

"Colonel Farrell."

"Sir, Captain Yaxley here. I think I have an answer to your question but because of the changing situation I can only come over this evening and explain everything if that is okay."

"Thanks Captain. We will see you at nineteen hours at Fifth Marine Regimental Headquarters."

Frank contacted General Rham and quickly briefed him, then said to Major Olney," Tell the sergeant major to be ready to go to regiment with us tonight. Let him know what this is about."

Major Olney nodded, "Aye-aye, sir."

At 1900 hours Captain Yaxley was surprised to see not only Frank and his officers but also General Lamb and all commanders from the Second Brigade. Since he was used to giving briefings he effortlessly moved on topic.

"Ladies and gentlemen, during the fighting in the tunnels on Planet Refuge, Colonel Farrell asked me if I could make something to clear tunnels before an assault. Thus, the Assault Pak came about and has since been extensively used.

"Recently, Colonel Farrell presented me with another problem in preparation for the attack on the space station. The issue was the need for something like a satchel charge that did not have any shrapnel, only explosive overpressure, but not enough overpressure to cause structural damage to possibly expose our troops to vacuum or begin losing atmosphere.

"After considering the problem I contacted a friend who is a physicist hiding in the infantry and explained it to him. He quickly came up with an idea that should do the job. We call it the Sonic Shock Satchel. It will send sonic shock waves down passageways and into spaces. It is in effect, an acoustic bomb, that causes a frequency that has extra-aural biofeedback's on the central nervous system. It will not immediately kill but it will disable everyone in a target area giving *you* enough time to get in and then kill them.

"If you encounter any exceptionally large spaces, we have a laser that can paint an invisible kill box in your specified area to contain our acoustic bomb to kill everyone inside the box. And we still have our pulse weapons."

After twenty minutes of questions General Lamb said, "Our

thanks to Captain Yaxley of Third Engineers, and Captain Boece of B Recon for their help. Now take ten and I will get on with some other issues."

Frank and Olney quickly got a cup of coffee and returned to their seats. "Well, what do you think of Yaxley's sonic device?" Frank asked Olney, who shrugged. "In theory it sounds good, sir, but I am still a little worried that some of our own people could be adversely affected by it.

"How so?"

"Sir, do you remember when Yaxley first gave us the explosive satchels on Pleasant? It was so successfully you wanted to breach the tunnel doors with one!"

Frank gave him a wry smile and nodded. "We solved that with a command detonation. Hmm. Let me get Yaxley again." He communicated with him.

"Captain Yaxley, Sir," he answered crisply.

"Colonel Farrell here. I'm sorry to bother you already Captain, but my XO asked a question I thought needed answered before we got ahead of ourselves with your devise. What are the chances of the waves from the sonic satchel coming back onto the troops who deploy it? We were thinking of that tunnel on Pleasant, where I asked you about using a satchel charge to blow down doors and you succinctly explained why it was a bad idea."

Captain Yaxley began to chuckle. "I remember sir. I began to address it at the meeting and I can see where it should have been in much greater detail. I addressed your issue in the context of putting up our spot marked laser fence in large spaces making a kill box. What I did not say was that the laser you use to mark the kill boxes you can use at the same time to put a blocking wall in front of whoever is deploying the device. Now that I think of it, we should consider issuing each person in the assault with a hand-held laser to avoid friendly fire issues if the troops call for the Satchel. I also recommend that the warning of *Fire in the hole!* still be used for safety. That will require a little training, sir. But I am sure if you get the word out it can easily be done in a one-day session. I guess we will know the first time someone uses one of them."

Frank contacted General Lamb and explained what Yaxley said.

"Colonel I will pass this up with the recommendation we get a lot of hand-held lasers, and my recommendation that it be done universally. And in a related matter we have recently learned that DMs routinely assigned to a space station are rearmed with Frangible ammunition for their weapons, for obvious reasons. With the exception of using slug type ammunition against War Beasts our troops have little experience with it. I will pass on to all the troops that a frangible will shatter on contact with a hard object and will only pierce one human target. It makes sense for operating in a closed environment in vacuum."

"That is good to hear, sir."

"Anything else on your mind colonel?"

"No sir."

L-DAY MINUS 7

UWS WHISPER.

Captain Sun Kee, sat drinking his coffee with his offices, and the chief of the boat, in the Ward room. "I have been considering the fact that the tunnel horizon on this side is the same one point five light minutes from the station as the one in andromeda. I suppose it makes good tactical sense. But since it is co close to us, I have been pondering the best way to keep Delta-Mike on their side after we capture this station. Anyone have an idea?

"I do sir," said the chief of the boat, "we should seed the Gateway ten light seconds deep outside the horizon on our side to at least destroy a first wave coming through the tunnel. The fragments from those ships may cause some problems to those behind them even with the slower velocity they will probably use coming out. Then we can have the fleet waiting another ten light seconds behind the mines to hit them again. When they come through that they face the Space Stations defense systems before landing."

"Good idea Chief, I have been thinking along those lines myself.

L-DAY MINUS 6.

UWE JOINT COMMAND HEADQUARTER, EARLY AM

General Hayduf the Commander in Chief of all United World forces sat at the head of a long table situated in the middle of a large well-lit room with one long glass wall facing lush woodlands and low hills in the distance. He was sipping his coffee while scrutinizing the others around the table with him over his cup. To his right going down the table was General Gimpsie his Chief of Staff, General Sing, Admiral Park and Colonel Martinez. On the other side sat the Marine Commandant General Thomas, General Lamb, Major Brown, Major Alicia Macalduie, and Navy Commandeer Dubni.

"I thank our ancestors we planted the chip in that Great Pack Leaders head when he was captured or we would have had a very unwelcome surprise when we hit the station, "General Hayduf said to the group.

"You are right about that sir," replied General Thomas. All the others nodded and made similar comments.

"Sir," Thomas continued, "Major Macalduie has the most knowledge of the dispositions and changes that SPL Glgoffen wants to make to the current DM assignments on the station. I suggest that she give the command briefing this evening."

General Hayduf looked around the table. "Does anyone disagree? No? Then prepare to give the briefing Major. Do you have any other recommendations General?"

"Yes, sir. I think we have a chance to cut the head from the sake with new information we have. Major Macalduie, Major Brown, Commander Dubni, and I have discussed this and developed what we consider a viable plan."

General Hayduf looked intrigued. "Go on."

"Sir, I will ask Major Macalduie to lay it out and Commander Dubni can comment and answer any questions."

General Hayduf approval.

"Sir," Alicia began, "we know that Supreme Pack Leader Glgoffen believes we are going to find him. He already suspects we may know where the Space Station and Tunnel are located; but he is yet not completely certain. So, he has not unequivocally pushed that narrative in his meetings on First world. Though he *has* been in contact with all of his key commanders ordering massive troop re-deployments for the short run. As fate may have it, he is returning to the Space Station, on L-Day, but he is not bringing any additional troops with him. His trip is considered a routine movement from one point to another. As such his ship will only have one escort destroyer with it.

"His primary reason in returning alone is, according to our intelligence, to assign where his three reconstituted Great packs will construct the strong points he wants for the additional three reinforced GPs left behind on their home worlds. Glgoffen seems certain they will be released to him if any fighting begins; because that will validate his fears to the Confederation Leadership.

"Our intelligence intercepts suggest that he still believes we are searching for the station in a Spinward, Coreward Quadrant from the Refuge system when, as you know, we are coming at him down and left from a Coreward, Trailing Quadrant. So, to continue that deception we are keeping ships searching up where Delta-Mike believes we are.

Alicia took a deep breath. "Since we know when he is arriving at the Space Station, we can plan to intercept and destroy him and his escort with stealth ships as he gets to the gateway of the tunnel."

Commander Dubni spoke-up. "Admiral Park has assigned four

stealth ships to this mission, the *Whisper, Shadow, Echo* and *Ghost*. The first three of them are veterans of this war and the fourth is a brand-new updated ship, UWS *Ghost*, that will use all their weapons and destroy both ships. At the same time we kill him, our Trojan Horse will be executing a controlled crash into the White Zone landing dock between Z-one and Z-four. By this time, our stealth ships will be dropping anti-ship mines all around our side of the gateway out as far as ten light seconds .Our sensors will be out to thirty light seconds, and the fleet ships can take care of any DM ships that happen to be in the area. At that point the invasion will be on."

Alicia continued. "With Glgoffen dead, it should add to their initial confusion somewhat. When we capture the station, we will heavily fortify the gateway of the tunnel with mines, and missiles, that will be backed up by the fleet against a counter attack"

The room took on a reflective quiet.

General Hayduf sat in thought for a long moment waiting for the Main Computer Entity to offer him guidance. When the Entity remained quiet, he looked at everyone sitting around the table for an additional moment. Finally, he asked "Are there any comments, suggestions, disagreement, or more discussion needed with this plan to target and, in fact, assassinate one man? If not, I'll query you one by one to decide if we should target Supreme Pack Leader Glgoffen.

"Major Macalduie. Yes, or no."

"Yes, sir."

"Major Brown."

"Yes, sir"

"Commander Dubni."

"Yes, sir"

"Colonel Martinez."

"Yes, sir."

"Admiral Park."

The Admiral nodded.

"General Lamb."

"Yes."

"General Sing." He nodded.

General Hayduf looked at his chief of staff. "General Gimpsie."

"Absolutely, sir."

"General Thomas."

"Yes."

General Hayduf nodded to himself. "It is settled then. Admiral Park, I will leave this to you to organize and coordinate with General Thomas."

"Aye-aye sir."

"How would you rate the condition of the fleet at this time admiral?"

"I would say five by five, sir."

Hayduf nodded. "Very well gentlemen and lady. Carry on."

L-DAY MINUS 6, LATE EVENING

Alicia and Frank sat on the couch they had just made love on, drinking wine. He had been surprised to see her at this time of the day; but he wasn't complaining. Now he watched her seemingly studying his wall collection of flags, helmets, and insignia. She sighed, "I only have a few hours to get some sleep and get back to work. So, do you, I assume."

"Yer right. With you running off this quickly I wonder if there is anything you can share with this poor grunt."

Alicia snorted. "Poor grunt! You're probably one of three persons in the galaxy that knows that term. But since I'm one of the other two I understand yur meaning."

Frank put his arm around her shoulders and whispered in her ear, "You know it arouses me when you use an Earth accent." He leaned over and kissed her right nipple. Later, after another quickie, Alicia hurriedly began dressing. As she dressed, she said, "All I can share is that we are picking up much more communications than we have been and are translating it almost in real time. Along with everything from the chip in our unwitting spy's head. You'll be called to a briefing at Division tomorrow. Don't be surprised at anything ya hear."

Frank watched her as she walked to the door and left. *Man, she looks as good going as she did coming,* he snickered to himself, *you're killing you. I wonder what she can't tell me?*

L DAY MINUS 5.

THE HURRY-UP DRILL.

"Attention on deck!" called General Sing, as General Thomas, Major Brown, and Alicia entered the large meeting room/ mess hall. The room had the 2nd Marine Division colors, along with each of its Regimental flags, displayed along with the United Worlds and Marine Corps flags sticking out on five-foot poles around the hall near the ceiling.

"As you were," General Thomas said.

He and General Sing took center stage while Major Brown stood off to the side with Alicia. The Commandant looked over the gathering of every commanding officer and XO in the division and began:

"A plan, however carefully conceived, is never safe from the first contact with the enemy, or any sudden change of intentions by that enemy."

Uh-oh. Frank and Major Olney glanced at each other.

"Intelligence has intercepted a flurry of communications to our target, and is constantly reviewing other sources about orders and other plans. Major Macalduie from Galactic Intelligence will now brief you on what has been learned."

Alicia walked to the center stage and looked around.

"Every time I think things will get better . . . but I'm not going to finish that statement because you all know the rest."

A low groan swept the hall.

"Supreme Pack Leader Glgoffen, having been exonerated ,and given back his command of the Expeditionary Forces, is being kept on their First World for several more days of discussions and meetings. As fate would have it, he is scheduled to return to the Station on our L-Day. Since his reinstatement, he has been in contact with all of his command staff continually giving them assignments and instructions. He has already made significant changes altering what we planned for; and according to our information he intends to plan an offensive action against us from the Station when he locates us.

"The good news, is he is giving his commanders on the station a few days to begin getting his changes in place so he can inspect them as soon as he arrives back to decide how to refortify the station. That will include positions for s three new great packs that will be arriving in Attack Pack contingents over the next month. After that he is going to have a meeting with his senior commanders to discuss strategy for the continuation of the war against us. Since we know his arrival is on L-Day, we are going to prevent him from arriving at the station by ambushing and destroying his ship."

Frank sat up straighter. *Holy shit! They are really beginning to play the game now. It's a good move and payback for the shit he's done to us.*

A murmur of conversation swept the hall. "Ladies and gentlemen your attentions please." Alicia waited util it was completely quiet again. "Because of these developments, I will give you the new order of battle that Commanding General Glgoffen has sent to his troops on the station. But before that . . ." Alicia looked at General Thomas who nodded to her.

"Before that . . . L-Day has been moved up and we will now begin your mount out to the ships in twelve hours. The units assigned to the Trojan Horse will leave in six hours."

It seemed to her that everyone in the hall took a collective breath at the same time, but remained silent. "Here are the changes we know of. . ."

Major Olney nudged Frank and whispered, "Did she mention any of this to you?" Frank shook his head.

Now I know why she was up tight he realized.

"You all know the Fifth Marines will begin the operation in the Trojan Horse, along with Second Recon and Raiders." Alicia continued. "Their mission remains the same except for the amount of resistance they will encounter. We now know that SPL Glgoffen has ordered a re-deployment of his forces. It is hoped that the new disposition will not be totally completed by L-Day. Remember, they do not know we found them. One can only hope they will be casual in the execution of any redeployments.

"The entire surviving Third Great Pack equals only Two thousand nine-hundred troops. They will be augmented by an additional one thousand troops from the Twenty-third AG of the First Great. They will all be defending the White Zone, and the CIC Hub.

"One change for the Fifth Marines is Colonel Blak's Three Five, and Colonel Tzu's Four Five will now have an active part in the clearing operation in White Zone. Units of the Third Marine Division will now follow the Fifth Marines in and initially take occupation and security of the Station. The Army's Second Infantry Division will stand by as reinforcements for any level of the Station that may need them.

"The First Great Pack is the only one that remained more or less intact after our other battles. They will deploy the Twenty-first and Twenty-second AGs in Blue Zone with four thousand troops. The remaining half of the Twenty-third AG totaling one thousand troops will be in Yellow Zone.

"The Sixty-first and Sixty-second AGs of the Sixth Great Pack will be in Orange Zone with four thousand troops. And their Sixty-third AG is in Green Zone. I know the veterans here remember these units from several past and hard-fought battles. So . . . you all know what to expect, and what to do. Good luck in the coming operation."

Alicia stepped back and General Thomas said, "We are fortunate to have the information we do; I am sure it will make the difference. Now when the ship reaches the station proximity while transmitting their Friend or Foe signal, and a message that they are trying to get back from the Refuge System with considerable battle damage, Commander Dubni will wake the sleeping EMPs in a rolling black-out toward the station that will be closely followed by the invasion force.

L-DAY, 0230 HOURS LOCAL.

TROJAN HORSE

As the ship moved toward the Space Station, Frank and Major Olney held a final pre-landing briefing in the officers mess with his company commanders and their executive officers.

"Well gentlemen and lady, we will be landing, or should I say crash landing, at 0730 Station time. Hopefully our ambush ships will be done killing Supreme Pack Leader Glgoffen. The ship's captain feels he can achieve a minor crash without causing major injuries to any of us.

"I know that with the exception of Captain Blanco, this will be yur first combat landing. Just remember things can get chaotic. Remember yur training and make sure yur platoon commanders and sergeants understand the mission. They're the ones who will make this landing a success or failure.

"When the ship hits the Zebra-One left side dock, we'll be the first out leading the invasion. We'll almost certainly have immediate contact with DM troops. Have your people kill every DM they see. Don't worry about prisoners until after we have secured our ring. Our information is that all the Great Pack, and Attack Group, Commanders will be mustered in a large meeting and recreational hall in Blue Zone to welcome their Supreme Pack Leader back. Try not to kill too many high-ranking officer who are not trying to kill you. They're the type of prisoners we want.

"Initially, expect contact with the Third Great Pack. They have the fewest troops because they have taken the brunt of most of our battles. Do not underestimate them! They are brave, aggressive fighters that Major Olney, Captain Blanco, and I have been up against more times than we like. Also keep in mind how massive this station is. I expect each of the four station spokes to be at least several hundred meters wide and have a divide or separation wall on both sides.

"Captain Sherington, your "A" Company will attack from the docks straight up the Zebra-One side of the Station spoke to the Center hub and CIC to link up with the Second Raiders. At the same time, Captain Woon's "B" Company will proceed up the Zebra Four side. The Raiders will leave the *ship* in Landing Boats to attack the CIC sitting on top.as soon as it approaches the station If we are lucky, the DMs will think for a moment that they are just getting off before a hard landing."

"Aye-aye, sir," both captains answered together.

"Captain Aeneas, "C" Company along with Captain Silvanus's "D" will attack to the left through the ring and will be backed up by "K" Three-Five. Myself, Major Olney, Captain Worrall, and the Sergeant Major, will initially follow "B" Company to the CIC.

"Aye-aye, sir."

"Captain Worrall I want H&S Company to assign one Platoon to each of the attacking companies. For this operation they will act as engineers if needed. Have an engineer sergeant with his bat drones with each of those platoons. You will be with the headquarters group to respond if called for by Recon. I want each of those platoons to have the ability to set up multiple laser dot kill boxes, and larger protective walls for our troops using the new sonic weapons. Your engineers will also blow strong points and keep the supply of Satchel charges.

"Aye-aye, sir."

Captain Blanco, I'm counting on you to limit any surprises as much as possible. Deploy your company as you see fit among the Battalion and in the station. I need to know strong points, who exactly we are fighting, and how many are there. You know the drill.

"Aye-aye, sir."

Frank looked around, "Any questions or comments? No? Alright, if you need supplies or anything else Major Olney and the Sergeant Major will take care of it. Have I missed anything? Right then. Major Olney do you have anything?"

"Yes sir. Everyone, remember that when we do take prisoners, we need officers. Send them back to the CP group for collection."

L-DAY 0728 HOURS STATION TIME
ABOARD THE TROJAN HORSE.

On *Pack Helper, aka, Trojan Horse*, the human bridge crew had been broadcasting its message continuously since they entered the sensor zone of the Space station. Commandeer Dubni had kept his word and was activating the tiny EMPs as the ship passed enabling a clear passage for the rest of the attacking force.

As the Trojan Horse neared the station, surprisingly, it went unnoticed at first. Then a DM crewman in the station CIC sat at his station to begin his watch and was the first to see it entering the sensor field that surrounded the space station. He was relatively new to the station and continued to watch his scope for an additional long moment to see if what he was witnessing would continue. When it did, he alerted his leader. "I have an anomaly indicating movement into the sensor field from the Rimward Spinward Quadrant and the Warbeast system that I can now identify as a ship that appears large."

The minor leader turned to another station and asked that crewman "Are you receiving any communication from this contact?"

"I am getting something I am trying to firm up and..." He was interrupted by his shipmate who said, "Leader as the contact passes our sensors become inert."

The Leader felt a jolt of anxiety and prepared to sound an alert of a possible attack when the communications crewman said, "Leader, the ship is now broadcasting the correct FOF. It reports to be the ship *Pack Helper* that needs assistance, and has suffered moderate damage to its structure and some fundamental systems. They have recently escaped from the Warbeast System and Sensors show they are losing atmosphere They report many wounded. Apparently, it is an automated message that is repeating every fifteen seconds."

The crewman who first noticed the ship added, "Perhaps the incoming ships system damage along with the broadcasted FOF are combining to have an effect on the sensors since the outages seem to follow the ship as it passes."

The shift leader in CIC asked, "Can either of you think of any reason this should be happening?" They both shook their head, and the communicator said, "No leader it is very strange."

At that moment a message from the landing dock was broadcast throughout the Station from the command station of the dock. "Crash and emergency units to Docking area One; the incoming ship has declared an emergency from battle damage and has suffered a loss of ability to control their approach to the dock. The crew predicts a hard approach."

Since Supreme Pack Leader Glgoffen had been called away all the senior leaders had been deferring to his deputy, Deputy Supreme Leader Herschel, to make any final decisions on the troop dispositions. He supposed it was because of his close daily contact with Glgoffen who more and more had been passing orders through him rather than his second in command. A role he found himself proficient at and enjoyed.

Herschel sat in his office reviewing the latest dispositions that Glgoffen requested when he was contacted by the Duty officer in the CIC. "Deputy Supreme Leader, we are receiving a message from another of our ships believed lost during the fighting in the Warbeast campaign."

"What ship?"

"Communications is not good; we believe it to be *Pack Helper*. They are broadcasting the correct FOF and report they have a number of wounded with them."

"Where are they now?"

"We are following their progress through the Sensor field. They will arrive here shortly."

Herschel sat in thought for a moment and said, "*Pack Helper* was a troop ship. How do you think they were able to break-out past the hoo-man's fleet?"

"If you ask me, they were very fortunate. I hope they were able to bring troops out along with the wounded"

"Yes. We can use all the veteran troops we can get. I am pleased they made it. Gather their officers and we can debrief them when I arrive." Herschel was still uneasy and considered: *Glgoffen was convinced the Hoo-mans would find and follow us. Pack gods! Could this ship be more than it appears? Are they that bold to try something like this? No, I know they are still searching in the wrong quadrant for this station. I am letting the Supreme Leaders fears influence me. But to be safe I must check.*

"Have any other ships been picked up on sensor?"

"As I was coming here, I was advised that three landing craft left the Pack Helper after they broadcasted the FOF."

"Why?"

"Deputy Supreme Leader, I was told they are bringing the most serious cares to the station as soon as possible."

"Do you find anything suspicious about that, or this ship? Something feels odd to me. I want you to have all troops go to their battle position and wait for further orders." The officer saluted and hurried away.

Deputy Supreme Leader Herschel's communicator alerted him to an incoming call, from the Supreme Pack Leader on his way back to the station from First World on the Destroyer *Hunter*. SPL Glgoffen greeted his Intelligence Chief saying, "I will be with you shortly and we can begin our work. Is there any news of the Hoomans?"

"Nothing. We know they are still searching in the wrong quadrants. And another of our ships has escaped from Warbeast and is bring wounded out."

"Good."

"Supreme Leader, I am suspicious of that ship and have put the Station on alert.

"Why! Demanded Glgoffen. What makes you suspicious?

"The sensors are becoming inert as the ship passes and I feared a possible ruse."

"I am glad you are attentive Herschel but don't worry too much. Did you forget that those sensors are dumb? They were for a quick one-time use when we first arrived to warn us of a broad front invasion. They were never designed, or intended, for repeated use. If one of our ships is broadcasting the correct FOF we should be glad that more of our packmates have escaped the humans. Is there any other reason this has you nervous?"

As Herschel began to reply he heard a burst of static and realized his communicator had malfunctioned. *Of all the times to have this issue!*

"My communicator has malfunctioned," he called to his aid who came right in. "Get me another quickly." Herschel said with disgust.

"May I see it leader?" The aid asked. Herschel handed the communicator to his Aid who checked it over and pronounced, "There is nothing wrong with this sir." He gave it back to him.

"Hmmm," Herschel nodded a thanks, and tried to reestablish contact with SPL Glgoffen without success.

"It could be from the conditions entering the gateway, sometimes it causes interference," suggested his aid. Just then he received a call from the watch officer in CIC. "Leader we have noted some type of a disturbance inside the gateway but are unable to distinguish what it was."

"Do your sensors show any other activity near there?"

"No leader."

Herschel turned to his Aid. "You are right, CIC recorded a disturbance at the gateway and my communicator seems to be working now. That will be all." Herschel went back to thinking about the incoming ship and imminent arrival of the Supreme Pack Leader.

" Leader!" Herschel's aid rushed back in. "A message drone has just arrived from the gateway, please listen in private mode." General Herschel felt slightly light headed as he listened, but he quickly recovered and began contacting his troops.

SHORTLY BEFORE:

SPL Glgoffen wondered *What has made Herschel suspicious. He usually has a good sense about things*

"Multiple incoming missiles and torpedoes!" yelled by one of the bridge crew on Glgoffen's ship. The *Hunters* captain, and the Supreme Leader, quickly checked the screen and looked at the plots again.

"Where did they come from? Can you take evasive action

Captain.!" Asked Glgoffen. The captain ignored him and yelled "Full power toward the gateway, begin evasive action.!"

After a minute he turned to Glgoffen with a resigned look. "There is no evasive action to be taken I am afraid. I will continue trying to out-run the missiles, but that too may be a futile gesture. I believe there are several stealth ships around us. It is the only explanation for how they attacked from so close with the number of missiles and torpedoes coming this fast from different directions. It seems we will die for the homeland, Supreme Leader!"

Glgoffen looked around him and sadly shook his head as he sat down. *Those cursed humans! I knew they would follo . . .* Were his last thoughts as the *Hunter* and its escort were both blown to pieces becoming a cloud of expanding gasses and debris.

CHAPTER 20

*"Every time I think things will get better; they get worse.
And when I think they will get worse; they do."*
Unknown Marine Grunt

Captain Sun Kee contacted god and reported, "It is done. Both targets
are completely destroyed"

The Main Computer Entity, god, passed the message to the
High Command who passed it down to the troops anticipating the
attack order.

At the same time, a DM survey ship was approaching the gateway
from a different azimuth inside the tunnel several light seconds away
and witnessed the destruction of the two ships. From his instruments
the captain recognized the signature of the Destroyer *Hunter;* but he
had no idea of its mission or passenger. The survey ship captain, an
old space veteran, realized the attack was almost certainly the work of
stealth craft since he had no readings of other ships in the quadrant
until he recorded the weapons fire. "Come about, reverse full speed,"
he said to his helmsman, "there are human stealth ships here! I do
not want to be their next target! Send a message drone to the space
station; and another to First World with all our readings; and notify

them of what we witnessed at the mouth of the gateway in case they were unable to make it back. *Ancestors protect me and my crew so we can escape from these hidden ships.*

His message drone arrived at the CIC in station just ahead of the Trojan Horse. As soon as Herschel was notified, he sounded the general alert and ordered "Monitor *Pack Helper*, destroy it if it does anything suspicious." His message to the commanders caused some initial confusion since they had been celebrating the arrival of more packmates from the Refuge System and the return of their Supreme Pack Leader.

It was the second half of his message communication to all senior leaders that sent a chilling through the ranks. "Our Supreme Pack Leader has been killed by humans on his trip here. Until there are different orders from First World, I am assuming command. Get your Packs in place and do your duty."

Third Great Pack Leaser Growlerrez received a shot of adrenalin when he received the news and knew the station had been found and an attack may already be underway with this mysterious ship and contacted his 30th AG commander. "Go to your new positions and prepare to repel an attack."

The Main Computer Entity knew as soon as Growlerrez did that the attack was no longer a surprise and notified General Gimpsie then sent the message to all in theatre commanders: "Enemy aware of our plans. Prepare for an opposed landing."

General Gimpsie alerted the Reserves to move up and join the fight, then ordered Admiral Park to implement his plan to mine inside and outside of the gateway per their earlier planning and have the fleet ready to destroy any DM vessels attempting to come through.

The troops of the 5th Marine Regiment along with the 2nd Raiders and 2nd Reconnaissance Battalion formed nervously inside the large DM troop transport. Each Marine lost in private thoughts of what waited for them if they got that far, and the consequences if their ruse was discovered. They all knew detection meant destruction. Plus, even a controlled crash could sometimes end up as deadly as a real one.

Inside the ship a calm, deep voiced pilot said in everyone's head, "Landing boats away." the three Raiders shuttles left and flew toward the landing dock broadcasting the intent to deliver serious causalities, then veered upward above the station and landed on the exposed portion of the Main Core sticking four meters above the top ring of the station where Breachers and Damage control personnel dressed in assault gear with a survival oxygen face shield off loaded and began to cut into the Main Core. They were surprised to unexpectedly hit a small maintenance hall with a second bulkhead, and were concerned when the hit a third one. It took them almost two minutes before they were through the reinforced bulkheads and were inside the CIC but it was a costly delay. The Raiders stormed into the CIC to begin their deadly work but immediately began taking fire and causalities. A soldier in the 30th AG alerted the station, "Knife Soldiers inside CIC," before he was pulsed.

At almost the same time on the *Trojan Horse* the pilot broadcast, "All hands. Brace, brace, brace, for impact."

When the ship began to broadcast the FOF code; the space station already had the entrance bay door opened replaced by a force field that allowed the *Trojan Horse* to enter. After passing through the force field the ship seemed to wobble and suddenly hit the bulkhead of the dock slowly sliding sideways through the immense ship bay seemingly out of control until it stopped after causing damage to the dock, station bulkhead and the ship.

A klaxon sounded and a loud speaker broadcast "Security team and medical team to main first ring forward bay." A moment later it was followed by "All Packs, alarm! the station has been invaded by Hoo-mans on First Ring!" Fire on the ship. All the senior leaders ran for their units when they heard "Alarm! Hoomans attacking first ring."

As the ship stopped sliding the Marines of "A" and "B" Companies began to disembark pulsing every DM they saw and moved as quickly as possible through the landing bay into a very wide divided spoke hall way engaging in numerous firefights in and around the various shops and other quarters as the resistance by the 30th AG began stiffening. The marines continued up the Z-1 white zone ring spoke, brushing aside all opposition. On more than one occasion they had to backtrack to clear snipers that lay hidden behind them.

Captain Sherington contacted Frank. "Alpha-six to One-five actual, over."

"Go Alpha six."

"Alpha-six be advised we are encountering many small alleyways going from Spoke to spoke and also attaching to the rings as well, break. . . they are just walkways but we have contact at each one, break . . . from what I can see there are a dozen or more that have multiple barricades each manned by a squad, break . . . We are clearing them but the further into the hallways in we go puts us further into a fatal funnel situation, break . . . so far, I have four KIA and ten WIA since landing. Until these are all cleared, we cannot be sure our rear is secured . . . break . . . we are using our new sonic charges on the walkways now to hold down causalities and it is a great help, but we are going to need more of them, break . . . Recommend some of the Third Marines reserves to begin clearing and securing these alleys while we continue with our primary mission. . . Alpha six out"

Frank contacted Brigade. "One-Five actual to Brigade Actual, over.

"Go colonel" answered General Rahm.

"Sir, we are going to need a large supply of sonic munitions, and more Bats, break." Then he relayed what Captain Sherington told him. "Over."

"Keep pushing them like you are colonel. I will check with Colonel Fromk to see if they are having the same issues. . . break . . . the rest of the invasion force has landed in their zones and are all in contact with Delta-Mike, break . . .I'll pass on to watch for these fatal funnel alleyways. . . There is more resistance than we expected. Brigade actual out."

The rest of the 2nd Marine Division that was sitting one light minute away in the area cleared of sensors now sped in and began landing in their assigned Zones as the other regiments began landing in their assigned areas of the station.

0740 STATION TIME.

Frank motioned to Major Olney, Captain Worrall and Sergeant Major Kim Young standing in a group. "Any ideas or suggestions?" he asked after passing the information to god even though he knew the computer already had it. "Send a bat along the ring to the Zebra-two spoke to report."

Frank nodded. "Do it."

"I'll check on the Bat." Major Olney said. Frank nodded again then asked Captain Worrall. "How many did you get from engineers?"

"We have six, sir. We are using the first of them now."

"Get them flying for the other companies if they need it. Pass them the word."

"Aye-aye, sir."

"C" and "D" Companies began the task of clearing from their Z-2 side around to the Z-3 section of White Zone along with K/3/5. They too were surprised to see numerous small alleys connecting the four spokes of the wheel that were unnoticeable from the earlier images they had. It necessitated more troops to fight down the narrow halls that were easily blocked and defended.

The Engineer sergeant with the command group said, "Bat away!" As it began the trip around to the left of the wide quarter of a mile section that was Z-1 . The sergeant followed its progress on the back of his eyes and so did Major Olney who saw multiple alleyways between Z1 and 2. He counted seven in Z-1 section alone. When the Bat reached the dividing spoke he saw the ring ended and was blocked by a wall. The Bat flew into the Z-1 side directly into a platoon of DM troops behind barricades defending in depth and immediately began drawing fire from them.

The Engineer sergeant controlling it began jinking it up and down to avoid the fire, then he spun it one hundred eighty degrees flying out and across the main ring throughfare toward the docks. The Bat continued to take fire so the sergeant directed it into a narrow, dimly lit, corridor on the outer side of the ring that it flew down then suddenly stopped, turned left and slowly flew toward the outer hull.

"What is it doing?" asked Major Olney. The sergeant still following it behind his eyes replied, "It is programed to investigate any obvious anomaly it encounters. This is another small corridor we did not know about sir,"

A moment later the Bat paused at a bulkhead wall on the outer ring side that had a small open maintenance door. It flew inside for three meters and stopped again at a second bulkhead with another maintenance door. "Are you seeing this sir? "asked the engineer as the Bat went through the second maintenance door and immediately met a third bulkhead.

"Bring it back sergeant," Major Olney ordered and the Bat began to backtrack. When it reached the first of the doorways it flew into another team of DMs that were obviously hunting for it and they quickly shot it down. Before they could recover it the sergeant hit the destruct command for the Bat and it exploded killing one, and wounding a second DM reaching for it.

Major Olney and the Engineer Sergeant quickly approached Frank. "Sir, we made several discoveries that need to be passed on," the engineer said without preface.

"Like what?" Frank asked.

"First: This ring comes to a dead end on the Zebra- two side of the spoke and we counted fifteen of the alleys between us in Zebra-one dock on both sides of this street to the Zebra-two side of the dock. Zebra- two is heavily fortified in depth by the Thirtieth AG, I recognized their insignia. But the surprising discovery is that the station is triple hulled and the DM were shooting frangible ammunition at the Bat they shot down. Another observation if I may sir. I had the thought when I realized what they were shooting, that we should be prepared to meet their rapid-fire guns."

Shit! he's right. We were so concerned about a hull breach we never considered them using the Rapid-fire guns. Frank turned to Major Olney. "Pass that info on to Colonel Fromk's people in Zebra-Two right away.

"What's your opinion Sergeant?" Frank asked. "Sir, I self-destructed the Bat so they will not get anything from it. The bulkheads are strong, I don't believe even regular ammunition would pierce all three to let in any atmosphere. But the DMs are being extra cautions by using frangible ammo. I would recommend everyone be notified they could walk into the Rapid firing guns the DMs have. I don't know if they will try using explosives. My gut feeling is they will not unless we get another surprise and they have some type of special grenades also."

"Captain Worrall?"

"I agree with the sergeant, sir" Frank looked at Onley. "Shit! Every time, Major . . ." Olney grimaced. "I hear that sir. I'll pass the word." Major Olney walked back to frank a few minutes later. Sir, Colonel Fromk said his lead company has hit the blockage also. It appears that entire half of the station on this ring is blocked off."

That's not good. We need more information!

Frank contacted General Rahm. "One-five actual to Brigade actual, over." When Frank finished reporting the General said, "Colonel, I need you to push hard to clear Zebra-One and get down the Hub to assist the Eighth Marines. They are in a brawl below you in Blue ring. I will worry about the rings being blocked later."

"Aye-aye sir. One-five actual, out." *Fuck! I'm worried about it now*

"One-fire actual to Alpha-Six."

"Go sir," answered Captain Sherington.

"What's your situation . . . Over?"

"We have cleared the main ring concourse, along with our side of the Zebra-one spoke, and dock area where we landed, Break . . . We are within several hundred meters of the CIC hub and fifty meters away from the first of the alleyways, break . . . We are hitting numerous barricades they set up. Break . . . Since landing, I have twelve WIA and two KIA. Break . . . Some of these DM are still using regular ammunition and do not care what it hits. We could use another Bat to help check it out sir . . . Over."

"I'll have the engineers get one up to you, break . . . Push them as hard as you can, you're doing good. One-Five Actual out."

"One-Five actual to Bravo-Six, over."

"Bravo-Six, I have been monitoring sir," said Captain Woon. "We are not meeting as much opposition as I anticipated, break . . . We had most of our contact in the dock area and it was primarily workers and just a few infantry types, break . . . I have moved around the Zebra-One ring and can see the Zebra-two docks to my left, break . . . . so far, we only have four WIA, no KIA, and have been clearing at least the mouth the alleys with grenades as we push past. I will be at the main hub soon"

"One Five actual to Charley- Six, over."

"Charley-six. Go Five-Actual."

"How do you look Captain?" Captain Aeneas had anticipated the question. "One-Five actual we have cleared five of these alleys into Zebra- Four, and only have three wounded no KIA. break . . . most of the alleys lead to the core but one goes to the Z3 spoke and another just ends in an office for whatever reason. We are checking for anything hiding, break . . . . we have picked up ten prisoners who surrendered when they saw us and most are female, not combat troops break . . . Delta company is clearing around the Zebra-Four ring. Charley-Six out"

"Keep up the good work, Actual out." At that moment Frank heard the distant *Rrrriiipp* of a DM rapid firing gun. *Fuck! Just what I need.*

"Sounds like they just woke up skipper," quipped the Sergeant Major. Frank grimaced. "One-Five Actual to Delta -Six, over."

"One-Five Actual, this is Delta-five. Delta six along with five others was just KIA with two more wounded by a rapid-fire gun shooting from behind a barricade, break . . . We are in a giant hall with lots of furniture, break . . .It could be a dining hall. We are setting up a fence to clear it with sonic grenades, break . . . This room is so large it will take a while to sweep it, and I expect to hit other barricades somewhere in here, break . . . We are taking quite a bit of rifle fire also . . . Over."

"Okay. Delta Five, you are promoted to captain, and you are now Delta Six.. break . . . Use your senior lieutenant as the Five. Break . . . I am sending two platoons from Kilo Three-Five to assist with your sweep, do you copy? Over."

"Delta-six, Aye-aye, sir. . . Six out." Frank could hear the continued firing of the rapid-fire gun.

"I knew it was too easy so far Sergeant Major."

"Not to worry Skipper, we are better than they are." Frank grinned. "Right you are Sergeant Major. Major Olney, contact Kilo-Six and have him send two platoons to help Delta Company clear out that large space."

"Aye-aye, Sir."

Captain Blanco contacted Frank "Recon-Six, I'm going to move down through the station if possible and will keep you advised break . . . we are seeing a lot of combat troops flooding into the area, break. . . from their insignia they are from the Twenty-Third AG of the First Great, break . . . they are supposed to be in a lower ring and it makes me wonder if we have already degraded the Third GP so badly, they need help, break. . . .. We think we can follow at least one of these small alleyways down to the next level and I have a team checking it out, break . . . the DMs have barricades set up at the top and bottom of the landings manned by at least a Platoon leading down to the next ring, break . . . The landings are two flights of twenty steps that are at least ten meters long, break. . .. surprisingly we have not seen any large elevators here. The only elevators encountered were in the CIC main core ring and we do not know if they just want to keep the troops fit by using steps, or, if each one of these rings could be its own base camp they infrequently leave, or perhaps we just have not found or recognized other elevators yet, over"

"Actual to Recon-Six are you sure they are from another GP, break . . . are you certain they are not Thirtieth AG troops, Over."

"Recon to Actual, absolutely sure, they are wearing a Red Triangle on the blue background, not the yellow Diamond of the Third GP. We have no causalities so far and will check out what we can on the Blue and yellow rings, Recon -six out."

Frank turned to Olney, "Blanco has recon moving and reports a lot of combat troops arriving from the First GP to assist the Third GP. Hoysaia's people are still cleaning out the CIC. Except for Delta Company we've been lucky so far."

Just then Frank received a communication from Captain Hoysaia. "Echo Raiders- Six to One-five actual . . . over."

"Go Raiders- Six."

"Be advised we are meeting more troops from the Thirtieth AG and have taken most of the CIC, but the resistance is stiffening with help from those First GP troops reported by Recon. . . . Over."

"One Five actual give me a cas rep . . . over."

"Raiders-Six I have sixteen, one six, WIA and Five KIA."

"Rodger that Raider-Six, I'll get some support up to you, break. . ..be advised that recon reports the top and bottom of the route down are fortified and heavily manned. . . Actual out.

One-Five Actual to Charley-Six."

"Go Actual," answered Captain Aeneas. Charley-six, send a platoon over to the Raiders to assist them, Actual out."

Raiders-six to One-Five Actual. We just hit a very large space we are clearing now by using some sonic grenades and a satchel. The DMs broke and are moving back to another established fighting position. We put a bat up and see about six of these ready-made positions in this space that cover each other, break .. this space looks more like a shopping district with shops and repair sheds, break . . . . It has stairways up and down along with several smaller elevators, break . . . When Charley company arrives, we will work through the barricades and begin to pursue, break. . . be advised there are two tiers of steps in this space also, break . . . We did a quick measurement and this space is one hundred fifty meters by seventy-five meters, Over."

Frank turned to Major Olney. "The Raiders are pushing the DM back down to Blue ring with sonic grenades. Get Captain Worrall and his engineers and have him get a Bat up to Raiders so they can send it where they need it. You and I are moving up behind the Raiders to set up our command post there in the short run, so we can move up and down the main core."

"Aye-aye, sir." Said Major Olney and began carrying out the orders as the command group moved toward the CIC behind "A" Company clearing the many rooms lining the exceedingly wide hallway on the 1/5 side of the spoke to link up with the Raiders.

As Frank and his command group moved to join the Raiders the other company commanders began to report the withdrawal of the troops facing them and it became apparent that the top white ring and the CIC of the Space station were mostly in human hands. But so far that was all.

Major Olney informed Frank, "The Bats are verifying that the majority of DMs have moved down a Ring to the Blue level. It seems we only have some technicians and non-combat types left behind here. They are armed but inclined to surrender; however the Bats are being shot down very quickly. We may have to re-think how we use them."

Frank stood in thought, "It's been too easy so far, and that has me worried. This place is huge we should be hitting more. Some of the spaces we've entered are as larger than a theater like space "D" and the Raiders are clearing. What's your opinion?"

"Olney took a long drink of water. "I agree with you. it feels like it did on Refuge when they disappeared then began to ambush us when we searched for them." Frank nodded. "Yep. Okay I'll contact Brigade and we'll have a quick CO's meeting when we get up to Raiders.

"One Five actual to Second Brigade-Actual."

"Go colonel."

"Sir, they are retreating from the White Ring down to the next one. On white ring and docks, it is mostly mop up. And we have the large blockage cutting off half of this ring, break . . .Can we get the Third Marines in to finish the mop up and secure the ring while we move further down, break . . . We are stopping in place to regroup and so far, have light to moderate causalities. I have Thirty-four, three- four, WIA and thirteen, one three, KIA. I lost Delta-six and promoted his Five . . .over."

"Very well. Colonel, it will probably get worse when you go down. The Eighth Marines are in a brawl and have thirty percent causalities already. The changes the DMs made before we got Glgoffen are costing us. They managed to fortify themselves like the underground fighting on Refuge. Contact is very close and causalities are mounting. I have ordered Two -Five to link up with you and the Raiders . . . Brigade Actual out."

On First World the drone message of Glgoffen's death shocked the confederation leadership; but they did not act rashly. The elected leader called an emergency meeting of all the Esteemed members of the confederation council and addressed the membership.

"By now fellow Esteemed members I am sure you know the Expeditionary Supreme Pack Leader was killed in an attack while traveling back to the Human galaxy. We do not yet know if our space station on their side of our bridge is being attacked, or if his death was just an unfortunate encounter.

"One of our first items is to name a new Leader of the forces on that station, then determine if the station is under attack. If so, do we need to send the original Packs back there. Now we must plan a course of action."

The elected leader of the Andromeda confederation watched the council members as they discussed and, in some cases, debated the issue. He found his mind wandering *Poor Glgoffen, he understood all along. Perhaps they did follow him, ancestors, what an epitaph.* He brought himself back to the conversation and called the meeting to order again then asked the senior military member, "Do you have any recommendations for a new SPL? And what course of action would you recommend to him."

"Esteemed Leader, we think it prudent to pass leadership to The Former Deputy Leader Herschel."

"If there no dissent it is done. Now what do we have him do?"

"If the Station is under attack, we should immediately send the Second, Fourth, and Fifth Great Packs back to help and we must convene the military advisers on how to continue against them. A fleet should be gathered and sent through the tunnel to land the return-ing Great Packs. Or to force the way if needed since that survey ship reported human stealth ships near the tunnel Gateway. If it is not under attack they can also prepare if the humans do come. Send a message drone through the tunnel to the station and ask for a situa-tion report. If there is nothing else, we will reconvene when we get a reply to our drone."

Herschel had been forced to re-locate his office to the Yellow ring because of the loss of the CIC and the fierce fighting around him in the Blue ring. He reestablished a temporary command center in a large meeting room then met with the 1st, 3rd and 6th Great Pack Leaders.

He looked at Woflazgl, "What of the Third Great?"

"Leader we did not have time enough to get to our newly assigned positions when the attack began. Now the Hoomans are using a new type of sonic device to force their way through. We have not yet discovered how to defend against it. The Third Great, has been fighting bravely in ever shrinking numbers and as a result. I withdrew the surviving units to regroup. I fear we are less than an understrength Attack Group and not combat effective as a Great Pack."

"Pulled back by a decision made by you alone?"

"Yes leader, I *am* the Third Greats leader and saw no value in having the remainder of the Third Great destroyed in place when we can regroup and continue the fight with another GP in a different location."

Herschel looked to the 1st GP Leader, "And you?"

The 1st GP commander a long serving veteran of the military bristled and faced Herschel. "And me? I do not understand the query. I sent the Twenty-Third AG to assist the Third Great and they fought bravely. The other two AGs stayed in their new positions on rings four and five, that are also under attack. And now Leader, I need to get back to monitor my troops while I am able, and not have any more unnecessary meetings while our brothers in the Sixth GP are in heavy fighting above and below us." The 1st GP Leader left the room, and after a pause he was followed by the 6th GP Leader.

Herschel's skills had always been with Intelligence. He was a valuable asset to someone above him, but he did not have any experience ordering these tough front line warriors of the pack. He knew his predecessor would have instantly removed from command, or executed, the 1st Great Pack Leader for his behavior. But Herschel hesitated for a few heart beats and the damage was done. In their minds he had failed his first test of leadership and was indecisive during a major engagement. It was enough to erode their confidence in him.

Herschel said "Leader Wolflazgl, assign the remains of the Thirtieth AG to the Sixth GP. I want you here with me sine you have the most experience with the Hoomans" Herschel held up a cautionary hand, "This is not open for discussion. You stay with my Headquarters."

The senior communicator for the intelligence unit approached Herschel. "Leader, I have an urgent communication sent from the Confederation counsel to the Station.

"Well, what is it." Asked Herschel still disturbed by the near mutiny of his subordinates. "The Esteemed members of the Confederation counsel informs of the death of Supreme Leader Glgoffen by a stealth ship as he returned through the tunnel. Because stealth ships are now known to be in the tunnel, they sent the drone to ascertain our situation if the Station is under attack. If we are in contact with the humans, they will send the Second, Fourth, and Fifth Great Packs immediately after gathering a fleet to escort them through the tunnel to this side. Leader you are appointed as the new Supreme Pack leader of this Expedition."

Heschel leapt from his chair and replied to the communicator, "Send a message back home that we are under attack, and that the humans have broken into the Station with heavy fighting on most rings of the station. We are fighting them level by level. Send all help soonest." As soon as the communicator left the room, he turned on Wolflazgl. "You are now appointed as my Assistant Supreme Pack leader. Send for the other two pack leaders and inform them of my new position. Have them come here immediately or they will be considered to be in mutiny and executed. Then have someone from engineering bring a display of this entire station for a briefing. Quickly, time is important."

A short time later Wolflazgl reported "They are on their way Supreme Leader; the fighting is heavy."

When the two Great Pack leaders arrived the engineer already had a hologram of the station floating in the room. SPL Herschel said," This is a communication I received from the home worlds. First: I am now the Supreme Leader of this Expedition. If you show any disrespect like the last meeting you will be executed. Nod if you understand what I told you." Both men, looking nervous, nodded.

Herschel then pointed to the display of the station floating in front of them and gave them the information he had on the reinforcements being sent from the home worlds and nodded to the 1st Great Pack leader. "Give me your honest thinking on how you see our situation and what you would do to manage it."

Surprised and pleased by the question the 1st Great leader said, "Supreme Leader I believe that our only chance with the forces we have at this time is to re-deploy down to the small group level of ten fighters and fortify behind obstacles and bleed them for every step they take. Our main fight will be on the second and third rings especially in the Forest/Hydroponics section on level three. We can dig in bunkers and other hard fortifications and try to discourage them with causalities and hold on until the arrival of the other three Great Packs from home."

Herschel nodded; *Ancestors I had not even thought about much less considered the hydroponics spaces. It covers over half of that ring. I am glad I did not have to execute him.*

"Does my Sixth Great leader have any suggestions to help us beat the Hoo-mans?"

"Supreme leader I suggest we regain the initiative to contain and direct this battle mainly to the second and third rings. My Sixth Great along with the remnants of the Third Great will hold them as long as possible on second ring by heavily blocking any way down from that ring top or bottom. We already pushed them back some since the invasion and we must isolate and deny them reinforcements.

"The First Great can do the same to block anything coming up from the lower levels and we still have our small forest and fields in the ship hydrophobics area. If we can stop them for three days our reinforcements should be here and beat back their fleet and we will re-take this station."

SPL Herschel looked at Wolflazgl. "Do you agree"

"I agree that if we can keep them isolated in the area we discussed it is possible for us to hold. I am sure everyone realizes that if they break through in any of those locations, we might not be able to beat them back. Furthermore, it could put us in jeopardy."

SPL Hershel was pleased to be getting out of the meeting with no further confrontation and had the support of the Great Pack leaders. "I approve your plan," he said to the First and Sixth GP leaders, "Go and begin its implementation."

Wolflazgl said, "Supreme Leader may I make an observation?"

"Is this in reference to your comment that the plan could put us in jeopardy?"

"Yes, Supreme Pack Leader."

"Why do you think that? Be concise."

Wolflazgl quickly replied. "Leader I am only an asset to you if I give you my true thinking when you ask. My reasons are three-fold, first: The humans have a disturbing knack of discovering and countering our major plans. Do we believe that the meeting and destruction of SPL Glgoffen's ship an accidental meeting? Secondly, it may already be too late to completely implement the blockade we want to try. Finally, if we do seal the humans out, we have in effect sealed ourselves in."

The Herschel gave him a wry smile. "And what does that tell you Deputy Supreme Pack Leader?"

"That we hold on those levels until our reinforcements arrive, or we die for the Homeland."

"No! That does not necessarily follow," blurted the 6th Great Pack Leader, causing the others in the room to stare at him in surprise.

"Explain!" demanded SPL Herschel.

"Supreme Leader it is well over two years since we were at this station, and that was for a brief stop as we passed through. Now we have come back in various, sometimes disorganized, groups. Spending our time sorting out Packs that do, or do not, remain. We have focused on keeping a count of arriving Packmates from the Refuge system and have stayed on the second level, except for the Third Great that had policing duties.

"Pack mates, have we forgotten there is a second deck on every level of this station except hydroponics?"I do not think most packmates, or the Hoo-man's, know there is a second deck in each level since the main elevator is in its own space, out of casual view, and it only leads to Hydroponics. All other movement is with the main stairways, or small supply elevators. At that earlier time, I befriended a crewman who told me of it and took me to her quarters on one of those upper floors of the station. I recommend we send warriors to the second decks and attack the Hoomans from directions they won't expect. We can fortify the Hydro deck and bleed the hoomans even more."

The dimensions of each of the five rings was one mile around. A quarter of a mile wide, One hundred feet high. That height broken into two levels fifty feet high each except for the hydroponics area that was the full one hundred feet to give the park a feeling of space.

The park and gardens were a half of a mile long, one quarter of a mile wide and one hundred feet high. The third level of the station was civilian residence and office spaces for the civilian contingent and the permeant station personnel and their families; that occupied half of the diameter of second floor of that level. The other half was a park land with trees, bushes, flowers ,walking trails and several small streams that in certain place were three meters deep allowing bathing. Some of the trails had benches and artificial hills. There was also two lodge type building on the grounds that permanent personnel and their families could stay at for a few days at a time giving them the feeling of a vacation. It was the only place in the station that did not have a second floor and was the full one hundred feet in height offering some feeling of an open sky and space.

When the station was built enough local dirt from the home worlds was brought in to enabled a forest floor ten feet deep. This area was off limits to everyone not permanently stationed on the Space Station and even the main elevator was out of general view and housed in its own room. Permeant crew who wished to use the space needed a special identification card allowing them access to the elevator.

SPL Herschel was bemused by that revelation and looked at

Woflazgl "Do you think that is possible? Does anyone disagree?" The Supreme Pack leader and all three Great Pack leaders realized they had an opportunity to surprise the hoomans and gain the initiative in the ongoing battle.

"Assistant leader Wolflazgl, get the Station Captain and visit this parkland then report back. In the meantime, I want half an AG from the First Great and Half from the Sixth. Quickly begin moving them up to the floor above us then toward the main landing bay. Attack any Hooman forces you come upon. Try to keep them engaged with you as long as possible until our reinforcements arrive. Also begin our blocking plan for the second and third rings. Go and do your duty by blocking the two rings and we will destroy them from above and behind."

TWO HOURS EARLIER

As the battle unfolded, the Main Computer Entity, still busy inside Great Pack Leader Woflazgl's head, continually disclosed information to the Human high command on the conditions of the three Great Packs fighting on the Station. It delineated the lack of confidence the DM command staff displayed in their new leader and that they did not have a unified strategy.

"Recon-Six to One-Five actual, Sit-Rep, over."

"Go Recon-Six, what do you have?" Frank asked.

"Be advised that Yellow ring ends at the beginning of yellow Zebra two, break . . . and my scouts report the same on the other side at yellow Zebra four, break . . . I have no idea what is in the space in what is Zebra two and Zebra three, break . . . Be advised that My teams report that a majority of DM troops are leaving Orange and Green rings and moving up to Yellow, break . . . squad size are the biggest units we have seen and they are fighting a delaying action. I am going to try to find out why the rings on these levels just end . . .over."

"Roger that Recon- Six. One-Five actual out." Frank called and beckoned Major Olney and the engineering sergeant over and told them what Recon had reported. "Any ideas or suggestions? You first, sergeant." Frank said.

"Sir, hidden spaces make me nervous especially after the Planet Refuge fighting. I was remembering how they were sneaking around on us back on Black Beach at Refuge.

"One of my team located a small elevator in the space we just cleared. It was almost hidden and looked to be part of a wall unless you inspected it closely. I was thinking I could blow a hole in the ceiling of the elevator and fly a Bat up the shaft to see how the elevator works and find out why they were so careful with it. At the very least sir we can see where it takes us."

"That is good thinking Sergeant," said Olney. Frank nodded. "I agree let's see what we come up with. Get to it Sergeant."

"Aye-aye, sir."

Frank and Olney continued managing the movement, fighting to get down to blue ring.

"Colonel!" Frank looked and saw the sergeant running toward him. He was out of breath when he arrived and took his bat out of the carrying case.

"What's up sergeant?

"There is another fucking level above us that no one knew about!" the Sergeant blurted. "It is as large as this one. Look at the play back, sir. We have to assume that this in the same on each ring level." Frank and Olney quickly plugged in and watched then they looked at each other.

Frank sighed. *I knew something was going to bite us in the ass!* "Every time major. . . Shit! it's the same dimension as this.one The good news is I don't see any activity up there."

Major Olney unconsciously looked up. "Do you think each ring has two decks?" Frank shrugged "We sure as shit have to get up there and check after I notify Brigade. Is there anything unusual about that elevator sergeant?"

The sergeant shook his head," It is a standard gravity type elevator, sir."

"Sergeant lase the overhead of this ring for me." The sergeant checked the laser reading in his head "15.24 meters, Fifty feet sir." Great job Sergeant. Your idea has saved us from a possibility of major problems."

"One-Five Actual to Brigade Actual . . . over"

"Go colonel."

"Sir, we discovered that there is another full deck above us in this ring that is more or less the same dimensions. We have to assume the same for each of the rings including height. We lased this ring and it is fifty feet in height. We're gonna need more troops sir. I'm gonna have our engineer send you the exact location he found the hidden elevator, break . . . Recon reports that Yellow ring, is sealed from the beginning of Zebra two to the end of Zebra three, a full half of that ring. break . . . sir, I recommend that every command begin a station wide search for elevators, and lase their overhead. If the fifty-foot number is the same we are missing a full half of this station. I intend to send a team above to see what it is."

"Very well, carry on colonel, Brigade Out."

"One-five to Recon -Six."

"Go colonel."

"Captain do you have any teams still in the white ring area."

"One sir."

"Send them to my HQ as quickly as possible, break . . . this is what we are facing." Frank briefed him on everything learned so far. "See if you can help."

"Aye-aye, sir. Sounds like it could be a mess sir."

"That's what I want to prevent . . . Actual out."

Only a few minutes passed when a Recon Corporal and her team reported to Frank. Major Olney asked "Did you run here Corporal."

"Yes sir, the skipper said it was important and to be quick, sir."

"Frank nodded, "He was right. It is extremely important corporal, and may be the most important, not to mention dangerous, task so far." He indicated the Engineer Sergeant; the sergeant will take you to the elevator and brief you along the way. Sergeant I want you to go topside with Recon, but stay at the elevator and fly the bat from there. You and the Corporal communicate on your tactical channel. Give the Corporal whatever coverage she requests. You both have my permission to contact me directly if you find anything noteworthy. Good luck."

The corporal saluted. "Thank you, sir."

The Engineer Sergeant approached closer to Frank. "Sir, I want to thank you also; I was just notified god awarded me a Galactic Cross in Silver for this." Frank smiled "You definitely rate it."

Two and a half hours later the Main Computer Entity Contacted General Gimpsie again. Things had just changed dramatically; and the DMs were going to attempt a break-out if they could not hold the human forces. It could have been worse if the human forces had not recently learn of the threat above them.

The recon team, and Sergeant Gupta, the engineer, huddled buy the open elevator door in the hitherto unknown portion of the station. The team leader said, "What do you think Sarge?"

"Corporal, my understanding is you are in charge, I'm just support, but I have done this kind of operation before and this is what I advise. You and I keep an open tac channel and I fly the Bat out ahead of your team movement. Have you ever operated with a Bat before?"

The Recon Corporal shook her head. "Okay. It is a great tool you will like working with it. I will check on any anomalies and give us eyes on everything it sees. Do you want a direct link?" The corporal shook her head. "Okay, in that case I will warn you of possible hazards. If the Bat makes contact then try to keep it from getting shot down and alert command to the contact while you do what you do. Ready?"

The Bat flew low so not to be spotted and began its journey around the top ring of White Zone sending images of mostly living quarters for stations Permanent Personnel. It also found several larger elevators and numerous smaller ones and several passages leading to the outer hull the same as below that Sergeant Gupta measured from his location and sent the co-ordinates to Major Olney who assigned troops to find the location on their level. The Bat made a quick transit. "Engineer-Five to One-Five actual."

"Go Sergeant Gupta"

"Sir no activity up here now but these are living quarters here and some offices. We should be able to match up the elevator shafts, break . . . the ring is blocked by a bulkhead here too, over"

"Roger that. I am sending recon to check other rings below; you and the Bat go with them."

"Aye-aye, sir. Gupta to Recon what elevator are you using I will meet your team."

"We are about one hundred meters, from you. You will see us."

"Sergeant Gupta met the corporal." Sarge, I been told to go down a few decks with you but to protect the Bat. I am going to bypass Blue and see what Yellow looks like. You follow after we are down."

"The way to do this Corporal is I can monitor the Bat with my chip, so can you. But I can self-destruct it if it becomes necessary, I will not come down until you are in places then we can do it again for another deck."

"The Recon Corporal took the bat and she and her team took the elevator down. Gupta followed in his head and was as shocked as the Recon team when the elevator stopped and they walked into a DM squad the immediately open fire killing them. The Recon team only fired one pulse in return. Sergeant Gupta detonated the Bat killing five DMs who went in among the bodies and pulled the elevator back to his location then reported to Command.

Frank realized it was critical to get some troops up to that deck.

CHAPTER 21

"If it is not advantageous, do not move.
If objectives can not be attained, do not employ the army.
Unless endangered do not engage in warfare. . .
When not advantageous, stop."
"Warfare is the way of deception."
Sun Tzu. Art of War.

The battle had changed again; and the two Army divisions were committed to the fight with two additional coming from Sunset. General Gimpsie convened an emergency command meeting after the Main Computer passed on the information of a second deck. He sat with Generals Thomas, Rahm, Hayduf, Lamb, and Sing, along with Fleet Admiral Park.

"General Rahm, do you have a report of this changing situation?"

"Sir, One-five made an independent discovery of the second levels of the station before the Computer Entity passed on the information it collected. Colonel Farrell had his Recon and the engineer who first discovered the existence of the additional floors to verify the situation. When they did so he had them continue down to get more info from other rings.

"The Recon team leader went down to the Yellow level where she and the entire team were killed as they tried to get out of the elevator. As the DMs attempted to get the bat from among the bodies the

Engineer Sergeant observing from white level detonated the bat self-destruct killing five DMs and pulled the elevator back up to white level before any more DMs arrived. At this point, we do not know if they realize we are above them."

"Thank you General Rahm. General Hayduf turned to General Gimpsie. Effective immediately, I want the Second Infantry Division to search and occupy the second floors of each ring on the station. Get them moving up in every elevator we have located. Keep away from the fortified stairways. Since we do not know what to expect in the Hydroponics area, I want Marine Recon to continue trying to get a look in there. We know the DMs are massing on Blue and yellow levels for their surprise attack. General Thomas, have your marines press them as much as possible. Keep them looking at you and not over their heads. Get this arraigned quickly. When we are ready we will attack them from above. Once we control the station we will defend the tunnel and gateway and prepare for their next move; whether it be diplomatic or hostile.

"Good luck gentlemen,"

END OF BOOK 2

Other books by the author:

The Annals of Time

We Marines

Knife Soldiers

Lightning Source UK Ltd.
Milton Keynes UK
UKHW042250251122
412742UK00029B/316/J

9 781039 100671